GROWING UP

"Your father worked hard," Gamma Angel informed them. "But, unfortunately, he seems to have forgotten the lessons I taught him in bringing you up. He has let this go on far too long. And now I'm putting a stop to it."

"A stop to what?" Madrid asked.

"Your checks," Gamma Angel answered.

"What?" Madrid asked.

"Say again?" London added.

"Until you two can show me that you know the *value* of money, beyond its buying power, you will not get another dime. You girls—you *ladies*—are turning thirty next year. Since the age of seventeen, you have drifted through your lives, spending money on things no one really needs. The money you have spent on yourselves, on your whims and desires, could be much better spent on doing good for others. I thought you would've learned this by now. But you haven't. Your insatiable lust for partying and throwing Antonio's hard-earned money away has made you both sick. Sick with a disease I have heard called the *affluenza*. You get and you spend, you get and you spend. What good is coming from this spend, spend, spend? Maybe you already know this, but I will say it anyway. Money can't buy happiness. It never has and it never will."

Gamma Angel rubbed her hands together and then smiled at her granddaughters. "And so, my darlings, there is no check this Christmas. There will be no more checks until you can show me, your father and your mother, by the time you turn thirty, that you both have learned what money really means. Then, and only then, will the checks resume . . ."

The Perils
of
Sisterhood

AMY ALDEN

KENSINGTON BOOKS
KENSINGTON PUBLISHING CORP.
http://www.kensingtonbooks.com

KENSINGTON BOOKS are published by

Kensington Publishing Corp.
850 Third Avenue
New York, NY 10022

All Kensington titles, imprints and distributed lines are available at special quantity discounts for bulk purchases for sales promotion, premiums, fund-raising, educational or institutional use.

Special book excerpts or customized printings can also be created to fit specific needs. For details, write or phone the office of the Kensington Special Sales Manager: Kensington Publishing Corp., 850 Third Avenue, New York, NY 10022. Attn. Special Sales Department. Phone: 1-800-221-2647.

If you purchased this book without a cover you should be aware that this book is stolen property. It was reported as "unsold and destroyed" to the Publisher and neither the Author nor the Publisher has received any payment for this "stripped book."

Kensington and the K logo Reg. U.S. Pat. & TM Off.

First Trade Paperback Printing: May 2005
First Mass Market Paperback Printing: December 2006
10 9 8 7 6 5 4 3 2 1

Printed in the United States of America

To Judy

PART ONE

Money is like fire, an element as little troubled by moralizing as earth, air, and water.
—Lewis Lapham

There is a gigantic difference between earning a great deal of money and being rich.
—Marlene Dietrich

Money doesn't talk, it swears.
—Bob Dylan

1

London La Mira slowly leaned forward and then smiled at the sound made by her body's contact against the soft leather seat. "Gosh, I love that," she breathed out. "It sounds so . . . *sexy*, don't you think?" she asked, and turned to the woman who was sitting on the far side of the seat, riffling through a paper-jammed briefcase positioned on the floor between her legs. "Do this, Lucinda," she urged with a sly grin as she shifted her slender hips from side to side against the seat. "You see what I'm doing? Just like that."

Lucinda glanced up at her and then shook her head. "I don't have to move like that to make that sound, Lonnie. If you haven't noticed already, my big, fat, butt takes care of that all on its own."

"Then the sound you make will be *much* better," London answered. "Come on," she smiled, then slowly inched her hips across the seat toward her. "Cinda, Cinda. Do it for *meee*."

Lucinda took in a deep breath. "I'll do most anything for you, Lonnie. But a butt-dance on the limousine's leather seat is not in my job description."

"Fuck the job description," London answered. "Right now you're not the manager of my nightclub. Right now you're a passenger in my fine limousine with its lush leather seats. Come on. Let's have some fun."

"I'm all set," Lucinda replied as she opened a fat notebook on her lap and began flipping through scores of papers. "I still need you to sign a few invoices before you take off today. I want to be sure our vendors get paid before the new year."

London flicked a hand against the notebook, causing it to slide to the edge of Lucinda's knees and balance there precariously. "They'll get paid."

Lucinda quickly grabbed the notebook and pulled it back on her lap. "I don't want any loose ends before we close for the holiday."

"How could there *ever* be a loose end when you do your job so well? What I want you to do is put that notebook away and loosen up *your* end. You're screwed on way too tight, Cinda."

Lucinda glanced at London, then flashed her a quick smile. "Which is why I do my job so well. Now, I've hired the six DJs you requested for the—"

"Do you know that Dior leather wrap coat I have, Cinda? The light brown one?"

Lucinda shrugged her shoulders and tapped a pen against the papers.

London shifted her eyes to the pen, then let out a quick laugh and lay back in the seat. She pressed her shoulders against the seat and splayed her long legs out at odd angles from underneath her way-above-the-knees, hip-and-thigh-clinging black Istvan Francer skirt. "One night, when I couldn't sleep, I called the driver and asked him to take me out for a long spin around the streets of San Francisco. I was wearing the coat, and nothing underneath. I just lay on the back seat as we went up and down the hills and around the corners. The sound! Leather against leather. And did it ever feel luscious against my skin. It was absolutely sensuous." She closed her eyes and sighed.

"It's just all creaking and squeaking to me."

London opened her eyes and chuckled. "It's like sighs and whispers to me."

"I've tripled all of our orders for the New Year's Eve party," Lucinda continued.

"Work, work, work," London scolded playfully as she sat up, turned to Lucinda, and held out a hand to her. "You should channel some of this must-do focus into the bedroom, my dear. Hasn't it been a long time for you?"

Lucinda uncapped and then placed the Aurora Afrika fountain pen in London's hand.

"No answer, huh?" London asked. "Your silence speaks for itself. Poor dear. I got off, of course," London continued as she scrawled her signature wherever Lucinda pointed. "In the car, that night. Just from the sound of leather against leather. I'll tell you what. Take the Dior coat while I'm gone and have George take you for a spin. That'll be my Christmas present to you."

Lucinda watched as London signed the last document, then took the pen back. She closed the notebook and slid it into her briefcase, which yawned wide with several other notebooks of varying sizes. "You already gave me my Christmas present, Lonnie. The holiday bonus to your club manager is, as always, quite generous."

London waved a hand in the air and let out a snort. "Money. Who gives a shit? This is more personal, don't you think?"

"Wearing a coat you got off in and trying to get turned on by the annoying sound of leather against leather?"

London raised her perfectly shaped eyebrows and widened her green-gray eyes at Lucinda. "Well, yeah!"

Lucinda shook her head, then ran a hand through her short, more-pepper-than-salt hair, trying to push it away from her face. "That doesn't do anything for me, Lonnie."

"Well, what else are you going to do for Christmas?"

Lucinda tipped her head to the side and looked at

London. "You really don't ever listen to me, do you? I spend time with my family. I'm very close to my family. We have some great Christmas traditions like—"

"That's good," London cut in, then reached forward and pressed a lacquered fingernail on the intercom button on the panel in front of her. "Take a right up here, driver."

"A—no, driver, take a left!" Lucinda nearly shouted out as she urged her body forward in the seat, extending an arm out as she strained to reach the intercom button.

"There's that sound, Cinda," London cooed as she watched Lucinda's hand flutter back and forth a few inches from the button.

"A left, a left, a left!" Lucinda barked out as she leaned forward and rapped her knuckles frantically against the window panel that separated her and London from the driver.

London saw the driver glance up in the rearview mirror, first at Lucinda, and then at her. She wagged a finger in the air at him. He eased the long limousine to the right.

"Shit!" Lucinda cursed as she turned to London. "Don't do this to me again, Lonnie. You make things that should be so simple so hard, you know that?"

London's full lips parted as they gave Lucinda a half-smile. "You mean we should've turned left? Oopsie." She tossed her head back, shaking her thick mane of wavy brown hair around her shoulders, then closed her eyes and leaned back in the seat. "You know I simply have to do this, Cinda. It's in my nature. It's my life. It's something that *has* to happen." She opened her eyes and looked out the window. "And there they all are. Right up ahead there. Like thirsty animals drawn to a watering hole. Or, as my sister and I often put it, Our Reason for Living." She turned to face Lucinda. "Now, why would you want to deny us that? Forget about my twin. God knows, *I* want to most of the time. Even though there are miles of separation between San Francisco and New York City, I can't forget the one who shares my beauty and charm. But I digress. Why would you want to deny *me* that,

Lucinda dear—your beloved boss who you live and breathe for?"

"I don't know that I'd go that far," Lucinda muttered. "I just have to think of you and your needs plus the club and its needs twenty-four seven. That's all. I can't remember if I do live or breathe during any portion of that time."

"Such a funny girl," London said as she let out a low chuckle. Then she slowly eased her body across the seat, away from Lucinda—"Here's me making that delicious sound," she murmured as she ran a tongue over her full lips—and settled herself back into the seat. "Y'all ready for this?" she asked as she unbuttoned the top two buttons on her white silk Oscar de la Renta blouse. She slipped a hand into the blouse, slid it underneath her flesh-colored silk bra—"They think you're not wearing one, but you are," she had once explained to Lucinda about her choice of under-garment color—and gently flicked a pointed fingernail first against one nipple, and then the other. Then she arched her back and tightened the blouse against her chest. "And there they are, folks," she grinned. "The best damn nipples anyone will ever see." She then slid a hand between her legs and under-neath her skirt. "Oh, my. Another oopsie. I forgot my underwear. Again!" She let out a laugh. "Just a little *Basic Instinct* action, I guess. Want to see, Cinda?"

Lucinda closed her eyes and slowly shook her head. "Saw the movie. Once was enough." She opened her eyes, but kept them averted from London's legs. "Now, can you please re-think this decision? This isn't going to give you much time to—"

"Time, time, time. Work, work, work." London sighed. "You need a vacation, Cinda darling. You are *way* too stressed out." She looked down at her chest and repositioned the Giorgio Visconti white-gold-and-gold necklace so it was centered on her chest, with the diamond-studded heart falling just to the start of her cleavage.

She turned to Lucinda. "Last check."

Lucinda sighed and then ran her eyes slowly from the top of London's head to her immaculately applied makeup, past her off-the-fashion-rack outfit, and down to the Giuseppe Zanotti black-strapped, five-inch heels. "Sunglasses?" she suggested. "To shield your eyes from the madding crowd?"

London grinned and pointed a finger at her. "Perfect. The Guccis?"

Lucinda nodded. "The Guccis." She reached down into her briefcase, dug around for a few moments, and then took the sunglasses out of a leather case and handed them to London.

London slipped the Guccis on her face. "Perfect, dahling," she cooed as the limousine negotiated a slow turn. London glanced out the window. "It's show time, Lucinda."

Lucinda sighed. "It's always show time with you, Lonnie."

London turned to Lucinda and smiled. "I know. Ain't it grand?"

Lucinda rolled her eyes in response and then, with a grunt, lifted her briefcase onto her lap.

As the limousine drew to a stop next to the curb, London shifted her hips until she made contact with the door. She waited until George had opened the door for her, and then paused as bright sunshine and even brighter flashes exploded around her. After the first round of flashes had died down, she lifted her legs and slowly placed them on the ground. Another flurry of flashes burst around her, and she stood up.

"LONNIE!"

"LONNIE!"

"LONNIE! LOOK OVER HERE!"

"OVER HERE!"

"*THE NEW YORKER*, LONNIE! OVER HERE! *THE NEW YORKER*! Is it true that your club's New Year's Eve bash will be the best yet? Have you made up the invitation list yet?"

"LONNIE! LONNIE! What are you wearing?"

"How did you feel about the *People* magazine piece about you and your sister?"

"What are your plans for the holidays?"

"Where's your sister been hiding? Is she still dating that Latin heartthrob?"

"What about you, Lonnie? Are you seeing anyone?"

"LONNIE! Is it true that you dissed the latest J. Mendel spring line?"

"How do you respond to PETA's contention that you want to start wearing seal fur?"

Out of the corner of her eye, London saw George bow slightly to her from the waist and then shut the door to the limousine without a sound when she had cleared it. *Perfect,* London thought. *He's showing me the right amount of respect even though he's nearly twice my age. That's what Mother Doodle had taught her and Madrid. "Always employ people who are older than you are," she had said. "And never—I repeat, never—employ minorities. It makes you look racist. Even though we know we're better than all those African-Americans and Hispanics and Iranians and Guatemalans and God knows what other riffraff those damn Democrats let into our country every day, and even though everyone knows Mexican gardeners are simply THE BEST at landscaping—I mean, I would KILL to get a good south-of-the-border gardener—always surround yourself with white faces. Swedes are fine, of course—damn! are they ever hard workers; must be the constant cold or their socialistic society—as are the Germans, who know what precision is all about. But my point being, of course, as long as they're white. Then, no one will ever make an issue out of that. You don't want to give people reasons to resent your wealth. Because they will. No matter how much good you do in the world."*

London slowly moved toward the crowd of photographers and reporters. She walked past a few, nodding and smiling, and then stopped in front of a young, attractive female re-

Amy Alden

porter who had her head down and was furiously scribbling notes on a pad of paper.

A few seconds passed as London watched the woman in silence. The crowd noise drew quieter.

"Are you writing about me, or composing a shopping list?"

The reporter stopped writing and looked up at London, who had a five-inch height advantage over her. The whir of camera film being advanced dominated the now-silent phalanx of society and fashion-page writers.

The reporter opened her mouth to speak. London leaned forward and raised an eyebrow at her. The reporter closed her mouth.

London grinned, then touched the reporter's jacket. "Chloe. Brown cotton velvet with suede trim. Almost a thousand dollars. How are you affording that, Sweet Cakes?"

The reporter's face reddened as she stared up at London in wide-eyed silence.

"The jacket?" London prompted. "You do know how to speak, don't you?"

The reporter planted the pen in her mouth and placed the notebook under her arm. With her free hand she extricated a price tag that had been tucked into the sleeve of the jacket.

London grinned. "Ah, a temporary purchase." She glanced down at the price tag. "A hundred dollars less than I thought. You got a bargain. So tell me, are you trying to impress me with this soon-to-be-returned jacket?"

The reporter gave a slight shrug of her shoulders.

"It's nice, isn't it?"

The reporter nodded.

"Never worn a better jacket, have you?"

The reporter shook her head.

"Good." London grasped the tag, positioned a hand against the sleeve of the jacket, and pulled. The crowd gasped. "It's yours now. Send the bill to my manager at the club. La Mira

West. You deserve a treat, don't you think? For reading my memo. You *did* read the memo, right?"

The reporter nodded.

"What rag are you from?"

The scribe started to answer, then realized the pen was in her mouth. She quickly removed it. "U-Cal. Berkeley. The . . . the student newspaper."

"Ah, she speaks," London smiled.

"I . . . I want to be a fashion writer after I graduate. Maybe for *Vogue*. You know. Or . . . well, whatever magazine will have me."

London leaned closer to the woman, and then bent down and brought her face close to the woman's ear. "Maybe I'LL have you," she whispered. "Does the thought of that make you hot?"

The reporter's face turned a deep shade of red as she nodded.

"Good girl," London told her in a soft voice, then pulled back. "Give me your notepad." The reporter obediently handed the pad to London, who took the pen and hastily scribbled her signature on a clean piece of paper. "You take this to my club on New Year's Eve. You come in. You see me. Okay? I'll give you an exclusive for your rag."

The reporter flashed an immediate ear-to-ear grin at London. "That . . . is . . . so . . . cool!"

London handed the pen and paper back to the reporter, and then turned back to the crowd. "Look at this," she said as she spread her arms wide and surveyed the group. "I am so impressed! Charlie? Is that a Marc Jacobs suit coat?"

One of the men nodded at London. "I got the memo, London."

London grinned. "Apparently you have all taken my message to heart—how you present yourself to the subject you want to speak with is of utmost importance. If you want to write about fashion, then you need to show that *you* know something about it. And you don't do that in jeans and a T-shirt. Now, what did I title that memo?"

"Reporters Who Have No Fashion Sense Can Never Write About Fashion," a voice called out.

"Brilliant, don't you think?" London chuckled. "Maybe I should be a writer, huh?"

The group laughed.

"I guess it helped when I enclosed a ten-thousand-dollar check with that memo, right?"

"Thank you!" another voice called out.

"But our editors won't let us keep the clothes!" another voice yelled.

London shrugged her shoulders. "Well, I can't have you all running around naked, then, can I?" she asked as she moved forward into the group. "Leave your business cards with my manager, and I'll make sure you have something to spend on yourself this Christmas. Something you can keep." London stopped before a male reporter. "Charlie. Good to see you."

"You, too, London."

"You look sharp, Charlie. Marc Jacobs suits you. But lose the tie, hon. Unbutton the top two buttons on your shirt. You're doing overkill. It's not even noon and you look like you're going to an evening cocktail party. Always dress to impress, but dress for the right time of the day."

"Yes, ma'am," Charlie responded as he yanked off his tie and stuffed it into his jacket pocket.

"Not there, Charlie," London said as she pulled the tie out of his pocket. She turned it over. "Christ, man, what are you thinking? It's like serving a black-pepper-crusted, standing rib roast au jus on a paper plate." London tossed the tie over her shoulder. "You can do better, Charlie."

"Yes, ma'am."

London winked at Charlie, then glanced around him. "People, never—*ever*—short-change on your accessories.

Charlie's Marc Jacobs needs a Charvet tie. Or something comparable. And while I'm on the subject of ties—men, don't do the my-tie-is-the-same-color-as-my-shirt look. That's so over. Or the Roy Rogers string-tie look, unless your second job is as a square-dance caller. My point being, don't spend a thousand dollars on a jacket and then expect you can get away with cheap visuals. Got it? Now, who's wearing Donna Karan's Black Cashmere?"

"I am," a voice answered from the back of the crowd. "*Time* magazine. I was wondering if you could tell me—"

"Here's what I'll tell you," London began as she stepped closer to the voice. "A—you're wearing too much. I shouldn't be able to smell your perfume in a crowd, outdoors, standing this far away. B—Black Cashmere is a romantic, sweet, subtle scent that's meant for the evening. It is a perfume of seduction, and although I know you'd all like to seduce me, it ain't workin', babes."

A few reporters snickered.

"Now, when you wear that scent, the message you're sending is, 'I'm putting out for you tonight.' Are you putting out for me, honey?"

"Sorry, London. I like men."

London grinned. "That's never stopped me before. Nor has it stopped the dozens of women who have said the same thing to me and then couldn't wait to feel my tongue on them."

"Who are you dating now, London?" another voice called out.

"Give it up, Charlotte," London answered. "I kiss and tell when I'm good and ready."

"Is it Monique?" another voice called out.

"Only if she's wearing Black Cashmere," London joked, then sniffed the air. "Suffice it to say, honey, you need to wear something lighter for the daytime. And you simply have got to stop dousing. Time and place, people. Time and place.

Those are the two words that should dictate what you wear and how you wear it." London paused as the reporters scribbled furiously on their notepads.

"As for your other questions," she began as she surveyed the group. "The PETA people need to eat more protein. I think half the things they say and do are based on the fact that they're all lightheaded from the lack of animal blood in their macrobiotic diets of kelp and kale. And they also need to realize that for centuries people have been wrapping themselves in animal skins and furs. This is not some new invention. What I simply said in the *Mirabella* article, which PETA took out of context, is that the new Etro stole, which is actually a wool-silk blend, feels as luxurious as seal fur. I was simply making an analogy. Perhaps I could've compared the soft Etro texture to some luxurious plant species, but I really can't think of a vegetable that warms you up when you wear it. I have, however, sent several cases of Oscar Mayer bologna to the PETA main offices."

"How did they respond to that?" a reporter asked.

London grinned. "I think it went something along the lines of, 'My bologna has a first name—it's O-S-C-A-R.' "

London's reply was rewarded with scattered groans.

"Now, today I'm wearing an Istvan Francer skirt with a simple Oscar de la Renta blouse, Giuseppe Zanotti shoes—who you know is my favorite shoe designer—and a Giorgio Visconti necklace. I'll be spending the holidays with my twin sister, Madrid, who I refer to as my worse half. Have you heard of her?" London paused as the group exploded into laughter. "I'll be seeing my parents and my beloved grandmother, Angelica Forcini. I don't know who Maddy is dating right now, but I do know that she prefers humans of the dick-persuasion. I am currently bedding a number of fine women, as I always do, including a few fashion models and a couple of well-known actresses, whose names I will not reveal, and I'm not wearing any panties right now. Okay? Who's here from the *San Francisco Chronicle*?"

"I am!" answered a voice.

"Is that you, Betty?" London asked as she slid her sunglasses down slightly, revealing her striking cat-green eyes and causing a collective whir of camera film and a renewed burst of flashes.

"It's me, Lonnie."

"Okay. Let's you and me take a walk. I promised that you'd be the first to hear about my club's New Year's Eve party."

"You have to admit, she knows how to wow a crowd! Y'know?"

Lucinda heard the voice of Dolores Fontaine burst forth from within the constant cloud of cigarette smoke she expelled from her lungs like a stoked smokestack.

Lucinda blinked her eyes in the smoke.

"Wow! Y'know?"

"I know," Lucinda replied.

"What's that you say?" Dolores nearly shouted.

"I said, I know," Lucinda replied in a louder voice, remembering not to bend her head down too close to Dolores, or she wouldn't be able to hear for a week. The two stood side by side several yards away from the crowd of reporters and photographers who had gathered underneath the DEPARTURES sign at the entrance to the San Francisco International Airport.

Lucinda glanced over at Dolores, who today matched her at eye level, at five feet, two inches. *Except Dolores is wearing heels,* Lucinda noted as she glanced down at the pavement, then smiled to herself. "*Spiker-dos,*" Lonnie would joke to her whenever they'd watch Dolores attempt to move around at her usual warp speed in a pair of Tina Turner-styled heels. "*They make her look rounder, don't you think? Like heels on a baby rhino.*" It was hard not to laugh at Lonnie's comments—her delivery was quick and cunning, not really laced with deliberate viciousness, and always quick to hit the mark. But sometimes Lucinda wondered if London whispered such things about her when she was out of earshot. She wasn't nearly as round as Dolores, but she was still thirty pounds overweight. And short.

Lucinda drew her loose jacket self-consciously around her belly as she listened to Dolores prattle on. She stood at a safe distance so she could avoid the lit cigarette, an ever-present fixture in Dolores's nicotine-stained fingers, which she constantly waved about her when she talked as ferociously as a conductor leading an orchestra in a performance of the *William Tell Overture*.

Her lipstick is garish, as always, Lucinda thought as she took in Dolores's overly painted face, then eyed the wisps of dark brown hair that stuck out helter-skelter from underneath a beret that was part of the army of assorted head adornments Dolores sported. *"I swear, she sleeps in a hat,"* Lonnie had once remarked. Mixed clothing styles and colors draped Dolores's wide, squat body and seemed to be thrown on without any clear thought or patience.

"How's the ulcer?" Lucinda cut in during a nanosecond lull in Dolores's monologue.

"Ah, well," Dolores answered as she rubbed her ample belly. "My migraines help to divert attention from the abdominal pain. I need to slow down, y'know? That's what my doctors tell me. My shrinks, too. I'm only thirty-three, y'know? But who can go slow with the Energizer Bunny over there? And her sister's even worse. I gotta get outta this business, y'know? Maybe do somethin' I really like, like grow orchids. But I hear they're a lot of work. Who woulda thought a plant could make you stressed? Or maybe I should just sit down and write the damn book. You know, the tell-all. But Lonnie and Maddy would wring my neck, because I'd be tellin' all about them, y'know? Geesch, what a goddamned life. You know I went to college to be a schoolteacher? A damn teacher. But I hear that's stressful, too. Those damn competency tests they got the kids takin' now. Like, geesch, I didn't have them when I was growin' up, and I turned out to be pretty goddamned competent. Well, stressed, y'know. But I'm the best publicist there is. I tell ya that Grisham called me? Ya, ya, he did. Wants me to represent him. Like I got time, y'know? I got double the trouble with the twins, y'know? All you got to handle is one."

"And the club," Lucinda added quickly.

"Okay, yeah, sure, the club, too," Dolores shot back. "But the club doesn't move around. You don't have to be goin' here and there and everywhere, y'know? If only they'd stay put, y'know? Speaking of which, I thought you were supposed to use the private jet entrance. She calls me last night, y'know, and says, 'Better be there, Fontaine. I invited the press.' Like, that's supposed to be my job, y'know? I'm the publicist. I arrange the press gigs. You'd think, right? I gotta have some control. Ha! Who can control her? And Maddy? Who knows what terror she's up to? Maybe she's doin' this whole goddamned press conference thing in New York and isn't tellin' me about it. I get on a plane to one coast to put out a fire, and then I gotta get back on the damn plane and go back to the other coast to put out another fire. Fuck. I'll probably read about Maddy's gathering in the papers tomorrow. That's when my ulcer's at its worst, y'know? Can't drink a damn cuppa coffee without feeling like I just struck a match to a bonfire. But I can't survive without caffeine, y'know? I tried to stop once, and bam! I get these goddamned migraines now. Like my brain isn't ever gonna forgive me for not drinkin' coffee for one goddamned week. I mean, y'know, come on already. And so I'm up all last night drinkin' coffee and popping the damn migraine pills and then drinkin' wine just to get a little bit of sleep. I mean, is that too much to ask, y'know? I thought I could depend upon you to reel Lonnie in before she flew to the East Coast. I got a dinner party tonight. Fifteen people. And those things just don't fall in place, y'know?"

"Nice talking with you," Lucinda told Dolores as she watched London toss an arm across a reporter's neck and steer away from the crowd.

"Ya, sure," Dolores bellowed out as Lucinda walked away from her. "We'll catch up soon, y'know?"

"I know," Lucinda muttered under her breath.

Sometimes, when Lucinda was out in public places, she got noticed. Not because she was the manager of La Mira West, London's posh, renowned nightclub in San Francisco, but because she bore a striking resemblance to the actress Kathy Bates. Sometimes she'd have fun with that, trying to replicate London's quick wit. *"Say, you know who you look like?"* she'd hear someone say, and Lucinda would raise her eyebrows at them (like Lonnie did) and quickly answer, *"Jennifer Love Hewitt. I get that all the time."*

But, more often than not, no one outside of the staff at La Mira West paid much attention to her. Even when she was standing next to London in some public place. She could see the eyes of the reporters or the glitterati or the general public skim right past her, as if she were invisible.

Who cares? Lucinda would often think as she saw the eyes of others look around her or even through her, but sometimes she really did care. In this world, she realized, only the beautiful and the powerful—the rich and famous—got noticed.

But not always in a good way, Lucinda thought as she passed by the small crowd that had gathered around London and the *Chronicle* reporter, and which had now caught the attention of the underpaid and overstressed airport security personnel who were fast-stepping to the swelling mob of people, walkie-talkies pressed to their mouths. The fashion writers and the ones who penned the society-page stories loved London and her sister Madrid. After all, the beautiful billionairess twins sold their papers and magazines. But the public in general was a different story. While drawn to the rich and spoiled like moths to a light, they also cheered at those times when the enticing light flickered—and then let out whooping hurrahs when it was extinguished.

"I'm someone people love to hate," London had once told her. "And please don't ask me how that feels. Because I've learned not to feel anything about that. Just as I've learned not to focus on the stares I get wherever I go, whatever I do. Just as I've learned not to blink when the flashbulbs go off, not to grimace if I'm in pain, not to look panicked when I feel like I can't breathe in a tight crush of people."

"That can't be easy," Lucinda had answered.

"It's not," London had replied. "But I have to make it look easy. It's what I'm supposed to do."

Yes, people love to hate the rich, Lucinda thought as she moved past the shops that lined the wide corridor of the terminal. Lower-level employees gleefully celebrate as once-powerful corporate executives fall from the top of the organizational chart. *Now you know what it's like to be out of work, you jerk,* they think. *Whatcha gonna do now without that big, fat salary?*

Sports fans read about the spoiled major league baseball pitcher who drained his savings and pissed his pampered life away because he thought he was God and could inhale anything up his nose, inject anything in his veins, ingest anything he wanted.

I knew that bozo wasn't worth that contract, they respond. *Heck, he lost us that big game—remember? We were ahead by five in the sixth—by tossing up a fluff ball. And man, did that sail right outta the park, or what? Grand slam homer. Bye-bye, playoffs. Million-dollar contract, my ass. He ain't worth a dime.*

And when the box-office draw gets arrested for breaking the law, her fickle fans couldn't be happier.

I never liked her films anyway, the woman in the hair stylist's chair proclaims as she cradles *People* magazine in her lap. *She was too whiney. Too thin. She couldn't act her way out of a paper bag. And I heard she always used a double in all those sex scenes. There's no way that scrawny little body could've supported breasts that size. She would've fallen flat on her face.*

Lucinda dodged the people who were running past her toward the announced area of a sighting of London La Mira.

I'd hate to be their lawyers, Lucinda thought, returning to her fallen-executive-pro-ballplayer-actress scenarios. *Because how do you tell the executive who owns estates scattered around the world and a garage full of cars and a yacht and a ten-thousand-dollar umbrella stand that, when all is said and done, he'll be lucky if he can hold on to a change of underwear after he dons the orange suit? How do you tell the professional athlete that after he completes his rehab program and squares up support payments to his ex-wife and half a dozen children—how the hell did that happen? he wonders; I can't ever remember seein' them bitches, let alone doin' nuthin' with 'em—he'll be lucky if he can grace the mound in the minor leagues as a relief pitcher? How do you tell the leading lady that she'll be watching the next five Oscar presentations on a low-reception TV in prison, sitting in an uncomfortable metal folding chair in a crowd of husky-tough women who don't know Jean Paul Gaultier from the Gap and, after she's released, she'll be lucky to be hired as an extra in the latest John Waters film?*

The bigger they are, Lucinda thought. But then she spoke out loud the way she really knew the sentence should be completed, based on her experience as London La Mira's long-time club manager.

". . . the less you really know them."

"I do give a crap, you know."

London's voice came into Lucinda's mind so clearly as she made her way through the airport terminal that she turned her head to see if London was walking behind her. With her head turned, she nearly slammed into a group of travelers who had stalled in the middle of the terminal and were staring up at the arrivals-and-departures flight board like rapt stargazers.

Those words had been spoken about a year ago by London—*on a Monday night,* Lucinda recalled, inwardly smiling at her ability to remember even the smallest of details.

It was the only day the club was closed. Lucinda had set up stacks of paperwork on the polished mahogany bar in one of the club's smaller and more intimate rooms. She had turned on the television to CNN and wasn't really paying much attention to it—just listening to the noise as she tapped numbers into her calculator—until she heard Larry King mention the guests on his show, who would be talking about "the latest antics of the La Mira twins." Lucinda stopped what she was doing and stared up at the television as Larry prattled on.

"Madrid La Mira ventured out of the Big Apple to the City by the Sea last week and, as we all know, made tabloid headlines with her equally terrible twin London by raising their individual, well-known levels of brattiness, excesses, and rudeness to even greater heights. The duo, who will soon turn thirty but often behave like male college freshmen on spring break, engaged in four nonstop nights of relentless partying that resulted in numerous arrests as well as the hospitalization of a young invitee to London's club, La Mira West. Have the It Girls—once the darlings of the fashion world and society pages—turned into the Shit Girls? With us tonight to talk about . . ."

"I do give a crap, you know."
Lucinda immediately swiveled around on the bar stool

and surveyed the empty table and chairs behind her. She was just about to turn back, thinking that she had heard London's voice on the television rather than in the room, when she saw the orange glow of a cigarette at a table near the back of the room.

"I didn't think anyone was here," Lucinda called out into the darkness.

"I wonder if he's going to have on that former employee of this club," London answered. The cigarette glowed orange again. "What's her name?"

"Let me turn this off," Lucinda said as she frantically pawed through the papers scattered on the bar, searching for the television remote.

"Leave it on. You know the one I'm talking about."

"I don't," Lucinda answered.

"The one you fired a few months ago—remember the one who had a hissy fit after you caught her stealing from me? You know. The one who was dipping in the till and, when you fired her, told you that she was going to get a gun and blow your head off. That shouldn't be too hard to forget."

"Lonnie, most everyone I have to fire says that to me."

"Oh. I guess that doesn't scare you, then. Because, after all, here you are. You still have your head."

"What scares me more is when they don't say they're going to get a gun and blow my head off. Then I wonder if that's what they're thinking and that's what they'll do."

"Well, you're still here."

Lucinda let out a short bark of a laugh. "Yes, I am."

"Anyway. You know the one I mean, Cinda. And if not her, Larry can find any number of people who would be more than happy to get their fifteen minutes of fame on his show by talking about all the skanky sex acts that go on in our private rooms. That's all the media cares about. That, and if there's an OD or if we've served a minor or if the police have to be called here."

"Do you mean Debby?"

"That's her name!" London declared as she stepped out from the shadows at the back of the room and walked slowly to the bar. "Debby the Dipper."

London moved unsteadily toward Lucinda. Her head was tipped slightly back, her eyes narrowed to slits, and a half-smoked cigarette was pressed between her lips. In one hand she held a bottle of La Grande Dame by its neck, dangling it casually by her hip; in the other was a half-filled glass held in front of her in a cocked arm. One shoulder and nearly all of one breast were revealed in a wide-strapped sleeveless sweater dress that had shifted to one side. She was barefoot.

London stepped up onto a bar stool a few feet from Lucinda and placed the liquor bottle on the bar. She removed the cigarette from her mouth, and then drained her glass.

"Bartender? I'll have another," she slurred as she slid the bottle in Lucinda's direction. "You pouring tonight?"

Lucinda grasped the bottle before it was about to tip over, righted it, and then shook her head. "Bar's closed. I thought you didn't drink on Monday nights, Lonnie. Didn't your doctor—"

"I don't *drug* on Monday nights, Cinda."

"Alcohol *is* a drug, Lonnie."

"No one told me that." London took a long drag on her cigarette, then snuffed it out in an ashtray and blew out a long, thin stream of smoke.

"Nicotine's a drug, too."

London placed an elbow on the bar, dropped her chin into it, and turned to Lucinda. "You done?"

Lucinda gave London a half-smile. "I'm done."

"Good. Since tonight's a complete drug-free washout," London began as she lifted her glass toward Lucinda, "hit me, babes."

Lucinda shook her head slightly, sighed, then lifted the bottle and filled London's glass.

"The thing is, I *do* give a crap," London said, then downed her drink in one gulp. "I don't want this—" she glanced up at the television and stared at it. "Oh, shit."

Lucinda looked up at the screen and saw the clip of film she had already seen aired a number of times.

They watched the clip in silence.

"I'm going to catch hell for this from Gamma Angel," London commented as the clip showed the interior of a crowded dance floor of La Mira West, accompanied by the deep thump-boom sound of a techno beat. "My parents, well, they're not going to be happy, but they won't say anything. Their life goes on for them, no matter what Maddy and I do. But Gamma. Gamma will have something to say. 'You don't abuse your fame and wealth.' That's the line she gives me and Maddy. Over and over again. But she never was in a fishbowl in her life. I tell her—Maddy tells her— how things are different now than they were in her day. Cameras are everywhere. She never needed legions of security. I can't do anything without someone watching me. Sometimes, even in my own house, I don't feel relaxed. Try taking a shit or picking your nose while you think you're being watched. People think the rich and famous surround themselves with people because they're lonely and insecure." Lonnie let out a snort, took a gulp of her drink, then turned to Lucinda. "What *is* lonely?" she asked. "How can I be lonely? Christ, I'm never alone. And insecure to me just means not having enough people to keep perfect strangers from touching me, from coming up to me in a restaurant when I'm eating, from not being able to window shop without being hounded. I mean, my life isn't *normal*. I can't help that."

"You can't help *that*?" Lucinda asked as she stared at the television.

London leaned back on the bar stool, extracted a Nat Sherman Mint cigarette from a gold-and-diamond-studded case, and then flicked a flame to life from a slim, 14-karat

hammered gold Dunhill lighter. She watched the clip of herself gyrating on a crowded La Mira dance floor, clad in a
bra, as topless women, who were shown sporting black rectangular bars across their breasts for the television viewers,
pulsated suggestively against one another and against
London. "Cue the OD," London muttered as, a few seconds
later, the eyes of one of the dancers rolled up and then she
toppled down, out of the view of the cameras. The camera
then zoomed in for a closeup of London, who was seen looking down at the floor and laughing, and then grabbing the
breast of a dancer underneath the black bar.

"Next clip, Maddy going down on the tennis pro on the
dance floor in her club, La Mira East," London said. "Turn it
off," she told Lucinda in a husky voice.

Lucinda pressed a button on the remote, and the screen
went blank.

"Being rich is a bitch," London said.

"Money doesn't buy stupidity," Lucinda replied. "You did
that all by yourself."

"Who do you think you're talking to?" London snapped.

"A person," Lucinda said. "You told me you give a crap."

"I do."

"How? How do you give a crap?"

London inhaled smoke, and then formed her mouth into a
circle and blew out a string of perfectly shaped smoke rings.
She watched the rings hold shape for a few seconds, and
then slowly drift apart. "I do give a crap," she answered. "I
care what people say about me. Some of the things I hear,
some of the things I read—I mean, it's like people don't
think I have feelings, that money provides me with some sort
of insulator. Which it doesn't. And I care what they think
about me. Believe it or not, Cinda, I try very hard—so does
Maddy—to live up to Gamma Angel's legacy. I've told you
all about that. But it's like I can't keep myself from, well,
from just doing crazy things. And when I'm with Maddy, forget
it. She ups the ante. And so at those times, I figure, why the

hell not just have as much fun as I can? After all, I'll never be Gamma."

"Lots of people your age have money, Lonnie—a lot of it—and they don't seek out headlines or live lives that are essentially out of control from the moment they wake up. They just go from day to day keeping busy with things that give them a sense of satisfaction and purpose in the world."

London turned to Lucinda. "Okay, Gamma Angel."

Lucinda met London's eyes, and they stared at each other in silence for a few moments.

"I do good things with my money," London broke into the silence. "I'm involved with orphanages and manatee rescue foundations and save-the-whatever cause of the moment and—"

"You write out a check," Lucinda cut in. "You throw money at a problem or a cause. That doesn't mean you get involved."

London took another drag on her cigarette, then drained her glass. She ran a fingernail slowly up and down the outside of the glass, and then gently pushed against it. The glass tipped over, and then rolled a few inches on the bar.

"I do give a crap," she said softly. "I don't care if you don't believe me."

Lucinda took in a deep breath and stopped at the security checkpoint. She collected her briefcase and large shoulder purse from the conveyer belt, and then strode down the quiet corridor to one of the waiting rooms for the passengers who would be flying out from San Francisco in their private jets.

She started to rub her nose, stopped when she remembered the makeup she had painstakingly applied that morning—it was nowhere near as nicely done as London's, but she had at least made an attempt—and then pushed open the door.

London's head shot up the moment the door opened.

"Lucinda," she stated in a tone that was part scold, part impatience. From her chair in front of a large plate-glass window, she held up her left arm, turned it, and tapped a manicured fingernail against the face of her Patek Philippe watch.

"I know," Lucinda breathed out and rushed to where London was sitting with the latest issue of *Vogue* opened on her lap. A cell phone and a drink sat on the side table.

"They said no one is flying out. Nonstop, at least. Unless you want to stop over—"

London held up a hand and tightened her lips.

"The storm," Lucinda added.

"On the *East* Coast," London cut in. "We're on the *West* Coast."

"And flying east," Lucinda pointed out. "You can't fly into a storm."

"Like hell I can't."

"That's right," Lucinda said as she dropped her shoulder bag and briefcase on the floor, then slipped into the seat next to London. "Like hell, you can't."

London turned to face Lucinda. "Do something about it."

"What?"

"Find another way."

"The only other way is a layover in—"

"Nonstop," London cut her off.

"You can't."

"Make it happen, Cinda."

Lucinda smiled at London. "I'm good, Lonnie, but not that good. Mother Nature trumps me."

London stared at Lucinda for a beat, then licked her fingers, slapped at a page in the magazine, and turned it. "No one trumps you. I thought that's what you told me."

"I don't think I ever told you that. I told you that you'd find no one better than me to manage La Mira West. But nowhere on my resumé did I boast of being able to manage the weather."

London continued to flip through the magazine. "This," she said as she tapped a fingernail against a picture.

"What?" Lucinda asked as she leaned closer to London and looked down at the magazine.

"The Narciso Rodriguez dress. Get it for Betty. The *San Francisco Chronicle* reporter I talked to today. It's a perfect color for her—matches her eyes—and is a great design for her body. And you know that guy Charlie?"

Lucinda nodded as she opened up a notepad on her lap.

"Betty told me his mother has cancer. It doesn't look good. His father passed away years ago, and he's the only child, so he's been working and then spending time at her bedside. Find out what hospital she's staying in and send flowers. And write Charlie a sizeable check. I guess there's a chance, with a more aggressive treatment, that her cancer could go into remission. Let's cover the cost."

"Okay."

"And this," London said as she flipped to the next page and pointed to a Martine Sitbon khaki jumpsuit. "Get this for that Berkeley chick. And make sure we send checks to all the reporters."

Lucinda scribbled down London's instructions.

"How's Dolores?" London asked.

"Her ulcer's still acting up. She has migraines. She's very stressed."

"So, the usual, then."

"The usual."

"Lonnie, she says she wants to get out of the business."

"I'm not surprised."

"She says she wants to raise orchids."

"To do what?"

"To raise orchids," Lucinda repeated.

"I heard you the first time. I'm asking, what does she want to raise them to do?"

"I don't know. Look pretty, I guess."

"Did she say Grisham called her?"

Lucinda nodded.

"Good. I told him she was the best."

"I don't know if she'll take him on as a client."

"She will," London said. "John let me read his latest manuscript, and it's his best work yet. And Maddy is working on getting Robert Parker for her."

Lucinda closed the notebook and slipped it into her briefcase. "Why are you and Maddy finding clients for her? She says she has enough to keep her busy with you and your sister."

"She's also slowly falling apart," London noted. "My lifestyle—my sister's lifestyle—well, I think it's too much for her. Her health is—let's just say her health would probably improve if she was doing something else. We don't really have a need for a publicist anymore. She's been terrific to us since we opened our clubs years ago, but Maddy and I seem to be publicly self-sustaining." London immediately held up a hand and smiled. "I know, I know. Not always in a good way. Anyway, Maddy and I talked about getting Dolores hooked up in a more low-key publicist's environment. Book signings, reviews, and the like. Landing a few big names like Grisham and Parker—maybe even Grafton, but she could be a hard sell—would launch her into that."

Lucinda smiled. "That's really nice of you."

"Me? Nice?" London laughed, then gave a quick shrug of her shoulders. "I told you. I do give a crap. Plus, someone once told me that throwing money at a problem doesn't necessarily solve the problem. So there. Contrary to what you say, I do pay attention to you. At your family's Christmas gathering, your mother makes a ham. Your grandmother stuffs the turkey with your favorite stuffing. You give each other small presents that have a theme that changes every year, which you open at the dinner table. You have about a dozen nieces and nephews—"

"Eight," Lucinda corrected her.

"I rounded up."

"So if you listen to me so well, why do you—"

"Now," London said as she closed the magazine and handed it to Lucinda. "What time are we leaving?"

Lucinda slid the magazine into her briefcase. "I told you. You can't fly out tonight. Tomorrow morning, possibly."

"I want to fly out tonight."

"You can't."

"You tell the pilot we're going tonight."

"Lonnie, all the airports on the East Coast are closed. From Washington on up. There are already ten inches on the ground, gale-force winds. The snow is falling at a rate of—"

"We're going."

"We can't."

"If the president of the United States—"

"Please don't try that argument with me," Lucinda sighed. "You're not the president. We can take off from here. We can land somewhere. But not at La Guardia. Maybe Atlanta, but they're getting pretty full."

"I'm not going to Atlanta. I'm going to New York. And then Maddy and I are driving to Massachusetts. For Christmas with the parental units. This is how it is."

"I realize that."

"Then make it happen."

"Tomorrow. Sometime. When the airports open."

"Then I'm the first flight out," London told her.

"You'll fly out when they tell you."

"I thought you were a manager."

"Of your club, Lonnie. Not of airports."

"I should buy an airport."

"Then you'd better buy two. Because you have to land somewhere."

"Now what?"

"Tomorrow you fly out. That gets you into New York a day late, but still three days before Christmas."

"Oh, Maddy's going to love this," London said as she

picked up her cell phone and started to dial. She reached for her drink, took a sip, and then grimaced. "This is not Old Potrero single malt. It has to be St. George. Which is far inferior. I thought I told you to have them stock Old Potrero."

"I did. I'll have someone fired."

"Good. You do that."

"Hey," London said into the phone. "Latest *Vogue*. Don't get the Yves Saint Laurent Rive Gauche black silk georgette lace-up blouse. Or the Giuliana Teso wrap coat. Espresso leather with raccoon collar. Which one? Fine. Get it. But you'll look like shit in it. Because. *Because*. Okay. You have a similar one, and your butt looks like a watermelon in it. You're not still seeing that Latin singer, are you? What's his name? Huh? Ricardo? Like Ricky? Stupid name. Huh? Because he's old news. His latest CD got crap reviews. It's time to move on. He's just a one-CD wonder. What was that song? *I Wed Your Eyes*? Well, it was I Wed something. No. I'm done with her. Jennifer Traum has way too many hang-ups. She hasn't had a decent meal since she was breast-fed. 'I can't eat because I'm a model,' she whined the last time I took her out to dinner. She nearly passed out on the Paris runway wearing MaxMara. The dress was terrific—didn't like the cut on the shoulders, though. Traum looked like a refugee who was one rice bowl short of starvation. And her skin was awful. That woman needs makeup over her entire body. Listen. Lucinda tells me I can't fly out. Well, if you knew that, why didn't you tell me? Because I don't pay attention to *your* damn weather. It's sunny and warm here. Well, it should be that way everywhere. That's why they call this the Best Coast. Yes, I thought that was funny. Yes. *Yes!* I know how to pack, you idiot, and I know that snow is cold. Listen. I want to fly out to Boston the moment I get in. Why not? What party? What? Emeralds and Elephants? What the heck is that, a fancy Jenny Craig ball? Huh? Why are we going there? How much? We're giving a mil to the Wildlife Conversation Society?"

"I think she means conservation," Lucinda told London.

London stopped speaking and glanced at Lucinda.

"You said Wildlife *Conversation* Society," Lucinda said. "I think it's conservation."

London gave Lucinda a grin. "Of course it is." Then she held the phone out in front of her mouth. "It's *conservation*, you idiot!" she yelled, then returned the phone to her ear. "No, you didn't. No, you *didn't*. You said *conversation*. You did. You *did!* Okay, whatever. We'll give the damn check to whatever society to save whatever damn animals, whether they're conversing or conserving, and then we're flying out. No, I'm not staying over. We don't have time. *Because.* Because we'll only have two shopping days before Gamma Angel's dinner and then Christmas. Where? Yeah, yeah. Definitely Chanel on Newbury Street. And Armani and Versace. And I want to go to Alan Bilzerian to see the new Yamamoto. Yes, Yamamoto looks good on you. But I get first choice this time. Because you got the one you wanted last time. Did you get the Revelion chairs delivered? What's the matter with them? Huh? Then tell them you don't want them. I told you they wouldn't match. I did. *I did.* Then you need to listen to me more. I did tell you. I *did.* Oh, fuck you."

London handed the phone to Lucinda. "Hang up on her, would you?"

Lucinda gave London a half-smile, then clicked off the phone.

"What?" London asked as she noticed Lucinda staring at her.

"You always make me hang up on your sister."

"Technically, I'm hanging up."

"Literally, I am."

"But it feels so much better when you do it."

"What do you do when I'm not around to hang up on her?"

London laughed. "Sometimes I hand the phone to a stranger and say, 'Could you turn the phone off for me? I just had my nails done.' "

Lucinda smiled and shook her head.

"Don't you hang up on your sister?"

Lucinda shook her head. "No."

"Never?"

"Never. We actually get along great. We're family, but we're also friends."

London shook her head. "Maddy and I, well, having an identical twin isn't like having a sister. It's like having a lover. Someone you hate. Someone you can't do without. Because a twin is just you in a different body. Sometimes— most times—I can't stand being around her. Listening to her voice. It's like listening to me. Watching her do things in just the way I do them, like I'm watching a movie of myself. It's annoying. But I can't live without her. Because without her, I think I'd die." London paused, and then laughed. "Oh, the drama of it all!"

Lucinda smiled at London. "That's pretty interesting. I don't know what it's like to have a twin."

"Well, there it is," London answered. "Now call George. You can tell him to take a left this time. My gift to you, since you're refusing to wear my Dior coat, is a quiet exit from the airport."

2

"**F**ucking bitch! Fucking asshole!" Madrid shouted as she stood up on the bed and flung the cell phone across the room. Then she yanked the top sheet from the bed, whipped its satiny softness around her naked body, and leaped onto the floor.

"Ayiee, Maddy! You almost step on me! Why you be crazy woman from the moment you open your eyes?"

Madrid threw a hard stare at the man who was lying in her bed. " 'Why you be'?" Madrid repeated in a perfect mimic of Ricardo's voice. "I keep telling you, talk proper English. You sound stupid when you don't."

"That *is* the English," Ricardo countered defensively, then scratched a thick patch of dark chest hair, leaned over the side of the bed, and pulled a blanket up from the floor. "Why you take the sheet?" he asked as he bundled the blanket around his naked body. "Why you throw the phone? You always throw the phone. How many phones you have? And why you keep swearing? Such stuff that comes out from your lips! I tell you, you are too beautiful to be having such ugly words coming from your lovely mouth."

Madrid rolled her eyes and shook her head, then walked

down the steps that ringed the bedroom area and over to the floor-to-ceiling windows that offered a city-wide view from her spacious, open-floor-plan New York City Tribeca loft. "Fucking snow. This screws up everything."

"Again, with the fuck," Ricardo called out to her.

Madrid switched her focus from the snowstorm that was rapidly blanketing the city to take in her reflection in the window. She was drawn to looking at herself whenever she could, if only to provide herself with the reassurance that she did, indeed, exist. She needed to see how she was different from her twin, how she was a unique individual in the world, but there were such subtle differences between her and Lonnie that she often had to take a close, hard look. And then there were those frightening times when she had had too much to drink or drug or was just not paying attention and caught a glimpse of herself in a mirror or store window, and her heart would race because she would see, at first, Lonnie, and then think that she no longer existed.

Even upon an acutely close inspection of their bodies, which she and Lonnie had conducted numerous times as they were growing up because they were infinitely fascinated by the fact that they were exact duplicates of one another, there was little to distinguish them in their physical appearance—not even a minute deviation in their height, in their slender frames, in their broad shoulders, in their dark brown, shoulder-length, naturally wavy hair, in their gray-green eyes outlined by perfectly shaped, no-need-to-pluck eyebrows, in the oval shape of their faces, in the way that their full lips formed smiles, frowns, and pouts. Even their voices were echoes of one another's, with the same inflections and tone—so similar that their mutual friends and even their family members who called them on the phone would always preface a conversation by first asking, "Lonnie? Maddy? Which one am I talking to?"

"Who the fuck do you want to talk to?" she would ask if she was the one who answered the phone.

Well, that's a difference, Madrid noted. *I swear more than Lonnie.*

If Lonnie answered the phone, Madrid continued on in her thinking, she would hear her quip, "You're talking to the more beautiful twin."

Lonnie did have the quicker wit, she thought with a twinge of jealousy, then recalled that it was a quality that oftentimes got her sister in trouble because she didn't know when to use her humor and when to shut it off. Nine times out of ten, after Lonnie had snapped off some quick, sharp retort to a query from a member of the press and the reporter had, of course, printed it, one of the parental units would reprimand her by saying, "Why can't you be more like Maddy? She always knows the right thing to say to the public. I swear, you're her age—you even beat her out of the womb by a minute or so—but you're years behind her in maturity."

And there's another difference, Madrid thought. *Not visible, sure, but a difference nonetheless.*

In their teenage years, she had started parting her hair on the left and told Lonnie that if she ever did the same thing, even as a joke—unless it was agreed upon by both of them as part of a trick they would play on someone—she would sneak into her bedroom and shave her head while she was sleeping. To this day, the differing parts in their hair were the only noticeable variation in their physical appearance and something that had turned out to be a brilliant solution that helped others to distinguish them as well.

When you're young, it's fun. Madrid smiled as she recalled the mantra she shared with Lonnie from their youth—a sort of personal, bonding affirmation they had created while experimenting with increasingly devious ways to dupe others into thinking that she was Lonnie and Lonnie was she.

As soon as they could walk and then manipulate zippers and ties and buttons and bows with some skill, there was no stopping one from assuming the other's identity, which brought them endless pleasure. Their nanny would dress them in matching outfits of different colors in the morning so she could distinguish one from the other, but once they were out of her sight, they would switch clothes and then giggle incessantly throughout the day as the nanny would look one in the eye and call her the name of the other. They would deceive their teachers by sitting in different seats and then, as they got older and were separated by varying class schedules, both to help their teachers educate them as individuals as well as to keep them apart because together they were too disruptive, each would attend the other's classes and do the other's homework.

However, as soon as they entered their first year at Concord Academy, their most distinguishing difference surfaced. Madrid took in a deep breath, and then sighed.

"I like girls," London had told her one afternoon during a class field trip as they were walking through a graveyard full of dead classic authors who had lived in Concord. Madrid closed her eyes as she remembered the flaming reds, brilliant yellows, and juicy orange glows bursting forth from the New England fall foliage around them and the sound their shuffling, school-issued oxford shoes had made as they crunched their way through the curled, crisp-brown leaves that had blanketed the pebbled pathway.

"But I'm not," she had answered.

"I know," London had replied with such sadness in her voice.

Madrid had felt scared for her sister—scared even for herself—and had grabbed Lonnie's arm and pulled her off the cemetery path, away from the rest of the class and their teacher, who predominantly talked in a monotone but then would suddenly emphasize one word with such unpredictability and loudness that the half-shuttered eyes of her students would fly open in fear, thinking that they were missing something truly significant.

As Madrid pulled London toward her, their teacher's voice droned in the background: "Ralph Waldo Emerson was, as you know, one of America's most influential authors and thinkers, a Unitarian minister who left his church because of doctoral disputes and settled in Concord, Massachusetts, where he lectured extensively about transcendentalism and the MYSTICAL unity of nature . . ."

London had smiled at Madrid then, forced her eyes wide open, and mouthed the word *mystical!*

She had frowned and repeated, "I'm not."

London nodded and returned her frown. "I know, I know. We're supposed to be alike in every way, but now . . ." She had paused, and then grinned. "At least we won't be fighting over the same boy, right? I guess this is what's going to make us different from each other. We always wanted to find something . . ."

"I know. But I wanted it to be a mole or a birthmark or a scar or something like that. Then I could say, 'I'm Madrid. I'm the one with the mole on my arm.' Then people would see and know that it was me. This isn't going to help. It's invisible."

"Except when I'm with a girl."

"Oh, like now you're going to be Velcroed to girls?" she had asked, and then stared at Lonnie with wide eyes. "Shit, Lonnie, shit!"

"What?"

"Now everyone's going to think I'm a lezzie, too."

"No, they're not."

"Yes, they are."

"Aren't."

"Are, too. I mean, duh, what happens when I'm walking around campus with a girl or going to a movie with one of my girlfriends—shit, I can't call them that anymore, can I?— or doing anything with a girl? Now everyone's going to think that I am."

London had returned her stare, then smiled.

"What?"

"We can have some fun with this, Maddy."

"What do you—oh! *Oh!*"

London placed her hands together close to her face and looked over them at her. "Can you *imagine?*"

She returned Lonnie's grin. "Wicked. Really wicked. But there's just one thing. I'm not kissing any girl. Not like that."

"And I'm not kissing any boy. *At all.* But can you imagine their faces when they make their move and then we say, 'Hey, you must have me confused with my sister. Because I'm not that way.' "

"I like it."

"Me, too."

And now, several years and several lovers later, Madrid thought as she focused on her reflection in the loft's window, ran a tongue over her full lips, regarded her eyes, and re-arranged her hair with a hand, *here I am. Find a lover, have sex, break up. Find a lover, have sex, break up. It doesn't matter, gay or straight,* she thought. *Lonnie and I are still alike. When I hate someone she's with, I tell her to end it. And she does the same with me.*

She refocused on the snow that was hurtling past the window at an angle and stinging the pane with muffled clicks. "Remember last night, Ricardo?" she called over her shoulder. "You didn't seem to mind when I told you I wanted to *suck* your dick, did you? And you didn't seem too upset when I said I wanted you to *fuck* me hard. I didn't hear you getting all upset when I used those words."

"Please, baby. In the passion, I *love* those words," Ricardo answered as he tossed his feet to the floor, wrapped the blanket around his tall, lanky body, and shuffled down the steps and over to where Madrid stood. "They make me hot, yes. *You* make me hot," he whispered as he came up behind Madrid, placed his hands on her hips, and leaned his chin against her shoulder. "But when you are just talking. Before even your coffee. It's fuck this. Fuck that. You are too pretty, too wonderful, to be talking like that. A woman is to be gentle and kind and—"

Madrid pushed Ricardo away from her and whirled around to face him. "Would you stop with your fucking Spanish male fucking romantic attitude of how women should fucking be? Because from day one, when I fucked your Spanish dick in that recording studio, I've been using *fuck* as a verb, noun, adjective, and adverb. It's part of my vocabulary. So get the fuck over it. Christ!"

"And now with Jesus," Ricardo commented as he did a quick sign-of-the-cross, shot a glance up at the ceiling, and then watched Madrid storm away from him and into the kitchen. She pressed a button on the coffeemaker, opened a stainless steel cabinet, and pulled out a mug.

"I'm done, Ricardo," she said as she peered through the clear glass door of the refrigerator, then opened the door and located a half-pint of creamer.

"Good. Good, good, good, Maddy. No fighting is a good way to start the day together, yes?"

Madrid turned to Ricardo. "No. I mean, I'm done, Rick. Done with being with you. I want you to leave."

"Because you are leaving today for home?"

Madrid waved an arm at the windows. "Does it fucking look like I'm going to be leaving for home today? Does it fucking look like Lonnie's fucking plane is going to be able to fucking land here?"

"So why do you want me to leave?"

"Because we're over."

"Over?"

"I don't want to sleep with you anymore."

"Ah, baby, no. You are just mad at me for talking about the swearing. You can say *fuck*. Say it all you want. Say *fuck, fuck, fuck*. I stay."

"No—*baby*—I am done fucking with you. When you had

that stupid hit song and you were on top of the charts, you were much more appealing to me. It was exciting to be with you then, to see all those women at your concerts lifting their shirts for you when you were on stage. They would've chewed off their right arms to have you fuck them, and all I could think was, 'Hey, bitches, I'm fucking him.' You rode the royalties for awhile, and now all you're doing is riding me. You haven't seen the inside of a recording studio since then, let alone even hummed a song in the shower. You're not doing anything with your life. Get out."

"That is what you're mad about? I tell you this before. It's because I didn't want all that fame, baby. It was too confusing, too much being out there night after night, too much not who I really am. I love to sing, but singing isn't riding on buses and flying in airplanes and waking up in places where you don't know where you are. Singing isn't doing the same song over and over and over until I want to puke, until the sound engineers finally say, 'Okay, that's a good one.' I want to say, 'What was wrong with the fifty other times I sang the song the same way?' I want to be with you. And you are right. I am not making any more money. So I want you to stop paying for all our fancy dinners and the theater and the concerts and the fine clothes that you buy me. I can pay my own way. I'll get a job. I have a brother who has his own business. It's a good business. Carlos can get me a job in construction. I like hard work. And I like you. No, I love you, Maddy. I want you to marry me."

"Oh, please," Madrid answered and emitted a short snort. "If I wanted a construction worker, I'd walk to midtown and take my pick. I don't want to marry you. I don't love you. I don't even think I like you. And I hated that fucking song of yours. Someday soon it will be elevator music and will drive everyone nuts. So get out."

Ricardo stared at Madrid as he shifted from foot to foot on the gleaming black linoleum kitchen floor. Then he gave a quick shiver and pulled the blanket tighter around him.

Madrid raised her eyebrows and then snapped out, "What?"

He flashed her a quick grin, displaying his perfect set of bright white teeth. "This is what they say, no?" he asked in a soft voice.

"What are you talking about?"

"This is what they say you do. You and your sister. You go through people like they are meaningless, yes? You break hearts."

"Don't be so dramatic."

"You. You're the one who breaks the hearts of men. Your sister, the one who fucks the women, she breaks their hearts. The two of you can break everyone's hearts. You are double trouble."

Madrid sighed. "Again with the drama. It's time for you to go, Ricardo."

"Because I do not measure up."

Madrid shifted her eyes down Ricardo's body and smiled. "You measure up. But . . ." She lost her smile, raised her eyes, and met his. "You are no longer a success. You are a one-hit wonder. Maybe you'll be on one of those shows. What are they called? The ones where you find out what a former star is now doing. They'll show you singing your silly little one hit and then the camera will show you standing at a construction site covered in mud, with a fucking beer belly sticking out over a pair of dirty jeans, a ratty old T-shirt, a bloated face and a sagging chin, and your butt crack showing whenever you bend over. You're finished, Ricardo. And so I'm finished with you. I require only one thing from a man, and that is success. No one can be with me without it."

"So if I have another hit song . . ."

"You just told me that you don't want to sing. You want to fucking pound nails all day."

"I'll call my agent. I'll go back to the studio. I will do that for you."

"I don't want you to do anything for me. Except get out. Now!"

Madrid sprawled on the unmade bed with a cordial glass of Godiva chocolate liquor in her hand and photo albums crammed full of newspaper clippings scattered around her. She surveyed the grainy pictures. "I've had him. And him. And him and him and him. Men from every sport but football. No, wait. Soccer. But who the fuck is a soccer star? And who the fuck cares about soccer anyway? I've had Mister Oscar-winner here. And what have you done since you held that statuette in your hands two years ago, Mister Leading Man? And there's Mister Moody Artist. 'If I cannot paint, then I cannot perform in bed. It's just that simple.' Remember what I told you when you said that? 'If you cannot perform in bed, then you're sleeping alone. It's just that simple.' And there's Mister Senator. God, were you ever a bore. Middle East crisis, water shortage in California, road repair budget overruns—who gives a fuck?" Her eyes stopped when she spotted the photograph of her with Ricardo Raminero at a New Year's Eve bash at her La Mira East nightclub. The headline blared out, big and bold: LATIN HEARTTHROB BEATS STRONG FOR MADRID LA MIRA.

"It's only day one," Madrid muttered as she opened an album and browsed through pictures of London with a variety of actresses and models. *Always allow three days to recover from a breakup,* she and London had vowed after breaking up with their respective love interests on the same Friday morning while in their senior year at Concord Academy and then spent the rest of the weekend moping around the house. They called their three-day heartbreak mender La Mira's Breakup Plan, which was formulated the following Monday afternoon to keep them from devouring everything in sight after their next breakup and from getting too distraught over what Lonnie called "the inconsequential people."

"Inconsequential?" she had asked her sister. "But I told him that I loved him. And I do."

"Do?"

"I mean, I did."

"And I told her that I loved her," London answered. "And I did. So what? People say that all the time. Although, point of fact, sis, it's a good idea to have them say it first. When you say it first, it's a sign of weakness. But once you say it, you have to keep on saying it. It's what you're supposed to say when you're boinking someone so you can keep on boinking them. But it doesn't matter if they love you or you love them. In the end, they're still inconsequential. Because if we're dumping them, then they can't be very significant, can they?"

Inconsequential, Madrid thought as she remembered how it felt to be held by Ricardo. Then she sighed and said out loud, "One day to mourn 'em, one day to miss 'em, and one day to move on."

Day one is always the hardest, she thought, then lay back against a pile of pillows and listened to the silence in her loft. She had given everyone on her household staff and at the club the day off, thinking that she and London would be on their way to Boston around this time. Now there was no one at the club to take her mind off of Ricardo, no one to cook for her, no one to drive her to wherever she wanted to go, and no one to clean up after her—*just how skanky are these sheets?* she wondered as she turned and stuck her nose into one of the pillows. She could smell Ricardo's cologne and a mix of their sexual scents.

"Rick was definitely a terrific lover," she proclaimed out loud. "And certainly more vocal." She remembered that at first she hadn't liked his constant murmuring while he was on top of her, telling her how good she felt, how good she made him feel, and, among many other things, how beautiful she was—*I mean, duh,* she had thought at the time. Later on, when she had called London and told her some of the things that he had said in the heat of passion, London had countered, "Can't he be more creative than that? I mean, your being beautiful is a no-brainer. Like you and I haven't heard that a million times. What do they think we're going to say in response? 'Gosh, you *really* think so?' "

But then, after their passion was spent and they were lying together as the drying sweat cooled their bodies, Ricardo would talk to her about how open his heart was to her and how the warmth of their lovemaking would even reach his fingertips. She closed her eyes and recalled the sound of his low voice whispering in her ear and those times when he had said those words—lying on top of her, still inside her, her legs wrapped around his. She normally wasn't someone who liked to do what she and her sister called "bed-lingering"—*"I mean, how much of a waste of time is that?"* London had once asked her and she had always agreed. But Ricky had made her feel safe and relaxed and just plain lazy, and she never wanted to get out of bed when she was with him.

London had laughed out loud when she had told her that Ricky made her feel safe. "Safe is having your boys use condoms, Mad. Safe is a security system in your house. Safe is how you feel with a substantial bank balance. Don't fall for that bullshit. Words are just words, and they matter even less when they bookend an orgasm. What are you, going through PMS or something? Get the fuck out of bed and get your face in the newspaper. Go shopping and spend lots of money. You're not with him to feel safe. You're with him to get press."

She reached for the phone and hit one of the buttons. "It's me. I dumped him. I know, it's what you said. You're right. I know. It's just day one, and I'm fucking bored. I know, I know. Two more to go. Huh? Drinking. Godiva. Well, what the fuck else can I do? It's a fucking blizzard here. Huh? I can't. I can't go out. *Because.* Because I gave everyone the day off. You were supposed to be here. Yes, I know what I'm wearing to the party tomorrow. Let me ask you something, Lon. Why is it getting harder? No, I don't mean being without a staff. I mean being without him. I mean, well, I don't know. I just mean, it seems to me that it's getting harder to break up. No, I'm not drunk. I mean, shouldn't we be with someone by this time? *Be* with someone. *Be, be, be!* Be, as in longer than a few weeks or a few months. Huh? Well, I don't know for how long. Long, I guess. But *be* with them. *Really* be with them. I feel like we're getting too old to keep doing this bullshit. Oh, fuck you! *Fuck you!* I *am not* getting all soft. *I am not!* Listen, don't try to tell me that you haven't asked yourself the same question. Don't deny it. Huh? I'll tell you what I mean. I recall you calling me after that sitcom actress dumped you. Didn't you buy matching rings with her? Weren't you thinking about having that, what do you call it, that—oh, come on, you know what I'm talking about. That's right! A commitment ceremony! Weren't you planning one of those with her? Yes, I know that you need two people. Wasn't that a switch, *her* dumping *you* before you could dump her? Well, it's just too damn bad I brought her up again, isn't it? *Don't* fucking hang up on me, Lon! I want you to listen to me. *Listen to me.* All I'm saying is, we're going to be thirty this year. No, I'm not rubbing that in your face. No, I didn't say there was anything wrong with that. I just mean, well, isn't it about time we had something more, I don't know, *consistent?* No, I *don't* want to have a baby! Why do you always ask me that when I'm bummed out after a breakup? *So?* So what are you saying? That we're going to keep doing this until we're fucking eighty years old? I am *not* getting weird on you. I'm just saying. I said, I'm just saying. Why don't you turn the fucking music down? Who?

How long you been fucking her? Fine. I said fine. Go. Just get off the fucking phone and go eat her. No, I'm not mad. I said I'm fucking not mad. Oh, *fuck you!*"

Madrid lobbed the phone out of her hands, heard glass shatter, and muttered, "What the fuck." She shrugged her shoulders, drained her glass, and then picked up the newspaper article with the picture of her with Ricardo. She stared at the picture, kissed it, and then slowly tore it into pieces.

"What in God's good three-letter name . . . is that you, Maddy? Jean-Paul—quick! Boil water! Do something! We have an emergency! Maddy is a human popsicle!"

"Raph-ph-ph-ael." Madrid squeezed out a greeting through chattering lips as she stood, shivering, in the entry-way of the first-floor brownstone apartment of her friends Jean-Paul Montrouge and Raphael Barthelemy.

"What in Frosty the Snowman are you doing outside in this weather, girl? And that blue shade of lipstick—*très gothique!*—but it simply *has* to go!" Raphael commented as he fluttered his long brown eyelashes at Madrid and grimaced at the snow that swirled in through the open door and all around him. He crooked an elbow and held an arm up to his face. "It's not snowing out. Little bees are stinging me. What a world! What a world!"

Madrid untangled her arms from her chest, slowly raised them, and then held out the shaking limbs to Raphael. "In."

"Of course, of course, of course," Raphael gasped as he grabbed an arm, pulled Madrid into the house, and then leaned a shoulder into the door. "Jean-Paul!" he called out as he pushed the door shut, then bolted it. "She's too weak to even move! I had to *carry* her into the house! Hurry!"

"Help Maddy take off her clothes," Jean-Paul called out from another room.

Raphael put a finger to his mouth and frowned as he regarded Madrid. "If she's *cold,* Jean-Paul, then *why* am I taking off her clothes?"

"Based on the weather outside, I'd assume that they're wet," Jean-Paul answered.

Raphael rolled his eyes at Madrid and then mouthed, *I'd assume that they're wet.* Then he shrugged his shoulders. "He's handsome, *and* he's smart. Well, you know what happens when you assume, right, girl?" he asked as he stepped toward her. "Undress a woman. This is something new for Raphael." He struggled to unbutton her snow-and-sleet-covered coat as she kept shivering. "Goodness, you're like one big vibrator, aren't you, honey?" he commented. "Batteries not included. Some assembly required. Have you been watching TV? That's all they say after every ad for a toy for the rugrats. All I want is another G.I. Joe-Boy." He undid the last button, danced around her as he pulled her coat off an arm at a time, and dropped it on the floor. "Shit, woman, is that a Christina Oxenberg cashmere?"

Madrid nodded. "M-m-musk ox, g-g-g-uanaco, and s-s-s-suri."

"Honey, I don't know what you're saying," Raphael answered as he patted her arm, then called over his shoulder in a frantic shout, "Hurry, Jean-Paul! She's talking crazy stuff. Isn't mental breakdown the first stage of that hypo . . . hypo . . . well, it's hypo-something. Hypo-cold?"

"I'm right here," Jean-Paul said as he walked down the hallway toward them, holding a wool blanket in his arms. He stopped and peered at Madrid. "My, my! You have got one red face, woman. Looks like a Botox treatment gone awry. Not to worry. You'll be your beautiful self again once the boys have at you. Here, hon, wrap this around her," he told Raphael as he held out the blanket. "But please take a deep breath first. You're going to make everyone have a mental breakdown."

Raphael took the blanket, and then leaned toward Jean-Paul. "She's using strange words."

"I'm-m-m n-n-not," Madrid said as she grabbed the blanket out of Raphael's hands and clutched it to her chest. "It's the s-s-s-weater. You asked. An-an-imals. In th-the sw-sweater."

"Who cares about animals?" Jean-Paul asked as he picked up Madrid's coat. "How did you get here?" He shook out the coat, stared down at the Oriental rug for a few moments, then draped the coat on a wall hook.

"The J-J-Jag."

Jean-Paul peered out of one of the long, rectangular windows that framed the heavy wooden oak door of the entryway. "Where did you park?"

Madrid pulled the blanket tightly around her shoulders with Raphael's help and then shrugged. "A s-sidewalk. S-somewhere. Couldn't stop. Sp-spun out. Kn-knocked over a parking meter."

"Oh, my God! And you've been in an accident as well!" Raphael exclaimed. "This is *so much* to take in at once! You have to come in and calm down."

Jean-Paul placed a hand on Raphael's shoulder. "*You* need to calm down. She just needs to warm up. I'm going to make some cocoa."

"Oh, what a delight!" Raphael exclaimed as he clapped his hands together and jumped up and down. "Me, too! Me, too! Cocoa in the snow—how perfect is that? Right by the Christmas tree. You should see the beauty we got this year, Mad. Long and wide, like a perfectly endowed lover. And maybe we can pop popcorn in the fireplace, too, Jean-Paul! It'll be a blizzard party!"

"Where's your driver?" Jean-Paul called over his shoulder as he walked down the hallway.

"N-night off," Madrid answered as she reached down to take off her boots, then stared at her bright-red hands.

Raphael took one of her hands in his, then immediately released it. "Iceberg dead ahead, Captain. I'm sure you had a reason for wearing *no* gloves *and* no hat, girl." Raphael put his arm around her shoulders and guided her to a chair in the hallway. "Sit. Lecture time. See the weather? And you went out of the house thinking, 'Oh, that's not so bad.' " He folded his arms across his chest. "Why even bother with a coat or—say, are those boots Sergio?" he asked as he glanced down at her feet.

Madrid sat and nodded. "First time I've worn them. But now look at them. They're ruined."

Raphael patted one of the boots. "These are show boots, love, not snow boots. You need those big ugly-ass furry things that make your feet look like you have elephantiasis. Of course, you have to live in Alaska to pull them off as a fashion statement. These leather boots aren't made for walking, unless it's from valet parking."

She held onto Raphael's thin shoulders as he struggled to remove one of her boots. "It s-seemed like I was walking forever," she told him. "There are no fucking c-cabs."

Raphael grunted as he gave the boot a few quick tugs. "Honey, you are as tight as an adolescent's butt," he said, then leaned back on his heels and pulled hard on the bottom of the boot.

Madrid gripped his shoulders. "Where are your m-muscles?"

"Slathered all over the chair at the store," he answered through clenched teeth. "That's all I do. Sit on my butt all day. Or wait on customers. I'm getting it," he groaned as he started to twist the boot from side to side.

"You do realize that my leg doesn't come off."

"But it would help," he answered, then paused in his exertions. "So would muscles. I *want* to go to the gym. I *should* be going at least three times a week. But how can I? Jean-Paul is twice my age and has more energy than I certainly have. Maybe what you do when you're young is store up all of your energy, then release it in midlife like one big tidal wave. A tsunami. I love that word. Anyway, he's up at first light every single day and doesn't go to bed until late. I say,

'You can hire someone to do the books' or to do whatever it is that keeps him moving, or—*heaven forbid*—I tell him that *I* can help, but he wants to do everything himself. My man is *very* hands-on." Raphael flashed his dark brown eyes at Madrid and gave her a sly grin. He repositioned himself and renewed his exertions on the boot. "And he's always flying here and there and everywhere to find the best antiques—spanning the globe, for Manhattan's exclusive Duettos on Lexington," he chuckled. "So I'm left to mind the store like a good wife. And, of course, we're always busy. Busy, busy, busy. It's all too much."

"When's he turning the big four-oh?"

"He's hanging on to his thirties by a fingernail until next spring, sweetie. There!" Raphael exclaimed as he successfully extricated a boot, then flung it over his shoulder and sat down on the rug, breathing heavily. "Oh, my. Let me just catch my breath here. Now I know what they mean when they say, 'I just have to catch my breath.' " He took a deep breath, then stared down at his light khaki slacks. "Look at me. Wet in the crotch, just like a girl! Or maybe I got all excited thinking about an adolescent's butt. No matter. I'm about done in. Can you live with the other boot on?"

"No."

Raphael stared up at Madrid. "Are . . . you . . . sure?" he asked slowly.

Madrid flashed him a smile and then slowly drew out her reply. "Yeeesss. I'm sure."

"*My Cousin Vinny,*" they said at the same time and laughed.

"I love that Marisa Tomei," Raphael told her as he urged his wiry body up from the floor. "Did I tell you that she came into the store? Maybe a week or so ago. Wanted an armoire for herself, for Christmas. Fell in love with two we had. So she bought both!"

"G-good."

Raphael gripped onto her boot, started to pull, and then

stopped and draped an arm across Madrid's lap. "So my man's going to be turning forty, right? And he says to me, 'Now you're going to want to find someone younger.' Like, he suddenly forgets that I'm positively *drawn* to older men. Or that I'm truly, madly, deeply in love with him. Did I tell you? We're celebrating our tenth anniversary right after his birthday! He's taking me to the Riviera. How romantic! I don't want to leave him, Mad. *Why* would I want to do that? I want to grow old with him."

Madrid took a hand out from under the blanket and placed it against Raphael's face.

"Fucking cold, honey," he said.

"Fucking trying to comfort you, honey," she answered, then started to run her fingers through Raphael's wiry, short brown hair.

"I mean, the older he gets, the more I want to be with him. And he doesn't look forty. He hasn't got an ounce of fat on him, has marvelous leg muscles from all the walking he does on his shopping trips, takes wonderful care of me, and is still a stud in bed. Sure, he's losing a little bit of his top hat—some of it's getting gray—and he has to wear reading glasses, but I find those things so hot. So why would I want to leave him? But he's been talking like this for months. It's driving me nuts."

"My boot isn't going to take itself off, you know," Madrid said.

"Here's a question, snow queen," Raphael began as he gripped her boot and tugged at it. "What if we hadn't been here tonight? Would we have come home and found you on our steps, frozen solid? Would you have tried in vain to keep yourself warm with your cigarette lighter, like the little match girl? That would've been so dramatic, you know."

"I think nearly freezing to death is enough drama for one night."

"But how would they get you in the ambulance?" Raphael continued. "You would be like this," he said as he fell back on the floor and held his arms out from his body and his legs splayed in the air. "Madrid La Mira. Found frozen to death on the steps where her best friends, Raphael Barthelemy and Jean-Paul Montrouge, live, in their magnificent, showcase apartment. Details at eleven."

"I wouldn't have been frozen in that position, Numb Nuts. I would've been frozen like this," Madrid said as she drew up her legs and folded her arms over them. "People who are freezing don't look like they're going down a water slide."

Raphael giggled, then returned to loosening her boot. "They would have to thaw your body—your fingers would be gripped like this, in claws," he said, demonstrating to her. "And if you're frozen solid in that curled-up position, they wouldn't be able to stuff you in the casket. It would've been all too much, your death at such a young age. So tragic. It would've been like the opening sequence to an episode of *Six Feet Under.* Pan the camera on the blizzard. It's ferocious! A big one! And then there you are, frantically trying to get here. Oh, no! There's an accident. Will that kill her? No, it won't, because there she is, struggling to get out of the car. But you know she's doomed because everyone at the beginning of the show dies. And so you struggle and struggle and struggle to get to your best friends' house. The camera pans away from you to me, a close-up, of course, as I sit in front of the fireplace, reading a fashion magazine, glancing up every moment or so to stare pensively out of the window like I know something isn't right, but I just can't put my finger on it."

"This isn't about you, Raphael. I'm out there dying, remember?"

"Yes, yes, but remember that I'll then be in the rest of the show because I'll have to attend your funeral and say some incredibly deep and powerful words about you."

"This isn't about you."

"Okay, okay. So you're struggling in the blizzard to reach

a point of safety—it's amazing, of course, and everyone who is watching is on the edge of their seats. They want to root for you, but they know it's all for naught."

"For naught?"

"For naught. I like that word. It's all for naught. Very emotive, don't you think? You finally crawl your way up our stairs—"

"I didn't crawl. I walked."

"But you were nearly spent. The sands in your hourglass were slowly slipping away."

"In the meantime, you two are in here thinking only of yourselves, while outside I'm slowly freezing to death."

"You don't have the strength to knock on the door. It's all too much for you. Jean-Paul and I can hear this feeble tapping sound coming from outside. I ask, 'Do you hear that, honey?' And Jean-Paul pauses for a moment, listening, and then says, 'Ah, but it's just the wind.' "

"He doesn't say *ah*. No one says *ah*. He'll say, 'It's just the wind.' "

"Not ah?"

"No."

"Shit. I put that in the screenplay I'm writing. Did I tell you that I'm writing a screenplay?"

"Did I tell you that I'm fucking freezing?"

"Oh, well, isn't it just always about you? See if I ever write about you. And once this boot is off, there is no way I'm taking off your clothes. Unless you'd like to give me that Oxenberg."

"You take off the boot, and it's yours."

"Oh, goody!"

"I'm finally getting the feeling back in my feet," Madrid said, then blew on a hot mug of cocoa she held cradled in her hands as she sat in one of the three Jean Michel Frank chairs set up in front of the fireplace.

"More lemon-dill pound cake?" Jean-Paul asked as he held out a plate of thin cake slices to her.

Madrid shook her head. "No. But everything's delicious, Jean-Paul. You are such an amazing cook."

"Now, remember that our next Sunday brunch is two days after the New Year's Eve party at your club," Raphael told her as he leaned forward and reached out to a bowl on the mahogany-and-marble coffee table. He scooped a dollop of fresh whipped cream into his mug and then sat back in his chair. "Since it's the first of the twelve brunches we hold each year and it's so near the holidays, the RSVPs have been simply flying in!"

"I'll be there," Madrid said, then added with a frown, "sans Ricardo."

Raphael patted her leg. "So sad. You do go through them, girl. Like orange juice during the cold season. He seemed to have such good qualities—handsome and hunky. He's not gay, is he?"

Madrid shook her head. "No."

"Then it just didn't work out?" Jean-Paul asked.

Madrid let out a sigh. "I broke all of the rules with him."

Jean-Paul sat back in his chair and crossed his legs. "What kind of rules?"

"Kinky sex rules?" Raphael asked with a grin.

Madrid flashed Raphael a smile, then looked at Jean-Paul and shrugged a shoulder. "I don't know. They're just rules Lonnie and I made up years ago. We had made a rule, well, a plan, after we had each broken up with someone, to help us not eat everything in sight and end up the size of a rhinoceros. And so we wouldn't get all caught up in someone and then be devastated when the relationship ended."

"Ah, the Three Days to Recovery Plan, right?" Raphael asked.

Madrid nodded.

"But if you're always dumping other people, then why would you even *be* devastated?" Jean-Paul asked.

"If you ever dumped me, *I'd* be devastated," Raphael told Jean-Paul. "My whole life is you."

"Am I ever going to be able to say that to someone?" Madrid asked.

"Sure you will," Raphael told her. "Start practicing now. Repeat after me. My . . . whole . . . life . . . is . . ."

"Besides Lonnie, no one else *is* my whole life," Madrid cut in. "And anyway, there are the rules."

"Ah. The rules," Jean-Paul said.

Raphael leaned forward in his chair, shot Madrid a quick glance, and raised his eyebrows. "Ah! You see? He *does* say it."

"Say what?"

"Never mind, sweetie," Raphael said as he waved his hand at Jean-Paul. "What rules are you talking about, Mad?"

"The Rules of Non-Engagement."

"Sounds positively nonintimate," Raphael commented.

"That's the La Mira way," Jean-Paul added.

"Kind of like a catch-and-release program," Raphael giggled. "Oh, I caught you! Oh, now it's time to let you go!"

"I liked Ricardo," Madrid said.

"Then why did you dump him?" Jean-Paul asked.

"I broke the rules."

"Bad girl!" Raphael scolded.

"What rules?" Jean-Paul asked.

Madrid took in a deep breath. "I told him I loved him before he told me. You're supposed to wait and have someone say it to you first."

"You are?" Jean-Paul asked.

"I didn't know that," Raphael added.

"I stayed with him even though he didn't keep singing. He didn't keep building on his success."

"So?" Jean-Paul asked.

"You loved him," Raphael told her. "It didn't matter whether he had another hit song."

"I broke the rule of success," Madrid answered. "The person you're with has got to maintain his or her success. They can't be someone who was once successful and now is just riding on their name or past fortune—or using my success, or my sister's success, to keep their names out there and their faces in the newspapers and magazines."

"Well, I kind of see the point of that rule, being that you and your sister are billionairesses," Jean-Paul said.

"And rule the social and fashion worlds," Raphael added.

"And then I bed-lingered with Rick. I can't be just hanging out, away from the crowds and the cameras. I have to be out there as much as I can. And then I actually dismissed the staff one night and made dinner for us. I mean, the point of having a staff is so that they can gossip about the people I'm with or who my sister's with. And the fact that I even set foot in the kitchen to make him something puts me in too much of a subservient role. And I also talked to him about really private stuff, which is something we're not supposed to do because that's the kind of stuff that you don't want to get out, and then—"

"How many rules are there?" Jean-Paul cut in.

Madrid thought for a moment. "I don't know. A few. Quite a few. A lot."

"No wonder you and your sister don't have deep, meaningful, long-lasting relationships," Jean-Paul said. "They're doomed from the start."

Raphael nodded. "Absolutely. I mean, if you're following those rules, which, God love you and your sister, sweetie, you do dream and scheme together well, but you have no real sense of what makes a relationship work, so why bother being with anyone at all? Those rules scream out, 'Stay away!' Why be with anyone at all? Except to have sex, of course. Why not just have one-night stands and not even get involved? And then you don't need the rules."

"Unless it's not all just about the sex," Jean-Paul said, then stared at Madrid. "*Is* it just about the sex?"

Madrid met Jean-Paul's eyes, then looked away. "It's supposed to be."

"Ah, another rule."

Raphael patted Madrid's leg and when she looked at him, mouthed *Ah!*

Madrid shook her head and grinned.

"Sometimes, Maddy, rules are meant to be broken," Jean-Paul said as he stood and walked over to the fireplace. He picked up a fireplace tool and poked at the logs. "And sometimes, well, let's just put it this way. You may think that in making rules, they protect you. You may think that they keep you safe. But life isn't safe. Neither is love. You can't be alive and love while you try to abide by rules you make for the course your heart really wants to follow."

He set the poker down, walked over to Raphael, and placed a hand on his shoulder. "I said I would never get involved with someone who was younger than I. And certainly not over ten years younger. I said I would never let anyone help me run my business. I wanted to do everything myself. I said I would never open up my house to people. I felt I really didn't need them in my life. And see what happened when I followed those, well, *rules,* that I had made for myself? Raphael is twelve years younger than I am. He has been my lover for almost ten years. He helps to keep my business going and my household in order. He brought with him a set of wonderful friends, and I have met others through his outgoing nature. You, for instance. Raphael is just so *unlikeable,* so shy and reserved! He has made some of my most select customers into some of my closest friends. So. There it is. There's advice in there for you. Although I have always said that I will never give advice to people, that I prefer to stay out of their problems. See how well I follow the rules I set out for myself?"

Raphael beamed up at Jean-Paul, then blew him a kiss. "My little rule-breaker."

Jean-Paul smiled at Madrid. "See what terrible things can happen when you break the rules?"

3

The front door of the La Mira twins' childhood home in Concord, Massachusetts—a two-story, two hundred fifty-year-old white Colonial accented with black shutters and a bright red door, flew open as the twins stepped out of the airport limousine and made their way up the oversized, heated-brick front walkway, which had effectively melted the recent snowfall even though it was bordered by several inches of snow. A single white light sparkled brightly in each of the front windows, through which the twins could make out the glowing dining room chandelier and the tops of the tall-backed mahogany chairs clustered around the table in preparation for the evening's holiday dinner. Thick velvet curtains hung from the floor-to-ceiling, narrow-paned windows, and an enormous Christmas tree was framed by the windows at the front end of the living room. Numerous household staff dressed in black-and-white uniforms—"the penguin patrol," London had once joked to Madrid—scurried back and forth between the rooms.

"Fa-la-La Mira," London muttered under her breath. "Let the holiday Festival of Fights begin. In this corner, weighing in at—"

"Don't start," Madrid hissed.

"Bets on when the first argument starts," London suggested.

"You already have your gloves on," Madrid snapped back.

A grand holly wreath interwoven with tiny white lights slowed its back-and-forth dance on the front door as the twins drew nearer. It was held open by Catharine La Mira, a tall, rail-thin, strikingly attractive blonde whose pale complexion, narrow shoulders, sparkling blue eyes, and constant orange-alert anxiety level and accompanying high-pitched voice were features that neither twin had inherited.

"She's the trophy wife, not our mother," London had once told Madrid when they were attending Concord Academy. "We were brought into this world by some lovely Italian woman living in Boston's North End in order to preserve our lineage."

Madrid had responded by tossing her biology textbook to London as they lay sprawled on the floor of the den, studying for an upcoming exam. "Read it, idiot. No wonder I have to take all of your science tests. Genetically speaking, dark trumps light, every time. Brown eyes trump blue, for example. She's our mother."

The limo driver rushed past the twins, breathing heavily, and up to the door carrying armloads of suitcases. They were immediately claimed by three older men in starched-stiff white shirts and razor-sharp pleated black slacks who stepped out to meet him and then whisked the luggage down the hallway and up a flight of stairs.

"Have you two *not* got cell phones?" Catharine screeched before the twins were even close to the door.

"And there's that melodious voice," London mumbled. "How I've missed it."

"Because that girl of yours, that *publicist*—what's her name, Cloris . . . Morris . . . something like that—has been ringing here *every* half-hour," Catharine continued. "For what seems like *forever.* Does she *not* know that it's Christmas Eve? It's like the world is coming apart at the seams or something for that woman. And does she have some sort of *hearing* problem? My ears are still *ringing* from that voice of hers. How can you *stand* it? Blah, blah, BLAH! Blah, BLAH! Blah, bl—"

"And it's great to see you, too, Kitty," London cut in as she walked up the front steps and past her mother. "I like the red dress. A Dolce & Gabbana, right? But what's the matter with your hair?"

"Oh, God! Maddy, tell me you don't like the color! I *knew* she was going too blond this time."

"It's the curl," Madrid said as she stopped on the steps and surveyed her mother. "Are those new earrings? They're sweet."

"Can we move along?" London asked as she turned, grabbed her sister's arm, and pulled her into the house. "It's fucking cold. All of the heat is escaping while you two gab away."

"Let me tell you about cold," Madrid responded. "Cold is when—"

"Oh, yes—*please, please, please*—tell me the story again about how you almost froze to death in a snowstorm. And how if it wasn't for the flaming fags coming to your rescue, you'd be dead. I just want to hear that story over and over and—"

"Cold to you is forty degrees," Madrid snapped as she wrestled her arm out of London's grip. "You wouldn't have survived for *one minute* in that snowstorm. Mother, it's the *curl,*" she explained as she reached out a hand to her mother's head. Catharine immediately leaned her head away from Madrid's hand.

London let out a snort and said in a high-pitched voice, "*Don't* touch the hair! You'll positively *ruin* it!"

Catharine glared at London. "I spend a lot of money to have my hair done."

Amy Alden

"In point of fact, I think you spend *Dad's* money," London muttered.

"The color's your usual nice blond, Mother," Madrid commented as she dropped her hand and smiled at her mother. "You know I've always liked that. You just have too much poof up on top. It makes you look too thin."

"It makes you look like the Eiffel Tower," London quipped. "And you look like you weigh twelve pounds. Are you still on that stupid shake-no-bake diet? The one where all you can drink are chalky shakes and you can't eat anything that's been baked?"

"I haven't dieted in *ages*," Catharine answered. "I guess I'm just losing weight from the *stress* of the holidays, Maddy. You *are* Maddy, right?"

"Mother!" Madrid groaned with exasperation. "Why do you always forget how to tell us apart?"

London locked eyes with Catharine and grinned. "I'm the *gay* one, Kitty. The little ditty goes like this: Madrid likes men. London likes ladies."

"Oh, *please!* We'll have none of *that* talk over the holidays."

"Okay. I'll save it for Mother's Day," London quipped. "By the way, do you know who our mother is?"

"Mother, you shouldn't be on any diet at all," Madrid cut in. "You need to *gain* weight, not *lose* it." She shrugged off her coat and handed it to a servant. "Are you Ingrid?"

"I bet you know the names of all of your servants, Kitty," London commented. "You just keep forgetting how to tell your lovely daughters apart. Funny thing about that, don't you think?"

The servant bent her knees slightly and then nodded her head once. "Yes, ma'am," she said, taking Madrid's coat. "Thank you, ma'am."

Madrid let out a laugh. She pointed to her mother. "You see her? Catharine La Mira? *She's* a ma'am. I'm not *that* old!"

"Then what is she supposed to call you?" London asked. "Babycakes? Girly-girl? Weren't you the one who reminded me that we're turning thirty next year?"

"Eff off, Lonnie. I think Mother's a *lady*. And we're *young* ladies."

"Well put, Maddy," Catharine beamed at her.

"And I *like* young ladies," London grinned as she laid her coat on Ingrid's extended arm.

"London, I said *none* of that."

London turned to her mother, took a step toward her, and met her blue eyes inches from her face. She raised an eyebrow at her. "Just a *joke*, Kitty. You do know what a joke is, right? That's where you think something is funny and laugh at it. Although, now that I recall, I can't remember the last time I actually heard you laugh."

Catharine held London's eyes in hers as her face reddened. "That's *enough*, London La Mira," she hissed. "I will *not* have your attitude in this house over the holidays. And you can *stop* calling me Kitty, thank you very much. I'm your mother, like it or not."

"Okay, Mommy Poo."

"London, you can be most *infuriating* at the *most stressful* times. Do you know how much *effort* the holidays take?"

"*Mother*, you have a household staff that takes care of everything. And groundskeepers that keep the yard immaculate. I think if we hadn't gotten snow, you would've had them make it. Or better still, import it. From Switzerland, perhaps. That way, you could do what you like to do so much—brag. You could tell all the neighbors, 'Why, *thank you!* It *does* look festive, doesn't it? *Our* snow comes from Europe, you know.' Because that's what you like to do, Kitty. You like to make a big show of—"

"And just who do you think *runs* the staff, Missy Smarty Pants?"

London burst into laughter. "Missy Smart Pants! Oh, them's fightin' words!"

"Will you two *stop*?" Madrid cut in as she walked away from them and into the living room. She surveyed a long table that was set up with a Rockwellesque village holiday scene—"I've always loved this, Mother,"—and then shifted her eyes to an enormous fireplace, which was throwing off a brilliant amber blaze from several thick split logs.

"Even Martha Stewart would envy this," London proclaimed as she followed Madrid into the living room and looked around her as well, taking in the fireplace mantel adorned with fresh greens and delicate red glass balls and a row of embroidered stockings, each identified with a different name sewn at the top. At the front of the living room was a gigantic blue spruce adorned with white lights, lace ribbons, and bright red faceted, elongated glass balls.

"Everything looks wonderful, Mother," Madrid gushed. "You've outdone yourself."

"Thank you, Madrid. Please be sure to give London some of your manners one of these days, would you? You know, those outfits you girls are wearing are quite striking."

"Everything is by Tom Ford for Yves Saint Laurent Rive Gauche," Madrid pronounced as she gave her mother a quick twirl. "Lush forest green silk-georgette ruffled dress with a silk-velvet jacket, enhanced with gold ankle-strapped sandals and tourmaline necklace."

"Enhanced?" London asked with a grin. "That's the first time I've heard that shoes *enhance* an outfit."

"Everything I'm wearing is enhancing *your* outfit," Madrid countered as she pointed from her outfit to London's. "Green, green. Gold, gold."

"And what are you wearing, London?" Catharine asked.

"A Valentino beaded gold halter gown, accented with forest-green sewn decals, same shoes as Maddy—over my protest, please note, as you know how much I can't stand matching anything we wear. But she *had* to have them when she saw that I was buying them, and the entire outfit is *enhanced* with pearl-and-diamond earrings by Jack Valentino."

"Well, it's all quite lovely," Catharine murmured as she took a glass of champagne from a tray Ingrid was holding out to her. "A drink, girls?" she asked.

"All this green has made me *crave* a grasshopper, Ingrid," Madrid said. "Would Manuel make one for me, please?"

"Why are you talking like Kitty?" London asked her.

"Yes, ma'am," Ingrid replied, and then turned to London.

"Sounds good to me, too," she told Ingrid. "But ask him to go light on the grass and heavy on the hopper."

"There they are!" a voice boomed out. Tall, dark, and ruggedly handsome Carlisle La Mira strode through the back entrance of the living room and spread his arms open wide as he approached his daughters. "Christmas can begin, now that my girls are home! My lovelies," he proclaimed as he took the twins in his broad-shouldered arms and gave them each a gripping bear hug followed by a kiss on each of their cheeks. "Visions of beauty! So lovely. It makes me so happy to see you both. Let's sit down and talk about what's been going on for you. I was just about to get another drink."

"Carlisle, I think it's time that you *changed*," Catharine told him as she stood a distance from him and the twins. "A sweater and slacks just *won't* do. Your mother will be *expecting* a suit."

"Then I'll lay a suit over my chair at the dining room table, if that's what she's expecting," Carlisle joked.

"Good one, Dad," London chuckled as she delivered a light punch to his ribs.

Carlisle kissed London on the top of her head, and then regarded his wife. "Kitty, you know I've been busy all morning. If the Arizona wildfires come any closer to that new development, we're out billions. Burned homes, no matter how grand they are, simply don't sell. And I'm trying to find temporary homes for those who have been burned out of their—"

"Your *mother* will be here in about fifteen minutes," Catharine cut in. "You know she's *always* on time."

"You say that as if she's being rude," Carlisle countered. "If you don't want her here at six, then tell her to arrive at six-thirty."

"We're early," London pointed out. "Kitty, do you want Maddy and me to leave and then come back in fifteen minutes?"

Catharine threw London a stony glare.

"Now, now, Lon," her father told her as he placed another kiss on her head. "Kitty, I'm going to have a drink first, and then I'm going upstairs to change."

"Fine," Catharine sniffed. "Have it *your* way. You *always* do."

"What do you mean by that?" Carlisle snapped. "Aren't we all operating within *your* time frame, having the holidays the way you want them? It's your show, or so it seems. It's been nearly impossible for me to get any work done with all of the comings and goings. You'd think we were having the house rebuilt from the ground up. All for one holiday! And every year you cut back on another one of my family's Italian dishes and add more of your own traditions. Mashed potatoes. That spinach dish that looks like something an animal spit up. And *squash*. I mean, doesn't that name tell you anything? And turkey! For Christ's sake, we just *had* turkey a month ago."

"Well, that didn't take too long," Madrid sighed as she squirmed out of her father's arm and walked over to the blazing fireplace. "Why can't you both just chill out?"

"I *am* chilled out," Catharine said defensively.

"Like a fucking iceberg," Carlisle muttered under his breath to London, who giggled and beamed up at him. "Ah, there's my drink," he said as he dropped his arm from London's shoulders and reached for one of the cocktail glasses from Ingrid's tray. "I see you girls are going for a festive cocktail this evening." Carlisle gave a lopsided grin to his wife, raised his glass to her, and then downed it in one gulp. "There! Drink done. And now it's off to my chambers to dress." He kissed London's head again, and then exited from the living room.

"Honestly!" Catharine declared as she stood by herself at the opposite end of the living room. "I just want tonight to be a *perfect* Christmas Eve."

"Kitty, we haven't had a perfect Christmas Eve. Ever," London answered as she joined Madrid in front of the fireplace.

"Well, one can always *try,* you know," Catharine answered, and then shook her head. "I'm going to see if I can get some of this—what did you call it, Maddy?—*poofiness,* I guess, out of my hair. Your grandmother will certainly have some comment to make about it. I can *never* seem to do anything right in her eyes."

London and Madrid watched Catharine walk out of the living room.

"So much for the adage, 'There's no place like home for the holidays,' " London muttered as she placed her cocktail glass on the mantel and held out her hands to the fire.

Madrid gave London a shove against her arm.

"Hey! What was that for?"

"Why do you always do it, Lon? Why do you always fight with Mother? And then you and Daddy are like two peas in a pod. You think he walks on water, when you know full well that this marriage has been nothing more than a piece of paper since we were—"

"I'm not going there with you, Mad," London cut in. "You know that Kitty and I don't get along. You two do, though. You're like sorority sisters. No, wait. *Clones* is a better way to describe it. You walk through that front door, and all of sudden it's like you've got some sort of stick up your butt. You get all tense and agitated and anxious, just like Kitty. And you take her side whenever she's critical of Dad. You know, she could've divorced him years ago for all of his infidelities—remember that year she hired a private detective to follow him, and the dick came back with all of those

pictures and she confronted Dad? It was a fucking scream-
ing session for hours one night that we listened to from the
top of the stairs. But you know what, Mad? She leaves him,
and she loses everything. She was a middle-class Faye
Dunaway lookalike when they met at college, and she became a billionaire the second the minister proclaimed, 'I
now pronounce you man and wife.' She's got a good thing
going with Dad, and so she decided to suck it up. In my
book, if you decide to put up with something, then you
should just shut up."

"But Gamma Angel has never really liked her," Maddy
countered. "That's been hard for Mother. And I really think
she loves Dad, and that's why she doesn't want to leave him."

"Oh, for God's sake, are you really that dense?" London
snorted. "I mean, do you lose all sense of reality when you
walk into this house? The last time our parents were monog-
amous was on their honeymoon. Kitty's been prowling
around on her own for years."

"No, she hasn't!"

"Of course she has!" London declared. "Shall I cite a few
examples? The tennis pro she was taking lessons from when
we were at Concord Academy. I assume that you improve
your tennis game when you're actually out on the court hitting balls, not while you're lying flat on your back in a bed
getting balled. The gardener who spent more time trimming
Kitty's bush than the holly bushes? Paulie the pool guy, who
you actually had the hots for. The—"

"All right, all right!" Madrid snapped. "Then why doesn't
Dad divorce *her*? Answer me that one."

"They've come this far, Mad. Everyone knows Carlisle
and Catharine La Mira. Their names are linked on countless
charity benefits, hospital wings, campus libraries—you
name it. They *can't* divorce. It's just that simple. Love each
other or not—and it *is* not, I assure you of that—they're in it
for the long haul."

"I find that sad."

"What did you say?"

"I said, I find that sad."

"Since when is *sad* a word in your vocabulary? Anyway, it's not sad. It's pathetic."

"No, it's sad."

"Okay, Weepy. Why is it sad? It works for them."

Madrid raised her eyebrows at London and shook her head. "Tell me, Lon. What did we ever learn about love when we were growing up that was positive?"

"That money buys happiness? That love is blind?"

"Be serious."

"What's gotten into you? Has breaking up with Ricardo gotten you all, oh, I don't know, introspective and emotional?"

"Lon, we grew up in a house where our parents slept in separate bedrooms, where we knew they were sleeping with other people, where we didn't see a whole lot of affection between them, where we never heard the words, 'I love you' or—"

"Dad says it all the time."

"To *you*. Not to me."

"Well, Kitty says she loves you. She can't stand me."

"Because you can't stand her."

London nodded. "You're right. I can't. Even before I told her I was gay, she always preferred you. It was always her taking you shopping when we were little, and me being left at home. Her doing your hair up, and me having one of the servants do it. Her—"

"And it was always you and Dad doing stuff together," Madrid cut in. "He'd get a new car, and off you two would go for a ride. I even heard you one night when you were in his office, making fun of the way Mother talks, and he was laughing so hard it was making me sick to my stomach."

"I think I was making fun of *you*," London countered. "Because whenever you'd spend the day out with Kitty, you'd come home talking like her and walking like her and being all prissy like her. That made me sick to *my* stomach. But once I came out of the closet, that was it for Kitty and me. But you, Mad, you could never do anything wrong in her eyes. I was always the bad guy. She's always blamed me for everything and you for nothing. Even when you were clearly at fault. Do you know how many times I was punished for things that I never did? And then I'd hear you say to Kitty, 'Oh, *that* London!' "

"Well, you're Daddy's little girl. Maybe that's why you're gay. Because no one can ever take the place of Daddy. He's your *man,* Lon."

"Harsh, Maddy."

"True, Lonnie."

"Well, maybe your unhealthy connection with Kitty is why you can't keep a man in your bed for more than a few weeks, Mad. Because you're an uptight little bitch, just like her."

"You shut up!"

"No, you shut up!"

"Why don't you just—"

"Are those Gamma Angel's little angels I hear?"

The twins turned from their heated exchange to see Carlisle's mother, who they had called "Gamma Angel" from the moment they could talk, standing in the hallway looking in at them. As Ingrid helped her off with her coat, they saw Gamma lean her face toward Ingrid, whisper something to her, and then slide something into her free hand. Ingrid blushed slightly, gave a quick curtsey to Gamma, and then placed a hand into the front pocket of her uniform before she exited the hallway.

Gamma Angel walked into the living room and gave each of her grandchildren a hug and a kiss. "Now, my darlings, you must tell me about all the wonderful news of your lives. Remember what I told you last Christmas, about how I wanted you to experience life more? So? Have you gone to new places? Done new things? Learned something new?

Because that's what you must do with your lives, you know. You must always be learning, always be seeing something out of fresh eyes."

London smiled at Gamma Angel. She surveyed the tall woman whose beauty and simple elegance were evident not just in the Carlisle Collection wool slacks, deep pink cashmere sweater, matching pink jacket, and simple black heels and pearl earrings she was wearing, but also in her clear, olive-skinned complexion, high-arched eyebrows, deep brown eyes, full lips, and brilliant smile. Her long, more-salt-than-pepper hair was tied back with a pink silk scarf, which she now adjusted with long-fingered hands.

London beamed at her. "Look at you! You look wonderful!"

"You *do,* Gamma," Madrid agreed.

"That's because I just returned from the jewel of the Italian Riviera, my darlings. Portofino was absolutely marvelous. There's nothing like sea air to restore your soul. I stayed at the Hotel Splendido and read in the evening after dinner, sitting out on my suite's seaview terrace. The view! It was breathtaking. But you know me, I simply couldn't sit and relax. When I wasn't out in the hotel's riverboats, I was walking around the Cinque Terre. I went on some exquisite hikes through the forests above the sea. Absolutely breathtaking! You two must go sometime. And then you can brush up on your Italian. Learning another language in school means nothing. You must go to the country and speak it, read it, savor it, to truly make it yours. It is in your blood, after all."

"You have much more time than we do, Gamma," Madrid said as she walked to the couch in front of the fireplace and beckoned to her grandmother to join her.

"I do?" she asked as she took London's arm and walked with her to the couch. She sat between the twins and crossed her long legs. "How much more time do I have than you do? I have twenty-four hours in each day, fifty-two weeks in each year. Do you not have that same amount? More? Or perhaps less?"

"Yes, we have that same amount of time, but there are the clubs," London replied as she turned to face Gamma and tossed an arm across the top of the couch.

"The clubs," Gamma replied, then shook her head. "I think that those clubs have fulfilled their purpose, have they not? Perhaps you have learned a bit about the business world through them, although you have managers for doing all that, don't you? Perhaps they have given you something to do to fill your time, although why young people have so much free time that they seem to want to piddle away is beyond my comprehension. What those clubs do, my dears, is this. They help get people drunk and high and then encourage them to dance and make fools of themselves in all ways imaginable. And unimaginable. What good are those clubs contributing to the world? Are you saving lives with them, perhaps?"

London opened her mouth to speak, but closed it when Gamma turned to look at her.

"You were about to say?" Gamma asked.

London shook her head.

Gamma Angel smiled and then ran her hands lightly along her slacks, smoothing out small wrinkles. "No, in your clubs there have been lives that have come in jeopardy, that have almost been lost because of the excesses that seem to be all in vogue these days. One doesn't simply party anymore. One parties quite hard, yes? As if it were do or die, so to speak. I have seen the video of that poor girl who took too many drugs at La Mira West. And I have also seen your concern and the lifesaving efforts you exerted on her behalf at the time, London."

London cleared her throat and looked down at the floor.

"Let me ask, because I really want to know. Are you proud of your clubs?" Gamma turned to Madrid. "What are you most proud of, Maddy? The fact that you give people, both famous and unknown, a place to go to behave badly?"

Madrid followed London's lead and stared down at the carpet. She shrugged her shoulders. "People have fun at La Mira East."

"Fun? Oh, my darling," Gamma said as she patted Madrid's leg. "You two don't know what fun is. Every trip I take is fun. My Portofino trip was fun. I saw many things I'd never seen before, spoke with people I'd never met, and learned of a culture rich with history. And all of the volunteer work I do throughout the year is—well, it's not fun, but it's joyful. Very positive. You see, I make a difference in the lives of others. I see the joy that I can bring people from the time and the energy that I give to them. So please tell me. Tell me about the difference your clubs make in your own lives and in the lives of others."

London and Madrid were silent.

"Yes. My point entirely," Gamma responded, and then surveyed the room for several moments.

"There's nothing wrong with the clubs, Gamma," London said, breaking into the silence. "They're very popular. We have only the best of everything. The best music. The best entertainment. The best food. And the best, well, liquor."

"And the best drugs, too, I bet," Gamma Angel said.

"The difference we make," London continued, and then paused.

"Yes?"

"Well, we give people something to do."

"Something to do," Gamma Angel repeated slowly, and then sighed. "Because they don't have anything else to do with their lives, correct? But you girls. You have something better to do in your lives, don't you think? You are privileged. Smart. You have riches beyond imagination. So many people in the world would give anything for your education, for the opportunities you have been given, for the opportunities that you're free to create." Gamma Angel stood up, walked to the fireplace, and then turned to the twins. She rested an arm on the mantel. "Yes, you *do* have something better to do in your lives. There are things that you should be doing. Yes. Yes, there are."

London raised her eyes from the carpet and slowly turned her head to look at Madrid.

Madrid felt London's eyes on her, and met hers. Then she shrugged her shoulders.

"Shall I tell you girls once again the story of your grandfather?" Gamma Angel asked. "Shall I remind you of the business he created that not only helped others, but which also helped to build the empire whose riches you two now enjoy? Perhaps I should regale you once more with the story of how an immigrant girl from Italy came to this land of opportunity and took advantage of all that she could. Of how she made something of herself—what is that phrase? How she turned lemons into lemonade? Perhaps I should remind you of how I earned the nickname Angel. Or do the stories this old woman tells you bore you?"

"Gamma, you're not old," Madrid answered.

"Then my stories are old. I see your face, London. You look like I'm about to inflict some sort of pain upon you."

London sighed. "It's not that your stories bore us, Gamma. It's just that we've heard them so many times before and—"

"We think they're wonderful and all," Madrid broke in. "But, no offense, Gamma, you were born in a different time and you lived under different circumstances."

Gamma nodded. "I see. So all the problems in the world have been solved, then? No one is illiterate anymore or goes hungry or is lacking basic needs? No one is homeless? There are no people in peril? No animals in peril? No natural habitats threatened? *Marvelous!*" Gamma Angel exclaimed as she slapped a hand against the top of the mantel. "I take great pride in knowing that I helped to resolve the sad circumstances that so many people, so many living things, once suffered. And I am pleased to know that no one in the world suffers anymore. Thank God you two don't have to see such things, have to know of such things. I feel so powerful, knowing that I played a role in making the world a better place for everyone, especially for my two grandchildren. I can die a happy woman."

"Gamma, of course those things still exist," Madrid countered.

"They do?" Gamma Angel asked. "Where, Maddy? Can you name three places in the world where unfortunate people are living in dire circumstances?"

Madrid shot a quick glance at London.

Gamma Angel smiled. "Yes, yes, that's a good idea, Maddy. Pool the intelligence that's in both of your brains and then tell me about those three places."

London cleared her throat. "Uh, Africa."

Gamma Angel raised her eyebrows at London. "Africa. Okay. What's going on there?"

"Famine," Madrid answered.

Gamma Angel nodded. "Famine. That's good. In which African states?"

"States?" Madrid asked.

"Disease," London blurted out.

"Okay," Gamma Angel said. "We'll forget about identifying the states for the moment. Which disease, Lonnie? Or perhaps there's more than one?"

"I don't know," London said. "Polio? Rabies? The one where—"

"I think you're just guessing now, Lonnie," Gamma Angel cut in. She showed them a sad smile, took in a deep breath, and then released it. "You two really don't know much about the world, do you?"

"Not the tragedies," London answered. "Who wants to dwell on the tragedies?"

"Dwell?" Gamma asked. "I don't think we were anywhere near dwelling on tragedies. I am merely trying to find out what you two really know about the world that exists outside of your tiny, pampered existences."

"Why?" London asked.

"Gamma, it's Christmas," Madrid quickly stated. "What you're asking us to talk about is, well, it's kind of a downer."

"What's a downer?" Catharine asked as she walked into the living room. "Angelica," she said as she nodded at Gamma Angel.

"Catharine. The house looks lovely, as usual. You have done a wonderful job."

Catharine showed Gamma Angel a stiff smile. "Thank you."

"Ma!" Carlisle exclaimed as he walked past his wife and over to the fireplace, where he embraced Gamma. "What's going on?" he asked as he surveyed the expressions on the faces of the twins.

"Just setting the stage," Gamma Angel answered as she placed an arm around her son's waist.

"Now?" Carlisle asked. "I thought we were—"

"Son, you look as handsome as ever," Gamma Angel cut in. "That's a very nice suit. Catharine, how did that recipe that I gave you turn out?"

"I think it tastes good, Angelica," Catharine replied. "Fine. *Delicious,* I mean. But I'd like your opinion."

"Of course. Let's give it a try, shall we?" she suggested as she walked over to Catharine and linked an arm through hers.

Catharine's body stiffened at Angelica's touch. But then she raised a hand in the air, hesitated for a moment, and placed it on Angelica's arm.

The two women walked out of the living room together.

London furrowed her eyebrows as she watched Gamma Angel and Catharine walk out of the room together, then looked at her father. "Dad, does this seem like a really strange Christmas to you?"

Carlisle walked over to the couch and extended a hand out to each of his daughters. "Strange? No. No, I wouldn't say that."

"Weird?" Madrid suggested as she walked toward her father. "I mean, when was the last time you saw Mother and Gamma—"

"Sometimes, my lovelies, change is good," Carlisle said as he walked the twins out of the living room. "Sometimes, it *has* to happen."

"So what's up with the gift certificates to L. L. Bean?" London asked the next morning as Catharine, Carlisle, and Gamma Angel sat in the living room with her and Madrid. Each person was surrounded by small mountains of Christmas presents they had spent several minutes opening—clothing, jewelry, shoes of varying styles and colors, perfume bottles, and fancy dishes and glassware.

"And what's this other one?" Madrid asked as she sorted through a pile of envelopes she had spread out in front of her on a table. She picked one up and squinted at it. "What's Eastern Mountain Sports? Is that some sort of health club?"

"Am I missing something?" London asked as she flipped through her own stack of envelopes and then turned to her sister. "Mad, did you get your check?"

Madrid shook her head. "I already checked."

London grinned. "Checked for the check, did you?"

Madrid returned her grin. "Check." Then she looked at her mother. "So where's the check?"

Catharine stared at Madrid, and then reached for her coffee cup and took a sip. "Anyone for more coffee?"

"Dad?" London asked.

"No coffee for me."

"That's not what I'm asking you," London said. "Did you forget our checks?"

Carlisle tightened his lips and looked away from London.

"What are you girls missing?" Gamma Angel asked as she stood up from her chair and readjusted her bathrobe.

"The checks!" Madrid exclaimed. "The checks we get every year at Christmas."

Gamma Angel walked over to them. "Do you mean the ones for several hundred thousand dollars that you are given each year, with which you can do as you please?"

The twins nodded their heads vigorously.

"Do you know where that money comes from?" Gamma Angel asked.

In response, Madrid and London pointed to their father. Carlisle quickly cleared his throat.

Gamma Angel shook her head. "No, dears. That money comes from your Gamma. Actually, from Grandpa Tony, who you never got to meet. But he's the reason why I live so well, why your parents live so well, and why you girls live so well. And do you know how he made his fortune?"

Madrid and London sat back on the couch and answered in unison, in a monotone, "Frozen foods."

"*Freeze-dried* foods," Gamma Angel corrected them. "And much more. Yes, Antonio La Mira was a brilliant chemist who perfected the process of freeze-drying foods like potatoes and coffee and fruits. Also, salad dressings and soups and even entire meals."

"Gamma, we *know* all this," London sighed. "And the world has never been the same since."

"But he also used the freeze-drying process for other things," Gamma Angel continued. "Like medicines. Penicillin, for instance. And blood plasma. And milk. *That* was a savior. Because by the time the Great Depression had paralyzed our nation, no one could afford to buy fresh foods, nor was much even available. His was one of the few companies that stayed in business during the Depression—actually prospered through such a difficult time—and we used the process he had perfected to help so many people who were going hungry at that time."

"Which is how you earned the nickname Angel," Madrid cut in, and then sighed. "Like Lonnie said, Gamma, we *know* all this."

"Yes, my dears, you do. But you will hear it again. For the last time, I promise."

"And so you set up food lines and fed the poor and starving, blah, blah, blah," London added.

Gamma Angel smiled at her. "Yes, we did. All we needed was water to reconstitute everything we had freeze-dried, and like a miracle, people had milk to drink and soup to eat. We used the great ovens in our companies to bake bread, too—loaves of bread every day. My, the aroma was incredible. And then we would pack up our trucks each night and our drivers would go as far as they could to cities on the East Coast. Antonio had been smart. He had installed a petrol station at the manufacturing plant, and so we had all the fuel we needed as well."

"And the rest is history," London sighed. "Now can we—"

Gamma Angel shook her head. "No, my impatient grandchild. The rest of the story gets even better. Right before our entry into World War II, Antonio had sold a number of freeze-drying patents to the government and to a number of other companies—the ones who had the ability to work with medicines and with plasma. Do you know the number of Allied troops who lived because of what Antonio had created?"

"And then he died," Madrid said.

Gamma Angel nodded. "And then he died. He didn't die a hero in the war. He was just another soldier who was killed while serving his country. But he died a hero to anyone who can recognize the importance of what he did. And after I buried him, I continued to run his company, to sell his patents, and to serve others as much as I could. And now your father has built his own company, Crowning Chateaus, which—"

"Gamma," London cut in with a sigh. "We *know* all this."

"Girls, I think what—" Carlisle started to say, then stopped when he saw Angelica raise a hand in the air.

"All you *know,* London, is that you and Madrid get a sizeable check—quite enough to live fabulously on—every Christmas, since you were seventeen," Gamma Angel said. "Every year, you each earn more than the richest CEO in this country. And for doing what, I ask? Your father works hard because I taught him to work hard. I taught him the value of money from when he was a little boy. He used to deliver newspapers in the morning and run errands each afternoon after school and sweep floors and—"

"You did?" London asked her father, who nodded.

"He worked hard," Gamma Angel continued. "But, unfortunately, he seems to have forgotten the lessons I taught him in bringing you up. He has let this go on far too long. And now I'm putting a stop to it."

"A stop to what?" Madrid asked.

"Your checks," Gamma Angel answered.

"What?" Madrid asked.

"Say again?" London added.

"Until you two can show me that you know the *value* of money, beyond its buying power, you will not get another dime. You girls—you *ladies*—are turning thirty next year. Since the age of seventeen, you have drifted through your lives, spending money on things no one really needs. The money you have spent on yourselves, on your whims and desires, could be much better spent on doing good for others. I thought you would've learned this by now. But you haven't. Your insatiable lust for partying and throwing Antonio's hard-earned money away has made you both sick. Sick with a disease I have heard called affluenza. You get and you spend, you get and you spend. *On your own desires.* Why? What good is coming from this spend, spend, spend? Maybe you already know this, but I will say it anyway. Money can't buy happiness. It never has, and it never will. But money does have a value that oftentimes can't be measured. And this can be found in love, health, charity, and giving."

"I don't know what you're saying," London said as she stood up and faced Gamma.

"Oh, I think you do, dear."

Madrid stood up as well and turned toward Catharine. "Mother?"

Catharine raised her head and looked at Madrid, and then nodded at Angelica. "I am in full agreement with your grandmother. Before I met your father, I worked every day of my teenage years. I went to college on a partial scholarship. I had to balance classes and studying with serving food in the cafeteria. I may not look like I've ever worked a day in my life, but I do know what it's like to smell like stale food all the time or to scrape dried mashed potatoes out of my hair."

"Dad, this is ridiculous," London said as she strode over to him. "I see no reason Madrid and I shouldn't get our checks. We *run* the La Mira clubs."

"You do?" Catharine asked.

"Oh, bug off!" London shouted at her.

Carlisle immediately stood and faced London, his face red with anger. "I will not tolerate you talking to your mother that way!"

"What?" London asked. "Dad, what is *wrong* with you?"

"Just give us our checks, and we'll do some good in the world," Madrid said as she walked over to London and stood next to her. "We'll give a lot of it to charities."

"Oh?" Gamma Angel asked. "Which ones, dear? Which are your favorite charities? How about naming three?"

"Again with the name-three game," London muttered. "What does it *matter?* You throw a little money at a charity, and people couldn't be happier."

"Good Lord," Carlisle exclaimed. "Is that how you *really* think, London?"

"I told you this already," Catharine said to her husband.

Carlisle glanced at his wife and then shook his head.

"Angelica and I *both* did," Catharine added, then turned to the twins. "You two are *spoiled*. Spoiled to the *core*."

"Oh, and like *who* spoiled us?" London snapped.

"I accept full responsibility," Carlisle said as he looked at Angelica. "I have allowed this to happen." Then he turned his attention to the twins. "I have shown you girls that money means nothing. I have shown you that the fruit that the La Mira money tree bears is endless. I have shown you that you have to do nothing in order to get quite a bit of something."

"We both have," Catharine added as she walked over to Carlisle and placed a hand gently on his arm. "We've thrown money at them. And all they've done is what any sane person would do. Catch it. And then spend it."

Gamma Angel rubbed her hands together and then smiled at her granddaughters. "And so, my darlings. There is no check this Christmas. There will be no more checks until you can show me, your father, and your mother, by the time you turn thirty, that you have both learned what money really means. Then, and only then, will the checks resume."

"Well, this fucking sucks!" Madrid exclaimed. She waved a hand around the living room. "Do you hear me? This *fucking* sucks!"

"There, there, dear," Gamma Angel said as she smiled sweetly at Madrid. "Enjoy this moment as much as you can. Because once this whole challenge to you and your sister sinks in, once you both start to get those wheels in your minds in motion to try to dream up ways of regaining those lush checks of yours, you will truly learn just how hard some of the lessons are that you need to learn.

"Then, my darlings, believe me. It *will* fucking suck."

4

London La Mira sat, shoulders slumped, in a leather chair at the black, marble-topped desk in her spacious office at La Mira West, resting her elbows on the surface and holding her head between her hands. She stared down at several sheets of paper and piles of notebooks Lucinda had left for her that morning and tried to ignore the steady and invasive thump-thump-BOOM, thump-thump-BOOM sound of the techno beat her DJs were spinning to entertain her club's raucous New Year's Eve crowd. They had arrived in taxis, luxury automobiles, and sleek limousines and formed a long, snakeline line that extended for several blocks outside the doors of the club hours before opening.

When it had first started up, the music had startled her out of her desktop reverie, which had begun earlier in the day after she had entered the club, seen scores of staff scurrying about as they prepared for the night's party. She'd answered several questions which, she had felt, were easy enough to figure out without her input—"I mean, use your *brains,* people"—and then grabbed a large mug of coffee and retreated to her office. She started sorting through the stack of mail she had let accumulate in the week since she had returned to

San Francisco. As she attacked the pile, she thought about what she would be wearing that night—*an outfit to both wow and woo,* she decided with a grin—the well-known personalities who couldn't *wait* to be seen at her club; *I wonder if Cher will make it this year,* and the fun she would soon be having.

It's a good time to get drunk and high, she thought.

"Fly me to the moon and let me play among the stars," she sang, laughed out loud, and then hummed the rest of the song as she took out a letter opener and sliced open the top of a letter. *No offense, Gamma Angel, but screw you. Screw you, too, Dad. And, as always, screw you, Kitty. I have ways of not missing your money. Which is really my money. Mine and Maddy's. It's just a simple matter of extending credit limits, you see. And taking out loans. It requires a little more work on my part than cashing my check, but I think I get the whole prove-you-know-about-the-value-of-money thing. You want me to learn how to get money, rather than just be given it. So I'm going to show you that by spending some of my time, admittedly quite tedious time, filling out forms, I can get more money than you give me each year. And that's the true value of money. Being able to figure out how to get it in the easiest possible ways. Lesson learned. And months before I turn thirty.*

Grinning, London reached out for her coffee and then spotted familiar handwriting on a card addressed to her. Gamma Angel's distinctive and elegant handwriting was visible within the pile of telegrams from celebrities who had sent their regrets for missing the club's New Year's bash, oversized glossy fashion magazines, brochures about a variety of travel destinations, and FedEx Letter packages containing personal notes from top fashion designers, who had sent along sketches of outfits for the upcoming spring lines that they thought she might be interested in. "Caramel is the new pink!" Steve Fabrikant had hastily scrawled in a personal note to her that accompanied his sketches.

"Caramel is a candy," London spoke out loud as she surveyed the sketches, then frowned. "And these designs look far from delicious," she concluded as she tossed them into the wastepaper basket.

London sliced open the envelope and pulled out the card. It was a Happy New Year card by Hallmark, decorated on the front with bright, festive confetti cascading down over twin champagne glasses that had boozy bubbles floating out of them. Gamma Angel had written each numeral of the new year in a separate champagne bubble. Inside the card, some faceless writer had penned, "Have a bubbly New Year's!"

That must have taken hours to think up, London snorted to herself. *Thanks for the card, Gamma. But I'm still mad at you.*

She glanced below the tagline and read, "All my love, Gamma Angel."

And none of your money, London thought. Her eyes shifted to the opposite side of the opened card, and she read a short paragraph penned in Gamma's hand:

My darling London,

It was so wonderful to see you this Christmas. Thank you so much for your lovely gifts. Since you left in such a hurry, I didn't have a chance to tell you that, in order to avoid any embarrassment, it would be best if you put away your credit cards for the time being. As you may recall, your father cosigned for those before you turned eighteen and both he and I felt, in light of our decision this Christmas, that it was best to close the accounts. Your rather hefty balances have been cleared. What do you spend your money on?!? I wish you all the best as you advance toward your thirtieth year of life. Learn as much as you can!

Your loving Gamma Angel

"Read your mail," London commanded as soon as she heard her sister's sleepy voice on the other end of the phone. She took a long drag on her cigarette, and then spit out the smoke as she said, "I *know* it's early. Open your fucking mail. Because I got a card from Gamma Angel, and you must have one, too. No, you're *not* going back to sleep. You need to read the card. Then go get it! Get out of bed and go get it. *Now!*"

London took quick puffs from her cigarette as she waited for Madrid to return to the phone, then listened as she tore open the card.

Seconds ticked by.

"So?" she asked.

"FUCK!"

London nodded and stubbed out her cigarette. "Same as mine, then," she said as she reached for another smoke.

"What the *fuck!* Did you read the fucking P.S.?" Madrid shouted.

"What P.S.?"

"It's on the fucking back of the fucking card."

London turned over her card and read:

P.S. Remember that per legal contracts drawn up when you were young, your father must cosign any bank loans or credit card applications you might wish to take out. This is done to protect you! Your properties and vehicles are paid for, my darling, but what you have now is simply all you have. I hope that you have been frugal and have saved up all these years! There was a time when every penny counted! But since I knew that you don't want to hear about those days, I send you sweet kisses instead.

"Sweet kisses, my ass," London mumbled as she sat back in her chair, readjusted her headset, and sighed. "Well, I guess I don't have to fill out the credit card applications I picked up. Or the loan applications I got yesterday from First Banks or The Federal Reserve Bank of San Francisco or the Bank of San Francisco. My plan was to take out loans that would total up to the amount of our yearly check, and then maybe donate a lot to a charity. I thought that would put an end to this insanity."

"That was my plan, too," Madrid answered. "I was going to fill them out after the new year, but . . ." her voice trailed off. "What the *fuck!* This is so incredibly insane! It's just not right, is what it is. Lon, you want to hear something pathetic? I ordered a pizza last night because my household staff is off until next year. I can't seem to work up the energy to get dressed and go out to dinner. Anyway, I called out for—"

"I haven't left the house until today," London cut in. "And I've got to tell you, even though there are a thousand channels on cable, there's *nothing* on TV."

"Whatever," Madrid responded. "So, as I was saying, I ordered a pizza. When the pizza dude arrives, I'm flying around here trying to find cash to pay for it. Do you think I had cash? I mean, the kid full well knew who I was, and here I am trying to *find* money to pay him for a frigging pizza! I mean, *really!* I finally found a twenty on the floor of my closet and gave it to him. I almost wanted to ask for the change, because I thought, 'Shit! That might be the last of my money, for all I know.' But I didn't. And then I went through all of my purses and turned the house upside down. I actually got excited when I found a buck in change underneath the couch cushions. Is that sad, or what? All totaled, I have about five hundred dollars."

"Four hundred and change for me," London told her. "I found a mother lode of change in the glove compartment of my Jag."

"Shit! I didn't think to look in the car. Oh, Lon—shit!"

"What?"

"How am I supposed to pay for the repairs to my Jag? Remember I wrecked it in the snowstorm on my way to Jean-Paul and Raphael's?"

"Why you did something that stupid is beyond me."

"Well, I did it. Now how the hell am I supposed to pay to get the car fixed?"

"Send the bill to Dad," London suggested. "It's the only thing you can do. How else can you pay for it? It's going to cost more than five hundred dollars, for sure."

"For sure is right. And I don't want to spend the five hundred, because I think that's all I have left. I don't know what Gamma Angel thinks we do with our money. Let it sit in a bank? I mean, *really*. There are things we need, you know?"

"I hear you."

"Money is *supposed* to be spent. That's what we've been doing. And then we get more money and spend that. I mean, why give us the money unless you want us to spend it? Am I being crazy? I just don't see why that should have to change. It's not like we're doing *nothing* in our lives."

London nodded. "My thoughts exactly. Gamma Angel went about this all wrong, with no feeling or caring for us at all. It's like she's got her life, and somehow she thinks we each don't have our own lives. I love her and all, but maybe she's getting a little loose in the brain. She was like a quiz-show host, asking us, 'Name three diseases. Name three charities.' I can tell you three names I'd like to call her."

"Don't be nasty to Gamma, Lon. She is our grandmother."

"I know," London sighed. "I'm just frustrated."

"Me, too. I admit, I did call her a few names. But old people are, well, old."

"What she ought to have done is given us a warning," London continued. "Like, *this* Christmas tell us, '*Next* Christmas you won't get a check.' And then we can do whatever it is that she wanted us to do to prove we're worthy of the check for *next* Christmas. Which, by the way, I'm still not clear about."

"Me neither. I've been wracking my brains, but I have no clue what she expects of us. She shouldn't take away money to teach us the value of it. What does that teach us? Absolutely fucking nothing! I think this is so unfair. We had no time to prepare."

"Right. If we *knew* what was coming, then we could just not spend as much from this year's check and we'd have some left over to take us through the year we wouldn't get the check. And then we could do whatever it is she thinks we need to do to get the checks going again."

"Now what? Now what are we supposed to do, Lon? We can't use our credit cards. We can't take out a loan. What does she expect us to do? Get a *job?* I mean, we *own* our own businesses. That should count for something."

"You'd think."

"You'd think."

Silence filled the airwaves between them. "We could write a book," London suggested. "A sexy tell-all. A kind of she said-she said. You spill the beans on all your lovers, and I could do the same with mine. We could get a big advance. I could talk to Dolores about it."

"We can't write."

"No, but we could *tell* our story to a ghostwriter. Do you think Hillary wrote her book? I mean, *really.* No one with a big name writes their own book. They pay some schmuck a few dollars to write it, and then cash in on the sales. We could probably get an advance in the millions."

"I don't think that's going to impress Gamma."

"So? We'll have millions."

"And then what? How long do you think that's going to last? I don't want to have to keep thinking of ways to make money, Lon. It's all too much. My brain actually *hurts.* I want this to be over and done with so we can get those checks again. I like my life the way it is. Was. You know what I mean."

"I was thinking, Mad, about getting back some of the money I lent out to people. It's not much, but it's something."

"Good luck. I already tried that. Do you know how many people laughed at me? Just *burst* into laughter. They thought I was joking. I wasn't about to tell them the situation. They'd believe that even less. Do you know that one of my friends actually had the audacity to say, 'You can't be serious. You *gave* me that money. What do you need it back for? If I had wanted a loan, I would've gone to the bank. Anyway, I was going to ask you for *more* money.' Jesus, Lon, what are we going to do?"

London thought for a moment. "I guess we'll just have to put our energy into our clubs. Maybe double our profits this coming year. That might convince Gamma that we know what we're doing with our money."

"Profits? What profits?"

"What your club makes, stupid."

"My club is losing money, Lon."

"What?"

"Losing money. I don't know why, but it is."

"That can't be. Is your manager stealing from you?"

"Nope. He showed me the books. He showed me the expenses."

"Maybe he's lying."

"He's *not* lying. Do you know how much my club loses, just on the New Year's Eve party alone?"

"Don't you have a full house?"

"*Of course* I have a full house. Lon, the numbers don't lie. Maybe you're doing something different, but my club has been sucking money out of me like a vacuum cleaner."

"Well, you must be doing something wrong. Between your club and mine, we've got the hottest tickets on each coast."

"So what are you saying?" London asked Lucinda as she rubbed her temples and stared at the stacks of statements, notebooks filled with numbers, and spreadsheets scattered about the desk in front of her.

"Let's start with the fiscal year again," Lucinda suggested as she picked up one of the spreadsheets. "This category—"

"Bottom line!" London cut in. "I don't give a crap about what our bartenders make and what the liquor supplier gets paid. I want the goddamned bottom line—not a lesson in business management 101. How much money does this club take in?"

"We're three hundred thousand—"

"That's not great, but it's not—"

"—in the hole at the end of each fiscal year," Lucinda finished.

"What do you mean?"

"I mean," Lucinda said as she showed London a patient smile, "that the club's expenses exceed what it takes in. Each year we're approximately three hundred thousand dollars in the red."

"But what could possibly add up to three hundred thousand more than what I give you? There's no rent or mortgage. The building is paid for."

"The utility bills come each month, Lonnie. Take the electric bill, for instance. What we use is pretty astronomical considering the lighting system, the central air conditioning, the venting, the kitchen appliances, the ice maker, the fog and mist machines, the rotating dance floors, the wall-sized aquariums. And then there's your staff. And then the food, the alcohol, the special decorations, advertising—you tell me what you want for this club, and I give it to you. You tell me not to cut corners, and so I haven't. I mean, it would be nothing to switch over to cheaper brands of liquor or to hire DJs who would work for less than those you hire or to stop giving out the gifts for all of the special parties. Last year's Good Gold New Year's Eve party favors—those thousand-dollar earrings you gave out to a few hundred people—set us in the hole a bit. This year, in fact, we're about twenty-five thousand more down than previous years, with this Diamonds Are Forever theme. I can lower that figure next fiscal year, Lon. Just say the word, and I'll start making changes."

"Then this place won't be La Mira West," London cut in. "It'll just be like every other club."

"I don't know about that," Lucinda countered. "Your

name is what makes this place. And you have so much more to offer than other clubs. I can cut down on expenses without sacrificing what has made this club unique. And then you wouldn't be losing so much money."

London shook her head and let her mind wander. *The yearly check is eight-hundred-and-fifty thousand. Three hundred thousand of that apparently gets consumed by this club. You do the math, idiot. You can't afford to stay in business with nothing to give the club this year. Jesus Christ! I can't pay the staff at my home! I can't pay the limo driver! Holy shit! No wonder I can't wait for the check each year. Nearly half of it goes to the club. I spend the rest. I could sell the club—well, maybe not now, in today's economic climate. Sell the building. Yes, that could bring in some money. Wait. No. No! I can't do that! People can't know about this. The press would have a field day if they found out Maddy and I have been cut out of the family's money. If I closed the club and put the building on the market, how would I explain that? The reporters would not stopping digging until they found out, no matter what I told them.*

"Well, you just let me know what you want me to do," Lucinda said.

Put a gun to my head? London thought.

"Because I can cut these expenses down in no time."

How about starting back five years ago? Can you go back to five years ago and then pull in a profit for me up to the present? Because we are so royally fucked right now.

"Just keep me posted on what you want me to do."

Fire everyone. Sell everything. But do it discretely.

"By the way, Lonnie, I need your annual check so I can deposit it," Lucinda said as she stood up. "I've got to write out some checks for last month's bills for the club."

"How much is left in the account?" London asked.

Lucinda shrugged her shoulders. "Offhand, I'm not sure. Maybe a few thousand. What you've got in there won't cover very much. The good thing is, you've paid the staff through this past year, so we won't have to write out checks for them until the second week in January."

Yes, that is a good thing, London thought. *It's a little ray of sunshine on this otherwise monsoon day.* London cleared her throat. "The, uh, the check is going to be delayed for a bit, Cinda. I guess we should just, you know, uh, divide up what we have and, uh, pay whatever we can."

Lucinda raised her eyebrows. "When do you think you'll get the check?"

When hell freezes over. Which is apparently the only thing Grandpa Tony didn't freeze-dry. "Uh, soon, I think."

"Okay. Because I don't think we can spread ourselves too thin, just making small payments. It doesn't look good."

Oh, I'll tell you what won't look good, London thought. *Me in an orange prison jumpsuit. Maybe that will be the new pink for spring. I can see the headlines now: "Daughter of billionaires into debt up to her eyeballs." Oh, that's a good one.* London forced a smile. "I'll let you know as soon as that check arrives. Thanks so much."

Here's what it's all about, London thought as her pounding head kept beat with the pounding music that infiltrated her office. *Soundproof, my ass,* she snorted as she reached into a drawer, pulled out a bottle of Advil, and shook out three tablets. She washed them down with the dregs left in her long-ago-poured morning cup of coffee and grimaced at the stale taste and bitter coldness.

So here's what it's all about, she resumed. *Gamma Angel lived through the Depression. When people lost everything. And so what she's doing is giving me and Maddy a taste of what that was like. I can see that now. People went from riches to rags in a flash. Just like she's doing with Maddy and me. What the no-check policy is really saying is, without money, you're screwed.* That's *the fucking lesson.*

London reached for a cigarette and lit it. *But what does*

Gamma now expect of me? Of Maddy? That we land in prison for—what's it called, nonpayment of debts? Because that's where this is certainly heading. There are a lot of people who are going to be pretty upset about not getting paid. They're going to sue us! Did she even think about that? Okay. So let's say that happens. Daddy isn't going to put up with that. Not for one minute. Because the press will not be kind to him about abandoning us. So he'll come to our rescue and bail us out. Mad and I will cry and hug our parents and say, 'We've learned our lesson. We're never going to take money for granted again.' And then we'll get our checks back. And I won't spend as much money. I'll cut up my credit cards. Well, most of them. I'll keep one. Or two. And I'll ask Cinda to cut some corners here. I wonder what I should wear when I'm taken off to prison? Something that's not too showy. And no heels. No jewelry, either.

London mentally surveyed her clothes closet and then stopped when she remembered the outfit she had planned to wear to the club tonight. She glanced at the clock on her desk and saw that the new year was thirty minutes away. Outside her office, she could picture the fun people were having.

Enjoy it while it lasts, she thought and then frowned.

I like this damn club. It's something to do. Somewhere to go. It keeps me occupied. If I didn't have it . . .

London's thoughts trailed off and she felt a sudden tightness in her chest.

If I didn't have it.

She took in a deep breath. *But I want it.*

She exhaled. *But I can't afford it.*

She closed her eyes, and then opened them.

If I didn't have it, what would I do?

The club music suddenly burst into her office in a loud blast.

"Hey! You're still in here," Lucinda shouted over the noise as she peered around the door. "It's almost time to celebrate—just minutes away from the countdown! And you wouldn't believe the crowd! I've got your favorite," she smiled as she closed the door and walked to London's desk with a champagne bottle in her hand. "Domaine Ste. Michelle. Shall I pop the cork and pour you a glass? And, and, and!" she said excitedly as she reached into a pocket of her red-and-black-trimmed velour jacket. "Your favorite chocolate, boss. Valrhona Limited Edition Chuao. Premier Cru. Believe me, this stuff is going fast. I think we've gone through six cartons already."

London watched as Lucinda placed the chocolate bar and champagne bottle on her desk.

"Do you have glasses in here? And I want to thank you for your Christmas present. This jacket," Lucinda smiled at her. "I used the bonus you gave me to buy it. I haven't bought myself something new in years. I know I haven't lost any weight, what with the holidays, but I feel good in it."

"How much did that set me back?" London asked.

"The jacket? It was on sale."

"Not the jacket. I mean the chocolate. The champagne." *People are out there sucking money out of me. Like vacuum cleaners,* she thought as she remembered Maddy's description. *I'm getting poorer by the minute.*

"And those smoked beers are a real hit. Have you tried the roasted vegetable and cheese stacks? I mean, *the food!* It's like everyone came here starving. We'll have to order more for next year, I think. And speaking of next year, I'm starting on a new way of life. I'm using the rest of the bonus you gave me to join a health club. I'm going to start working out and shedding those pounds! The second day of January—like ninety percent of Americans! Oh, I feel positively giddy. I think this is the best party yet. It was worth it to get DJ Crystal Joye. No wonder she's the priciest DJ around. She's worth every penny. She's awesome! Her dance floor is packed."

There was a time when every penny counted, London thought. *Like now. Wait. Lucinda said people were starving. So I'm feeding the hungry! Like in the Depression. That's a good thing, right? I could call Gamma Angel now and say, 'Gamma. I'm feeding the hungry. I'm giving drink to the thirsty. Doesn't that count for something?'*

"So why are you still in here? The party's going on out there. Do you know that I danced with Helen Hunt? Well, I didn't really dance *with* her. But she and I were on the dance floor at the same time! Oh, oh, oh! I forgot to tell you. That reporter from the student newspaper is here. Where *are* your glasses?" she asked as her eyes wandered around the office while she used her fingernails to pick at the foil wrapper at the top of the champagne bottle.

"What reporter?"

"You know," Lucinda said. "The young one from U-Cal, Berkeley. The one who was at the airport. The one you took a fancy to. You wrote a note on her pad of paper. So she could come here and interview you tonight."

"Tonight?" London asked, then shook her head. "Not tonight. Just tell her to enjoy herself."

"You want her to stay? You do know that she's a sophomore, right?"

"So?"

Lucinda began to untwist the wire on the top of the bottle. "We weren't going to let anyone into the club who was under twenty-one."

"She's twenty-one?"

"Younger than that."

"Younger than twenty-one," London repeated. "Let her stay. Let her have some fun. In another ten years, life won't be fun for her anymore."

"Good glory—someone's not in a very good mood. What's going on with you tonight?" Lucinda asked as she abandoned her work on the bottle and sat down in the chair in front of London's desk. "You've been holed up in here for hours and look like, well, you look like you haven't slept in a week."

"I haven't."

"Why?"

"I've got . . . got some things on my mind."

"Like what?"

London shrugged her shoulders and then glanced down at the piles on her desk.

"Hey, listen, don't worry about all this financial stuff, Lon. That's my job, to worry about that. And I'm making another resolution for the new year. I'm going to try to take things a little easier. Not get so serious. I mean, I will be serious about managing the club. And cutting down expenses, if you want me to. But you told me before Christmas that I was, I think your words were, screwed on too tight. You're right. I haven't had a good time in I don't know how long. Tonight I'm having the *best* time. Because I'm thinking, 'How would Lonnie enjoy this evening?' And that's what I'm trying to do. Well, I'm certainly not doing *everything* you'd do. I mean, you're too wild for me! But you—you should be out there, Lon. That'll get you out of your gray-cloud mood. You need to get out there and do what you love to do."

"What's that?"

Lucinda laughed. "Party hard, boss. Drink, dance. Mingle with the rich and famous—the ones just like you. Do you know how many people keep asking, 'Where's Lonnie?' There are reporters and camera crews. Since when have you ever shied away from publicity? It's New Year's Eve. It's time to celebrate!"

London opened to the society pages of the morning's newspaper and groaned as she read the headline to the lead segment in the daily *Star Talk* column:

LA MIRA—DISAPPEARA?

Party girls pull vanishing act at their New Year's Eve clubs

Rumors were flying as fast as clothes were being discarded in the sex rooms of the infamous La Mira East and La Mira West nightclubs, owned by the often trashy twins **London** *and* **Madrid La Mira,** *at last night's New Year's Eve bashes. My sources, who were posted inside each club, tell me they spotted neither twin during the entire night. I mean, there was not even a sighting! Managers for both clubs said that their respective bitch-bosses were most certainly on the premises, but the funny thing about that is that there are no pictures of the La Mira beauties in any party photographs taken inside the clubs. And since when have those publicity hogs ever run out of sexy smiles for the ever-present cameras?*

So what happened to the La Mira twins? Theories of alien abduction aside—I guess stranger things have happened at the stroke of midnight prior to a new year—one source tells me that Madrid's crashed Jag was being kept under wraps at a Manhattan foreign car repair shop. But a check of hospitals up and down the East Coast revealed no admissions. Is Madrid wandering around somewhere with amnesia? Has her sister gone off in search of her? Oh, that would be so dramatic, wouldn't it?

With curiosity building up inside of me until I could no longer contain it, I broke down and called the La Mira home in Brit-free Concord, Massachusetts. The lovely **Kitty La Mira,** *mother of the twins, was most gracious in answering my questions. She assured me that the twins are fine—"in perfect health and as beautiful as ever"—and she double-assured me that* *they are often quite busy during the holidays. "They may have even taken a trip out of the country," she offered up, but my money is on what some have suspected for years.*

My theory is that the fast-lane lifestyles and the mostly liquid-and-pill diets the two have been imbibing over the years have finally spelled impending health disaster. My guess is that they're behind the closed doors of Betty Ford. Or perhaps Hazelden. Maybe these gals, who are often higher than kites, are learning how to twelve-step their way back to earth, one day at a time.

Now, as much as I'm all for that wonderfully rehabilitative program, Alcoholics Anonymous, I must confess that such a change will not bode well for the La Mira twins. Some of my closest, dearest friends are in the AA program of recovery, but I'll tell you, my dear readers, what I often tell them. "Get over it and get back to the way you were!" Because reformed drinkers are worse than reformed smokers. You just can't throw a good party with punch and expect to have a raucous good time.

Lest you think, dearest devoted fans of this column, that I might be grabbing for straws, I recently confirmed that the twins' long-suffering publicist, **Dolores Fontaine,** *has signed* **John Grisham** *as a client and is in negotiations with several other big-name authors. Shall I let the name* **Jacquelyn Mitchard** *slip, for instance? Or* **Scott Turow?** *Or* **Elizabeth Berg?***

Now you tell me, avid readers. Why would the twins' publicist fly the coop, unless the chickens had already left?

"The chickens are still in the coop," London muttered as she tossed the paper on the floor. "They're just now scratchpoor."

* * *

London lay motionless on the couch in her living room that afternoon with a cold facecloth draped over her eyes. "And I don't even have a hangover," she muttered every few seconds, which she then followed up with an exasperated sigh and a moaned, "What the *fuck* am I going to do?"

As she got up to rewet the now-warm facecloth, the phone and the doorbell rang at the same time. She stopped on her way to the kitchen and looked back and forth from the phone to the door.

"Neither, either, both?" she asked herself.

The ring-buzz, ring-buzz kept pounding in her head, much as the club music had the previous night. She rubbed her forehead, picked up the phone, and walked with it to the front door.

"You are *not* going to fucking believe *this!*" Madrid shouted through the phone as soon as London had placed it on her ear.

London sucked in air and closed her eyes for a few seconds. "Mad, I have a splitting headache right now. So stop shouting."

"I can't help but shout, Lon. Because this *really* takes the fucking cake!"

"What?" London asked as she opened the front door. "Lucinda?" she asked as she opened the door, and then quickly stepped aside as Lucinda burst through the door, thrust a manila envelope into her chest, and shouted, "So *this* is how you communicate with me? Through paperwork?"

"Why's everyone shouting at me?" London asked.

"So Lucinda's there?" Madrid asked. "Why didn't you tell me? Since you already fucking know, why the fuck aren't you fuming about it?"

"About what?" London asked. "What am I supposed to know?" She glanced down at the envelope. "What's this?" she asked Lucinda.

"You tell me," Lucinda answered.

"About Gamma Angel handing over our clubs to our managers," Madrid answered.

"Huh?" London asked.

"Why didn't you tell me about this last night?" Lucinda asked. "With the way you were acting, I knew something was wrong. Don't you remember that I asked you what was wrong? We could've at least talked about it."

"So basically we have *nothing,* Lonnie," Madrid continued. Abso-*fucking*-lutely nothing. First the check, then the—"

"I mean, I thought you would've had the courtesy to at least give me a head's up," Lucinda continued. "I mean, this is a great opportunity for me. It would've been something we could've talked about, and then we could've celebrated with that bottle of champagne."

"I have no idea what—"

"Don't get me wrong, Lon," Lucinda broke in. "I'm really grateful for the opportunity. I'm thrilled about the possibilities this opens up to me. I mean, I'd be a fool not to be. But I mean—come on! The least you could've done would've been to—"

"—no fucking possibility of getting a loan, and so the last thing in the world I expected—" Madrid continued.

"It's not that I *can't* do it, Lonnie," Lucinda broke in. "I mean, who *wouldn't* want this? So it's not that I *won't* do it. But I would've liked some explanation from you last night. I thought we had a better relationship than that. That's why I'm here now. She said—"

"Who said?" London asked Lucinda.

"No one said anything to us about this," Madrid answered. "I mean, why didn't she tell us this at Christmas?"

"Who?" London asked Madrid.

"Your grandmother," Lucinda answered. "She had a courier deliver this to me first thing this morning with a note—"

"Gamma Angel, you idiot," Madrid continued.

"—she wanted me to call her the moment I opened the package, and then she took me through the whole thing," Lucinda finished.

"What whole thing?" London asked.

"Lonnie, are you listening to me? Huh?" Madrid demanded. "You tell me what we're going to do now."

"How do I know what to do?" London asked. "I don't know what's going on."

"Once the press gets hold of this, Lon, it's not going to be pretty."

"Your grandmother told me you were in full agreement with this," Lucinda said. "It was my understanding that you knew—"

"I DON'T KNOW ANYTHING!" London shouted into the phone and at Lucinda.

"*Now* who's shouting?" Madrid pointed out. "You have a talk with your goddamned manager, why don't you? Because I've already had a talk with mine. And then you and I have got to think long and hard about this whole surreal thing and what we're going to do about it. Oh, and by the way. Our dedicated publicist is nowhere to be found. Or, she's not returning phone calls. Great idea, to hook her up with new clients. Like, where is she when we really need her? I bet Gamma Angel has gotten to her already. Told her, 'The girls will no longer be needing your services.' Which means that we're being hung out to dry. No, to *fry* would be a better word. We are so royally screwed. You ask Lucinda. You find out from her who owns our clubs now."

"According to this document, you're now the temporary owner of La Mira West," London said as she sat on the couch next to Lucinda and perused a sheaf of papers she had taken from the envelope Lucinda had given to her. "For the next two years."

Lucinda nodded. "That's it, in a nutshell. I thought you knew all this, Lon."

London shook her head.

"I feel bad," Lucinda answered. "Your grandmother said if I didn't want to do it, she'd find someone else. But the way she explained it to me, well, she implied that you knew all about it. That it was something you wanted. And so . . . so I signed a copy and sent it back before I came over here."

London closed her eyes and nodded.

Lucinda put a hand on London's arm. "I can keep it going, Lon. You know I can. Though, well, not in quite the way it has been. Because, well, if you look at—" Lucinda flipped through the papers and then settled on a sheet and tapped a finger to the page. "See how she says that the sex rooms are to be closed along with some of the smaller dance floors?"

"She's a hundred fucking years old," London snorted. "Of course she doesn't want the sex rooms."

"I never really wanted them, either. But they were what you wanted."

"Not just me, Cinda. *People* wanted them. They're what *made* the club."

"Sometimes, Lon, things got too wild."

London shrugged her shoulders. "So? That's why the club's so popular."

"But just with a limited population. That's why having a dance club and a restaurant under one roof will draw in a bigger crowd."

"A what?"

"A restaurant."

"People don't go to La Mira West to eat."

"Just hear me out, Lon. You know that my father owns a restaurant in Sausalito. It's been in the family for years. It's never gotten less than a three-and-a-half-star rating, and that was only because the regular chef had quit on the night when—"

"La Mira West doesn't have a kitchen," London argued. "We don't *prepare* food. We serve food. At catered parties. By some very fine catering companies, I might add."

"You're right," Lucinda agreed. "But part of the club can be made into a really nice restaurant—in fact, it *will* be. That's what your grandmother wants, and she's given approval for a full kitchen with—"

"Christ, who gives a crap what she wants? She's taken this whole thing way too far. Just because she and my father signed off on everything . . ." London took a deep breath, then let out a long sigh. She turned to Lucinda. "La Mira West is going to be a restaurant?"

"*And* a nightclub," Lucinda added. "It's still going to be a fun club."

"A *fun* club?" London snorted. "You mean like Disneyland? Why not put in a ride while you're at it?"

"It's not going to be family dining," Lucinda said. "It's going to offer up the finest dishes, prepared by top chefs. It will be great. And more people will come to the club." Lucinda smiled. "Lon, I *know* the restaurant business. My father had me working at the restaurant from the moment I could carry a tray with a cup of coffee on it and not spill a drop. And when I was in high school, I was the manager and I helped to—"

"My fucking club isn't going to be a restaurant!" London shouted.

Lucinda sat in silence for a few moments. "She said you—"

"I don't care what she said."

"Not that much is really going to change, Lon."

"Good Christ, *everything's* changing!"

"La Mira West is going to still be a great place to dance. And it will be a great place to get a fantastic meal."

"No, it's *not*."

"Lon, I don't know what to tell you. That's what your grandmother wants, and now, well, she's my boss."

"Thanks for the loyalty, Lucinda. By the way, you're fired."

"I *am* loyal to you, Lon. I have been all these years. I know your club like the back of my hand. And I also know how to run a restaurant. I'm being given the opportunity of a lifetime. I'd be a fool to refuse the chance to do this. I'm losing nothing."

"And I'm losing everything. You're fired, Lucinda."

"Lon, I don't know what's going on between you and your grandmother. That's none of my business. But my job is my business."

"You don't have a job. You're fired."

"No, Lonnie, I'm not. Only your grandmother can fire me."

"You're a little shit. Here I thought that you were my most dedicated employee, and now you just—"

"Lonnie, I *am* your most dedicated employee. Think about it. I'm sticking with the club. Your grandmother said that if I didn't want to sign the papers, she'd find someone else. Who knows what they'd do with it? But I'm going to be the temporary—remember that—temporary owner. Because at some point this thing with your grandmother is going to blow over. You two will patch it up, work it out—whatever you have to do. In the meantime, I'll be running the club for you. I'm not running out on you or stabbing you in the back or anything like that. I'm trying to make sure that you still have the club, and that I can still be there for you.

"And, Lonnie. I *am* there for you."

PART TWO

We all need money, but there are degrees of desperation.
—Anthony Burgess

Preoccupation with money is the great test of small natures, but only a small test of great ones.
—Sebastien-Roch Nicolas de Chamfort

Money is better than poverty, if only for financial reasons.
—Woody Allen

PART TWO

5

"Who was the fucking bozo who said we'd get used to this fucking heat?" Madrid asked her sister as she bounced up and down in the back of the pickup truck that was bringing them and five other Habitat for Humanity volunteers to the Miami site they had been working at for two weeks. "It's inhumane to be working in this fucking heat. We should be called the fucking Habitat for *Inhumanity* volunteers."

"Inhumanity," London snickered. "That's a good one!"

The truck slowed and then drew to a stop under an early-morning sun that blazed down from a cloudless sky. A high-humidity haze obscured the distant horizon and filled the air with a thick blanket of dampness. As a cloud of dust settled around the truck, the twins alternated between emitting fits of staccato coughing and waving their hands frantically in the air while the rest of the crew gathered up tools and equipment.

"Bo be dat fuckin' bozo," replied a large black man who was wearing a well-worn, dirty pair of baggy cutoff jeans that hung below his belly and down to his kneecaps. A glistening layer of sweat covered the rest of his shirtless body.

He grabbed an enormous water container between both hands, lifted it up to his chest, and turned to face the twins, displaying a gold front tooth as he spoke. "All Bo gonna say is, you two's better be pullin' your weight today. Bo be hopin' you break all dem fancy nails a yers. Then mebbe you can work like the rest a us."

"Do you know how much these nails cost?" Madrid asked as she displayed her hands to Bo, and then peered at them and sighed. "Well, what's left of them. Believe me, you pay top dollar in the city for this kind of work."

Bo snorted. "That don't be no work. Bo knows work."

London glanced down at her own hands. "Mad, we're going to have to schedule manicures when we're done here. This damage is not going to be easy to fix."

Bo slowly lowered the water container, released his grip, and then placed his massive hands on his broad hips. "Bo knows dem nails a yours are 'spensive. Each little bitty finger a yours probably cost more dan dis here house we be buildin'. Bo don't care. Bo works hard. Bo don't like people who don't work hard."

"Second that sentiment, Bo-man," piped in a short, athletic-looking woman who was wearing cutoff jeans coveralls over a shocking-pink jog bra, a pair of high-top construction boots, and a matching bright pink bandana across the top of her head that held back a tangled mane of long, dirty-blond, tightly-curled hair. "And I'm tired of hearing your constant gripes. If you two don't want to be here, then leave. Go get your damned manicures. We'll get the job finished in no time."

"We're doing *stuff*, Sally," London told her.

"*Sandra*. It's Sandra." Sandra tossed a toolbelt over her shoulder and shook her head. "As if I even care that you know my name. We've got two more weeks at this Overtown site—thanks to you two princesses, we're a week behind schedule. After that, I'll never have to deal with your spoiled attitudes again. You brats are as vacuous as they say."

"They?" London asked. "Who's they?"

"We put up that wall-thingy yesterday—Sandra," Madrid pointed out.

"Which we had to take down on account a ya didn't use the right nails," gasped a pear-shaped, overweight, heavy-breathing woman who was wearing a massive pair of dark-blue shorts and a grey T-shirt that had already darkened in several areas from sweat. "I got six kids I raised on my own, and they ain't stupid like you two. I mean, how easy can we make it for ya? Your brains cain't seem ta take in the number of the nail, so Bo an' me made up a board with all them nails on 'em with color codes. Yesterday was them blue nails. *Blue.* We tol' ya and tol' ya it were blue. But you two's used the yella. All it was gonna take was a teeny puff a wind afore that wall jus' fell on down. And if'n ya know anythin' 'bout Florida, you know there ain't no gettin' 'round hurricanes packin' wind."

"Dat right," Bo added. "Bo be here wit' Mrs. Mac hours after you two left. Bo an' Mrs. Mac fixed stuff an' make it right. Dat there wall not be comin' down no matta what de wind be."

"Hey, a nail's a nail," London retorted. "Blue, yellow—they all look the same to me. At least what we're building has a floor, four walls, and a roof. I mean, it's better than these poor schmucks that are going to live here had before, right?"

"Oh, I've been waiting for you two to open your big, fat, rich mouths and say something like that," Sandra said as she tossed the toolbelt onto the truck bed, where it landed with a loud clang, and reached into the front pocket of her cover-alls. "You guys wanna see just how these tramps live?" she asked as she unfolded several pages she had torn out of magazines. "This is from *Town & Country,* folks. A high-class magazine about working stiffs like these twins."

"What does it matter to you where we live?" Madrid challenged her. "That's our business."

Sandra shook her head. "No, honey lamb, it's my business. It's real important to me who I work with, whether it's on the job in the schools where I teach or in the groups I volunteer for. People have got to be in sync with one another, share in the common purpose, so to speak, in order to make something work well."

Bo nodded his head. "Bo likes makin' friends when he workin'."

"Once I found out that you twins were going to be joining our crew, I wanted to find out everything I could about you. Just think of me as the crew's social director. Oh, wait. Your *hospitality administrator*. Do you understand that term better? As I said, it's important to me that I enjoy the people I'm working with. After I read up on you, I knew you two would be trouble with a capital T. Because you chicks have no clue about what these houses mean to the families that will live in them. How could you, when you both live in places like these?" Sandra tapped the pages she held open in one hand.

The crew gathered around Sandra. "Pretty fancy, huh?" she asked. "This one here's where London lives in San Francisco. Shall I read what it says?" she asked as she glanced at London.

London moved closer to her sister and folded her arms across her chest.

"Read it," Mrs. Mac answered as she let out a sigh and leaned against the side of the truck bed.

Sandra looked down at the pages. "Uh, blah, blah—oh, yeah—'soaring, twenty-five-foot-high, perforated fiberglass-paneled ceiling with three new skylights arches above the multiuse great room.' *Multiuse great room*. Got that, people? Shit, I don't even know what a multiuse great room is, let alone what I'd use it for. Plus, there are four bedrooms and a guest suite, a living room, a dining room, a massive kitchen, and a huge master bedroom. All for just one little person. Well, one little person with an ego the size of the city she lives in. Oh, and—get this—there's also, and I quote, 'an oak-and-stainless-steel staircase that provides access to the study/library and the guest suite.' "

"Fuckin' A!" exclaimed a short, deeply tanned, muscle-bound twenty-something.

"You got that right, Jimmy," puffed out Mrs. Mac. "I have me a multiuse great room, but I call it my mobile home." She let out a long, gasping laugh, clutched her chest, and then drew in a deep breath. "And we don't have no *li-brar-y* in my house. But my kids know how to *use* a library. Ya see, London, my kids cain't afford no books a their own. We hasta borrow 'em."

"I bet you don't even read the books in your library," Jimmy snorted. "I bet you just have them there for show. Just so you can impress people."

"I read—" London began, but Sandra cut her off.

"And then Madrid here lives in New York City, in a penthouse apartment in Tribeca," Sandra continued. "That's a very fancy section of the city. See this? This is an elevated living room area on a steel platform. And there are nine-foot-tall windows overlooking the city. You see this chair?" Sandra asked as she pointed to a picture on one of the pages. "It's a—let me read this now—a 'low-backed, slatted chair in oak from Armani Casa.' Retails for six hundred bucks, people. She owns twelve."

Bo whistled. "Bo could make quite a few car payments jus' wid dem chairs."

"I could put some 'a that good food in my kids' mouths for a change," Mrs. Mac added. "I've tried six ways ta Sunday to make macaroni 'n' rice 'n' hot dogs interestin'. Believe me, it ain't never gone be interestin'. But my kids, they be good. They eat it. Just a leg 'a one of them chairs would buy me some steaks—um, boy, my kids'd sure love them a steak ever' once in a while. A nice, thick juicy piece, with lotsa meat on it."

"I could buy new textbooks for my classes instead of used," added Jimmy as he moved away from Sandra and sat down on the side of the truck bed next to Mrs. Mac. "There's nothing worse than reading a book that's filled with high-lights someone else put in it. I think to myself, are those things really important, or just what someone else thought was crucial to know? Yeah, new books would be good. And then maybe I wouldn't have to put in as many hours as I do working so I could hit the books more. I'm so dog-tired by the time I start to study, my eyes close without me even knowing it. Believe me, my grades are reflecting that I'm not reading my books—I'm usually using them as pillows."

"So what the fuck are you doing here?" snapped a tall, thin Hispanic woman as she glared at London and Madrid, then sat down next to Jimmy and crossed her long legs. "You're a long way from your palaces, and you don't seem particularly happy to be here. It's pretty clear that you couldn't give a crap about the Haitian immigrants who are going to be living in the homes we're building. Do you two even know where Haiti is?"

"Don't you know their story, Nicie?" Sandra asked as she refolded the pages and slipped them back into her chest pocket. "These two are billionairesses. Yes, they are."

"You mean million, don't you?" Jimmy asked.

"*Billion,*" Sandra emphasized.

Jimmy whistled. "It's like winning the lottery."

"And then spending it all," Sandra added as she shot the twins a sly grin. "I know a lot about you two. Believe me, I spend a lot of time in the hair salon with this mane. That's the time when I get to catch up on all the magazines I can read. For free."

"Don't believe everything that's printed in those maga-zines," London muttered.

Madrid nodded. "There's not a lot of truth in them."

Sandra flashed them a smile. "Oh, I think there's enough truth in there to make my point. You see, folks," she said as she turned to the rest of the crew. "These two trust-fund ba-bies were cut off from their yearly check this past Christmas.

Want to know how much it was? Just a few hundred thousand short of a million. *Each year!*"

A pained expression flashed across Mrs. Mac's face, and she shook her head. "That's a education for all my kids. Ever' single one a them. And nice clothes. New clothes—not bargain basement ones or hand-me-downs. A decent home, too. Not one up on concrete blocks that're so uneven that if'n ya drop a apple on the floor in the kitchen, it rolls right smack-dab to the middle of the living room. And with that kind a dough, I could afford me a car that don't break down jus' when I need it the most. Ya cain't be goin' on job interviews when your engine don't turn over."

"Why were they cut off?" Jimmy asked Sandra.

"Why don't you ask us?" London replied. "We're right here."

"Like you'd tell us the truth," Nicie snickered.

"Their grandmother," Sandra began, "who I guess did a lot for people during the Great Depression, providing free food and setting up bread lines for those who needed it the most, told these two that they had to learn the value of money before they got another cent. You see, they've never had to work a day in their lives. They've just been handed their checks each year on a silver platter. They've never earned a penny from puttin' in a hard day's work."

"Bo knows a hard day's work," Bo said. "Yes, he do. Bo works hard ta bring him home a paycheck."

"We all know about hard work," Mrs. Mac said.

"So now they're trying to find the . . ." Sandra placed her hands in the air and wiggled two fingers on each hand up and down, "*meaning* of money. This is—what?" she turned to the twins "—the fourth or fifth attempt to earn your grandmother's respect so you can regain your fortunes?"

"They've been at other Habitat for Humanity projects?" Jimmy asked.

Sandra shook her head. "Nope. They've . . ." Sandra stopped as she began to laugh. "They've . . . well . . ." Sandra clutched her stomach as her laughter continued. "Oh, my. It's just so unbelievable that you have to laugh."

"I don't see what's so funny about what we've been trying to do," Madrid hissed at Sandra.

"Tell us," Nicie prompted Sandra.

"Okay, okay," Sandra said as she took in a deep breath and wiped the corners of her eyes. "These two have pretty much screwed up everything they've volunteered for. You think their not knowing the right nails to use is bad, Mrs. Mac? Why don't you tell them about the sea turtles, Madrid? Or, you, London. Why don't you tell them about the fashion show you staged at a Salvation Army?"

"Why don't you fucking shut up, Sandra," Madrid snapped.

"The Salvation Army thing was blown way out of proportion," London countered.

" 'Fess up," Nicie asked Sandra.

Sandra turned to Nicie. "So London goes to all of her rich-bitch friends and asks them to donate clothing they don't want to the Mission Hill Salvation Army in San Francisco. So what kinds of donations does she get? Dior gowns and Rive Gauche sandals and Kate Spade tote bags. Okay, so that's bad enough, right? I mean, like some homeless woman pushing a shopping cart filled with her possessions and as many soda cans as she can scavenge out of trash barrels is going to be tooling around San Francisco in a ball gown and heeled sandals saying, 'Look at me! I'm homeless, but I'm fashionable!' "

"That's cruel," Mrs. Mac glared at London.

"I wasn't trying to be—"

"To add insult to injury," Sandra continued, "London decides to enlist all of her friends—who wear, like, a size two—to *model* the donated clothing. Sort of a 'How to Dress for Homelessness Success' seminar."

"What are you, fucking stupid?" Jimmy asked the twins. London tightened her lips and lowered her eyes.

"And then Madrid here," Sandra chuckled as she swept an arm in Madrid's direction. "Oh, I shouldn't laugh, because this one's really pathetic. She decides that saving sea turtles will help her regain her money. So she goes to the Mexican seaside village of Rancho Nuevo to help bring the Kemp's ridley sea turtle back from the brink of extinction. She travels down there with Green Nature, a group that's trying to educate the villagers to prevent them from harvesting nearly every egg the turtles lay on the beaches because the people consider the eggs to be an aphrodisiac. This year, the group was thrilled because they found more than a thousand nests and were able to keep the majority of the eggs intact. So they were more than ready for all of the volunteers to arrive to help escort the hatchlings safely to the sea."

"Bo had a turtle once, when he was a kid. Bo loved him, dat dere turtle."

"How hard can a hatching rescue be?" Jimmy asked.

"How hard can it be to bang in a nail?" Nicie quickly responded.

"Bo don't think very hard. But Bo be wrong."

"Anyway," Sandra said. "By the time Madrid gets down there with the rest of the volunteers, the hatchlings are ready to be born. Her job was simple—guide the babies in the correct direction. You see, the hatchlings are attracted to light and move toward it. Before villages were built near the seashore, the turtles had no problem moving toward the moonlit sea. Without guidance, however, they head toward the lights on land and then die. So all Madrid had to do was walk along next to the babies and keep them going in the right direction until they made it to the safety of the ocean."

"Bo don't think that be too hard. Bo thinks he be wantin' a turtle again."

"No, Bo, it really shouldn't be too hard," Sandra agreed. "But apparently—what did that newspaper article say that quoted you, Madrid?"

Madrid met Sandra's eyes for a brief moment and then turned to face London.

Sandra waited for a few seconds, and then shook her head. "Well, I guess she won't tell anyone, so I will. To paraphrase, it was something along the lines of, 'The damn turtles were moving too slow.' And so what did she do?"

"I don't think I'm going to like to hear this," Nicie said with a groan.

"She picked up the hatchlings in her care and flung them into the ocean!" Sandra declared. "*Dozens* of them. *Flung* them! Of course, when they've just hatched, their shells haven't had a chance to harden. So when they hit the water—"

Mrs. Mac frantically waved a hand in the air. "I don't need ta hear any more. *No more.* Killin' baby turtles—I never!"

"I thought I was helping them," Madrid said defensively. "It was just taking them *forever.*"

"They're *babies!*" Mrs. Mac exclaimed.

"Bo knows a story," Bo interjected with a broad smile, " 'bout how a turtle be beatin' a rabbit in a race. The rabbit, he be fast. The turtle, he be slow. But de bunny done take itself a nap, an' de turtle crawled on right by him while he be snoozin'. Slow 'n steady, is how he won. Bo likes dat dere story."

"But they were taking *forever,*" Madrid repeated. "And one would go this way and another would—"

"Mad, just drop it," London cautioned her as she glanced at the faces of the crew.

"Let me finish!" Madrid snapped at her. "I want to make sure these people understand just how *hard* the job was. I mean, one would go this way, and another turn another way, and there were hundreds of them just skittling about here and there like it was some sort of goddamned turtle free-for-all, and it was just all too much. The damn things were just not doing what they were supposed to do. So I got them to the ocean as fast as I could. I thought I was helping them."

"Just like you thought you were helping in that soup kitchen?" Sandra challenged her.

"God, don't even mention that place!" Madrid exclaimed. "I can still *smell* it. *I* wouldn't eat that slop. So why should I expect anyone else to? Runny mashed potatoes—they weren't real, of course, but made from flakes—"

"Thanks to Grandpa Tony," London mumbled to her. "Hard to believe Gamma got rich off of that."

Madrid nodded. "And there was some sort of soup that smelled like someone dropped old sneakers in it and had a funky color going on and meat that was all grey and gristly. It made me nauseous just being around it. And the people— they smelled just as bad as the food."

"Which you made certain to point out before you ripped off your apron, ran out of the kitchen, and puked," Sandra added. "I'll never forget the headlines in the papers the next day. My favorite was 'From Soup to Nut.' One writer said that the only thing that was spoiled in that soup kitchen was you. The mayor's office was apparently flooded with phone calls of complaints about the quality of the food being served. It turns out, of course, that what was being served had been prepared by volunteer dieticians and was quite good. However, it was apparently not up to Madrid's four-star restaurant standards."

Nicie shook her head at Madrid. "No wonder you two don't eat any of the food we make at night."

"Ain't you two never been hungry before?" Mrs. Mac asked them.

"I just didn't think—" Madrid began.

"And let's not forget London and her interview at the Big Sisters program in San Francisco," Sandra broke in. "The case worker who interviewed her said—and this is pretty much a direct quote—'I have never, in all of my years on this

Amy Alden

job, meeting all kinds of people from all walks of life, met someone as pompous and selfish as that woman.' When the case worker asked her what she was looking for in a little sister, London said something along the lines of, 'Someone who comes from a good home and likes the finer things in life and can pretty much just do what I tell them.' And it doesn't end there."

"Christ! There's more?" Nicie exclaimed.

Bo placed his massive hands over his ears. "Bo don't wanna hear no more."

"Me neither," Mrs. Mac agreed.

Bo dropped his hands. "Bo feels mad."

"It's okay, Bo," Mrs. Mac said. "We probably all do right now."

Jimmy stood up. "I guess that saying is true after all. Money can't buy an education. You two are proof-positive of that."

"But it can certainly buy stupidity," Nicie added.

"Our hearts were in the right place," London said defensively.

"Hearts?" Mrs. Mac gave out a quick laugh and then sucked in air with a wheeze.

Nicie stood up and faced the twins. "You think that anyone believes you two actually *care*? You killed an endangered species and couldn't even serve soup to the hungry! You staged a fashion show for people who simply want clothing to put on their backs! All you big babies want—all you *care* about—is getting your money back. You couldn't care less about the people or the animals you say you have a heart to help. I mean, do you even know *anything* about Habitat for Humanity? You don't know a thing about simple, decent, affordable housing. You two live in palaces. You wear top-of-the-line designer clothing. You live the life of luxury. The people we're building these homes for will, for the first time, have indoor plumbing and electricity and a stove to cook their food on. They'll have beds to sleep in. They'll have shower stalls. These homes couldn't hold a candle to where you two live, that's for sure. But it's more than these worthwhile people have ever had in their lives. In fact, they're going to feel like *they're* billionaires just by living in a little over a thousand square feet."

"Fuckin' filthy-rich do-gooders," snorted Jimmy. "My parents don't have much. But they worked hard to give me the basics in life. My father's a long-distance trucker and my mother's a nursing assistant. They never went to college, but they saved as much as they could to make sure that I could go, so I could get a good education and a good job and not live from paycheck to paycheck like they did. I'm on scholarship to the university, work at a convenience store at night, give half of what I make to my mother, and I *chose* to do this for my spring break and a semester credit. You don't see me out there on the beach getting high and stoned with the rest of the spoiled brats. And all you two have done since you got here is complain. Complain about the heat. Complain about the dust. Complain about the fact that we sleep on the floor of the Methodist church, cook our own meals, and share a shower and two bathrooms. You probably have twenty bathrooms in your homes, have people who cook whatever is your hearts' desire for you—no puking there, I bet—and sleep on the best mattresses money can buy, all tucked in with the finest linens. You couldn't give a crap about anything outside of your world. You don't see me complaining—or anyone else here complaining—and believe me, I think all of us could do a lot."

"You two girls need to grow up. And fast," Mrs. Mac said as she shook her head at them. " 'Cuz there's a lot of difficulties in the world, a lot a sufferin', that needs the help of others. Them who rolls up their sleeves and takes action—them's the ones that has their hearts in the right place."

"Bo likes Mrs. Mac. Bo says Mrs. Mac is right on. Mrs. Mac jus' like Bo's mama. An' my mama—God please be restin' her soul in dat grand heaven a yours an' may she be through wid her pain an' her sufferin'—she be only thinkin' a hersef. Worked hersef straight inta a heart attack, she did. Bo misses his mama. Bo heps others 'cuz his mama hepped him. Bo big an' strong, an' so Bo build houses an' work wid his hands. You work wid your hands, ladies, an' you be doin' good in da world. You work up a sweat, an' you be sweatin' for da good a others. Bo sleeps like a baby at night—yes, he do. Bo ain't afraid a no hard work. An' now Bo wants ta go ta work."

The rest of the crew muttered in agreement. In unison, they gathered up their tools and equipment, jumped from the truck, and set off to the work site.

Madrid walked to the edge of the truck bed, then slowly squatted in her pair of tight-fitting designer jeans and sat down. She dangled her open-toed-sandal-clad feet off the end and lifted her light blue Anne Klein crop-top off her stomach. "I am so goddamned fucking uncomfortable."

"That's why I suggested that you buy a pair of overalls like mine," London said as she sat down next to her sister. "And a tank top."

"Lon, you look like fucking middle America. You look like the person who's interviewed on the news after some natural disaster has hit her home and cries out, 'I seen it! I seen it! It done tore ever'thin' down and our lives are rooned.' "

"Well, I'm probably ten degrees cooler than you."

"In temperature, maybe. But not in looks. You went to frickin' *Wal-Mart* to buy the damn clothes."

"So? They were cheap. And who cares about looks? I mean, take a look around you at the fashion senses of the people we're working with. And let's not forget that we're walking around in dirt, breathing in dirt, and building a fucking house."

"Well, you're a dyke. Dykes do tank tops."

"I'm *not* a dyke. I'm a very feminine gay woman."

"Well, you look like one in that outfit."

"I'm just trying to stay cool."

"I know. But please promise me you'll never wear that outfit again."

London held up an open-palmed hand. "Swear."

Madrid sighed. "Lon, did you think it would ever come to this? I mean, *Wal-Mart!* And the food we ate last night. What the fuck is lentil pie? I had gas all night. And, of course, I can't get any sleep on the floor."

"I saw a spider the size of a mouse in the bathroom. It had these enormous hairy legs—"

"Oh, great. I haven't taken a satisfying shit in two weeks, and now I've got to worry about a huge spider in the bathroom!" Tears sprang into Madrid's eyes. "I hate this, Lonnie," she cried as she wrapped an arm around her sister's arm and laid her head on London's shoulder. "I really, really do. Why couldn't we have written out a check for a couple hundred dollars? That would've bought nails—who cares what the fuck color-code they are! Or a kitchen door. Isn't that what the brochure said? That a donation would go to paying for part of a kitchen door? Or roofing materials. We had enough money after we sold most of our jewelry to just write this off with a check."

London shook her head. "What we got was about half of what we paid for the jewelry, and we don't know how long we're going to have to make that last. You and I are both getting a few thousand for renting out our places for the time we're here, and that's got to keep us afloat for awhile. It's only February."

"And three months until our thirtieth birthday."

"And then seven months until Christmas."

"Maybe we'll get a check on our birthday."

"I wouldn't count on it."

"Lon, I hate these people."

"I don't think they like us very much, either. And they're

mean. They're like the people in the hospital I worked with as a volunteer orderly. I told you about them and what they did."

Madrid sniffed and then smiled. "You have to admit, what they did was kind of funny."

"Funny, my ass!" London exclaimed. "They made a fool out of me. They would make up phony assignments and the names of people I was supposed to pick up and take somewhere. I'd be standing there with a wheelchair in a room calling out, 'Mrs. Dee Cup. Is there a Dee Cup in here?' Or 'I'm looking for E. Reckshawn. Is there an E. Reckshawn here?' "

Madrid burst into laughter.

"Shut up!" London snapped at her. "Christ! Sick people are *so* much work. Help them into a wheelchair. Help them out of a wheelchair. Help them onto a stretcher. Help them off of a stretcher. And there's nothing worse than picking up someone from radiation therapy and bringing them back to their room. All they do is vomit. I mean, if it's *that* bad, then just fucking die already."

"People are just too needy," Madrid said. "Why can't we find something to do that isn't so . . . so . . . *disgusting!*"

"You know, Mad, we're getting horrible press. Horrible. This volunteering crap is killing us."

Madrid nodded. "I know. It's scandalous."

London shook her head. "It's worse than that. We're a joke. Do you realize that everyone is laughing at us?"

"They're not just laughing at us. They're being nasty and vicious. Remember that one article, the one that called us the haughty heiresses?"

"Don't forget the one that called us cold-hearted bitches."

Madrid sighed. "We are fucking up big-time."

London nodded her head. "Big time."

"Maybe we can just get done with building this stupid house—I mean, what we're building is barely inhabitable, don't you think?—and then take a picture and send it to

Gamma Angel and say, 'Okay, we did it. We busted ass to build a flippin' house for the goddamned needy. Now give us our money.' Or something along the lines of that."

"It might need to be toned down a bit."

"Fuck! This sun is relentless. Why are there no trees here?"

"Hey, m'ladies!" Sandra called out to them as she stood next to a stack of lumber. "Can you see if you have time in your busy itineraries to lend four useless hands? And grab the rest of those toolboxes out of the truck, would ya?"

"Would ya," Madrid muttered. "These people can't even speak correctly. And what's up with someone who always refers to himself by name? There's something really strange with that. Unbalanced, I think. And that Mrs. Mac. Can someone get the woman an oxygen tank? And, quite frankly, if Sarah Jessica Parker can have a baby and look that good afterwards, why can't everybody? And that Spanish chick. Christ, she scares me. She has got one big, fat fucking stick up her butt."

"So does Sandra. She is a one-woman demolition crew. Someone like her, Mad, doesn't have many friends. Believe me."

"If you ask me, Lon, this crew is needier than the family that's going to be living in this rat hole we're building."

London nodded her head. "And everyone has the intelligence of a gnat. I mean, think about it, Mad. If this is how they choose to spend their time, building shacks for the poor—and, believe me, a college boy who would choose to do this over spring break has got a screw very loose in his brain—then they must have pretty useless lives. We are so much better than these people. Just keep remembering that. We *know* about life. They don't."

"That's right," Madrid agreed. "They haven't been to all the places in the world that we have—"

"Nor have they done the things that we have," London added. "We have got so much more than they do. We know more, and we've done more. And it's just their loss if they can't see that."

"Right."

London slid out of the truck and held out a hand to Madrid. "It's not much longer, Mad. Now come on and help me get the toolboxes. Why there are so many damn screwdrivers with different names and purposes is beyond me to understand."

"Why isn't this wall ready?"

London stopped tapping her hammer against a bent nail and looked up to see Rico, the Habitat for Humanity project leader who checked on the work site twice daily.

"We had a nail issue," London said as she slowly stood up and wiped a gloved hand over her brow. "Man, it's fucking hot! This house is going to have air conditioning, right?"

Rico stared at her, then lifted a yellow hard hat from his head and cradled it under one arm. He rubbed a hand over his unshaven face. "Which one are you? The capital of Spain or the capital of England?"

"I'm London."

Rico nodded his head. "London. Okay. Well, yes, London, this house will most certainly be outfitted with central air conditioning. We're installing that just as soon as we dig out the spot for the Olympic-size, inground pool."

"A pool?" Madrid asked as she sat back on her heels and gently raised and lowered her hammer against a nail. "Don't you think we should've put that in first? Then we could take breaks and cool off in it."

Rico slowly ran a tongue over his teeth. "Well, we still aren't exactly sure *where* to put the pool. Because there's the putting green to consider. And the tennis courts."

"You're making fun of us," London said as she tossed her hammer onto the wood floor. "You know, we're volunteering *our* valuable time to work on this rinky-dink house."

"And we're going as fast as we can," replied Madrid as she kept up a slow, weak cadence against a nail. "In this fucking heat, I might add. I think once the thermometer hits a certain temperature, work should be suspended. People weren't meant to live in extreme temperatures, let alone work. It's unhealthy."

"That nail's bent," Rico said as he wrapped a gloved hand around the nail Madrid was attempting to drive into the two-by-four and yanked it out of the wood. "So's yours," he told London. "Despite the fact that this is what you call a rinky-dink house, that doesn't mean we put rinky-dink labor into it. You need to do things right. And if you don't know how to do something, you ask someone. There are all different skill levels on this crew, so that's why we work together."

"Well, it's hard," London said as she gripped the bent nail and tugged weakly on it.

"You thought this would be easy?" Rico asked her.

"We didn't think it would be so fucking hot," Madrid answered. "I mean, if it was cooler, maybe it wouldn't be so hard. I'm practically melting."

"Melting, huh?" Rico said as he narrowed his eyes at Madrid. "Well, then, I'm glad you feel that way. Because the family that's going to live in this house—hey, Sandra, this is unit twelve, isn't it?" he called over to Sandra, who was halfway up a ladder balancing a long bundle of roofing shingles on one shoulder.

"Twelve!" Sandra called out the confirmation to him.

"You see, unit twelve will house the Manzuela family," Rico said as he leaned a shoulder against a wall frame of the room London and Madrid were in. "Or what's left of it. Several of their family members didn't make it to this country alive. They died, along with the members of other families, as they were kept locked in a truck container under the blazing heat. There were no windows, no water, no food, no bathrooms. The heat inside that container during the day reached over one-hundred-and-twenty degrees. The oxygen began to be slowly depleted as the days wore on. Finally, someone discovered the container and opened it up. Out of one hundred or so people that were crammed in there—people who had paid dearly for safe passage to this country—only a little over half made it. Babies and the elderly didn't stand a chance of surviving. There were ten members of the Manzuela family who took that journey. Only six are alive."

London and Madrid stared wide-eyed at Rico.

"What do you think of that?"

London shook her head. "I can't believe that six people are going to fit into this postage-stamp home."

"And there's only one bathroom," Madrid pointed out. "Maybe you should give them two homes. You know, divide up the family so they're not so crowded."

Rico thought for a moment. "Yes. What a good idea. Because what they really want is not to be together as a family under one roof. They would much rather be separated. Or perhaps we could build each member of the family their very own home. Let them know what it's like to have all the room in the world. I'll tell you what. I'll take the pools out of the plans and then we'll be able to build those extra homes."

London crossed her arms and locked eyes with Rico.

Rico returned her stare for a few moments, then shook his head.

"Do I make fun of you girls? Yes, I do. Shamelessly, I do. I should not. Quite frankly, it has never been in my nature. I only try to see the good in people. But it is a better response than being angry at you, which the crew you work with has felt, with a very strong passion, for the past two weeks. They, like me, want to scream at you, shout at you, shake you until you can understand what life is like for so many impoverished people—the people we are here to serve. But anger at you will do no good. Because you cannot see what you have never allowed yourselves to see. Those who have riches only see their piles of money and the good things in life—the luxuries. Those who are poor, who are struggling each day to get by, rarely get to see their money because every penny in a paycheck is spoken for, and the only good things in life they see are on television or in the movies. If they can even afford the luxury of cable television or a night out at the movies. But what they see isn't real. It's a dream. You two are living the dream of so many, and yet you are too blind to see that."

From above them, London and Madrid could hear the pounding of nails.

"The roof is now being put on," Rico noted. "We are days behind schedule. We made a promise to the Manzuela family, and we need to keep that promise. You two are not helping us. I need a crew of seven hard workers. I have a crew of five who are pulling more than their weight. Unnecessarily so, I might add. On behalf of the Habitat for Humanity, we extend our thanks for volunteering. But we no longer wish to have you involved in this project."

"You're firing us?" London asked. "You can't fire volunteers."

Rico shrugged his shoulders. "We can hire 'em. And we can ask them, politely, to leave. Which I am now doing."

"Fine by me," Madrid said as she stood up and grabbed London's arm. "Come on, Lon. Let's go pack our things and head home. I need a long soak in the bathtub, clean clothes, and a soft bed to sleep in."

"You know, our father knows Jimmy Carter," London said as she pulled her arm out of Madrid's grasp and took a step toward Rico. "All he has to do is make one phone call, and *your* ass will be fired. We can effectively end your association with the Habitat for Humanity forever."

"Really?" Rico asked. "I'm impressed."

"You should be," London answered.

"Although, you're wrong about one thing," Rico said as he pushed his hands into the pockets of his jeans. "You see, my family and I live in a Habitat home. I was so grateful for the gift that was given to my family when we had nothing that I wrote to Mr. Carter and said whenever he needed someone to build more homes, he could count on me. And that's what I did. I went all over the country, building homes for other families like mine. Well, one day Mr. Carter called me. He was very impressed at the number of homes I had volunteered to build. He offered me a job as Habitat project leader in south Florida. I've had lunch with him a few times—even stood right next to him building homes. He's a wonderful man. I'm sure your father has told you that."

London stared at Rico.

"You know, young lady, I really don't like playing the 'I Can Top You' game. Because, in reality, it's a game I will always lose with you. I really can't top your wealth or how you live. But what I can do is ask you to leave. For the good of this project and for the Manzuela family."

Rico placed his hard hat back on his head. "And I'm sure Jimmy Carter would agree with me."

6

"I can't do anything that has the word *green* in it," Madrid told Raphael as she stood behind him, resting both hands on his shoulders and peering over his head at the results of his Google search of volunteer opportunities in New York City. She perused the list, and then looked up when the bell above the door to Duettos on Lexington jingled.

A tall, handsome man wearing an Armani suit, black tie, and light-colored purple shirt stepped through the doorway. "Raphael, my sweet young man! Is Jean-Paul around?"

"He's on a shopping trip to Asia this week, George. It's just li'l ol' wifey me taking care of business. But he'll be back late Saturday afternoon, so we're still on for the Sunday brunch. You're coming, right?"

"Wouldn't miss it!" George beamed a smile as he played with the gold rings on his fingers. "That's one of the first things I do with a new calendar at the start of the year—put in the dates of all the brunches."

"Great! Because I have been a domestic goddess extraordinaire this week. After I close up here, I scurry home and cook up a storm. Well, I don't actually cook—I am *so* stove-challenged—but I shop for things on the list Jean-Paul made for me and do all the prep work. Naturally, I'll be his assistant in preparing the entire meal, including the *Galette de Pommes au Calvados*, which we're having for dessert and which is way, way, *way* over my non-Martha head."

"What's a *Galette*—whatever you said?" George asked as he ran a long-fingered hand through his short, lightly salted dark brown hair.

"Basically, a fancy apple tart. That's the *pommes*, my non-French-speaking friend. *Pommes*, apples. Apples, *pommes*. Now the Calvados—that's a different story. Talk about running my tiny heinie off! Try finding a bottle of *that* fancy French apple brandy. I had to make an emergency call to Jean-Paul to say, 'What the fuck, honey?' I got my time zones all messed up and woke him up in the middle of the night. Of course he gave me the entire history and purpose of the brandy before he told me to put in a special rush order at the liquor store."

George let out a chuckle. "Well, you *are* talking about The God of All Antiquity. I told you how he was a pain-in-the-butt roommate in college. I can't tell you how many nights he kept me up because he just *had* to tell me something he had learned about some ancient civilization. Sometimes he'd wake me up from a sound sleep to go on and on about something that I could make no sense out of. He was a walking encyclopedia of the history of the world. And brilliant. I'd study for hours—accounting, management, business ethics—and never get above a B. He seemed to be reading for pleasure and just sailed through his exams."

Raphael let out a playful snort. "Well, *I* know the man's brilliant! And he's the cutest thing that I ever done see. But *really!* Who knew that food and drink even *had* a history?"

"Once you eat it and drink it, it *is* history," George joked.

"So what's the history and purpose of Calvados?" Madrid asked Raphael.

Raphael clapped his hands together in excitement. "Oh, goody! A pop quiz. Madrid, George. George, Madrid."

George waved a hand in Madrid's direction. "Pleased to—"

"Okay, students. Settle down. Let me just clear my throat—ahem!—and put on a pair of Jean-Paul's glasses so I look positively professorial—there! Now, class, Calvados is a French apple brandy from—anybody? Anybody?—"

Raphael glanced up at Madrid and then George, who each met his eyes with blank expressions on their faces.

"Well, then I'll tell you. Normandy, France. And the Calvados region is named after—anybody? Anybody?" Raphael paused. "And the brandy is aged for how many years? Anybody? Anybody?"

"Would you stop asking us and just tell us?" Madrid said as she flicked an index finger against the back of Raphael's head.

"Ow! Detention! Detention!" Raphael exclaimed, then giggled. "Okay. Where was I? Let's see Normandy—oh! The Calvados region is named after a Spanish Armada galleon, *El Calvador*. Oh, can't you just picture all those dark-haired, deeply tanned Spanish men with their big, strong arms and legs, wearing next to nothing, pulling on those oars of the *El Calvador*?" Raphael smiled and then shook his head. "Fantasy over. Returning to present time. Now the brandy is aged for . . ." He paused for a moment. "For. For, for, for." He grew silent, put a finger in his mouth, and thought. "And I was doing *so* well. All I know is that it's aged. One year, three years, a century—I don't know. But I guess that makes it taste good. Although sometimes I think recipes just get all stuck-up. I mean, what's the difference between any old apple brandy and Calvados French apple brandy? I wish we had an empty bottle of it at home. Then I'd go out and get the cheap stuff and see if Jean-Paul even notices. Anyway, *that* was the brandy drama. And then I had to deal with the whole scallop fiasco! I mean, just how—"

"We're having scallops?" George cut in. "Like the kind we've had before?"

Raphael nodded his head. "We're starting out with pear champagne cocktails and *Camembert aux Nois Amuse-Bouches*—'cheese and walnut pastries,' quipped the translator—and then, since no one will stop talking about them since we last served the dish, the main course will be *Coquilles St.-Jacques*. But of course one can't go into *any* reputable fish market to purchase said coquilles. No, no, no, no, *no!* One must go through a broker, who then puts in an order with a seafood company, which then ships, next day, dayboat Nantucket scallops—only from November to March, mind you. Again, I had to make a call to Jean-Paul and ask, 'How much should we order?' Because he had written down for me on the To Do list, 'Order enough for twenty-five people.' Okay, all well and good, Mister I Can Cook in My Sleep and, When I'm Actually Cooking, Not Measure a Thing. Well!" Raphael exclaimed as he patted his chest. "The scallops *finally* arrived yesterday, and I am simply exhausted."

"Sounds like it'll be a wonderful meal—as it always is," George said.

Raphael nodded. "Oh! And it will all be accompanied by a simple watercress-and-Belgian-endive salad. I've got to pick up the greens on Saturday morning. Remember, remember, remember," he said, tapping two fingers against his head. "And, and, *and!* Raspberry-hazelnut scones, which Jean-Paul will get up to make, along with the tart, before the sun's up on Sunday morning."

George patted his stomach. "Looks like I'll be eating low-fat yoghurt for the rest of the week."

Raphael swept a hand through the air. "Oh, as if you've ever had to worry about your girlish figure."

George laughed. "You need me to bring anything?"

"Not to the house on Sunday. But here. Georgie Porgie, puddin' and pie, I need more customers. It's been dead in here all week. The days just drag."

George nodded. "I know what you mean. It's February vacation. The phone barely rings at work. No one's in town.

The bars last night were smoke-free, but also pretty much patron-free. Very dead. Very depressing. I'm never going to meet my next Mister Wrong."

Raphael giggled. "Hang in there, my sweet, handsome man. It won't be long before someone new will come along and break your heart again."

"Thanks! I needed that cheering up."

"Anytime."

"Catch you on Sunday," George said as he waved to Raphael and Madrid, and then exited the store.

Raphael waved his hand loosely in the air, then turned to Madrid. "I ask him not to bring anything. But do you know what he'll do? He'll bring a case of expensive wine. Or dozens of fresh flowers. He is just the most thoughtful person in the world. George Richardson. Stock broker. *With ethics.* Good looks. Great charm. Smart. Witty. Mr. Personality. That's the upside of Jean-Paul's dearest friend. The downside? He keeps hooking up with youngsters who break his heart. He asks me, 'Why can't I find someone like you?' Well, that's what everyone says, right?" Raphael laughed.

Madrid smiled at him. "As soon as you turn straight, Raphael, you're mine."

"But of course. As long as Jean-Paul can be our cook."

"Whatever you want, dear."

"Anyway, George says he wants to find someone like me. He says, 'There's a huge age difference between you and Jean-Paul, and you make it work.' So I say to him, 'I was ten years older than my age when I was born.' The fact is, I've always been way more mature than men my age. Plus, I remind him that I *did not* meet the love of my life in a club packed with sweaty, shirtless men who dance, get a blow job, dance, get a blow job. No one is going to find true love in a crowd like that."

"I forget—where did you meet Jean-Paul?"

"I met him at the candy store. He turned around and smiled at me—you get the picture?"

Madrid rolled her eyes. "Seriously."

"Jean-Paul has *got* to turn off that oldies radio station on Saturday mornings. Anyway, I met *my* leader of the pack at a flea market. I was looking for cheap furnishings for my very first apartment. Oh, the kitsch that was there! It was stuff right out of *The Brady Bunch*. I kept looking around for Greg. I felt like I was regressing to a past I had never known, but only read about in magazines or seen in sitcom reruns. I bought a beanbag chair for two dollars because it was so retro. So here I am, making the big, fat mistake of buying the beanbag chair plus a half-dozen Flintstones jelly jar glasses—one was chipped, but it was Pebbles, not Bam-Bam—and lugging it all around with me while I continued to shop. *As if* I could carry anything else! I ran right into Jean-Paul. He was looking for the real antiques that sometimes show up at flea markets. He said to me, as he picked himself up off the ground—"

"You knocked him to the ground?"

Raphael nodded his head. "I told you. I *ran* right into him. Wiped him out. So he says to me, 'Are you moving into the attic with Greg?' Remember that episode?"

Madrid shook her head. "I didn't watch much television growing up."

"TV was my babysitter *and* my best friend," Raphael said. "So Jean-Paul helps me to my car with my stuff, we go back to the flea market to shop around some more, and then he took me out to dinner. We spent the whole day together. And then, later on that week, we had our first date. He showed up at my apartment with a present—a Partridge Family lunchbox, *with* a thermos inside. I fell in love with him right then and there." Raphael sighed. "So anyway, I keep telling George, 'You're forty years old now. It's time to leave the *Real World* crowd and get into the real world.' But he positively melts whenever he sees a sweet, young thing who just started growing facial hair. Kidding, of course. He doesn't like them *that* young. But he is *so* into that just-graduated-college, oh-my-God-what-am-I-going-to-do-with-my-life-now crowd. Those boys are cute as all get-out, but they have no money and no direction in life. They're like deer caught in headlights, and George is the one who always stops the car and rushes out to rescue them. He thinks he can show them what life and love are all about and, of course, get that in return. They move in with him faster than you can cook a Hot Pocket in the microwave. He treats them like the gods they believe themselves to be. They endure the theater and the opera and the museums with him, and then, after a few months of that, decide that sex is really what they were after all along. I wish I could fix him up with someone nice, but I've been in a relationship for so long that I've lost touch with the singles scene."

"Oh, he'll find someone," Madrid said dismissively. "Everyone eventually does. Now can we—"

"Oh, do they?" Raphael cut in as he clicked on the mouse and closed the Google search.

"Hey! We haven't—"

Raphael ran his fingers lightly over the keyboard. "Oh, be still for a moment. I just want to prove a point." He moved the mouse, then pressed it. "*Voila*, my darling who believes that eventually everyone finds someone. This is just one on-line singles site for gay men. And now I'll focus in on the New York City area and . . ." Raphael opened a palm at the screen and sat back in his chair. "Look. All of these single men, all looking for love. Hundreds of them. And this is just one site. There are dozens of others, with an equal number of people on them who are posting profiles and trying to look for a long-lasting love."

"Well, they're gay men. Everyone knows that gay men don't settle down." Madrid quickly patted Raphael's shoulder. "Except for you and Jean-Paul."

"Hey, Missy-Girlfriend, weren't you the one who was complaining about the lack of a meaningful relationship in your life not two months ago?"

"Oh, I'm so over that. I've got more important things to deal with than finding my next bedmate. I've got to do something that will convince Gamma Angel that I know what money's all about."

"It makes the world go around, the world go around," Raphael joked.

Madrid tightened her lips. "Not if you don't have it."

"True."

"I'm trying my darnedest to do something impressive."

"Oh, yes. You've done a good job so far, according to the press."

"Tell me you haven't been reading those stories!"

"How can I not? The headlines positively scream at me whenever I walk by the newsstands. 'La Mira Reflects Twins' Cold Hearts.' That was kind of clever, you have to admit. And then there was 'The Fools and Their Lack of Money.' "

"I'm not a fool," Madrid said.

" 'From Soup to Nut,' with a picture that made your face look like a sphincter muscle." Raphael sucked in his cheeks, pursed his lips, and then crossed his eyes.

"Will you stop already! I see what's being written. I was just hoping you hadn't."

"How can one pass up such things? If they *scream* scandal, you simply must pick them up! And every talk show— well, I can't *help* but listen. You're my very best friend in the whole world. What people say about you matters to me. And, oh, are they *ever* having a field day with you and your sister. I mean, they are positively relentless."

"Aren't they?"

"But you two—I mean, did you really hurl baby turtles into the ocean, to their *death?* That is *so* not *Finding Nemo*-ish. *Free Willy*-ish. Whatever-ish. You're supposed to *love* the creatures in the sea. Take good care of them. You're like *Jaws* on land."

"That's pretty harsh, my friend."

"Honey, you *killed* an endangered species."

Madrid sighed. "I didn't *mean* to kill them. I thought I was helping them."

Raphael looked up at her. "And you were a tad inconsiderate during your short stint serving food to the homeless."

"I wouldn't call what was being served *food*."

"Mad, people are starving. Does it matter that the food didn't measure up to your high standards?"

Madrid raised her eyebrows. "Hello, Mister We're Serving *Camembert aux Nois Amuse-Bouches* and—"

"Hey, *I'm* not serving the homeless."

"It was slop, Raphael. It smelled inedible, and it looked inedible. Believe me." Madrid sighed and dropped her chin so she could rest it on top of Raphael's head. She wrapped her arms around his chest. "What am I supposed to do? I'm not used to such people, such circumstances, such *things*."

"Who is, honey? The majority of the people who volunteer have never lived like the people they help. It's all about—"

"I mean, you should've *seen* the people working at the Habitat for Humanity. They were, like, *so into* what they were doing. Like they were some sort of superheroes who were saving the world. But they were lowlife. Overweight. Unattractive. Dirty. Smelly. And they couldn't even speak correctly. One of them—"

"Aren't we getting a bit hoity-toity?"

"Raphael, Lonnie and I *knew* we were so much better than them. But all they did was ride us and—"

"Well, you couldn't have been *that* much better than them. After all, you were asked to leave."

"Oh, who cares? I can't wrap my brain around the *point* of building a cheap house or ladling out stomach-turning food or crawly little creatures that have to be walked to the ocean by taking the minutest of baby steps. If that's what your life gets reduced to, then you might as well pack it in."

Raphael glanced back at her. "Is this *really* you talking?"

"What?" Madrid snapped at him. "My world and those

worlds have *never* intersected. So how the fuck can I even *begin* to care?"

"Excuse me, but are you made up of flesh and blood like a human being or put together with nuts and bolts like a robot?"

"Raphael, it's not as if getting *that* involved in helping others has ever been something my parents instilled in Lon and me. Gamma will do things like that. She serves meals to the homeless and helps stock food pantries and goes on walks for breast cancer and abused children and I don't know what else. But you'd never see my parents doing things like that. My family may donate millions to build a children's cancer wing in a hospital, but Carlisle and Kitty wouldn't be caught dead spoon-feeding Jello to some bald kid with sunken eyes. The money they give certainly helps those who need it, in very big ways, but they don't get involved beyond that. Maybe if I had had some previous experience with people in, well, dire circumstances, I might be better at this serving-the-public crap."

Raphael shook his head, then placed his hands on top of hers. "Honey, when you do things that help others, it's not what previous experience you bring to the table that matters. It's, well, you have to kind of feel it inside. You bring *yourself* to the experience. It's not just all about what you can do for others. It's about how it makes you *feel* doing things for them."

"I don't feel anything," Madrid told him. "Now hold on a minute here," she said as she slipped a hand out from underneath Raphael's and moved the mouse.

"What are you doing?"

"I'm finding George a date."

"We were talking about you."

"What about me?"

"How do you feel—how *did* you feel—doing the volunteer work you failed so miserably at?"

"How did I feel? I didn't feel anything. I don't feel anything."

"Nothing?"

"Well, in Florida I was hot. Really hot. Here's an interesting—no, he seems too self-absorbed. Listen to this, 'I'm not into head games, baggage, insensitivity, dishonesty, selfishness, lack of good judgment, abuse of drugs or alcohol, manipulative behaviors'—Christ, it goes on and on and on. What do you think he'll bring into a relationship, other than negative energy and an excessive need to control someone else's behavior? Get over yourself, bozo."

"So all you felt in Florida was hot?"

"What else does someone feel in Florida? Yes, I was hot. Being hot makes me feel miserable. In the soup kitchen, I was mostly nauseous."

"Honey, those aren't feelings. Those are physical responses. I mean, how did you feel *inside* about the people you were serving the meals to, the people you were building the homes for?"

"How about this one? He's twenty-eight years old, owns his own business, is—"

Raphael pulled out of Madrid's grasp and pushed his chair back. "Would you *stop* looking at the screen and pay attention to me?"

Madrid stepped back from the computer and stared at Raphael. "How am I *supposed* to feel?"

Raphael met her stare. "I think you answered my question."

"What does that mean?"

Raphael shook his head.

"No, tell me."

"In here," Raphael said as he placed one of his hands against Madrid's chest. "How do you feel in your heart?"

Madrid shrugged her shoulders.

"Do you feel sad for the people you've met who have had a much tougher life than you can ever imagine?"

"Not really. I actually think they're kind of pathetic. I mean, Lon and I are down and out now, and you don't see us begging for food or asking someone to build us a home."

Raphael raised his eyebrows. "You think you and your sister are down and out?"

"Hey, we don't have much money left. That's the reality. As for the turtles, well, I felt they were pathetic, too, but kind of a cute pathetic. You know what I was thinking? I was thinking that maybe I could adopt a dog. From one of those rescue organizations. I was considering something small, like an Elle Woods dress-up dog. I could take it for walks and get all cuddly with it. It would come from some sort of really bad background, and I'd rescue it. It'll be skin and bones, maybe a bit mangy-looking when I first get it, and then it will look terrific because of the care I give it."

"And what, exactly, do you think is involved in taking care of a dog?"

Madrid shrugged her shoulders. "How hard can it be? You open a can of food and scoop some out in a bowl. You hire a dog walker to take it for walks. You take it to a groomer."

"That's assuming you have the money to pay for such things."

"It can't be all that expensive."

"Oh, you'd be surprised. But let's forget about that for a minute. What do you plan to do with the dog?"

"Do? Feed it."

"All day?"

"What else is there to do with it? It eats. It sleeps. End of story."

"Where does it sleep? In your bed?"

"No way! I don't want some little filthy creature on my nice linens!"

"What happens when it starts chewing up your Faryl Robin embroidered sandals? Or your Lambertson Truex camel crocodile clutch?"

"Why would it do that?"

"Because that's what dogs do. They like to chew things. They like to play. They like to run around. They like to be cuddled. They like to go wherever you're going."

"Dogs need all that?" Madrid exclaimed, and then shook her head. "Why is it that people—that *things*, even—are so fucking needy?"

"Sweetie, we're all needy."

"I'm not needy."

"Really? You need nothing?"

"Well, I need my yearly check."

"And nothing else?"

Madrid shook her head. "That's about it."

"So you don't need me?"

"Of course I need you."

"But I thought you didn't need anything or anybody. Except for money."

"Raphael, I don't know what I'd do without you. Or Jean-Paul."

"Ah. So you *need* friends."

"Okay, so I *need* friends."

"What about love, Mad? Do you need someone to love you?"

"Well, I need to have *it*. We all need to have it. I like getting off with someone. Especially if he's a really good lover."

"So you don't have to love the person you sleep with?"

"Of course not!"

"Have you ever been in love before?"

"I have crushes all the time."

"That's not what I asked. I asked—"

"Why are you throwing all these questions at me? I thought you were going to help me find some organization I could volunteer for."

Raphael stood up, grabbed Madrid by the shoulders, and then leaned close to her. "Have . . . you . . . ever . . . been . . . in . . . love?"

Madrid stared at Raphael. "Yes! No! I don't know. I don't know, okay? What does it matter?"

Raphael showed Madrid a hint of a smile. "Because, my dear, if you've ever had a heartfelt investment in someone, and then, say, lost that person you cared so deeply for, you would have an understanding of how to give to another. But if you haven't, then you don't know how to feel for them on a deeper level, one that goes beyond hammering a nail or ladling out a bowl of soup."

"Oh, I can tell you about loss! Lon and I have just taken a huge loss—and I mean *huge*—selling off our jewelry. I lost two Ritmo Mvndo watches, my Charles Garnier gold-and-diamond earrings, my Bellarri rings, several Baraka bracelets—"

"Those are *things,* Mad. Just things."

"They're very important things."

Raphael closed his eyes, and then opened them. "Do you know what the first—and, usually, the only—thing people take before running out of a home that's burning to the ground?"

"Their jewelry?"

"No."

"Their wallet? Purse? Money?"

Raphael shook his head. "Their photo albums. They can't bear to lose pictures of their precious memories—of weddings, children, pets, friends, vacations."

"Why? They're just pictures. But if all your money burns up, then what do you have?"

"Sweetie, you know that I lost my mother when I was a teenager. I was brokenhearted over that. I can still feel the loss in my heart. You have your parents. You have your grandmother. Even though you lost your grandfather, you hadn't even been born, so you didn't develop a close bond with him. You've never lost out on the dream of going to the finest private school or the best university in the world.

You've always gotten everything you've ever wanted. I guess the only thing you've ever lost in your life is this year's check."

"And the jewelry."

"Okay, *and* the jewelry. Certainly your financial losses are great. But I'm sure that you'll find a way to prove yourself worthy, to redeem yourself in your grandmother's eyes. So the loss that you're experiencing right now is temporary. Losing a parent or a lover or a best friend, on the other hand, is permanent. That's why some of the most giving people in the world are those who have lost something or someone very dear to them. They understand the pain, they understand the emptiness, they understand the ache in their heart that never really goes away. They can give, because they have room in their heart, an empty room that they need to fill."

Madrid thought for a moment. "So that's why Gamma did what she did. Why she does what she does. She lost her husband. Interesting." Madrid took in a deep breath. "So what you're saying is that I need to lose something in order to gain something?"

"Actually what I'm saying is that you need to lose something so you can *give* something. The giving allows you, at least in some small measure, to regain what you've lost."

Madrid laughed. "I could lose the sister. I could kill London."

Raphael raised an eyebrow. "Imagine that, Mad. Imagine how you'd feel if you lost London."

"Oh, for God's sake, Raphael, lighten up. I was only kidding."

"Think about it."

"I don't want to think about it."

"Try."

"No."

"Mad, think of what your life would be like without

Lonnie to call, to be with, to share things with. Imagine that you'll never see her face again, never hear her voice, never—"

"Shut up!" Madrid said as she squirmed out of Raphael's grasp and stepped back from him.

"She's like your other half, isn't she? It's that twin thing. You're linked psychically to one another, even though you're thousands of miles apart. If she ever died, you'd be devastated, wouldn't you?"

"Will you stop with this psychological mind-fuck thing? It's not funny."

"It's not meant to be funny. What would your life be like without London? Without your parents? Without your Gamma?"

Madrid took a step toward Raphael and gave him a quick slap across the face.

Raphael immediately grabbed Madrid's hand, raised it to his lips, and gently kissed it.

"*That* was an expression of a feeling," he said softly. "And that's just the tip of the iceberg, of how you'd feel if you ever lost someone dear to you."

"You're an asshole."

"Call me what you want. But if you want to be able to give to others, you have to feel what it would be like *not* to have someone dear, not to have someone you cherish, not to have someone you love. You *understand* pain if you've lost someone, and that enables you to ease the pain in others. But, if you're lucky enough to have made it through nearly thirty years of your life without experiencing deep loss, then you have to go to a place where you can feel the *potential* of loss. Then, whatever you do for others is filled with passion. Because then you know what it's like to be missing something very important, very significant, in your life. And passion, my dear, is really what makes the world go around. Not money. The greatest artists in the world—the writers, the painters, the actors—have a passion that oftentimes springs from great loss. Sure, they'd all like to get rich from their passion. But, more powerful than that is the drive to create, to make something out of what they're missing. Loss makes you feel. I believe that's the lesson Gamma wants you to learn. How you figure that out for yourself, and then how you find it, are what's going to change your life."

"So no green, huh?" Raphael asked several minutes later as he scrolled down the list of volunteer opportunities in New York.

Madrid nodded her head as she peered over his shoulder. "That means no Greenstreets. And no Greenthumb Urban Gardening."

"Well, honey, I should think so," Raphael answered. "Those are just silly little jobs. More like 'Let's-Keep-the-Parks-Clean-and-Pretty-and-Dog-Poop-Free' projects than doing some sort of good in the world. You want to find something that does some good for others, and for you, too. What do you think you'd like to do?"

Madrid let out a sigh. "That's just it. I don't want to do anything. I couldn't give a crap."

Raphael drew his lips together and wagged an index finger at her. "Too harsh."

"Hey, I could do this one," Madrid said as she pointed at the screen. "I could be a Big Apple Greeter. I know about all the places to go around town."

"Yes, honey, that's a real lifesaving, meaningful volunteer opportunity."

"Well, it's *something*," Madrid shot back and then walked over to an antique chair and slumped in it.

"You need to do something that makes a difference in people's lives," Raphael said as he moved the mouse and clicked. "Or even one person's life. You could get involved in the elder read-aloud program."

"Bor-ing! That would be like reading to my grandmother."

"Or check in on a person who's really sick."

"I don't want to catch anything."

"You don't catch anything," Raphael said as he sat back in his chair. "I did check-in visits a couple of years ago. With Shaun. Such a nice man. He had AIDS. His partner dumped him as soon as things started going downhill. I helped him to remember his pills. I held his hand when he was depressed. I fed him when he was too weak to even open a can of soup. And sometimes I sat up with him for hours and read him his favorite poetry, on those nights when every second that ticked by was filled with pain and discomfort."

"Do you really picture me doing something like that?" Madrid asked as she raised her eyebrows at Raphael.

Raphael shook his head. "Sadly, no. Mad, you're a whole lot of fun. You really are. And you're very generous with your money. But you would run for the hills in a situation like that. And that makes me very sad."

"Oh, God. Tell me we're not going back to talking about feelings again."

"No. Getting bitch-slapped once was enough for me."

Madrid tightened her lips and sighed. "I'm sorry, Raphael. I didn't mean—I don't know why I did that to you. What you were saying was making me *so* upset, and I just wanted you to stop talking."

"Which I haven't done."

"That's okay. I know you're trying to help."

"I am."

"I know. You're a good friend. A really good friend. A lot of people wouldn't put up with my shit. Raphael, I know I'm spoiled. I know that I think the world revolves around money. I know I can be shallow and heartless and mean-spirited. I just don't know how to be anything different. But I know that I have to be, if I'm ever going to earn Gamma's respect."

Raphael nodded. "I do believe the old woman gave you a

mighty big challenge. But, girl, you're up to it. I know you are. You'll figure it out."

"I just feel like the clock is ticking faster and faster to my birthday in May."

"You can't think about May right now. You just think about today. Right now. This moment." Raphael glanced down at his watch. "Well, my clock says it's time for lunch. I'll put up the OUT TO LUNCH sign on the door. You can stay here and browse around the Web if you'd like. See if you find anything you'd like to get involved in. Okay?"

"What's all this?" Raphael asked as he set a large brown paper bag down on a table behind the computer desk and nodded toward a pile of papers Madrid was organizing on her lap.

"What's all *this?*" Madrid asked as she took in a deep breath and smiled. "It smells delicious!"

Raphael grinned and reached into the bag. "There's nothing like a little Jewish comfort food—oy, vey!—to make everything right in the world. For you, my dear," he said as he handed her a wrapped sandwich. "I chose a thick, juicy pastrami sandwich on a chewy bulkie roll, heavy on the spicy mustard. For me, corned beef on rye. I got us a container of extra pickles, a side of slaw, and a side of potato salad. Plus two large cream sodas."

Madrid set the papers aside. She unwrapped her sandwich, took a bite, and then closed her eyes and emitted a low moan as she chewed. "Unbelievably good! Marry me, Raphael. Right now!"

"Honey, you're not a very good catch. You're broke. I don't want to have to support you for the rest of my life."

"So you're only interested in my money? How shallow!"

"Sorry, my darling. But gay boy not do fucky-fucky with straight woman without good incentive."

Madrid sat up in her chair and stuck out her chest. "So these breasts don't do anything for you?"

"Honey, I've seen much bigger—and much perkier—on drag queens. But if you have a nipple ring, I might just take a peek."

"No nipple ring. And may I just add, ouch."

"So what's up with the paperwork? Looks like you found a lot of things to volunteer for."

Madrid shook her head, wiped the corner of her mouth with a napkin, and took a sip of her soda. "It's not for me. It's for George. I found him some potential love interests."

"You were supposed to be doing your homework while I was out. Bad girl!"

"I looked, Raphael. First I eliminated all the soup kitchens and homeless shelters."

Raphael nodded. "Probably a good idea."

"Then I eliminated any type of building activity. I don't think I ever want to see another tool. What was left was a lot of programs for needy children, but since I'm obviously capable of killing off baby turtles, I figure any at-risk kid I come in contact with would be at an even greater risk. Who knows where I might fling them. Perhaps into the harbor."

"Or off a tall building."

Madrid nodded. "Yes. The poor, the disenfranchised, and the young should be kept away from me, because I'll only make things worse for them. And I don't want to work with the elderly or disabled, so . . ." Madrid shrugged her shoulders. "So I figured I could make more effective use of my time by trying to find George a match. I have a pretty good idea of who he is."

"You do? But you only met him for a few minutes."

"Well, if there's one thing I'm pretty good at, it's reading people. When you're in the limelight as much as I am, people are attracted to you like moths to light. You have to know who's real and who's not—who's just out for the best story or who wants to befriend you for their own benefit. I've learned how to pay attention to everything about someone—even the smallest of details."

Raphael dipped a fork into the potato salad. "I just take everyone at face value. My philosophy is, 'What you see is what you get.'"

"I wish I could live by that philosophy. It would be so much easier. But I can't. I've got too much to lose. I mean, look at my reputation now. It's pretty much shot. People just love to see someone who is successful fail. So whenever I meet someone, I think, 'What do they want?' And then I try to figure out how they're going to try to get it."

"So what did you learn about Georgie?"

"Well, I know that he's health-conscious. He's obviously in good shape, but he was also concerned about watching his weight with your upcoming brunch. I saw the way he was dressed and the jewelry he was wearing. Impeccable and expensive, so that tells me that he cares a lot about his appearance. He was very polite and kind and respectful in how he spoke with you about the brunch. He is also generous. Remember? You told me that he's the type who brings flowers or wine to your brunches even when they're not expected. He enjoys cultural events—you told me that he loves the theater and opera and museums. And he's someone who's loyal and values his friendships."

"How do you know that?"

"Because he went to college with Jean-Paul, and they're still friends—over two decades later."

"Good observation."

"Finally, he's someone who likes to have things planned ahead of time rather than being spontaneous. He probably lives a very structured life."

"How did you come up with that?"

Madrid grabbed a pickle and tapped it on the side of the container. "Because he said that he had marked his calendar with the dates of your brunches as soon as he knew them. And, since you told me he likes cultural events, I imagine he probably has season tickets to such things and therefore knows ahead of time what he'll be doing."

Raphael sat back in his chair. "Wow! You're like Miss Marple. Jessica Fletcher. Agatha Christie. *Very* observant."

Madrid shrugged her shoulders. "There are three things I know in this world. I know how to spend money. When I have it, of course."

"Of course."

"I know fashion, inside and out."

"I agree. You outshine the gay boys. In fact, you might even be a gay boy in drag."

Madrid grabbed a breast in each hand. "These wouldn't be real."

"Guess not."

"And I have a pretty good idea of what makes people tick."

"I would agree with all that. So who did you find for Georgie-Porgie?"

Madrid handed Raphael a pile of papers. "These are possibilities. I think that George should contact each of these people and see what he thinks. But although these guys are close matches to him, *this* is the one who is going to steal his heart." Madrid held up a sheet of paper.

Raphael glanced through the profiles Madrid had given him. "Honey, these men are all in their thirties. I told you that he likes younger men."

"And he's done real well with them, hasn't he?"

"Good point."

"If he still wants to satisfy his craving for youngsters, he can go out to the clubs. But if he wants to meet someone who wants to be in a relationship—and every person's profile I've run off says they want one—then this is where he should start looking for something more meaningful."

"Okay, so you say these are all possibilities that I'm holding in my hand. But the one you have is . . ."

"The one for him."

"And he would be?"

"His member name is Snugglebunny. He's white, athletic build, five-eleven, about one hundred and eighty pounds, brown hair, blue eyes, great smile."

"George has a great smile."

Madrid nodded. "He does. Snugglebunny writes that he's all grown up from his adolescent years—he's thirty-three— and has, how does he put it, 'cleaned house' of all toxic friendships. He's done with bad nights out at the bars, experimentation with drugs, and drinking to excess to make someone look better. He's gotten rid of the orange crates and futons, posters of hunky men, and piles of dirty laundry and now has a lovely set of dinnerware and matching drinking glasses, nice furniture, and artwork on the walls of his apartment."

"He sounds okay."

"Oh, I'm saving the best stuff for last. Here, see?" Madrid said as she moved the profile closer to Raphael and pointed. "He says that he strongly believes in the most important things in a relationship. He calls them the Four Cs: chemistry, compatibility, communication, and commitment."

"That's what George believes in!" Raphael grinned.

"Snugglebunny says that he's a good soul who's looking to be a best friend, partner, and lover to someone who is in the same place."

"Just where Georgie is."

"And here's the kicker," Madrid smiled. "He says, 'Thank you for taking the time to read my profile. If you think we'd hit it off, please contact me. If not, I wish you all the best in life, in love, and in everything that has deep meaning for you.' Now isn't that gracious and polite?"

Raphael patted his chest with a hand. "Oh, how sweet!"

"So," Madrid said as she crumpled the wrapping paper from her sandwich. "There you have it. Maybe I didn't find something I could do, but it was a whole lot of fun trying to fix George up. And who knows? Maybe I helped him find his true love. What I did is certainly nothing to write home about, but—"

"But nothing," Raphael broke in. "You did something nice for someone. See? You're not such a bad person after all."

7

London stood outside the last remaining sex room located on a long corridor near the back of La Mira West. The corridor, which once led directly off of one of the more intimate dance floors of the club—"So there's an immediate outlet for the bump-and-grind that inevitably starts on the dance floor," London had once explained to Lucinda—now served as a passageway to the club's kitchen-supply storage areas. London had opened door after door to rooms that had once been well known to her and other club patrons as chambers for lustful encounters. But she didn't see the familiar dimly lit rooms, with a variety of themes, painted in dark, rich colors and furnished with a king-size bed made up with silk sheets that were changed frequently throughout the night and a bedside table with drawers kept well-stocked with a variety of sex toys, harnesses, and lubricants. Instead she saw brightly lit, eggshell-painted storage areas filled with towering shelves containing paper products, or enormous containers of olive oil, tomato paste, sauces, spices, and mixes, or bins of kitchen utensils, or cases of liquor.

"This is like some bad fucking nightmare," she muttered

as she opened and closed each door, and then wondered, *Where'd all the goddamned sex toys go?*

The corridor was no longer accessible from an intimate dance floor—one in which the DJ played sexy-slow music, the strobe lights pulsed to what London called "a thrust-thrust rhythm," and no-back couches lined the dance floor to facilitate foreplay. Lucinda had told London there now was "a romantic dining area" when she had taken London on a quick tour of the club that was not only no longer hers, but barely recognizable.

"Does that mean they can fuck on the table between courses?" London had asked Lucinda as they stood next to a small, round table draped with a deep burgundy tablecloth and centered with a small pewter candleholder and a tiny vase with sprigs of dried flowers.

"Listen, I know you're upset about your grandmother handing the club over to me—"

"Upset?" London shook her head. "Nope. I'm not upset. *Seething* would be the word I'm looking for. You've taken this club and made it into . . . into . . ."

"A dinner-dance club that's gotten really good reviews, Lon," Lucinda finished. "We've been in 'Talk of the Town' each week, and *Gourmet* and *Bon Appétit* magazines have scheduled interviews. And last week on the news—"

"I saw it," London cut her off. "Hooray. The club *finally* gets good press. Isn't *that* a relief! It's like the conversion of Hitler into a Big Brother to some poor, inner-city, single-parent Jewish boy. What was it that the *Chronicle* printed a while ago? Something about the club formerly being a damsel in distress, and you're the knight in shining armor who has shown up to rescue it?"

"I didn't really—"

"And then there was the headline—let's see if I remember it correctly—'Love at First Bite: Reformed La Mira West Replaces Party Passion with a Passion for the Palate.' "

Lucinda smiled. "That was a nice article."

"Nice?" London asked, and then wrinkled her nose. "The writer talked about the club's past as if it were bordering on the criminal."

"Lon, I don't think that was too far from the truth. We got into trouble a lot, for the things that went on here before. There were arrests, and there was the time when it was shut down for a week because—"

"Police are called to *other* clubs, too, Lucinda. To the corner bar and grill, when one of its regular drunks gets a little too well-lit one night and decides to break a chair over a random customer's head because he was talking when the drunk's favorite song was playing on the juke box. Or to someone's house, because they're playing music too loud. Even the bars near the colleges get shut down from time to time when they serve minors. But the way the article was written, the implication was that the club used to be *so* criminal when I ran it that it ranked right up there with serial killers and rapists and child molesters. And now, under your highly moral, highly watchful eyes—your fucking high-road attitude—it's gone through some sort of magical *reformation*. It's like the club has rediscovered Jesus or something—you don't hold church services in the basement on Sunday mornings, do you?—and now hallelujah, praise be to the Lord, sister-friend, you done saved the world from a scummy establishment and turned its reputation around."

"Lonnie, you *know* what this club was like. You know what its reputation was. You *wanted* that reputation. Fostered it, in fact. But it was a bad reputation."

"*Bad* club. *Bad* me," London said as she slapped a palm against her arm. "So what, Cinda? To quote the infamous Joan Jett, 'I don't give a damn about my bad reputation. Oh, no. Not me.' "

"If things had kept on in that insane direction, Lon, the club probably would have been permanently shut down."

"Oh, for God's sake, Cinda, get a dose of reality, would you? This club was no worse than any other club."

"You can't be serious."

"I am. So things got a little out of hand from time to time. It's only because of—"

"From time to time? A *little* out of hand? Lon, if you can't admit that the things that went on in here were bordering on the very, very bad—"

"There's that word again," London cut in and slapped her arm again.

Lucinda shook her head. "You are in big-time denial, Lon. *Big-time*. And contrary to your opinion, I'm no savior. Your grandmother could've put the club on the market for a bargain price, and then someone else would've come along and changed it."

"No one else had that opportunity."

"You're right. Because I *agreed* to do it. But your grandmother wasn't holding a gun to my head. I *wanted* to do it, Lon, because if she had passed it off to someone else, it would never be yours again. And it *will* be yours again someday."

"I don't want a fucking dinner-dance club. Eating out, for me, has a much different definition from yours. La Mira West is done. Over. You should just change the name—call it Good Eats or Lucinda's Fine Dining Establishment or Chicken Soup for Saving Souls. Just leave my name out of it."

"Lon, we're making money."

"We? Yes, I can see bundles of cash rolling in every day to my bank account."

"Okay, the club's making money. More than it did before."

"Goody for you. Maybe my grandmother will adopt you. Or, better still, maybe we could rush off to Vermont and have a nice little lesbian commitment ceremony and you could support me in the lifestyle to which I was once accustomed."

"Why don't you work here? I can pay you."

London glared at Lucinda. "Work here? *Work here!* As what? A bus boy? A waitress? Some sort of sideshow attraction? Oh, I can picture that. Me walking around from table to table—'See, honey, that's the reformed *criminal,'* the diners would whisper—wearing my What Would Jesus Do necklace, a sensible yet tasteful dress, and making sure everyone's water glasses were filled. *Don't* fucking insult me!"

"I'm not trying to insult you, Lon. There's a lot you could do here that you might enjoy. You'd still be involved in the club. And if you don't have any money—"

London raised her eyebrows at Lucinda. "So *you'd* pay me? I'd become *your* employee? I'd take orders from *you?* Christ, who the *fuck* do you think you are?"

Lucinda sighed, pulled out a chair, and sat down at the table. "Lon, I'm your friend. I care what happens to you. Over the years, you've supplemented my terrific salary with very generous bonuses, given me a great job as your manager, and now I'm just trying to repay you for all that you've—"

"You're an ass, Lucinda. You know, at one time I thought you were a terrific person. But you're no friend. A friend doesn't help to pull the rug out from underneath someone. A friend doesn't insult someone who's down and out. A friend—"

"I'm doing this for *you,* London," Lucinda broke in. "You still have the club. And maybe, well, maybe if you work here, stay involved, even for a short time, your grandmother would see that as a good thing. You don't have to work here full-time. You can do it part-time."

"Oh, good. Then maybe I could go to school and get my professional waitressing degree. Maybe I could even, *someday,* become the head waitress."

"Lon, you've *got* to do something. You work here for a bit, put in some hours in steady employment, and then maybe your grandmother will start giving you your yearly checks again. You could work in the kitchen if you wanted to, prepping food."

"Prepping it for what? Its eventual demise?"

"You could help make salads. Cut up vegetables. Do soup stocks."

"Don't even mention soup to me. My sister already had a bad experience with that."

"Or you could help me to plan menus. Or handle the reservations."

"I have reservations about handling reservations. Unless you've installed a public address system and I can interrupt the dining experience all night long by making announcements like, 'The Jacksons? Party of five? Your table is ready. Donner party? Time to eat food instead of people. Joel Ditmire? Paging Joel Ditmire. Please call your babysitter. And I'd like to fuck your wife while you're on the phone.' Yeah. I think I'd be good at that."

Lucinda flashed her a scowl. "I'm just offering, is all. Face it, Lon. You haven't really been doing so well on the volunteering scene."

"A friend would also not throw someone's failures in their face. And, quite frankly, you couldn't pay me enough to afford my tastes, let alone to do any of this drudge labor you're offering up."

"You're right," Lucinda said. "I couldn't. But it's *something*. And I'm not trying to throw your failures in your face. I'm worried about you. I care."

"Oh, yes, I know all about caring," London snorted. "What's that called? Tough love? My Gamma cares about me *soooo* much. My parents care about me *soooo* much. Yeah, I got this caring concept down. Just please don't say that what they're doing is for my own good."

Lucinda reached across the table and pushed out the other chair. "Could you sit down so we can talk about this?"

London folded her arms across her chest and peered

down at Lucinda. "Why? So you can conduct a job interview? Ask me what my strengths and weaknesses are? Ask me about my past work experience? Names of references? My availability to work nights and weekends? Put my celery-chopping skills to the test? I don't want to own a restaurant, and I most certainly don't want to work in one. "

"If you would just sit down, I would tell you that things really haven't changed that much around here," Lucinda said as she placed her hands on the tablecloth. "We served food before. Fine food. From the best caterers. The only change is that we cook the food here. We still have dance floors. Not the two largest, because the focus isn't on dancing. We still have the bars for mingling and meeting people. The only things we don't have any more are the sex rooms. And you know how I felt about them."

"Having never been in one with you, I have to answer, no, I don't know how you felt about them."

"I told you a hundred times when I was the club manager that I thought they were skanky."

"They were cleaned top to bottom every day and several times during the night."

"What went on *in* them was skanky."

"How do you know what went on in them?"

"When more than two people are having sex at one time, I call that skanky. When two people who barely know each other are using handcuffs and God knows what else to sadistically—"

"Don't knock it unless you've tried it, girl."

"I'm not about to try it."

"There's a surprise. Just because you want to be a nun for the rest of your life, you expect everyone else in the world to be one, too?"

"There are a lot of people who don't think making love should involve more than the person. There are also a lot of people who need a strong emotional attachment to another person before they sleep together."

"Are you sure that you're only a little older than I am? Because I'm getting the distinct impression that you grew up in the fifties."

"It's called morality, Lonnie. It's called having respect for yourself and for another person. It's called—"

London held up a hand. "It's called the train keeps leaving the station to take you into the present time, Lucinda, and you're not getting on board."

"Lon, the world you live in is not real. Your money has afforded you membership in a world that most people regard as another planet—one that they'd like to visit, but they'd be just as likely to ride a rocket to Mars. The world I live in, along with most of the rest of the world, is real. It's on planet Earth, and it requires working for a living."

London shook her head and sat down in the chair across from Lucinda. "The world I live in—lived in—was real. My money was real. The things I did with it were real. Just because others can't enjoy what I once enjoyed doesn't mean such a world didn't or doesn't exist. And now my lack of money and the things I can't do are real. They're very, very real to me."

"The sex rooms are real?" Lucinda asked as she raised her eyebrows at London. "Come on, Lon. What those sex rooms offered up was no more real than porn films, the breasts on most *Playboy* models and starlets, the smooth complexion of the fifty-plus Hollywood set, the full lips of—"

"Okay, okay," London cut in. "In a way, you're right. What went on in the sex rooms wasn't real. Those rooms are—*were*—just for indulging in fantasies. *Fantasies.* That's all. And it can be fun to make a fantasy come true."

"But why? Then they're not fantasies anymore, are they? I mean, if you fantasize about participating in an orgy, and then you do it, the fantasy is over."

"I guess. So what?"

"What's the point, then? What's the point of having something you fantasize about become a reality? Once you lose the fantasy—"

"You lose that particular one, perhaps. But there are a lot of other fantasies."

"Why do you even have to indulge in a fantasy? Why not just let it remain a fantasy? Isn't that the reason for having a fantasy—to dream about it, rather than to act it out?"

London smiled. "Ah! So the nun *admits* to having fantasies. Why don't you tell me one? Sexual in nature, please. Not the fantasy about finally getting a pony."

Lucinda stood up slowly. "My fantasy, London La Mira, is to build this club into a successful enterprise and then hand the reins over to you—"

"I knew it. You *do* want a pony!"

Lucinda sighed. "Hand *the club* over to you as a money-maker. I want to make you happy."

"A supper club isn't going to make *me* happy, honey. Not in the way that you think. But if it makes *you* happy, then by all means, have fun with it. Get off on it. Let it make you wet."

Lucinda tightened her lips at London, and then placed her hands on her hips. "Get over yourself, would you? Losing an enormous check that could feed an entire country, a check that was handed to you on a silver platter for doing nothing, is far from the end of the world. I'm proud of what I'm doing at your club—and yes, I still think of it as *your* club. You know, earning someone's respect comes from more than just doing good for others. It also comes from letting others do good for you."

"I'm not some sort of charity case," London snapped.

"I never said you were. I said you were my friend. And I treat my friends with respect. Especially when they're bending over backward for me. I've worked incredibly long hours here, Lon. Your club is successful and getting good publicity. You may not realize it, but some people are starting to look at you differently. It's time for you to start acting differently.

It's time to get out of your own head and look around you. See something—see someone, *anyone*—other than yourself for a change. You might find that the world is more interesting than you think."

Lucinda pushed in her chair, and then reached into the breast pocket of her white starched jacket. "For your reading pleasure," she said as she dropped a newspaper clipping on the table, turned, and walked out of the room.

London watched her leave, and then slowly unfolded the clipping and read it.

LA WONDERFUL LA MIRA

Club's New Theme Reflects New Vision, Positive Energy

Who'd a thunk?

La Mira West, a club that was once dubbed Studio 108, with the explanation that it was twice as raunchy, twice as debaucherous, and twice as detrimental to one's physical, emotional, and spiritual health as New York's infamous Studio 54, has done a pronto-turnaround in focus and become the place to enjoy a great night's dining and dancing experience. Last night, I finally caved in to the good press it's been receiving and the numerous raves some of my most trusted friends have been giving me. Now I can't stop talking about this new and improved club.

There's still the same superior valet parking and a spacious coat check room. But what I noticed immediately upon entering the club is the relative quiet. No loud thumping of dance music, with the bass volumes set so high that the window panes would rattle and your chest would vibrate so much that you would think you were in the early stages of an impending heart attack. I was told that the reason for the peaceful entrance atmosphere was the installation of thick soundproofing between the dining areas and dance floors.

A very attractive maître d' guided us into the main dining area, converted from what was formerly the club's largest dance floor and the scene of the infamous drug overdose caught on tape.

Now, I'm not a food critic—as you know, my nourishment comes from the nibbles of gossip I can share with you—but I must say that I had the best meal I have ever eaten. In my life! We started out with citrus champagne cocktails and smoked salmon barquettes. All were excellent. This was followed by the soup of the night, butternut squash with star anise and ginger shrimp. The main course, which was served with sweet potato gaufrettes with duck confit and cranberry-and-black-pepper chutney and horseradish mashed potatoes, was buffalo prime rib with orange balsamic glaze. Positively scrumptious! We barely had made our way through the beet-and-goat-cheese salad with pistachios before we were offered a sample plate from the evening's dessert selection, prepared on the premises by baker **Cindy Freeman,** a longtime friend of the new club owner and former baker's assistant at the four-star restaurant at St. Michael's-on-the-Hill Hotel. She wowed us with chocolate chestnut torte with chocolate cognac mousse, lime custard tart, and meringue petits fours with anise cream and pomegranate. Absolutely out of this world!

We could've sat there for hours, taking in the intimate atmosphere and listening to the strains of Vivaldi played by one of the city's finest quartets. But we didn't just sit there all evening digesting our incredible meal and sipping the best cup of coffee I've ever had—new club owner **Lucinda Claremont** responded to my ravings about the java by telling me that it was a blend made especially at the club and complemented by spices such as cardamom, cinnamon, and a light touch of nutmeg (and no, there are no plans to market it outside of the club, although I told Ms. Claremont that it would make the club a bundle). We got up after our meal and went to one of the dance floors, where renowned DJ Elle Note was playing some great music mixes. The crowd was lively, but controlled—obviously having a good time, but without the bad behaviors of the past.

We left the club way past my bedtime. Time just slipped away!

So who do we have to thank for this refocused **La Mira West?** According to Ms. Claremont, none other than big, bad billionairess **London La Mira** herself. I guess there's hope for the nearly thirty-something after all, who has been the subject of numerous columns I've written in the past—none of them complimentary! Like **Angelina Jolie,** who refashioned herself from Hollywood freak and gossip-column fodder to humanitarian extraordinaire and loving single mom to children in need, London gave Ms. Claremont the explicit instructions to transform the club from its former reputation as a house of ill repute (we've all heard about those sex rooms, haven't we?) into a cathedral of heavenly cuisine. The dance floors are still hopping, but gone are the added cheap thrills such as flavored mists or whipped cream sprayed over the crowds or body painting contests. Verboten is any sort of nudity, and all bartenders, who are following London's law down to the letter, are keeping a close eye on inebriation.

London, my hat's off to you! This former party girl is finally becoming a woman.

London reread the clipping, and then slowly refolded it and dropped it on the table.

Why would she do that? London asked herself. *Why would Cinda give her all the credit, when she hadn't put an ounce of energy into the club?* London reached for the clipping and opened it. She skimmed through the article, and then read out loud, "So who do we have to thank for this refocused La Mira West? According to Ms. Claremont, none other than big, bad billionairess London La Mira herself."

Why would she do that?

London furrowed her eyebrows as she recalled the La Mira philosophy—*Well, actually, it's Kitty's philosophy,* she reminded herself—which she and Madrid had learned about when they were twelve years old.

They had been sitting at the kitchen table one summer afternoon, eating sandwiches that had been prepared by the household cook staff, when Kitty had burst in through the kitchen doors waving a newspaper.

"The nerve! The nerve of these people! What in the name of I-don't-know-what is it going to take to get them to realize that enormous donations *do not* just fall out of the sky!"

She had slammed the newspaper down on the table, making her and Madrid jump. "If there is one thing I want you girls to learn, and to learn well, it's that you always—*always*—let people know who butters their bread. For that matter, who *buys* the damned bread. You let them know nicely and discretely at first, of course. You say, 'That donation to the Museum of Natural Arts is from the La Miras. Because we *believe* in the arts.' Remember to emphasize that you believe in the causes that you support. Then, if they're not completely brain dead, they will write a story that says something about the generosity, the good heart, the giving spirit, of the La Miras."

"What's a natural art?" Madrid had asked her.

"Who knows?" Kitty had snapped. "Who cares? I'm not talking about the arts, either natural or unnatural. Pay attention to what I'm saying. Then, if that offhanded, kind of casual strategy doesn't work, you tell them point-blank—and quite firmly, I might add—the only reason why the Museum of Natural Arts has a new exhibit that will attract numerous patrons and raise funds is *because* of the La Mira donation. It's spelled L-A space M-I-R-A. But now . . ." Kitty had slapped the back of her hand against the newspaper. "Now I'm going to have to call this dolt of a writer and say, quite forcefully, that she needs to give credit where credit is due. There's no mention in this article on the new exhibit about where the money came from to purchase it. Your father and I just don't hand out our money without full well expecting something in return. And we will *never* be anonymous donors. As if that isn't the stupidest thing in the world. Then don't give away your money, is what I say. We give away our money gladly. What we want to get in return is very simple. We want *credit.* We want recognition. Our goal is always to keep the La Mira name out there in the public eye. We must let people see that we're not some egocentric, selfish family. We are very generous and good-hearted."

"Is a natural art something like—"

"FORGET THE GODDAMNED ART, MADRID!" Kitty had screamed at her. "Have you *not* heard a word I've said? You're as airheaded as this writer. I will repeat, girls. Do not ever, *ever,* let people forget the good that your money does for them or for others. *Do not!* Understood?"

And so, from the moment that she and Madrid had started to follow in the La Mira tradition and write checks to charities, hospitals, and nonprofit organizations, they had heeded their mother's advice to make certain that their generous spirit got the publicity it deserved. Just seeing her that day with her bulging, furious eyes, her pale complexion deepened to a shocking crimson color, and her neck veins pulsating through her nearly transparent skin like a 3-D human road map had given the lesson that she was imparting to them great weight.

But how can I take credit for something I didn't do? London asked herself. *And why—why—would someone put so much work into something and then not want to draw recognition to herself, not want to take credit? Isn't that the point? To let people know what you did?*

She slowly got up from the table, and started to walk away. Then she stopped and looked around the dining area. She surveyed the small tables and their simple centerpieces, the soft-colored artwork on the walls, the floral arrangements set on tall, narrow pedestals and tastefully lit with overhead spotlights, the stage where Lucinda had told her that musicians played classical music. She imagined the room filled to capacity, the bustling about of the wait staff, the aromas, the conversations voiced by candlelight. Smiles. Laughter. Hands reaching across tables and gently touching.

Who do we have to thank?

London heard Lucinda's voice in her head. *Lon, I'm your friend. I care what happens to you.*

She returned to the table, picked up the clipping, and slipped it into her pocket.

London stood outside the last remaining sex room and peered in through the open door at walls and a ceiling that were painted in royal blue and decorated with drawings of tropical fish, a coral reef, a shipwreck of a wooden sailing vessel laying on its side on the bottom of the ocean, and numerous aquatic plants.

Ah. The Oceans of Orgasms room, she remembered. *Soon to be deep-sixed.*

She stepped in through the door, flipped a switch on the wall, and then closed the door.

A dim, gently flickering light, designed to replicate the rays of the sun as they undulated through the ocean's depths, provided enough light to make out the contents of the room.

London then turned a knob next to the light switch, and the sounds of ocean surf and seabirds blended with the strains of gentle calypso music.

London closed her eyes. She remembered breasts. Breasts that were firm. Breasts that were fleshy. Breasts that sagged. Breasts that saluted. Breasts with nipples the size of goose-bumps. Breasts with nipples as hard and long as miniature Tootsie Rolls. Breasts that came in twin packs of small, medium, large, and economy-sized—"My, what beautiful globulars you have," she would say as she grasped one of the economy-sized breasts between both of her hands. She remembered the many flavors of skin—vanilla, almond, berry-fruit blends, citrus. The young ones would sometimes taste of patchouli; the older ones of lilac. She remembered warm, smooth wetness. She remembered firm, round buttocks. She remembered soft pubic hair. She remembered groans and moans, cries of pleasure, urging voices that begged and pleaded, gasped. She remembered entering and being entered, slaps, tickles, pleasure laced with a tinge of pain. She remembered being tied up and tying others down.

"If these walls could talk," she whispered into the room.

I remember . . . well, I remember a lot.

A lot, and a little, she added. *I remember the activities. But the faces? The names? And where are they all now? The actresses who struggled to keep their sexuality hidden but stealthily followed her into these rooms because the passionate nonintimacy afforded within the walls kept their secret intact but allowed them to give temporary voice to their desires. The models who craved feeling normal, if only for an hour—who wanted to be touched and to be able to respond to that touch, but for whom starvation diets, constant lightheadedness, and drug addiction oftentimes kept them from achieving orgasm. The twenty-somethings who adored her and then tried too damn hard to please her. The hordes of unknown names. Faces that were now a blur to her.*

London opened her eyes and sat down on the bed. *Where are they all now?* she asked herself again, and then let out a soft snort. "Probably in a better place than I am. The young thangs have graduated college and are starting out in their careers. The older, rich women are still rich, but now older—probably with a few more nips and tucks than before. And the models are still getting rich by starving themselves."

The thing of it is, London thought, *they're all somewhere. Doing something. Making a living, for instance. Denying their sexuality in a marriage while they raise their first child and have another warming up in the oven. Following the rules of rehab. Living with a lover. Getting on with their lives. Whereas, I'm nowhere. Stuck in some club I no longer feel a part of, stuck in a life that's like a circling jumbo jet, somewhere up in the sky in a perpetual holding pattern, waiting for the go-ahead.*

"The go-ahead to what?" she asked the room.

If only things could get back to the way they were, she thought. *Get back on track.* She surveyed the room, and then imagined herself in it with any number of beautiful women.

She yawned.

Anyone, Lon, she prompted herself. *You can be in here with anyone. Imagine the most beautiful women in the world, lying here, naked on the bed, waiting for you to touch them, to taste them, to take them. You can do anything you want to them, anything you desire.*

She yawned again.

She closed her eyes. *I'd rather take a nap. Alone.*

She opened her eyes and raised her eyebrows at that thought. *Why do you even have to indulge in a fantasy?* she heard Lucinda ask. *Why not just let it remain a fantasy? Isn't that the whole point of having a fantasy—to dream about it, rather than to act it out?*

"What more can I do in this room that I haven't done before?" London tossed the question into the empty room. "It was fun while it lasted, ladies. But once the fantasy is over . . ." London sighed, stood up, and turned off the background noise. "I'm bored. Bored out of my fucking mind."

She opened the door, flicked off the light switch, and re-called a conversation she had had with Madrid the night be-fore their lives dramatically changed.

"Mad?" she had whispered across the guest bedroom late on Christmas Eve. "You awake?"

"I think I'm going to be sick. I drank way too many grass-hoppers."

"So go make yourself puke. But then I want to talk to you about something."

"What?"

"Don't you want to throw up?"

"Not really. Just talk to me."

"Okay. Well, it's like this. I can't really figure it out. But I'm not having, I don't know, I guess, *fun* anymore. Like with people. I mean, with the women I've been seeing."

"So dump 'em. My stomach *feels* green."

"I'm not seeing anyone now. But the thing is, I don't know that I *want* to. See anyone, I mean. It's all gotten . . . gotten—oh, I don't know."

"Gotten what? Do you think my puke will be green?"

"It's usually the color of whatever you eat."

"I didn't eat much. But I drank. Those damn grass-hoppers."

"So it will be green, then."

"Yuck. That's making me sick just thinking about it."

"Then don't think about it."

"Keep talking."

"Okay. I'm bored. I'm bored seeing the people I've been seeing. Being with them. I'm even bored in the sex rooms, if you can believe that. The last time I was in there, I'm getting it on with some woman—who knows who it was—and I re-alize, as I'm getting *her* all hot and bothered, that I'm not even conscious about what I'm doing, and I'm most definitely not getting turned on. I realize that instead of thinking about who I'm doing and what I'm doing, I'm thinking instead about an article I had read in *W* on Gwen Stefani's new line

THE PERILS OF SISTERHOOD 181

for LeSportsac. It was like I wasn't even in the room, but at home in my living room, sitting on the couch listening to music and reading the magazine."

"Keep talking. I'm not feeling so sick anymore."

"It's like I don't care whether I'm fucking these women or not."

"Like you can think about better things you could be doing with that time?"

"Exactly."

Madrid sighed. "I know. I'm feeling the same way. The last time I was in one of the rooms, and this guy's hammering away at me, I'm not even feeling anything. Nothing. Like I was numb. I kept thinking, 'Just *come* already.' And I thought the guy was hot, too."

"Do you think there's something wrong with us?"

Madrid got out of her bed and walked over to London's bed.

London pulled back the covers, and Madrid settled into bed next to London.

"I think it's just all too empty," Madrid told her. "I mean, what's the point? You get off, and then what? I've been feeling like I want something more. I was saying that to Raphael and Jean-Paul. I want to feel more than just a physical attraction to someone. I'd like to spend time with someone doing . . . I don't know . . . doing things, I guess. Simple things. Shopping. Walking around town. Going out to a movie. Sitting in a café somewhere reading the paper."

"Like in a relationship."

"Yeah, I guess. Although I don't know what that would be like, having never really been in one before. But I see Jean-Paul and Raphael together, and they just seem so . . . so . . . happy. So *together* with each other. They're two people, but they're a unit. I don't know if I could ever be that way with someone. But it just seems so nice."

"We've never been with anyone long enough for it to become a relationship."

"We decided not to."

"I know. The thing is, I get tired of people so fast. Most of the people I've had as lovers aren't very interesting out of bed. It's like sex is the only connection."

Madrid tossed an arm and a leg across London. "I feel the same way. I still miss them when they're gone, though. It's like they leave behind a hole, an empty space inside me."

"Then someone else comes along . . ."

"Fills the hole. So to speak."

London snickered. "So to speak. And then they're gone and the whole thing starts over again."

"It *is* getting a little old, isn't it?"

"Yeah. But I don't know what to do about it. I do know that I don't have any desire to be with anyone. Right now, at least. I kind of just want to be left alone for awhile."

Madrid let out a yawn. "I know what you mean. Me, too. Tell you what. After we get our checks tomorrow, we'll make a plan to go traveling together. Just you and me. We'll spend some time doing the things we want to do. Maybe talk about this more."

And they never got to go on that trip, London thought as she closed the door to the sex room.

"There you are. I have something to say to you."

London turned in the direction of the voice.

"Yes, you. I want to talk to you."

"Okay," London said to a tall woman of average build who was dressed from head to toe in bright-white clothing and shoes and standing in front of her with her hands on her hips. Strands of long, dark hair spilled out from underneath a tall white cap, and streaks of white covered her hands and one of her cheeks. "And you are . . . ?"

"Cindy Freeman. I work here."

"Then you need to see Lucinda Claremont. She's the owner."

"I *know* she's the owner. I'm her head pastry chef."

"Well, that explains your outfit," London said as she

brushed a hand against her own cheek a few times. "You have a little something on your—"

"It's just flour," Cindy snapped, ignoring the signal to wipe her face. "I live it, I breathe it. I want to talk to you about Lucinda. I want to know what the hell you said to her."

"When?"

"I don't know *when*. It had to have been a little while ago. But she came into the kitchen in tears. When I asked her what was wrong, she said that you told her she might as well be a nun."

"I didn't say—"

"You *do* know what happened to her, don't you?"

"Susie, I have no idea what you're talking about."

"*Cindy*. It's Cindy. She got dumped, is what happened. The woman hasn't dated anyone in years—I mean, how can she, when you made her work more hours as your manager than an aspiring lawyer trying to make partner in a law firm. So I finally convinced her, when you were out of the picture, that she needed to get out more. Meet someone. Her confidence level was finally better than it had been in a long time—hell, it was about sky-high because of what she had started doing with this club and with you not around to kick her ass all the time and make her feel that she's nothing."

"I don't think I ever—"

"Let me finish. She's been my friend for years, ever since we were kids and I worked at her family's place. So I care about her. She's the nicest person I know. Not into games. Generous—a true giver, not a taker. Just a down-to-earth, sweet, sweet woman."

"I agree. I don't know what I would've done without her. I've always felt that—"

"Focus on *me*, would you please? Christ, you're as self-absorbed as they say."

"Hey, I'm just trying to—"

"*As* I was saying, she goes out to a bar with me after she signs for the ownership of this club and meets someone who seems like a pretty nice person. She dates the woman for about a month and really likes her. I finally see Lucinda smiling and happy. Going out, doing things. And then, right out of the blue, she gets dumped. The bitch completely blindsides her—breaks her beautiful heart—and so Cinda throws herself into making this dinner club great. She tells me that she's not going to date for a long, long time. She spends all of her free time here. She stops eating. You *did* notice that she's dropped about fifteen pounds, didn't you?"

London thought for a moment.

Cindy tossed a hand in the air. "No matter. What do *you* care, right?"

"I don't know why you're so upset with me. I didn't dump her."

"No, but you didn't have to tell her that she might as well be a nun."

"I don't know that I phrased it quite that way. And we were talking about, well, we weren't talking about her getting dumped."

"Do you know that this has been the first week that she hasn't broken down into tears at work? That she hasn't been miserable? That she hasn't asked me, for the hundredth time, 'Why did I get dumped? What did I do wrong?' Lucinda didn't do anything wrong. It was that jerk she was dating. For the first few weeks, everything was going fine. They really seemed to hit it off. But then the ex waltzed back into the picture, and Lucinda became history."

"That seems to be pretty common in the lesbian community."

"Oh, is it? Suddenly you're an authority on lesbian relationships?"

"I didn't say I was an authority. I was just making an—"

"The fact of the matter is, now Lucinda is in the kitchen crying her eyes out because she thinks she's going to end up alone for the rest of her life, thanks to you."

"I didn't say she was going to be alone for the rest of her life. We were talking about something that had nothing—"

"You don't tell someone who finally gets up the courage to shed the protective shell she's been hiding under for years, someone who then takes the chance on opening up her heart to another person—only to get coldly and harshly dumped—that she might as well be a nun!"

"I said I didn't say that! We were on a totally different topic. And how am I supposed to know any of this? I was in Florida for—"

"Yeah. Good job there, by the way."

"Listen, I don't need you to—"

"What you need to do is treat Lucinda better. I mean, this woman has busted butt for this place—not because she even believes for one minute that it's hers, mind you, even though it technically is, but because in her mind she wants to make it right for you. Why, is anyone's guess. But all she's thinking about is you. How you'd like this. How you'd like that. You ought to show more appreciation when someone's doing something nice for you."

"I didn't realize that she had been doing anything for me," London answered as she crossed her arms and leaned against the wall. "She did tell me that today. But I had no idea. How could I?"

"Maybe if you paid more attention to your club, you'd—"

"It's not *my* club!" London told her. "And I've got more pressing things on my mind than—"

"Oh, yeah, boo-hoo, you lost your bundles of money."

"My life is none of your business."

"No, it's not my business. I couldn't care less about you. But apparently every time you pick your nose it's some sort of major news event."

"Well, I can't help that."

"No, I guess you can't. But I make you my business—I pay attention to you—because your life intersects with

Lucinda's. And since I care about *her* life, how you treat her is my concern. She's making this club into something you can be proud of. And with the press the club has been getting under her leadership, you're getting good publicity as well. But when you take cheap shots at her when she's doing all of this good stuff for you, then I feel like I have to defend her."

London uncrossed her arms and took a step toward Cindy. "Would you tell me why? *Why?* Why is Cinda doing all of this for me? Why is she giving me the credit? It's not my club. It's hers. Why is she not taking her well-deserved bows? I can't seem to wrap my brain around that."

Cindy shrugged her shoulders. "Beats me. My guess is that she likes you. Although I can't wrap my brain around *that.*"

London met Cindy's eyes for a few moments. "You know, I wasn't taking a cheap shot at her. I was . . . I was upset, but it had nothing to do with her."

"You hurt her."

"I didn't mean to."

"Mean to, don't mean to. Hurting someone is hurting someone."

"Well, what can I do about it?"

"Talk to her. Give her a little compassion, a little respect. If you know how, that is. Show her that you care what she's doing with the club. Help her see she's not a miserable failure in your eyes."

"She's not."

"Then *tell* her that. Because I don't think you've ever shown her that. Maybe it's about time."

"Okay."

"Oh, and one more thing."

"What's that?"

"If you ever—*ever*—make Lucinda cry again, I will stake you to the ground near some anthills and smear frosting all over you."

"That actually doesn't sound that bad."

"I haven't said what else I'd do. But it wouldn't be pleasant."

London watched as Cindy turned and strode down the corridor.

Revenge of the pastry chef, she thought. Then she grinned and said out loud, "Now that's one tough cookie."

"Sure smells good in here," London called out as she stepped in through the swinging kitchen doors and waved at Lucinda, who was standing in front of an enormous stove.

Lucinda tossed her a quick wave with a spoon and then turned back to the stove.

"What are you making?" London asked as she walked over to Lucinda.

"Corn-and-lobster chowder," she answered through a cloud of steam. "It's tonight's soup."

London stood next to Lucinda and took in a deep breath. "When will it be ready?"

"It's got to simmer for several hours. By tonight, it will be perfect."

"That sounds about right. It's how you do things."

"Pardon?" Lucinda asked as she rubbed a handful of dried herbs between her palms over the soup.

"You always do things perfectly, Cinda. That's how you did things for me as my manager. And now this supper club. It's all . . . it's all perfect."

Lucinda tossed her a quick, puzzled glance, and then clapped her hands lightly together. "I don't know about that."

"It is. After we talked, I really looked around the dining room. Everything looks so nice. The artwork. The tables. The flower arrangements."

Lucinda turned to her. "Why are you talking to me in that voice?"

"What voice?"

Lucinda shrugged her shoulders. "I don't know. It's . . . it's just not really your voice. Not how you usually talk to me."

London sighed. "Maybe it's my contrite voice. I feel bad about our conversation a little while ago. *My* end of the conversation, that is. I wasn't very . . . well, very pleasant. And I don't think, well, I don't think I've told you how grateful I am for everything you've been doing here. I don't understand why you don't want people to know about all the hard work you've put into this. Into the club's transformation. But even if they don't, I do. And what you've done is really impressive. I liked that article, too, by the way. Can I keep it?"

Lucinda shrugged her shoulders. "It's for you. I have my own."

"Thanks."

"You're welcome."

"So, uh . . ."

"What?"

"I don't know. What are you doing now?"

"Well, right now I'm talking to you. But I'm really busy, Lon. I've got to start making the marmalade-horseradish glaze for the baked ham and peel the Yukon Gold potatoes that I'm going to mash with fried sage leaves."

"Can I help?"

"Ha, ha. Very funny."

"I'm serious."

Lucinda stared at London. "I thought such work was beneath you."

"Well, I don't know what I'm doing. So you're going to have to show me what you want. But I can try."

"How are you at peeling carrots?"

"Carrots are peeled?"

Lucinda smiled. "Maybe you should just watch."

"You sure seem to know what you're doing. I never knew you could do all this."

Lucinda shook her head and sighed. "I actually told you, Lon. Several times. Here goes the story, one more time. My family had a restaurant in San Jose. It was family-style cooking, but it was good. We were always busy. From the moment I could carry a tray, I would work there serving customers. But what I really loved was the kitchen. After high school, I went to cooking school, courtesy of my parents. I graduated, and then I got my business degree. To put myself through college, I worked in a restaurant."

"You told me that?"

Lucinda nodded her head. "I did. Every time you mentioned what you wanted the caterers to prepare for the club. I told you I could do all that myself."

"And what did I say?"

"Order it."

"Oh. Well, I should've paid closer attention."

"Doesn't matter. Now I have my chance to prepare the food."

London watched as Lucinda dumped a large sack of potatoes into an enormous stainless steel sink. "What are you doing with those?"

"These are the Yukon Gold potatoes. I'm going to peel a small batch and then do a trial run of tonight's potato dish. Sometimes the potatoes can get runny when you mash them, so I need to know the moisture content of this batch. My assistants will be along in an hour or so to peel the rest."

"That's good. So . . ."

"So?" Lucinda responded as she rubbed the potato peeler quickly against a potato.

"So what do you do after work?"

Lucinda sighed. "Go home and sleep. I don't leave here until about two in the morning. And then I'm back before eight."

"What about on weekends? What do you do on weekends?"

"Lon, I'm here. When you own a business, it's twenty-four seven." She turned to London. "Except when you have me to be your manager."

London smiled at her. "You *are* a terrific manager. And a good cook. And you're a good person, too."

Lucinda tossed a peeled potato into a small pan and turned to London. "What is *up* with you?"

"Nothing."

"Nothing, my ass. You're acting really strange. Are you high?"

"No. I can't afford it anymore."

"Well, that's one way of getting clean and sober. Although I think it's addled your brain a bit. This is a weird conversation."

"I'm just telling you things I should've told you a long time ago. I should've told you that you're a giving person. That you're very kind. And very generous. Have you lost weight, by the way? Because you look terrific."

"Okay, that's it," Lucinda said as she tossed the potato peeler on the counter. "I'm really busy, Lon. Go find something else to do with your time."

"I don't have anything else to do."

"I'm sure you can find something."

"I could peel carrots. If you show me how."

"Fine. I'll show you how to peel carrots. But you have to do it quietly. You can stop trying to make up for what you said before. You're forgiven."

"I'm not trying to make up for anything. I'm just being truthful. And I thought it was time to tell you how I felt."

"I never thought I'd be saying this to you, Lon, but stop it. Just focus on yourself and your own planet. What you're saying to me sounds phony."

"I'm saying it truthfully."

Lucinda tossed her hands on her hips. "Why now? Huh?"

London shrugged her shoulders.

Lucinda closed her eyes and let out a short grunt. "Ah,

ha—Cindy!" She opened her eyes. "Did Cindy put you up to this? Did she tell you that I was upset about what you said to me? Did she? When I see her, I'll wring her neck. I swear. Sometimes she just gets too overprotective."

"Cindy who?" London asked as she picked up the peeler. "Do you think I'll be able to peel as fast as you do?"

"For about ten seconds. Before you cut off the tips of your fingers."

"I don't think I want to do that."

"Are you sure Cindy didn't talk to you? Because it seems odd, your whole conversation with me."

London shrugged her shoulders. "I don't know any Cindy. I'm just starting to appreciate things more, what with losing the check and all. And then having a hard time—well, actually, a pretty easy time—screwing most things up. I'm starting to see things, see people, differently. That's all. I just thought I'd try voicing that appreciation. I guess I probably don't sound all that sincere. But I mean it. You *are* a very, very good person, Cinda."

Lucinda bit her lip for a second, and then smiled at London. "Thanks, Lon. I needed to hear that. I really did. Now, are you ready for those carrots?"

London nodded her head. "But the question is, are they ready for me?"

8

"You two are *harder* than *hellcats* to track down, y'know?" Dolores Fontaine's voice blasted at London as soon as she emerged through the arrival gate at Hanscom Field Airport in Bedford, Massachusetts. "Not that I haven't been keeping tabs on you two since you decided I was better off as a literary publicist, but—" She stopped talking when her cell phone rang, pulled the phone out, and barked a loud "Speak!" into the phone.

"Can you hear me now?" London muttered.

Madrid walked quickly over to London, opened her arms, and pulled London toward her.

"How is she?" London asked as she shifted her shoulder bag and returned the hug.

"I think I'm deaf," Madrid whispered into her ear. "I'm also ready to pull out my hair. You try spending two hours trapped in an airport waiting room with Dolores. And check out those awful shades of red she's wearing. If I were a bull, I think I would attack her. Thank God your flight was on time."

"I meant Gamma, you idiot."

"Oh!" Madrid pulled her head back but kept her arms

around London. "She's fine. I called her doctor myself because Mother was absolutely no help. He said it was just an episode. Nothing to be concerned about, although he's keeping her at the hospital for a few days."

"Well, that's a relief. The way Kitty was going on—"

"Tell me about it! That's why I haven't gone to see Gamma yet. I wanted us to be together when we saw her. You know how Mother can't handle anything out of the norm. It just gets her all in a tizzy. I tried talking to her after my flight got in—she's been at the hospital since yesterday morning—but she's using that high-pitched tone of voice—"

"Ah, yes. The one that can shatter glass. And annoy every dog within a hundred-mile radius."

Madrid nodded. "She's also talking at about a hundred miles an hour. She sounds like Mickey Mouse on speed. I don't know if we should be more concerned about her than about Gamma."

"Maybe we could get *her* sedated and put her in the hospital instead. Is Dad here?"

"He's flying back tomorrow because of a—"

"But I *found* you both, didn't I?" Dolores's loud voice broke into the conversation as she slapped her cell phone against an enormous thigh and slipped it into the pocket of a bright red serape-style cape that was draped loosely over her body. "Tracking down's what I do best, y'know? I've got a nose like a bloodhound."

"And the body of a Saint Bernard," London mumbled to Madrid.

Madrid raised her eyebrows at London and shook her head.

"Now don't you two worry about *a thing,*" Dolores continued. "I've got *everything* under control. Newspapers, television. The cell's been ringing off the hook, y'know? I mean, this is *news.* Well, not *good* news, that's for sure. But news is news, and it's no time to be without a publicist, y'know?" Dolores hoisted her weight closer to the twins and then threw her short, plump arms around them. She laid her head against Madrid's back. "It's a sad, sad situation, y'know? But don't you two worry about a thing. I've got it all under control."

London met Madrid's eyes, and then glanced down at Dolores and let a smile play on her face.

Madrid returned the smile to London. "All right, then," Madrid said as she rubbed London's back and started to release her.

But Dolores gripped the twins harder, pushing Madrid back against London.

"Dolores!" Madrid complained. "You can—"

"We'll get *through* this, girls," Dolores assured them. "We *will*. And we *must*."

"Dolores, it's really not that big of a deal," London said. "Gamma is going to—"

"Of *course* it's a big deal," Dolores snapped as she released her hold on them. "Now don't start being Cleopatras and sail on down that river called Denial. Your grandmother's in the *hospital*. The matriarch of the La Mira family suddenly collapses and is rushed off to—"

"She just fainted," Madrid broke in.

"I never thought of Gamma as a matriarch," London commented. "That sounds so regal, doesn't it? *So* Jacqueline Bouvier Kennedy Onassis."

"I think Gamma's more like Katharine Hepburn," Madrid suggested.

London nodded. "With a lot of Audrey Hepburn thrown in, for the humanitarian—"

"Your grandmother is the *glue* that holds your family together!" Dolores nearly shouted at them. "And when something *happens* to that glue—a heart attack, for instance—things can dramatically fall apart."

"Dolores, it wasn't a heart attack," Madrid told her.

"I don't actually think of Gamma as *glue*," London said.

"Who *knows* what will happen now to the La Miras?"

Dolores continued. "With Angelica Forcini La Mira fighting for her life in a nearby hospital, the family draws together and—"

"She's *not* fighting for her life, Dolores," Madrid cut in.

"Well, *that's* the type of thing that people will write and publish, if you don't have an astute publicist, such as myself, who's giving them the truth, y'know? Rumors fly, innuendos are cast about, lips wag, and then, before you know it, everyone is reading a story with the headline, 'Bedside vigil for the La Miras—family matriarch suffers major heart attack, clings to life.' Y'know?"

"It wasn't a—" Madrid began.

Dolores waved an arm in the air. "And *then* the papers will find *the worst* picture ever taken of your grandmother and run it, along with the story, to convince readers that she'll never, ever recover from her heart attack."

"Will you *stop* saying *heart attack*?" Madrid nearly shouted at Dolores. "It . . . was . . . an . . . *episode!*"

"Kind of like a sitcom, but without the laugh track," London added. "Now, could you just—"

"Well, *why* didn't you say so *before?*" Dolores grilled Madrid. "I can't *say* what I don't *know.* You *have* to keep me in the loop."

"You *are* in the loop," Madrid replied. "I've been trying to tell you that for the past—"

"And *now* I know," Dolores broke in. "Good. *Good.*" She waved a hand in front of her flushed face. "Hoo, boy! I was really sweating that one. *Big time!* I mean, that is one big, fat *whew!* don't you think? We certainly dodged *that* bullet, y'know?"

"Yes, we know," London answered.

"Everything will be fine, then," Dolores said.

"It *is* fine," Madrid assured her. "She's only going—"

Dolores suddenly exploded into a fit of coughing. She slapped her chest a couple of times with a hand that was adorned with numerous rings, then inhaled deeply. "I'm okay, I'm okay. Now. I already talked to the Boston and New York papers." She quickly held up her hand. "Don't worry, don't worry. I didn't say *heart attack.* But I didn't say *episode,* either. I really don't know what that means. I just said that your grandmother was taken to the hospital for *observation.*"

"Sounds like she's a caged panda at a zoo," London commented.

"Or an amoeba being viewed through a microscope," Madrid added. "Can't you—"

"It's a standard term," Dolores snapped. "Now, I'm gonna talk with Frisco and LA later on today. Time difference and all, y'know? I'll tell them *episode,* but then someone's going to ask, 'What's an episode?' and I'm damned if I know. And in my business, you don't say what you don't know or the papers'll make their own guess at it. I'll check in with you after you get to the hospital. Then you can let me know what you want me to say. But for right now your family needs to focus on the personal grief it's going through. I'll take care of the press grief."

"What personal grief?" London asked.

Madrid placed her hands on her hips. "Dolores, Gamma's not *dead.* Nor is she dying. She just had an *episode.* Not even an itty bitty stroke. We have *nothing* to grieve."

"Well, okay, I know that *now.* But, *really,* anything to do with the ticker, you gotta be careful, y'know?"

Madrid turned to London. "Why is she *not* getting this?"

"Our grandmother is *fine,* Dolores," London emphasized.

"But the fact is that—" Dolores began.

"Listen to me, Dolores," Madrid broke in. "They're just going to keep her in the cardiac unit at Emerson Hospital for a few days. They're going to *monitor* her heart and run some tests. But she just had a checkup a few months ago—she has checkups every year—and everything was fine. The doctor even told her that, on paper, she has the health of a teenager. Which means that she has a very, very strong heart."

"That's because Gamma is pretty active," London added. "And she takes good care of her health."

"Good heart, good health. Got it," Dolores responded.

"Now you might want to also say that—" Madrid began.

"We'll have time to chatter in the limo," Dolores boomed as she steered her body behind them. "I gotta have a smoke, y'know." She pulled the strap to her oversized purse up to her shoulder, held each of her arms out from her body, and quickly herded the twins toward the airport entrance.

"We're going to the hospital now, right?" London asked Madrid as Dolores kept them moving at a quick pace.

"I think—"

"We're having a smoke first," Dolores answered. "You two smoke, don't you? Join me."

London shook her head as she continued to be pushed forward by Dolores. "We quit," she called back over her shoulder. "We couldn't afford our brand anymore. Nat Sherman is pretty darn expensive."

"Who's Nat Sherman?" Dolores asked.

"It's a brand of—" London began.

"Don't bother," Madrid told her, then called back to Dolores, "I thought *you* were quitting."

Dolores had her cigarette lit and a cloud of smoke spilling out from her lungs before the second set of automatic doors behind her had closed. She stepped up next to the twins. "I *am* quitting. This is all part of it."

"Smoking is part of quitting?" London asked.

Dolores nodded. "That's the plan. I tried that hypnotism. Oh, yeah, right. Like I'm gonna be programmed to do something, y'know? I'm much better off *giving* orders than taking them. I tried the patch. A Band-Aid, is all that was. I tried acupuncture, even. I said hooey to all that when it wasn't working. Then I heard about this other thing. See, I got this here little computer that tells me when to smoke, y'know?" Dolores rummaged through her massive purse and then fished out a credit-card-sized piece of plastic. "See here on the screen? I'm at zeros, and the SMOKE sign is there. That means I can smoke. I'm actually about a minute behind, y'know? That's why I was going crazy. Then all I do is press the button. See?" she asked as she held the monitor toward the twins, who glanced down at it. "Now I have to wait another fifty-six minutes for my next smoke. I'm in stage two. Each day, the monitor makes me wait longer and longer between cigarettes. I got nineteen more days until I'm smoke-free, y'know? By that time, I hope to have another vice in place to help me deal with this anxiety. I never know what to do with my hands anymore, and this withdrawal is killing me. I mean, you try quitting when the world is crashing down around you."

"Dolores, we could've handled the media," Madrid told her. "You didn't have to come out here and—"

"It's the *least* I can do," Dolores answered as her cigarette wagged up and down in her bright-red painted lips. "The limo driver should be along shortly. I thought your plane might be late, y'know? Anyhoodle, I got a ton of time on my hands. Working for those writers is a piece of cake. All they do is sit in front of a computer all day and write, y'know? They're as quiet as mice. Gone are the days of Dorothy Parker and her sharp tongue, which was always getting her in trouble—know how many times I sometimes ask, 'What fresh hell is this?' whenever the phone rings—and Ernest Hemingway's grand 'round-the-world adventures. Today's writers might as well be librarians. They're actually pretty boring. No drinking. No drugging. No setting fires that I need to put out. And they *hate* to talk. Period. I know they're screening me when I call. They read, they write. *Yawn*, y'know? I've got some signings lined up for Grisham, because his new book is coming out in the fall. But other than that, I've got nothing to do. All I've been doing, really, is smoking when this goddamned thing tells me to, y'know?"

"Well, thank you for arranging the flights and for—" London began.

"I mean, I sit at home and read all this negative publicity you guys are getting, and it just breaks my heart," Dolores continued. "Makes me mad. I could've put a positive spin on *everything* if I was still working for you, y'know? I did research on those turtles, for instance. It turns out they aren't as endangered as you'd think. In fact, they're only a few thousand short of *not* being endangered. Plus, there's an annual mortality rate of fifty percent, whether you fling 'em into the ocean yourself or they get there on their own. Same mortality rate as squirrels, who nobody really gives a crap about and I think are just one step above pigeons. You don't see the papers writing about *that,* do you? But I would've fed the wires that info, y'know?"

"Well, we certainly appreciate—" Madrid began.

"And I could tell you other spins I could've put on things," Dolores ran on. "Puking at the soup kitchen. You just had the flu, that's all, Maddy. A twenty-four-hour, stomach-cleaning bug. Hells bells, we've *all* been through that at least once in our lives. And that Habitat for Humanity project. I heard about one site that was using substandard materials, and I could've said you gals didn't want to work on a house that wasn't up to snuff. I could've taken care of it all."

"We're not planning on doing those types of things in the future," London said.

Madrid nodded. "That's right. We're going to find something else we can fuck up pretty badly."

"I grated carrots and didn't fuck it up at all," London told her. "Well, just the first one. I didn't know you were supposed to stop at a certain point."

"Why were you grating carrots?" Madrid asked.

"I helped Lucinda make dinner at the club."

"Why?"

"I don't know. Because I had nothing else to do, I guess."

Madrid sighed and nodded. "Sad to say, but Gamma being in the hospital is a welcome respite from sitting at home and being bored out of my mind. Although I haven't tried grating carrots yet."

"Put it on your to-do list," London suggested. "It helps to pass the time. They're also a nice shade of orange. Could be that they're the new broccoli."

"Okay," Dolores said as she dropped her cigarette butt on the ground and slowly emptied her lungs of the smoke. "That was a *good* one. Now I have about fifty-two minutes to go until my next smoke. You talk about carrots! Someone said I should be walking around with a bag of carrots and then whenever I found myself craving a cigarette, I should reach into the bag and chomp on a carrot instead. I know someone who did that. She started turning orange, y'know? Too much beta carotene. That just proves that even health food can fuck you up. I started chewing gum, but my dentist told me to stop. He said that I'm too hard a chewer, and that if I kept that up for too long, I'd be grinding down my teeth in no time flat. You're damned if you do, and damned if you don't, know what I mean? Like you guys and your volunteering. You *tried* to do good, but it all turned out bad. I'm just sucking up the cravings and dealing with them. That's what you gals've got to do, too. This, too, shall pass—and all that, y'know?" She glanced down at the monitor. "Fifty-one minutes. And so will this episode with your grandmother. It *will* pass. Go see her, and trust that everything will be fine. Your gal Dolores is on the case. Y'know?"

"She's sleeping," Kitty warned in a hushed voice as she looked up and saw London and Madrid walk through the door to Gamma Angel's private hospital room. "She's so *pale*. I mean, *look* at her," she urged as she stood up and waved an arm at the bed. "She *does not* look good."

London walked over to the bed and looked down at Gamma Angel.

"You see?" Kitty asked.

"She looks fine," London answered. "Peaceful as can be. She looks pale because her nightie is white, the bedsheets are white, and the pillowcase is white. *Anyone* would look pale against that background. Good fashion dictates color contrast, and there's none there."

"She *does not* look good," Kitty insisted.

"Mother, no one looks good in the hospital," Madrid answered as she gave her a quick kiss on her cheek, and then walked over to the bed. "That's why they're in the hospital." She looked at Gamma. "She doesn't look bad at all."

"Oh, *I* think she does."

London let out a sigh. "You've said that three times already."

"And I meant it each time," Kitty answered. "You know, she's going to be *eighty-five* this year."

"She looks terrific for eighty-five," London said.

"Eighty-five is *eighty-five,* London," Kitty replied.

London looked at Kitty. "Yesss, it is," she drew out. "And my age is my age, and your age is your age. What *is* your age, by the way?"

"It's none of your business. The point I'm trying to make is that Gamma is eighty-five. She's no spring chicken."

"She's not a chicken, period."

"Could you two please stop?" Madrid asked. "You can't be in the same room with each other for more than two minutes without starting this bickering."

"She's *not* a spring chicken," Kitty repeated. "She's eighty-five years old. And that means that we need to look at the *reality* of this situation. Sure, *this* one incident isn't serious. We can be thankful for that. But it signals the *beginning* of the ride down that slippery slope. There *will* come a time when your Gamma will no longer be with us."

"Now *there's* a positive attitude," London commented.

"I'm just *saying*. These things *always* start out as inconsequential. But she's an elderly woman. One inconsequential thing leads to another, and then to another, and then, before you know it, she has the *big* one."

London let out a snort. "Yeah, Kitty. Like a scrape on the knee eventually leads to a leg amputation."

Kitty wagged a finger in London's direction. "Sass me all you like, missy. And stop calling me Kitty. You know how I hate that. But I for one am *not* going to ignore this. This is a *warning* that your grandmother's health is going to start failing. Sooner? Later? Who knows? It's just a question of time. And that means your father and I are going to have to make some tough decisions."

"Like whether or not to put a pillow over her head and put her out of her misery?" London suggested. "Or toss her on an ice floe and wave to her as she drifts out to sea?"

Kitty took a step toward London. "Would you *stop* with the sarcasm? You are *so* immature."

"And you are so doom-and-gloom," London retorted. "Lighten up, would you? Gamma's doctor said this was nothing to worry about."

"What does *he* know?" Kitty snapped.

"Well, he does have a medical degree," London answered. "From Harvard, I believe."

"There's going to come a time—and I *do* hate to say it—"

"But you will anyway," London finished.

"I *will*. Your father and I are going to have to make some *tough* decisions. Such as whether or not we put her in a nursing home."

"For God's sake, Kitty, Gamma just did the three-day breast cancer walk last month," London argued. "Before Christmas she walked every day in Italy. She goes for a morning swim at Walden Pond when the weather's warm. She's always busy in her garden. She does a lot of volunteer work—and *at* a nursing home, I might add. This woman is nowhere near becoming a nursing home *resident*."

"Mother, why are you even thinking this way?" Madrid asked.

Kitty patted her chest and let out an exaggerated sigh. "Because *this* is what you do when someone is as *old* as she is and ends up in the *hospital*."

"For a *few days,*" London countered. "And for nothing serious."

"Maybe not *today.* But it's just a question of time before your grandmother will *have* to be put in a nursing home."

"NO!" Madrid and London shouted in unison.

"*Don't* wake her," Kitty warned as she stood on tiptoes and glanced at the bed. "Face it, girls. Gamma is getting on in years. And then there are other decisions we're going to have to make as well. Such as, do we encourage her to sell her home and move to a place without stairs, without so many rooms?"

"Gamma didn't fall down the stairs or end up here by crawling on all fours from room to room in her house," London said. "There's nothing wrong with her heart. The doctor said so."

"Gamma Angel is going to live in her house for the rest of her life," Madrid added.

"*If* she can," Kitty answered. "And then there's the whole question of who will take over her financial affairs. You know, there's a lot of money that belongs in this family that she still controls. I don't want there to come a time when she's so mentally incapacitated that she decides to rewrite her will and give all of her money to her damn—what do you call them?—azaleas."

London let out a snort. "You wouldn't know an azalea if you fell over one."

"Mother, none of this has to be decided now."

"None of this has to even be *considered* now," London added. "Have you talked to Dad about this?"

Kitty tossed a hand in the air. "Oh, you know your father. Unless Carlisle is *confronted* with a situation, he just doesn't pay too much attention to it. When he gets here tomorrow from the real estate development site in Santa Fe, we're going to have a long, serious talk."

"For about two seconds," London told her. "And then he'll tell you that you're overreacting. Just like you always do whenever something unexpected happens. If everything doesn't go along swimmingly, according to *your* plans, Kitty, you think it's the end of the world—just like you're thinking this little episode is the end to Gamma."

"Mother, Gamma *will* die. We know that," Madrid answered.

"We're *all* going to die," London added, then looked at Kitty. "Is that a happy enough thought for you?"

Madrid frowned at London. "But Gamma's not going to die today or tomorrow or even sometime soon. She probably just overdid it. You said she was working in her garden?"

Kitty nodded. "Which she *shouldn't* be doing, of course. Because she's got enough money to hire people to take care of that."

"Kitty, gardening is a passion for Gamma. It's not work. It makes her happy. You only hire people when you don't want to do the work. Like you, for even the smallest of tasks. You can't turn on a faucet without a plumber and you can't change a lightbulb without an electrician."

"Now you *know* that's not true, London," Kitty sniffed. "I'm perfectly capable of handling *some* things. But you *know* your Gamma. She's got to do *everything* herself. *Planning* a garden. Reading book after book after book. *Choosing* the flowers. Fine. Go to the nursery and pick out all the damn plants you want. *Those* things I can understand. Maybe even watering from time to time. But, no. Your Gamma has got to spread her truckloads of mulch and dig here and dig there like she's some sort of yard worker."

"It's what she likes to do," London repeated.

"But it's going to do her *in!*" Kitty exclaimed. "Do you know what she was doing right before she sprawled out on the ground? She was on her hands and knees *weeding!* In the dirt, mind you."

"That's where weeds are," London muttered.

"It was getting to be a hot day," Kitty continued. "She was right out there in the sun. *For hours!* I guess she fainted. But how was I to know that? It's not like I've got a crystal ball. One of her neighbors called me when she looked out and saw Gamma flat on her face on the ground. I called the ambulance, of course, because I didn't know what to think. By the time the ambulance had arrived, your Gamma was sitting up and sipping lemonade and gabbing away with the neighbor and the ambulance people. Of course, once she saw me, she told me that I had *no* business calling the ambulance. She scolded me—*right* in front of everyone, including Evelyn Daniels, who, by the way, has most certainly been burning up the telephone wires since this whole thing happened, and I'm sure that what she's saying is *not* complimentary to me *at all.* So Gamma says to me, right in front of Evelyn, 'Catharine, why didn't you just *come over* here and *see* what was wrong? I could've had a hangnail, for all you know.' You see, girls, it's *always* my fault with her. It always has been, and it always will be. I can never do anything right in her eyes."

"Do we have to get into this topic now?" London asked.

"I'm just saying, that's all," Kitty answered. "It's no big secret that your grandmother and I have never really gotten along. But you'd think she'd be grateful that I erred on the side of caution in this situation. What did she *expect?* That I'd just leave her lying out there in the yard?"

"You did the right thing, Mother," Madrid reassured her.

"Of *course* I did," Kitty sniffed at her. "Will she *see* that, though? No, she won't. She was so mad at me that when they loaded her into the ambulance—under much protest, I might add—she told the driver, 'You'd better turn on those goddamned lights and the siren and floor it, buddy. Because there's no way I'm riding in this thing like I'm going out for a drive.' "

London laughed. "Good for her!"

"Oh, sure, you think *that's* funny. Then you try living each day of your life knowing that no matter what you do for that woman, you're always going to be wrong. You're never going to measure up."

London rolled her eyes. "Oh, please, Kitty. Would you put a cork in it?"

Kitty slipped a tissue out from underneath the sleeve of her Rena Lange pink-yellow-and-orange-striped cashmere sweater and started to dab at a corner of an eye.

"Here we go," London muttered. "Release the dam."

"God knows I've *tried*," Kitty said in a wavering voice as her lower lip quivered. "It annoys Carlisle to *no end* whenever I complain to him about the way your grandmother treats me. But who else can I talk to about it? It's like I'm an outsider in my own home, in my own family. It's always been that way, and it's never going to change. And then when I try to show that I care what happens to her, and . . . and . . ." Kitty's voice faded and the sound of soft sobs emerged.

"Mother, I know you're really upset," Madrid said as she walked over to Kitty and placed a hand lightly on her arm. "But I think you might be overtired. You've been here since yesterday. Why don't you go home for a while? Take a nap, maybe. London and I will be here when Gamma wakes up. We'll call you later."

"It's just . . . just so *hard*," Kitty whimpered, then blew her nose. "It's *always* been hard. I'll never make that woman see the *good* I do."

"She knows what you do," Madrid assured her. "She knows that you mean well. Just go home and get some rest. Do yourself some good."

"Do *everyone* some good," London muttered.

"You'll call me when she wakes up, Maddy?" Kitty

asked. "All she's been doing since they admitted her is sleep. I keep waiting for her to wake up. I want to tell her that I'm sorry I called the ambulance. I want to tell her that I was only looking out for her. But I . . . I . . ."

"Kitty, just go home and get some sleep," London said as she plopped down in a chair. "And if you have any chill-pills left, take one of those as well."

"If she wakes up when I'm gone, Maddy, could you tell her that I've been here the entire time?" Kitty asked as she gathered up her purse and jacket and stood up. "I don't want her to think that—"

"I promise I'll call you, Mother," Maddy said as she guided Kitty to the door. "And when Gamma wakes up, I'll tell her you've been here and you'll be right back. Now go home."

"Is she gone?"

London turned from the hospital room window where she had been standing since Kitty left and glanced over at the bed. "Gamma?" she asked, and then walked to the bed and looked down.

"Is she *gone?*" Gamma asked again, with one eye open.

"Who? Cat woman?" London grinned at her.

"Lonnie!" Madrid scolded.

Gamma opened both eyes and smiled up at London. "I like that. Cat woman."

Madrid reached for Gamma's hand. "Mother just left, Gamma. I told her to go home and—"

"I *know* what you told her, dear," Gamma replied. "I've been awake the whole time."

"You have?" London asked.

"Since we got here?" Madrid followed.

Gamma nodded. "And long before. Who can sleep in a hospital? But no matter where you are, I've always found that *pretending* to be asleep can be a pretty interesting experience. Especially when you're an old lady like me. People leave you alone. It's amazing the things you hear, when people look over at you and think—sometimes they even *say*— 'Oh, the old biddy has nodded off. She can't hear a thing.' They think that because your eyes are closed, you can't hear a damn thing. Just like babies, who cover their heads with a blanket and think that because they can't see *you,* you can't see *them*."

"Well, aren't *you* the sly one!" London grinned at her.

"Sometimes you *have* to be."

Maddy stared down at Gamma. "So you heard *everything?*"

Gamma nodded. "Yes, dear. *Everything*. By the way, Lonnie, you have a marvelous sense of humor. I think that's the way I want to go out of this world, when I'm good and ready to kick off. Just toss me on an ice floe and send me on my way."

"She was just kidding, Gamma," Madrid assured her. "We don't want you *ever* to go. Period."

Gamma reached out for Madrid's hand, and then clasped it in hers. "Of course she was, dear. But it was hard not to laugh at that one. When you do the pretend-sleep game, you have to be sure not to react. Whether things are funny or . . ." Gamma furrowed her eyebrows ". . . infuriating. So, yes, I heard it *all*. How your mother wants to put me in a nursing home. Put me in a nursing home, *my ass!* How she wants to *sell* my home! Sell my home, *double ass!* I can take stairs two at a time if I want to! *Backwards!* How she wants to try to convince your father—good luck to her, is all I can say— that my brain's getting addled. Addled brain, *triple ass!* The woman—forgive me, Maddy, dear," Gamma stopped and locked onto Madrid's eyes. "I know you have a very special, very close relationship with Catharine. You always have. Lonnie," she said as she turned to London. "You've always been closer to your father. But girls, Catharine's your mother nonetheless and has given me two beautiful, marvelous grandchildren." Gamma let out a long, slow sigh. "So shame on me for saying this."

"Saying what?" London asked.

"Saying that there has only been one focus on that woman's mind ever since she first laid eyes on my Carlisle. The woman sees green. Always has, always will. And that makes me see red."

"What are you talking about?" Madrid asked.

"Put the head of this bed up, would you, Lonnie?" Gamma asked as she pressed her hands against the mattress and shifted her position.

London glanced down at the side of the bed, then pressed a button.

"Okay, that's good," Gamma said as Madrid adjusted her pillow behind her back. "Let me tell you a little story about your mother. I think it's time you both knew the truth. But . . ." Gamma paused and wagged a finger at them. "If she *ever* found out that I told you this, she would be very upset. So it's our little secret, okay?"

London and Madrid nodded their heads.

"Before you girls came along, your mother was going to have a baby boy."

"What!" London and Madrid exclaimed in unison.

Gamma nodded. "That's how she got your father to pop the question. You see, she met him for the first time at a silent auction for charity—she was working for the auction house, setting up displays, keeping track of items sold, and so on. She knew that Carlisle was not only rich, but eligible. He was like the John Kennedy, Jr., of socialite society at that time. Handsome and wealthy, well-spoken and well-educated. He could've married any woman he wanted to—and believe you me, there were *long lines* of beautiful and intelligent and interesting women who I would've approved of as my daughter-in-law in a heartbeat. But then he met Catharine. She's certainly beautiful, I'll give her that, and she turned many a head back then. But once she noticed Carlisle, and he, in turn, noticed her, that's when I discovered that she was a manipulative woman. Because, you see, she got him interested and then turned right off to him. Blink, *blink!* Just like she had flipped a light switch on and off. She wouldn't give him the time of day after that. He'd call her, and she wouldn't return his calls. He'd go to the auction house when he knew she'd be working, and she wouldn't see him. Say she was too busy. Now, to a man of Carlisle's upbringing and social status and, to be truthful, with the youthful cockiness that comes from having such things—from knowing that you can, indeed, have any woman you want—the fact that a beautiful woman *didn't* want him was all that was needed to keep his attention. Because he saw her as a challenge. Someone he *had* to have. If she had just gone out with him on one date—or even on a few—then I don't think she would've wound up being your mother. But, you see, Catharine wanted it *all.* She didn't want to date Carlisle or be his arm candy for a few months. She wanted to be his wife. She wanted to be Mrs. Carlisle La Mira, both for the social status it would give her and for the riches it would bring her. And because she wanted to be his wife, she played that catch-me-if-you-can game quite well with him. Poor Carlisle! He was absolutely obsessed with trying to get her to notice him. Sometimes she would even agree to go out on a date with him, and then she would make herself somewhat available to him. But it wasn't long before she would slam the door shut again, and the game would begin anew. She had him hooked."

"I can see Kitty doing that," London commented as she sat down at the end of the bed.

"I can't," Madrid said. "You're just prejudiced, Lon, because you've never seen eye-to-eye with her."

"Mad, don't you remember Kitty doing something similar with the editor of *Town & Country,* when she was having the whole house redecorated? We were freshmen at Concord

Academy. She wanted the house featured in the magazine, so she spread the word through the grapevine that the house was going to be magnificent."

"Which it turned out to be," Madrid added.

London nodded. "But whenever the editor called the house, don't you remember that she'd never take the call? She'd tell whomever had answered the phone to say she wasn't there. I had to do that a couple of times. That went on for about a month, and then when the editor stopped calling, she returned the calls, and then the whole process started over again."

Madrid shrugged her shoulders. "She got her wish. The house was featured."

London frowned. "Yeah, but why not just take the editor's first call? Why play the I'm-not-home game when it's something she really wanted and clearly had the right person interested?"

"*That's* the game of cat-and-mouse, dear," Gamma pointed out. "It works with just about anybody."

"But that was with a magazine editor," Madrid said. "I can't picture Mother doing that to Dad. I mean, she may have her faults—"

"Yes, she does," London cut in.

"But I really can't believe that she would be so . . . so . . ."

"Manipulative," Gamma finished. "Yes, she was manipulative. *Quite* manipulative. Because her on-again-off-again, cat-and-mouse game with your father went on for months. And just when Carlisle was starting to lose interest in both her and the game—I'm sure she knew that he was nearing the end of his patience because he began to see her less and less—she threw open the door. She agreed to see him— might have even asked *him* out, if I recall—because he had stopped doing that. And then, well, one thing led to another. One night, your father told me that he was going to ask Catharine to marry him. I said, 'Carlisle, she isn't good enough for you,' and proceeded to outline all the reasons why I felt that she wasn't worthy of being his wife. After I had finished my long—and what I had thought to be convincing—speech, he said to me, 'But Mother. I *have* to marry her. She's pregnant with my child.' And so I gave him my reluctant approval—what else *could* I do? And they were married within the month."

"What happened to the baby?" London asked.

Gamma sighed. "The baby was premature, and there were numerous complications. It didn't survive for very long. Your father was devastated. But I thought that the loss of the baby, as sad as that was—after all, it was *my* first grandchild as well—might actually be a blessing in disguise. So I talked to your father once things had settled down, tried to convince him that Catharine wasn't a wife worthy of him, who would do right by him. I pointed out that she was cold and aloof and—"

"*That* certainly hasn't changed much," London commented.

Madrid sighed. "I know she is."

"And I reminded him that she was quite focused on spending his money—*my* money," Gamma added. "You see, your father was just starting Crowning Chateaus when they married. I financed him for years until his corporation started to make money. I gave him and your mother all the money they needed. Even though he never told me all the things Catharine wanted, I knew she was asking him for more and more and spending it as fast as she could get it." She paused for a moment. "But there was no talking to him. He told me that he loved Catharine, told me he had spent far too much time courting her to lose her, said that they would have another baby, and then things would be fine." Gamma smiled at them. "And she *did* get pregnant again and brought into this world my two little angels!"

"So it's a good thing that they didn't divorce," Madrid pointed out.

Gamma sighed. "Well, yes, for the gift of you two. But,

no, for the fact that . . . well. There's more that I need to tell you. From the moment that I started writing you your trust fund checks, Catharine objected strongly to you girls receiving them. She wanted me to give *her* the money so that she could then dole out an amount that she felt was best for your own use. Now, I knew what would happen to that money if I had done what Catharine had requested—you probably wouldn't have seen much of it. Because, you see, I was already quite familiar with how she spent your father's money. She used money to impress others. It wasn't something that she would use to do any good in the world. It was something that she used to improve her social status, to get her pictures in magazines and her name in the society pages. The final straw for me came when I asked her to donate money to the burn center at Mass General Hospital. She asked me, 'What do they burn there, that they need four million dollars from us?' I explained to her that the burn center treated burn *victims,* especially children. And do you know what she said to me?"

London rolled her eyes. "This should be good."

"I don't think I want to hear this," Madrid said.

Gamma shook her head. "No, you really don't. But I must tell you because there is a very important point that I wish to make with this story. She told me, 'Why bother spending so much money on people who are scarred for life? No amount of treatment can make them look better. They just need to move on with their lives—and hopefully, out of everyone's sight.' "

"Ouch," London said and then tightened her lips.

"I know, my dears, that Catharine can't wait to get her hands on my money when I pass away. She suspects—and she is quite right in this suspicion—that I am worth far more than anyone imagines. Not even your father knows the total value of my estate—and neither will you girls. Until I die, that is. I've drawn up a will in which your father receives a quarter of my estate and you will split three-quarters. You may end up being richer than your father when I pass on, and that, of course, will infuriate your mother to no end. She will not see the value of me giving you that much money, and so that's why you are both experiencing this terrible withdrawal from your funds this year. To be perfectly honest, Catharine was all for this, for me stopping your checks. But not for the same reasons as I was. She'd much rather see you fail in this endeavor—sorry to tell you this, Maddy. But the less of my money that I use in the years I have left, the more she feels will be available for her to squander when I take that journey out on the ice floe. *You* are the ones I want to carry on the La Mira name, in a way that will make me proud. I want you to learn how to give from your heart, not from your wallet. That's how I've lived my life after I lost your grandfather, and that's how I want you to live. So now, my darlings, do you finally understand why you're living in this check-deprived year of yours? Why I want you to become more focused and more mature, more aware of the world around you, more cognizant about the value of money?"

Madrid sighed. "So we don't become like Mother."

Gamma nodded her head. "That's right. So you don't look at a child who has burns over ninety percent of her body—and is, in fact, scarred for life—and think that giving money for her care and treatment is a waste. So you can see the good in the world that your money can do, and not the good that your money can do for you. So you can understand that there's more in this world than, say, owning not just the latest Lambertson Truex clutch, but dozens of them."

Madrid shook her head. "But we just don't know how to see the world in the way that you do, Gamma. You know how we've been royally fucking up—sorry—just *screwing up* in everything we've tried to do."

Gamma smiled at her. "Oh, yes. I *do* know how you've been doing."

"We're hopeless," London sighed.

"Hopeless?" Gamma echoed. "Oh, I think not, girls. You're just trying to find your way. I pretty much expected you would start off in the way you have."

"But we're not any closer to being the kind of people you want us to be," Madrid said.

"You must be so disappointed in us," London added.

Gamma reached out for London's hand and smiled at her. "I'm not disappointed at all. The fact is, you're trying."

"Badly," London responded.

"You're *trying,*" Gamma emphasized. "You need to find something that excites you, that gets you outside of yourself, that takes you to a different place so that you can see things differently. That doesn't happen overnight. It's all just trial and error."

"More error," Madrid stated.

"No, more *trial,*" Gamma corrected her. "To find what you really want in the world, you have to first figure out what it is that you *don't* want. And that can be hard to do, because more often than not, the things you want simply aren't right for you. So you find that out, one thing at a time, and then you look for something different. And you keep doing that until you find what it is that you are truly looking for, something that resonates with you."

"But we don't have much time left until our thirtieth birthdays, Gamma," London said. "The months are just flying by, and we really have nothing to show for the things that we've been doing."

"Except for bad press," Madrid added.

Gamma closed her eyes and sighed. "Ah, to be thirty again." She opened her eyes. "Of course, being thirty again wouldn't be fun unless I could go back to that age with all the knowledge, all the experiences, all the maturity that I now have. You're both right where you need to be. It may not be exactly where you want to be, but you're doing fine. Don't worry about reaching your birthdays without having all of this figured out. The beauty of growing older is that you acquire an amazing amount of patience. I'm not in any hurry. And neither should you two be. Because you won't find what you're looking for by moving too quickly. You'll find it by sitting back and letting it unfold before you. Chase after butterflies, and you never catch them—I forget who once said that. But stand still, and one will softly alight upon your shoulder."

London cleared her throat. "We'll keep trying, Gamma. We *will*. But . . . well—"

"But what, dear?"

"It's just that . . . that . . . we're not just running out of time. We're running out of money."

Madrid nodded her head. "We are. We've sold a lot of our jewelry and are trying to figure out—"

"Not to worry, dear," Gamma said as she patted Madrid's hand. "I put a little something in each of your bank accounts. Just to take care of necessities. That should buy you a little more time. But you might want to think about those cars of yours. How many vehicles does one really need? You can only drive one at a time, after all. And I assume that you each let go of your household staff and chauffeurs."

Madrid and London nodded their heads.

Gamma smiled. "Good. Who needs all that help? Help with *what*? Things you can take care of quite well on your own. Now you can start to learn how to do the basic things you need to do to take care of yourself. God knows you didn't learn anything from your mother. You're going to have to learn how to do your own laundry, how to iron your clothes, how to cook for yourselves, how to clean. And, as another suggestion, while you're cleaning take a look around your homes at all of your decorations, all of your art. If you don't know anything about the artist or the potter or the sculptor, then you might as well sell those things, too. You should surround yourself with things that have some sort of meaning to you. You should value the work of the creation. A hefty price tag means nothing. What it does for you inside, however, means everything."

"Where's Mother?" Madrid asked Ingrid as she followed London in through the front door of the La Mira house in Concord.

"She's sleeping, ma'am," Ingrid replied. "She said for me to wake her by five. And then I think she plans to return to the hospital to visit your grandmother. How is your grandmother doing?"

"She's doing well," London said.

"Very good. Do you have any bags that you wish to be taken in?"

"I brought my things here earlier," Madrid replied.

"And I just have this bag," London said as she set her shoulder bag down on the floor.

"I'll call Henry to take it up to your room," Ingrid said.

"I can carry it up later on," London told her.

Ingrid clasped her hands in front of her starched black dress. "We need to keep the hallway free of clutter, ma'am. That's the way your mother likes it."

London surveyed a hallway filled with an array of antique tables, American Federal period mahogany side chairs, Early American jugs and flasks filled with fresh flowers and dried floral arrangements, and several gold-gilded mirrors. "It seems pretty cluttered to me the way it is."

"Lon, don't give Ingrid a hard time."

London shrugged her shoulders. "Sorry, Ingrid. Call Henry to carry my one bag up to my room." She turned to Madrid. "This is what Gamma means, Mad. We grew up with someone on staff whose job is to take bags and suitcases up a flight of stairs. Gamma does that herself, and there's no reason why we can't, too. Don't you think that it's a bit ridiculous that Kitty has—"

"I don't know what to tell you, Lon," Madrid quickly cut in. "And I really don't think I can hear another thing about Mother. My mind is in overdrive as it is, just trying to digest everything that Gamma told us."

London stared at Madrid for a moment, then took a step toward her. "Are you okay?"

Madrid looked down at the floor and then shrugged her shoulders. "I don't know. I guess."

"I know you get along well with Kitty. And what Gamma said—I mean, if she said those things about Dad, I think I'd be devastated."

"I *am*. I am devastated. But why don't you get along with Mother just as well as I do? If I get along with her so well, does that mean that I'm just like her?"

"Mad, you're *nothing* like Kitty. Trust me on that. Neither one of us is, although Gamma is putting us through all this to make certain that we *never* turn out like her. Which is a good thing, don't you think?"

Madrid sighed and then nodded her head. "I don't think I can look Mother in the eye again, Lon. I wish . . . I wish I was closer to Dad, like you are."

"Dad has a lot of love in him, Mad. And I think he'd like nothing more than to be able to show his love to you. I guess my being close to him has let me see Kitty in a different light than you over the years, made me not want to get close to her. What Gamma told us today—well, some of the things, at least—didn't surprise me. Because I've kind of seen Kitty through Dad's eyes. And you know something?"

"What?"

"Sometimes she's not very nice to him. That has never sat right with me. Because Dad's a lot like Gamma. He's got a heart of gold. Kitty's, well, Kitty's heart needs a lot of polishing."

"I'm sorry, Lon."

"Sorry for what?"

"For getting on your case so many times in the past, when

you were being mean to Mother. I would get so mad at you. And sometimes I would tattle on you to get you in trouble."

"Oh, gee, was it *really* you? I had *no idea!*" London laughed, and then tossed an arm around Madrid's shoulders. "It's no big deal, Mad. You've always accepted Kitty for the way she was. I never have. Now we're seeing her through the same set of lenses. Now you and I are in the same boat."

"This time, with two oars."

London nodded. "Yeah. I think that'll help us move along a little better."

Madrid drew her arm around London's waist. "I'm selling the Jag."

"Oh, really?" London asked. "Well, I'm selling the Lexus—*and* the Jag, *and* the Beemer."

"Get out! So what are you going to drive?"

London grinned. "I think I'm going to get me one o' them economy cars. Maybe a Hyundai!"

"Oh, *pleeeze!*" Madrid giggled. "You in a Hyundai? Fine, then I'll sell *all* my cars and buy a used Chevrolet! And then I'll take a car repair course and change my own oil!"

London burst into laughter. "Okay, you win. At least you'll be able to find a job at Jiffy Lube."

Madrid held up a hand. "Not with these nails, I won't. I guess I'll have to keep the Lexus after all."

"And I'll keep the Beemer. Now let's go find something to eat. I'm starved."

"Shall I get Gretchen to make you something to eat, ma'am?"

London peered over the open refrigerator door and saw Ingrid standing on the opposite side. "You're everywhere, aren't you?"

A smile flickered and then disappeared from Ingrid's lips. "It's my job, ma'am."

"To be everywhere?"

"Yes. So I can anticipate anything. I'll get Gretchen for you."

London closed the refrigerator door and turned to Madrid, who had sat down at the kitchen table, pulled a fruit basket toward her, and was eating cherries. "I could just make something myself."

"Oh, that should be fun to watch. When was the last time you made something to eat? And I'm not talking about a snack, Lon. I mean a *real* meal."

London thought for a moment. "Remember Cook's-day-off on Wednesdays during that one summer when we were in grade school?"

Madrid smiled. "Oh, yeah. I remember that. Sometimes we'd have pizza."

London grinned. "And sometimes, darling sister, I would make us dinner. Peanut butter and jelly sandwiches or Fluffer-nutters. Hot dogs, once in a while."

"I wouldn't call that cooking."

"Hey, you didn't starve, did you?"

"Why didn't we have a family dinner?"

London pulled out a chair and sat down. "Because, if I recall correctly, Kitty had joined the historical society, which met on Wednesdays. She was trying to get our house listed in the Concord Historical Registry. She wanted to make nice-nice with the historical society, but then discovered that to be part of the society, she had to actually show up at meetings. And the meetings ran from the morning through the evening, because they had to go on house tours, research the history, fill out applications. Since she couldn't be here to supervise the dinner preparations and Dad was usually working late, she decided that we could just fend for ourselves. I think her commitment to the group lasted all of a month or two—long enough to get the house registered. Mission accomplished, and Cook was back on the job. So what about you? Do you know how to cook?"

Madrid shook her head. "I know how to order out," she

answered as she chewed around a cherry pit. "And reheat leftovers in the microwave. I don't think I'd like to cook. I like to eat, but not to cook."

"It's not so bad."

"How do you know that? Because you grated carrots once? That doesn't make you Julia Child."

London flashed Madrid a smirk. "Funny girl. I watched Lucinda prepare some of the dishes she was serving one night at the club. It looked like fun. She's a really good cook. And I helped her with other things, too. I measured stuff and chopped some other things."

"Sounds boring to me."

"You should see some of the things on the menu at the club. And people are packed in there all the time. It's gotten four stars and great reviews."

"Does that bother you? With it not being your club?"

London shrugged her shoulders. "Yes. And no. It seems weird going there and knowing that it once *was* my club. And thinking about what it was like and then not seeing that anymore. I had a good time there. But I feel like those days are over. I have no desire to be back in that scene."

Madrid nodded. "I know what you mean. I guess we're getting older, Lon."

"I guess. But Lucinda's done great things with the club. It's still a hip place to be, but it's a different sort of hipness. Speaking of clubs, what's going on with yours?"

"Well," Madrid said, and then spit out a cherry pit and placed it on a napkin. "The club is no more, but the space is nearly totally filled with small businesses. It's kind of got a theme to it, although the guy who purchased the place and is handling the rentals wasn't intending that. There's a hair salon, a day spa, a nail place called The Painted Pinky, and two massage therapists' offices. The space is still called La Mira East, but there's nothing left over from the club there. I actually go to The Painted Pinky now. It's as good as New York Nails, but cheaper."

"Does it bother you to go back there?"

Madrid shook her head. "No."

"Me neither."

"You would like something to eat, Miss London?" Gretchen asked as she stepped into the kitchen.

London looked up at her. "Oh, sure."

"Anything in particular?"

London shrugged her shoulders. "I haven't really eaten at all today. Just had a bagel on the flight out here."

"Would you like a sandwich? An omelet, perhaps? I could make you a western-style omelet, with peppers and onions."

"That sounds good."

"Very good. It will be ready in about twenty minutes. I'll serve you in the dining room, if you wish."

"Do you mind if I . . . well, if I watch you make it? Or maybe I can even help you? I kind of like cooking, but I don't really know how."

Gretchen stared at London for a moment. "Whatever you wish."

"Great."

"Anything for you, Miss Madrid?"

Madrid shook her head and stood up from the table. "I'm all set, Gretchen. I'm going to use Dad's computer to check my e-mail. Did I tell you, Lon, that I met one of Raphael's friends, who's single and looking to find someone to date? So I matched him up with another single guy from this online site, and it seems they're really hitting it off. Now Raphael's got another friend who wants me to do the same thing for him. Raphael said he'd e-mail me today and tell me what his friend is like."

"What are you, becoming a matchmaker?"

Madrid shrugged her shoulders. "I'm not doing anything these guys couldn't do on their own. But it's kind of fun."

Gretchen pulled out an omelet pan and set it on the oven.

"Don't start without me, Gretchen," London said.

"I'm not, ma'am. I'm just taking out the pan."

"And then what are you going to do?"

"Take out the eggs, ma'am. And beat them."

"Do you think I could do that?"

"It's really not that hard, Miss London."

"Well, Lon, I guess that means that you can do that," Madrid grinned. "Have fun, Julia."

PART THREE

Having money is like being a blonde. It is more fun but not vital.
—Mary Quant

Being moderate with oneself and generous with others; this is what is meant by having a just relationship with money, by being free as far as money is concerned.
—Natalia Ginzburg

While you have a thing it can be taken from you . . . but when you give it, you have given it. No robber can take it from you. It is yours then forever when you have given it. It will be yours always. That is to give.
—James Joyce

9

This is the best vacation I've ever had, London thought as she felt a peaceful, lighter-than-air feeling settle comfortably into her mind and body. *I'm relaxed beyond belief, just lying here, floating on the ocean, off the beaches of Anguilla. Ah, the Caribbean! My favorite vacation spot.* She smiled and let her thoughts create an advertisement for the enchanting island destination. *Anguilla! You'll swoon at the eighteen-mile slice of an Edenic paradise, with its powdery white sandy beaches and shimmering turquoise waters. Come, come, to Anguilla! Be seduced by its friendly warmth.* She felt her hand drop limply off the side of the float, felt her fingers drift through the silky-soft water. *Must be about eighty degrees,* her mind calculated. *Warm—but still perfect, quite relaxing. I've never felt so relaxed in my life. I'm just floating. Just . . . floating.* Her skin felt damp, a little sticky, and she imagined that she must have just emerged from a swim in the warm, salty waters. *And now I'm floating so peacefully. I can smell the fish cooking for dinner, and freshly chopped mangoes, and an enticing aromatic mix of tropical floral scents and spices.* She heard the watery sound of the surf somewhere in the background, felt the warm sun beating down on her, felt beads of perspiration trickle down her neck, her arms, her legs. She ran her hand slowly back and forth through the water. *I'll just lie here for a little while longer. Feel that wonderful feeling of having no place I need to go, nothing I have to do. Then I'll swim back to shore. Walk across the bleached-white sand. Return to my air-conditioned room. That cool air will feel really nice. Then I'll take a long, steamy shower. Cleanse my body of the sweat, of the oily, damp feeling. I'll towel off on the deck overlooking the beach, stare out at its pale blue waters. Let the sunlight shimmering off the waters mesmerize me. Then, later on, after dinner, I'll keep the sliding glass doors open so I can be lulled to sleep by the sound of the waves gently lapping the shore. So peaceful. Soooo peaceful . . .*

"Lonnie?"

London felt herself drift up on a gentle wave, and then down.

"Lonnie?"

London drifted up again, and responded with a low moan.

"Lon? Wake up."

"I'm awake," London mumbled without opening her eyes. "Just relaxing. Just . . . relaxing. I'm not too far from shore. I can hear people near me. I just want to stay out here a little while longer. Okay?"

"What shore? Hey! Wake up."

London felt someone touch her arm, and then pat her shoulder. She slowly opened her eyes.

"Are you okay?"

London looked up at Lucinda, ran a tongue over her lips, and then blinked her eyes a few times. "Hey, Cinda. What are *you* doing here in Anguilla?"

Lucinda furrowed her eyebrows at London, then reached up and removed her chef's hat and squatted down next to London. "You're not in Anguilla, Lon. You're at your club. In the kitchen. You're sleeping on sacks of flour. And, from the looks of it, spreading a good amount of it all over the place with your hand, from a tear in one of the bags. Why are you doing that?"

"What flower? Are there flowers? Are they pretty?"

"Not *flower*, like what grows in the ground. But *flour*. As in cooking flour."

London closed her eyes. "I don't know what you're talking about."

"And I don't know what *you're* talking about. But you need to wake up. Everyone's gone. I'm closing up."

"But the beaches never close on Anguilla."

"Lon, you're *not* in Anguilla. You're at La Mira West."

London opened her eyes and shook her head. "I'm not at the club. I'm on Anguilla. I just don't understand what you're doing here."

Lucinda smiled at her. "Lon, I would *love* to be in Anguilla right now. But I'm in San Francisco. *You're* in San Francisco. At La Mira West. See?" Lucinda turned her head and waved an arm in the air.

London let out a long sigh, slowly lifted her head, and then looked around her. She frowned. "I'm at the club?"

Lucinda nodded her head. "You're at the club."

"Oh, my God!" London suddenly exclaimed as she quickly scrambled to her feet. "Order up! Order up!" she called out and raced to the stove. She stopped and stared at the burners, then turned to Lucinda. "Where's the soup pot? Where are the vegetables?" She turned her attention back to the stove and pulled down the oven door. "It's empty! What's going on here? I've got orders to fill. Don't tell me we're out of everything already!"

Lucinda picked up her chef's hat and slowly stood up. "We're done for the evening. We finished a couple of hours ago. It's almost midnight."

London stared blankly at Lucinda, then slowly blinked her eyes. "We're done?"

Lucinda nodded her head.

"We *are?* There aren't any more customers?"

Lucinda shook her head. "No more customers. Everything's been cleared up and put away."

"What happened to me?"

Lucinda grinned. "You, my dear, have experienced your first full week—and your first busiest night of the week—in a restaurant. You've been quite the trouper, too, coming in every morning bright and early and staying here all day, working for hours in a hot kitchen as my assistant. Takes a lot out of you, doesn't it?"

"We're *done?* But it seems . . . but I just got here! How can we be *done?*"

Lucinda walked over to London. "I find that working in a restaurant is like entering a time warp. Once things get busy, you lose all concept of time. You've been serving up meals for the past six hours. And quite well, I might add. You kept right up, didn't slow us down at all."

London turned her back to the stove and leaned against it. "Six hours?"

Lucinda nodded her head.

"Tonight's *done?*"

Lucinda nodded again. "You can go home now, Lon. You did *really* well. Believe me when I say that. I've worked with a number of people since the club switched over to a restaurant. A lot of them had considerable past experience in the field, too—"

"Unlike me."

Lucinda nodded. "Unlike you. But they're no longer around because they couldn't seem to get out of their own way, let alone mine. You can't have that in a kitchen like ours. We're not some sort of family-style restaurant or quaint eatery. What we prepare here changes on a daily basis. La Mira West is experimenting with culinary traditions and creating imaginative dishes. That means that the work environment has to be fluid, and sometimes unpre-

THE PERILS OF SISTERHOOD 231

dictable. I'd work with you any day. You're smart, can figure most things out on your own, and seem to be tireless. Until now, that is," Lucinda smiled. "But *everyone* reaches their limit."

London returned the smile and crossed her arms. "Does that mean I get a raise?"

Lucinda laughed and shook her head. "Nice try. But no. You put in more hours here than I ever thought you would, but you'll be paid the same hourly rate as everyone else. I really appreciate the help, and I hope you enjoyed the experience."

"Of course I enjoyed it. I mean, I'm tired. But I liked it. And I'm ready to——"

"Good. I'm glad. The good news is, I'll have a check ready for you tomorrow if you want to stop by sometime and pick it up. It won't be anything near what you're used to receiving or even close to what you'd like to have, but it'll be something I'm sure you can use."

"Stop by? I was planning on being here anyway. To work. I have to help get the food ready for tomorrow night."

"Tomorrow's Monday, Lon. The restaurant is officially closed."

"But isn't there something to do?"

Lucinda let out a soft chuckle. "Oh, yes. There's always *something* to do in this business. But you've been working here every day for the past week. You've earned a day of rest. Think of this past week here as something you can file in your scrapbook of new adventures, courtesy of your grandmother. So go home. Go to sleep. Return to your dreams of Anguilla."

"Is that what you're going to do?"

"Dream about Anguilla?" Lucinda asked with a smile. "I've never been there, so I wouldn't know what to dream about. No, first I'm going to make the Sunday night delivery. Then I'll go home and catch a few hours of sleep, come back here in the morning and place some orders, take in deliveries, do the books, and cut the payroll checks. My usual Monday routine."

"What delivery are you making tonight?"

"It's just a food—a meal—drop-off."

"Where?"

"At a shelter. Not anything that would interest you. But I need to get going. They're waiting for me."

"At the shelter? They're eating dinner now?"

"No, it's for tomorrow."

"What food are you delivering?"

"My, but you're full of questions."

"I'm just interested."

"Okay. I hate to throw food out—it's such a waste. So I do what a lot of restaurants in the city do—donate leftovers. Those containers over there are what I'll be delivering."

London glanced at the oversized, stainless steel counter where Lucinda had pointed. On top of the gleaming surface were several stacks of take-out white Styrofoam containers.

Lucinda walked over to the counter and opened up one of the containers. "Each is filled with some of the leftovers from this week—Thursday through Sunday dinners. There's soup in this covered bowl, a main dish, potato or rice, and veggies. It helps us to clean out the refrigerators and not toss out a lot of food, and it really helps out the shelter."

"How many—"

"One hundred," Lucinda quickly answered, and then sighed. "Give or take a few. I'd like to have more meals to drop off. Sometimes, if we've had a busy week, I can't put together one hundred meals. But that's usually what we end up with. And it's enough for the women, their children, and the staff at the four Home Safe Homes, located in the city and in Marin County. And sometimes there's enough left over for the homes to deliver to those women and their children who are living in temporary housing in motels."

"What motels?"

Lucinda shook her head. "I can't tell you that, because I don't even know. But the women who are in that type of situation have usually left extremely abusive situations, and so they're moved from motel to motel until a safe residence can be found for them and their kids."

"That doesn't sound like fun."

"I'm sure it's not. But it's probably better than living every day in fear for your life and the lives of your children. The meals the restaurant contributes to them and to the residents in the homes aren't much, but at least they're something. Six days a week, the residents cook their own meals. They make nutritious dishes, but they're pretty basic—pasta, soups, sandwiches, things like that. Kind of bland, and a lot of repetition. The meals the club gives them are considered their special Sunday dinner, even though they eat them on Monday. One of the residents told me that our meals make her think that she's eating out at a fancy restaurant, which, of course, is something she can't do." Lucinda showed London a sad smile as she closed the container. "She told me that on Monday night, when they heat up the meals, she dresses herself and her kids in the best clothes they own. She says it helps make them feel like it's a special occasion. I was pretty touched by that."

"What kind of people are at the homes?"

"Home Safe Homes is a step above a homeless shelter, for women and their children. It's hard for them to get into the city's shelters, because they're not taking up one bed, but usually three, four, sometimes even five. Homeless families can wait for a space in a shelter for up to five months. That's a pretty long time to be living on the streets. And then, if they're lucky enough to get in, they can only stay for about a month. That means the whole process then begins all over for them. It's tough on the mothers, but even tougher on the kids. I don't care what anyone says about kids being resilient. Being homeless means having very little opportunity to be a kid—to play, to explore, to have a full belly so they can learn. More often than not, the kids don't attend school regularly, and they certainly don't have the space or the resources they need to do their homework."

"So when can the families in this Home Safe Home place go back home?" London asked.

"What do you mean?"

"This shelter—it's just temporary housing, right? It's just a place to stay until the families can move back to their own places, isn't that it?"

Lucinda stared at London.

"What?" London asked.

"A shelter isn't a place people go when they can't go home. It's a place people go when they have *no* home. These people have nowhere to go, nowhere to live. Sometimes the women have jobs, but what they make isn't enough for them to afford the rent on even a tiny place."

"Don't they have friends or family they can stay with?"

Lucinda locked eyes with London again.

"Cinda, please don't look at me like that. Maybe my questions are stupid, but I *am* trying to understand."

Lucinda sighed. "I know you are. It's just . . . it's just that I forget how removed you are from the rest of the world. Do you know that there are over *five thousand* homeless children in this city alone? Most are about nine years old. Their mothers are usually high school dropouts and, if they do have a job, they don't make much more than minimum wage. About fifty percent of the women at the home have taken their children and themselves out of extremely abusive situations. These families, well, they're fighting for their lives. They don't have friends with guest rooms or family members who can take them in, and they certainly don't want to return to a space in which a boyfriend or husband is going to beat the crap out of them. It's either get themselves to a shelter or to a place like Home Safe Home, or live out on the streets. Surely you've seen this city's homeless people when you've been out and about."

"Of course I have. It's just that . . . well . . ."

"It's just that you've never really *noticed* them," Lucinda finished.

"No, I've noticed them. It's just that I've never understood *why* they're homeless. I've always thought . . . well, I've always thought that it was like the people who don't have jobs. The newspapers are filled with job opportunities, and yet there seem to be people who have no jobs that don't even want them. That makes me think that they're just plain lazy. And I guess, well, I guess that's how I've viewed homeless people. That they're homeless because they're lazy. Or because—okay, I *know* this is going to sound ignorant. But I thought they might actually like the . . . the freedom of that way of life. The easiness of it all."

Lucinda unbuttoned her chef's jacket and tossed it on top of a pile of dirty white tops and slacks stacked in a corner of the kitchen. "The easiness? Lon, maybe you're seeing a whole different set of homeless people than I am—kind of like the hippies at Woodstock partying it up in the mud and the rain—but on those cold, drizzly San Francisco nights when the wind's howling off the bay and I'm snuggled up under a comforter in my apartment, I can't imagine what it would be like to have no place to go and to have to try to stay warm and dry. Homeless people are far from lazy. It's the circumstances they're in. It's hard to rise above poverty level when you have nothing in your life that can give you a lift."

"There's no one who can help them?"

Lucinda shook her head. "Just the city. But that's far from enough. Budget cuts have really had an impact on services for those who are most in need. That's why organizations like the shelters depend upon whatever donations they can get from others. Clothing, basic supplies like soap and shampoo, blankets and sheets, toys and games for the kids, and, most of all, food. The meals the club gives to this one program help out a lot, even though all it really adds up to is one less meal that has to be prepared. But the price of feeding one hundred people is pretty high."

London shook her head. "It's still hard for me to understand what it's like not to have a home."

"No one understands better than those who are living in the shelters. But I can give you an idea of how tough things are for the homeless, even when they have a job or even two jobs. After I give you your paycheck tomorrow, take a look in the papers for apartments to rent. Even rooms to rent. See what you could afford to pay for, based on what you're making. Then factor in food, utilities, laundry, transportation. See how much of your check is left. And then imagine having children. No, not children—just one child. How would you feed and clothe your child, based upon what's left in that check? *If* there's anything left at all. That'll give you a good idea of what these women were going through every day of their lives until they got into the home."

London removed her own white jacket, which was covered with stains of many sizes and colors, and tossed it on top of Lucinda's. "You must think I'm pretty spoiled."

"I don't know whether or not you're spoiled."

"I *am*. I never thought I was before. Actually, I had never really thought about it at all. I just expected my check each year. I did whatever I wanted to, whenever I wanted to. How spoiled is that? And I thought of little else but myself. *That's* spoiled. Spoiled and selfish."

"Are you done?"

"Done?"

"Yes, done. Are you done beating yourself up?"

London thought for a moment. "No, I could probably continue for quite a while. Focusing on myself is what I do best."

"Well, don't. So what if you don't understand what it's like to be homeless, Lon? A lot of people don't understand it. And those are people who have far less than you do. Most people don't even want to think about it, except maybe during the holidays, when their tables are overflowing with food and the shelters are making public announcements for help."

"It doesn't help that I've lived in an ivory tower all my life."

Lucinda shrugged. "Ivory, gold. Mud, brick. It doesn't matter what the tower is made of. At some point in every-one's life they build their own tower, put on their own blind-ers, so they can remove themselves in some way from seeing things that are too difficult for them to see. Don't be so hard on yourself. Sure, you've lived a life that's out of the normal ebb and flow. Most people who are rich do. You live in a world few inhabit. I don't fault you for that."

"I fault *me* for that," London answered. "I've been so busy partying and traveling and shopping—just *pissing* away tons of money—that I haven't paid any attention to what goes on in the real world. I thought my world *was* the real world."

"It is—was—to you. It's the world you live in. But it's a world in which built-in buffers oftentimes keep you at a dis-tance from the difficulties others have just getting through each day. You have to make an effort to see something out-side of that world. Some of the rich do—most, however, don't."

"I wouldn't even be having this conversation with you if it wasn't for Gamma."

Lucinda smiled. "Nor would you be standing in front of me with your hair in a hairnet, your makeup smeared, and your clothes looking like you haven't changed them in a week."

London reached up and slowly pulled the hairnet from her head. "I'm a mess, huh?"

"Well, you're not your usual model of fashionable perfec-tion. But it's not a bad look for you. You look . . . well, you look almost human. Not like a picture out of a fashion mag-azine."

"I imagine I don't look alluring at all."

"It depends on what your definition of *alluring* is. You've got a down-to-earth look going on. Some people find that alluring. But what I find most attractive about you right now is that we're actually having a conversation. Do you know that in all the years I worked for you, we never really talked? Most people who work together have conversations from time to time."

"And I never talked with you?"

Lucinda shook her head. "Not *with* me, really. You told me what to do, and I did it. I tried to give you advice, and more often than not you'd choose not to pay attention to me. Sometimes you asked me a question about something in my life outside of work, but I don't think you ever really listened to me, ever really cared what I had to say." Lucinda paused. "Did you?"

London sighed. "Before this past Christmas, I only cared about three people in this world. Me, myself, and I. And those three came before my sister, my father, and my grandmother. Pretty sad, huh?"

Lucinda shrugged her shoulders. "At least you found that out."

"Yeah. Now what do I do about that?"

"That's an easy one to answer."

"It is?"

"Yup. You start to care about others."

"How do I do that?"

"I don't know the answer to that one, Lon. That you have to find out for yourself. But at least you have three people who can help you out with that."

"Who?"

"You, yourself, and you."

"Very funny." London ran her fingers through her hair. "This is hard."

"What is?"

"This whole thing that Gamma's trying to teach me and Maddy. I thought it would be easy, doing some good in the world just to get back my yearly check. It's not. My brain feels . . . feels stuffed. All I do lately is think."

"Ah."

"After Maddy and I were booted out of the Florida Habitat for Humanity project, I read that if you give a kid a reasonable weekly allowance, that's a good thing, because it teaches them about the value of money. But if you give a kid a million-dollar check every year, it's a curse, because what it teaches them is that money has no value. All along, I thought it had. Imagine coming to the realization that the one thing that you thought was meaningful in your life has no value, has no true meaning. With an allowance, the meaning, the value, lies in conservation. You learn to save your weekly allowance, for example, so you can afford something you want. But you don't have to learn that lesson when you get a million dollars every year. You can just consume all the fun and comfort you want, without restrictions."

Lucinda thought for a moment, and then nodded. "That makes sense. I came from a large family. Everything we had, everything we did, was about conservation. In fact, one of the first things I did, after I moved out after college, was take a very long, very hot shower because there was no one else waiting in line for the hot water. Don't get me wrong—we weren't poor by any means. But we had to work for anything we wanted. And we had to learn patience, too. Sometimes it took months to save up for something, only to discover that when I finally had the money to buy what I wanted, it was no longer available or had been replaced by a more expensive model or had gone out of fashion."

"I couldn't have done that. Wait around to get something I want. I'm not a very patient person. I want what I want when I want it. I've never had to wait for anything."

Lucinda nodded again. "When I was your manager, nothing could happen fast enough for you. But I've seen a different London this past week. You've been very patient dealing with all the chaos that comes from working in a stressful, busy kitchen, and you've been patient with yourself, too. A lot of times I see assistants get more down on themselves than I ever could. I worked with a woman years ago in my family's restaurant who tried to kill herself because she couldn't make the perfect tomato rosette."

"I don't think I'd kill myself over a tomato rosette."

"No, you wouldn't. But you stayed very even-keeled, and that can be hard to do in the heat, in the confusion, in the stress. Out there on the dining floor, the atmosphere is relaxed. The diners don't see what happens behind those kitchen doors. I've been quite impressed with how you handled everything."

London smiled. "Thanks. It's nice to hear that I might actually be learning a good quality. But I have a long way to go. Sometimes I feel like a foreigner in my own country. The other night I couldn't sleep, so I flipped on the TV. I watched one of those cable news shows and was completely blown away. Is there nothing good going on *anywhere* in the world?"

"Sure there is. It's just not something that would make the news. There's a staff of dedicated volunteers at Home Safe Home, for instance. Some of them are part of the mentoring program, which provides tutors who help the children with their homework and with other educational activities. There are people who run food banks, which distribute food to the poor and out of work. There are humane societies and animal rescue organizations, elder caregiving programs, services that provide recordings for the blind—I could go on and on. But those things aren't news. Those are just things that go on every day."

"Those are the types of things that my grandmother wants me to find out about. How other people live. How other people make their way in the world. How other people serve others. And those are the types of things that my sister and I have gotten involved in and have screwed up badly."

"Well, you've certainly gained some experience this week, working as a chef's assistant and seeing what it was like to put in a full workweek. To be quite frank, there was a good deal of betting going on among the kitchen staff that favored your not lasting here a day."

"So who won the bet?"

"Ramero. He put his money down on two days. That was the most anyone had you sticking with the job."

"What about you?"

"What do you mean?"

"How many days did you think I was going to show up?"

"Honestly?"

London nodded. "Honestly."

"I didn't think you'd show up. Period."

"Oh."

"But you proved me wrong. If you ever want to come back and work a shift or two—"

"What do you mean, if I ever want to come back? I *am* coming back. I thought I had a job here. I thought you *offered* me a job."

"Well, I did, but I didn't think you wanted it."

"I didn't. But then I realized that I didn't have anything else to do, and so I came here. And I liked it. Now I want to stay."

"Lon, you're not going to be making any money. Not taking home more than—"

"It's not about the money. It's about *doing* something. I need to be doing something, Cinda, or I'm going to go crazy. Being inside my head is driving me nuts. And I'm a shit at volunteering. I don't even want to think about trying something else. But I'm pretty good at this—"

"You're *very* good at this."

"So, I want to stay. I want to work for you."

"You can work *with* me."

"*For* you."

"Okay. I don't care how it's defined. You have a job here,

Lon. Now it's after midnight, and I'm already late with this delivery. If you want to talk more tomorrow, we can." Lucinda slid a tiered stack of Styrofoam containers toward her and cradled them in her arms.

"Can I help you with those?"

Lucinda shook her head. "I've got 'em. I do this every Sunday night."

"By yourself?"

"Yup. You can open the door for me, though."

"Can I come with you?"

"To the home?"

"Yes."

"Lon, I do this all the time. It's not going to take me long at all."

"So? I'd like to come."

"Aren't you wiped out?"

London shrugged her shoulders. "Not really. I had my nap on Anguilla."

"Okay. I'll load the van while you clean up the flour—I'm not even going to ask what you were doing with that. But making the delivery is on your own time. I can't pay you because it's not part of your job at the restaurant."

"That's fine. Let's just hope I don't fuck up *this* volunteer opportunity."

"Sorry I'm late, Rhonda," Lucinda apologized as she peered in through the back screen door of the Home Safe Home main residence and spotted a large-breasted African-American woman dressed in a faded orange, oversized T-shirt with a black Nike swoop on it and a pair of paint-splattered brown gym shorts.

Rhonda looked over to the door, snuffed out a cigarette, and then heaved her weight up from the kitchen table. She shuffled over to the door in a pair of dirty pink slippers, and held it open for Lucinda.

"Girl, you done saved my butt," Rhonda breathed as she watched Lucinda squeeze by her. "I been settin' here since afore midnight—when you was *supposed* ta be here, mind you—an' then watchin' dat clock tickin' away an' thinkin' I was gonna have ta tell ever'one we was gonna have tuna casserole for our Monday night special. I think that woulda been the end 'a me."

"Things got a little crazy at the restaurant tonight," Lucinda lied as she slid the stack of containers on top of a worn and pockmarked, faded-pink linoleum counter next to a deep, double-sided stainless steel sink.

"It wasn't crazy at the restaurant. It's my fault we're late," London explained as she stopped on the back steps and gently nudged the top two containers in the stack she was carrying back into alignment with her chin.

"Rhonda, this is London La Mira," Lucinda said as she walked over to London and took the top two containers from her stack.

"Oh, I done know who she is," Rhonda said as she narrowed her eyes at London. Her head swayed slightly and was accompanied by a dull clinking sound of wooden beads braided into several long strands of hair that hung loosely on either side of her round face. "She be dat rich bitch."

London met Rhonda's eyes and then squeezed past her through the doorway.

"You be here doin' yer good deed fer th' day, white bread?"

"Rhonda, be nice to her," Lucinda said as she directed London to the countertop. "She actually helped me to prepare these meals. She's been working at the restaurant."

"Oh, she be *workin'* fer ya, is she now? Didn't know she knew how ta do dat. *Workin'*, dat is."

London set the containers on the countertop, and then returned to the back door.

"I sure hope dem meals'll be fine," Rhonda hissed as she

glared at London. "Was dat you or dat der other white bread who be likin' dat soup kitchen food soooo much?"

London stopped in front of Rhonda. "That was my sister."

Rhonda leaned her body close to London. "She done *puked* in the soup, is what I heard."

London cleared her throat. "She didn't puke in the soup. But she did get ill."

Rhonda gave a quick laugh and then waved a hand in the air and lifted her chin. "She did get *ill,*" she echoed in a close imitation of London's voice.

"Rhonda—"

"I'll get the rest of the containers," London said as she started to move past Rhonda.

Rhonda leaned her body forward against London, pushing her shoulder flush against the door jamb. Then she moved her face close to London's. "Wanna know how I be endin' up in dis here house, white bread?"

"Rhonda! Would you leave her alone! She's helping."

London turned her head and met Rhonda's eyes. "Sure."

"My grandmama done stopped mah yearly check!" Rhonda slapped an enormous hand hard against London's shoulder and emitted a long, loud cackle of laughter.

London turned her head away from Rhonda.

"What'sa matta, white bread? Cain't you see th' humor in dat?"

"Rhonda, stop calling her white bread!"

Rhonda pulled herself back from London and leaned against the opposite side of the door. "What d'ja think, white bread? Dat I cain't read no newspapahs? Dat homeless people is dumb an' stupid?"

London slowly turned her head and placed her face close to Rhonda's, until their noses were almost touching. "No. I don't think homeless people are dumb and stupid. Rich people like me are dumb and stupid. Haven't you heard the saying? Money can *buy* an education, but it can't *teach* you a thing."

Rhonda stared at London for a few moments, then slowly nodded her head. "Ain't dat th' truth."

"And just for your edification . . ." London paused for a moment.

Rhonda tilted her head back and wagged a finger at London. "Oh, don't you be thinkin' I don't know what dat der word done mean."

"I'm here because I *want* to be."

Rhonda let out a short snort and shook her head. "Honey, ain't *no one* here dat wanna be. I kin rouse ever'one out of dem beds, an' dey all tell ya the same thing. We all done dreamed 'bout dat white picket fence an' a nice house, a good man, kids dat be able to be playin' in the yard an' swingin' on a tire strung up to a tree."

"I just meant—"

"So don't you be sayin' dat you *wanna* be here, white bread," Rhonda continued. "Yer doin' the things yer doin' jus' ta get back yer tons 'a money. *We* all are here jus' 'cuz we gots ta survive."

"I'm sorry."

"What you be sorry about?"

"That I can't . . . I can't do more."

Rhonda lifted her lips into a sneer. "Oh, yeah. You be wipin' yerself out, white bread, movin' dem containers from the van into the kitchen. You be a regular meals on wheels, sweatin' hard, ain'tcha? I ain't seen the inside 'a restaurant since I was workin' at McDonald's in junior high school. You think you bein' so kind an' so—"

"Rhonda, I think that's about enough," Lucinda scolded as she walked over to London.

"No, she's fine," London told Lucinda, and then turned to Rhonda and leaned back against the door jamb. "Continue. I want to hear what you have to say."

Rhonda met London's eyes. "You want me ta be sayin' what I be thinkin'?"

"Yes."

"You never be knowin' what a life like mine be like."

"No, I won't. I never have, and I never will."

"You kin thank de good Lord for dat."

London shook her head. "No. I have my grandmother to thank for that."

"And she be the only reason you be here tonight."

"Yes."

"Then mebbe your grandma be smart. Mebbe her money done taught her stuff."

London nodded her head. "I think she's very smart."

"Time fer you ta be gettin' some o' dem smarts."

"Yes, it is. And time for me to be getting much more than that. I may have a beautiful home and nice clothes and a fancy car and so many other things that most people would love to have. But there's a lot I don't have in my life. I don't have common sense. I don't have maturity. I don't have values. I don't have dreams. I don't have sensitivity to others. But I bet those are just some of the things you have, right?"

Rhonda crossed her arms across her chest. "Dat be right, white bread. I do."

"Money can't buy them for me."

"No, it cain't."

"So I'm trying to learn them on my own. Maybe you don't think working at the restaurant or helping Lucinda tonight is a big deal. But it is to me. So don't fault me for at least trying."

Rhonda met London's eyes for a few moments. "Well?" she finally asked.

"Well what?"

"Dat de end 'a yer speech?"

London nodded her head.

"Den what'cha waitin' fer? Get yer sorry ass outta de door an' git dem containers. I ain't got all night."

* * *

"I got me three kids. Three of th' best kids ever," Rhonda said as she blew on the mug of coffee she had just brewed, pulled in a noisy slurp, and then took a long drag on her cigarette.

"Can I have one of those?" London asked, nodding at the pack of cigarettes as she sat across the kitchen table from Rhonda.

"Gonna cost ya."

"How much?"

"A carton." Rhonda tapped out a cigarette from the pack and then held it up in her hand.

London reached for the cigarette. "Deal."

Rhonda quickly pulled the cigarette out of her reach.

"An' a liter a' Coca-Cola. Not Pepsi. Coca-Cola."

"Rhonda, stop it," Lucinda said as she placed her coffee mug on the table. "Just take it, Lon."

"What choo mean, 'jus' take it?' She made o' money! I ain't."

"If you've been reading the papers, Rhonda, then you know she doesn't have any more money."

"Oh, yeah, right. She be poor ferevah and evah. She be livin' in a shelter fer de rest o' her life. She be lookin' in on bare closets ever' day. I tell ya what, white bread. Forgit about de carton an' de Coke. You done get me a pretty dress—one dat fits me, mind you. Not one o' dem size-six petites like you an' dat sista a' yers wears. You git me dat dress, so's I kin eat mah fancy dinnah in style, even if it be in de dinin' room here. You kin take what you want now, if'n dat be de payment," she said as she tossed the pack of cigarettes across the table.

London pulled out two cigarettes, slid one behind each of her ears, and then tossed the pack back to Rhonda.

"Color?" London asked.

Rhonda immediately widened her eyes and rocked her head. "Yeah, I be colored, you moron."

London sighed, and then slowly lit a cigarette. "Color of your dress. Moron."

Rhonda immediately flashed London an ear-to-ear grin and then let out a long, low chuckle. She turned to Lucinda. "I done like her."

Lucinda rolled her eyes. "Yes. I knew that was how you felt from the moment you laid eyes on her."

"I jus' had ta feel her out, is all," Rhonda answered as she sat back in her chair, placed her cigarette between her lips, and narrowed her eyes at London. "I be thinking 'bout somethin' wid yellows in it, white bread. And pretty flowers'n all. Sumpin' dat says *special*. Ain't no one be seein' me in it but us all in here an' mah kids. But it'd be sure nice wearin' it, no matter."

"What are you looking at?" Lucinda asked London as she drove the van to Home Safe Homes the following Sunday night.

"The seating plans to the restaurant." London held up the oversized sheet of cardboard so Lucinda could see it and pointed to a spot with a pencil. "Do you think we could put in two more tables in this room here, the largest dining room? Enough to fit in about twelve more people?"

"Twelve more customers aren't going to make a big difference in per-night profits, Lon. We'd have to add another room to see anything appreciable, and we don't have the staff to handle that. Plus, I think it's too soon to expand. We should turn a profit for a while before we even think about adding on."

"I'm not thinking about expansion or increasing profits," London answered as she turned over the pencil and erased something she had written on the seating plans. "I just need space for twelve more people to eat at the restaurant on one particular night."

"Why?"

"Well, here's what I was thinking. You know how you deliver these meals to the home, right?"

"Right."

"And they're not fresh meals—I mean, they're not coming right off the stove or out of the oven. They have to be reheated."

"Right."

"Well, what if we brought the residents of the Home Safe Homes to the restaurant one night and served them dinner? That way, they'd have a chance to go out to a nice restaurant and not have to eat leftovers. Even though they're good leftovers, I think food tastes much better when it's fresh."

"I agree. But what about the regular customers? There wouldn't be room for the residents and the customers."

"I know. We'd have to close the restaurant for a night. Or, if that means that we'd lose too much money, we could do this one afternoon."

"But how would the people from Home Safe Homes get to the restaurant?"

"Well, I actually thought about that, once dawn cracked through my thick skull and I realized that the residents don't have their own transportation. I mean, that was a real duh! 'Sure, Lon,' I said to myself. 'They're homeless, but they *own* cars.' "

"So how are they going to get to the restaurant?"

London tapped an end of the pencil against the plans. "By limo."

Lucinda eased her foot off of the accelerator and looked at London. "By *limo?*"

London looked at Lucinda and grinned. "Pretty cool, huh? I got the limo service I've been using for years to agree to donate a fleet of vehicles and drivers, on whatever date we give them. They can write it off, and the ladies and their children can come to the restaurant in style."

"Get out!"

"No, I will not get out. This is a moving vehicle."

"Lon, that's pretty neat."

"I thought so. So all we have to think about is—well, two things we have to think about—first, can we fit in seating for twelve more people?"

Lucinda nodded her head. "We'll *make* room. It might be crowded, but we'll fit them in."

"Well, three things, then. The second is, can we get the staff of the club to donate their time for this dinner? Actually, now that I think of it, there are four things."

"You can tell people what we want to do, and see how many want to work in the kitchen, wait on tables, clean up afterward," Lucinda answered. "If we find that we're short-staffed, I'm sure I can call around and get other volunteers to sign up."

"Okay, then maybe there are five things. This one just came to me."

"Let's go back to three, then."

London held up three fingers. "Three. We have to decide on a time when this can happen. And I thought that once we did that, I'd get really nice invitation cards printed up. I've already got a printing company lined up to donate those. Maybe we can even print the menu on the card, as sort of a keepsake. Four. I've actually taken care of this. I made several calls to people I know on Nob Hill—known to most as Snob Hill—and they're willing to pay for whatever food we want to prepare for that meal. So I was thinking, we should go all-out on this. Something really fancy, something the ladies and their kids wouldn't probably ever get to enjoy. Like lobster. Filet mignon. You know, things like that."

"That sounds good."

"Great."

"Was there a five?"

"Well, maybe it's not such a good idea."

"What is it?"

London shrugged her shoulders. "I don't want the residents to think that we're treating them, I don't know, like charity cases. You know how I made that stupid blunder of holding the fashion show for the homeless."

"You're *not* thinking of doing that again!"

London shook her head. "No. But what I was thinking was to see if we could get gift baskets made up for each of the residents. Have things in it donated from different places. The baskets would include some of the stuff you told me about before. Toiletries. Maybe perfume. And the kids would get baskets, too, with toys and things that they need."

"Lon, I think that's a wonderful idea."

London grinned at Lucinda. "Sometimes it's nice to play that *rich* card. You can make some phone calls and shame wealthy people into giving you anything you want for a worthy cause, because they know that if they don't, you'll make a big stink about how they refused to help out with even a dime. Rich people hate for anyone to know that they're stingy, even though they are."

"Lon, I am really, really impressed with this idea."

"You are?"

"I *am*. Your grandmother's probably so excited about this."

"Oh, she doesn't know anything about it. I wanted to . . . well . . . first I wanted to run it by you and see that this whole idea even made sense. And then I kind of wanted to see how it all worked out. I don't want to make a big deal about it. Because—well, this is going to sound weird—but I just want it to be between the restaurant and the people at the homes. I'm not doing it to get Gamma's praise."

Lucinda placed a hand on London's leg and patted it. "That's nice."

"So, all we have to decide on now is the time when this can happen."

"I have an idea."

"Shoot," London said as she slid the seating plan between her legs.

"We're doing this for the mothers and their kids, right? May is right around the corner. Mother's Day is in May."

London thought for a moment. "I like that."

Lucinda nodded. "So do I. We'll close the restaurant to the public on that day and have a nice afternoon dinner prepared for them. Why don't you tell Rhonda about it tonight?"

"Oh, I'm not going to mention a thing to her," London said. "I want this to be a surprise. And, anyway, I have the dress she requested. I hope it looks better on her than on the rack, but it's got everything she says she wanted. *And* I bought her a carton of smokes and Coke with my paycheck. I think that's all the shameless sucking up I want to do for that woman in one night."

10

"Georgie Porgie, puddin' 'n pie, kissed his Snuggle-bunny, and now he's going to live happily ever after," Raphael announced as he raised his wineglass in the air and flashed George a grin and a wink.

"I owe it all to you," George replied as he tipped his raised wineglass toward Madrid, who was sitting across the dinner table in Raphael and Jean-Paul's dining room. "I've never been happier."

Madrid smiled at George. "Of *course* you are. I *knew* this would work out."

"So modest," Raphael grinned at Madrid.

Madrid shrugged her shoulders. "I'm just telling it like it is. And there's the proof of what I'm attesting to—the happy couple—right in front of you."

"To her—and to *us,* Mr. Elliot House, aka Snugglebunny, and the love of his life, Mr. George Richardson, aka Georgie Porgie," said Elliot as he kissed George on the cheek, and then took a sip of his wine. "We have decided to name our first child after you, Maddy—a Jack Russell terrier that is soon to be born out of the pairing of an extremely elegant line from one of the country's top Jack Russell breeders.

Madrid Richardson-House, who will be better known as 'Sit, Maddy,' 'Stay, Maddy,' 'Down, Maddy'—"

"And 'Oh, you've been a *baaad* girl, Maddy,'" Raphael added.

"Our baby will *never* be a bad girl," Elliot proclaimed with feigned indignation. "She'll be residing in canine luxury in Georgie's apartment until we find our Connecticut dream house in the country, where she'll be able to romp about to her heart's content."

"You'll have your very own *Frasier* Eddie dog!" Raphael exclaimed. "Jack Russells are *so* gay, don't you think?"

"And smart," George added. "They can learn a lot of tricks."

"No wonder they're gay dogs, then," Raphael grinned. "Because gay men know *all* about tricks."

"Tricks are for kids—take it from me, the former pursuer of boy-toys," George joked.

"I'm glad those days are over," Elliot told him.

"What's that dog that lesbians like?" Jean-Paul asked as he poured himself a glass of wine. "The tall, long, thin ones? The ones that look like they haven't eaten in weeks?"

"Greyhounds?" Elliot suggested.

"Yes, yes, that's the one," Jean-Paul answered. "You always see lesbian couples walking them around town. The lesbians look a bit depressed, as lesbians often do, and so do their dogs. It's as if the dogs *want* to be back at the racetrack instead of being doted on by their two mothers. I'm sure the lesbians process everything with them. 'Is your bed *comfortable?* What about your food—do you *like* your food? Do you *need* any more toys?' " Jean-Paul chuckled. "The dogs are probably thinking, 'Chasing that fake rabbit around the track was simple compared to this. See the rabbit. Run after the rabbit. *Now* I have to think about *everything!*' It's funny how dogs take on the personalities of their owners. There are straight couples with babies. They usually have golden retrievers. They're such a spunky breed, all happy and energetic. If I were going to have a dog, I'd probably pick a boxer. Very elegant. Or maybe a Saint Bernard. Big, but low-key. However, you can't love antiques and own a dog. I guess I just can't be a dog person."

"Uh-oh," George said. "You're *not* a dog person? We were planning on asking you to be Maddy's godfather."

"Dogs have godfathers?" Madrid asked.

"She'll be our baby girl," Elliot answered. "*Every* baby has got to have a godparent."

"But it's a *dog*," Madrid argued.

"Now, don't get all technical on me," Elliot said with a grin. "It doesn't matter if our baby is gay, straight, bisexual, transgendered, or of the canine persuasion."

"It's not that I'm *not* a dog person," Jean-Paul said. "I *like* dogs. I grew up with beagles."

"I thought you had human parents, honeybunch," Raphael quipped.

Jean-Paul delivered a quick slap to Raphael's arm. "I *do* like dogs. I just don't think my décor would fit in with having one in this house."

"That décor being known as mid-seventeenth-century European breakables," Raphael explained.

"And irreplaceables," Jean-Paul added. "And with my crazy travel schedule and Raphael at the store so much, we're never around. It wouldn't really be fair to own a dog."

"But could you be Maddy's godfather?" Elliot asked. "Or should we find someone else?"

"Pick me! Pick me!" Raphael told him. "I've watched all the *Godfather* movies. I could teach Maddy how to fend for herself in that hard, cruel doggie world. I can be *very* Tony Soprano-ish when I want to be." Raphael formed a sneer with his mouth and began to scratch his belly. "Yeah. I'm in da waste management biz-ness."

"No offense, Raphael, but I think you're less of a *Godfather* or Tony Soprano type and more of a *Best in Show* or an Elle Woods Bruiser lover," George said. "We love you—we really do. But we don't want our Maddy being used as some sort of dress-up doll. I know how many Barbies you have in your bedroom."

"Damn!" Raphael frowned. "And I had the *perfect* outfit picked out for her. It's cute, but with an attitude. It's something that says, 'I am dog. Hear me bark. But see how pretty I am, too.' "

"We want you to be Maddy's godfather," Elliot told Jean-Paul. "We believe that you can respect Maddy's dogness and not see her as some sort of living plaything."

"What a strange conversation," Maddy commented. "I keep hearing my name, but it has nothing to do with me."

"What, exactly, does a dog godfather do?" Jean-Paul asked.

"Or is it a god dogfather?" Raphael grinned.

"Just come to visit her often," George answered. "Bring her treats. Take her for walks. Let her know that she has the best parents in the whole world."

"I can do that," Jean-Paul said. "I'll bond with her. Maybe I'll even make doggie treats for her. I hear there's a booming business in bakeries that cater to pets."

"Oh, goody!" Raphael declared. "A place in the country for us to go visit. But what to wear, what to wear? I'll have to start shopping now for my country outfits." He turned to Madrid. "Is my fashion consultant ready?"

"I know nothing about country outfits," Madrid said. "But I do have an unused gift certificate to L. L. Bean I got for Christmas. Don't ask me why, because when have I *ever* shopped there? I have very little use for a kayak in the city. But it's yours, if you want it. I did glance through the catalog once. My goodness, but everything's so *plaid*. So plaid and so, well, flannel and fleece. Although now that I think of it, they had these cute little dog beds with dog paws on them. Maybe I should get one of those for my namesake."

"Oh, no, no, no, sister-friend," Raphael said. "You just

promised the gift certificate to *me*. I'm not going to be up-staged by a dog, even if she *will* be named after you."

"That's no way to talk about my godpup," Jean-Paul said. "My little Maddy poopie doopie doggie—"

Raphael rolled his eyes. "Oh, please! Save that baby talk for me, when we're in the bedroom."

"He calls you Maddy poopie doopie when you're in bed?" Madrid asked.

"Anyway, *enough* puppy talk," Elliot said when he saw Raphael open his mouth to shoot back a reply to Madrid. "You'll all get to see our little Maddy when the bundle of joy arrives in a couple of months. For now, however, this toast is to you, Maddy La Mira—"

"Who is not of the canine persuasion," Raphael joked.

"Will you let me get out this toast?" Elliot asked. "I think I started it about a week ago."

"Toast away," Raphael told him.

"To Maddy! For bringing Georgie and me together."

"To you both," Madrid replied, and then drank some of her wine. She set her glass down on the sheer, white-lace-edged, embroidered tablecloth. "But, as I said, I *knew* this would work out. Matching you two up was a piece of cake."

"I still can't quite figure that out," Jean-Paul said as he passed a bread basket to Raphael. "To paraphrase Bogart in *Casablanca,* out of all the profiles in the world that are posted on the Internet, you went on-line and found the perfect partner for my best friend. I know people who go on-line all the time and never seem to have any luck finding a match, let alone a good one. And I can't begin to tell you all the horror stories I've heard from my single friends about the guys they've met on the Internet. More often than not, things don't go beyond the first date. Or, if they do, each time they get together it's like some sort of psychological meltdown that slowly descends into insanity."

Raphael let out a quick laugh and grabbed Jean-Paul's arm. "Honey, remember the one who met that who's-he-what's?"

Jean-Paul stared at Raphael. "Can you be more specific, love?"

Raphael waved a hand in the air. "You know the one. The—oh, gosh, is it Tim? Was Tim the one who went out with the guy who was obsessed with his ex-lover?"

"Right. Tim." Jean-Paul nodded and then smiled. "You know, it got so out of control that you could only laugh at the situation. After a few dates, even when Tim knew things would never work out with this guy, he kept seeing him because it was so entertaining. And then he'd come home after the date and call me. We'd laugh so hard it would hurt. Of course, you had to realize that the guy he was seeing was simply *dying* inside ever since his partner dumped him. He just could *not* get over it, and, unfortunately for him, he became sheer entertainment for Tim and me."

"So what happened?" Elliot asked as he speared a fork into his salad bowl.

"The guy's lover's name was Francis," Raphael began.

Jean-Paul nodded. "Except the guy would pronounce it *Fraun* Sisss. Like it was two words, and with a snaky hissing at the end of it."

"Everywhere Tim would go with the guy, the ghost of Fraun Sisss was always with them," Raphael explained.

"Yes," Jean-Paul agreed. "They met at the Crab Legs Café for their first date. I think the guy suggested the place to Tim. They spotted each other, shook hands, grabbed a table, and then the guy says to Tim, 'This is where Fraun Sisss and I would go for lunch on Saturdays. We'd meet up at noon, after Fraun Sisss had finished his workout at the gym and I had run some of our errands. Fraun Sisss and I had our own little routines, you know, as most couples do.' And then the guy launched into a long and boring saga about all the places he had ever gone out to eat in the city with Fraun

Sisss. Tim made a second date with him, even though the guy didn't seem much interested in who Tim was. But Tim, being the sweet, sensitive guy that he is, told me, 'Hey, we've *all* had hard breakups. I'm gonna cut this guy some slack.' But then every place Tim met up with the guy, there was some long and bittersweet Fraun Sisss story to go along with it. 'This is the theater where Fraun Sisss and I saw our first play. This is the restaurant where Fraun Sisss and I shared a piece of Black Forest cake. This is where Fraun Sisss and I bought a cute little antique pewter teapot. Fraun Sisss got it in the divorce, you know, and I can't bear to get a replacement. This is the same Central Park path I used to walk on, holding hands, with Fraun Sisss.' "

"How maudlin," Elliot commented.

"And then the guy got *really* strange, right?" Raphael prompted Jean-Paul.

Jean-Paul nodded and echoed, "*Really* strange. Tim had told the guy—"

"Does the guy have a name?" George cut in.

"I'm sure he does, and I'm sure Tim knew it," Jean-Paul answered. "But he never used it with me. It was always, 'Fraun Sisss's ex.' That seemed to fit him much better anyway."

"So how did he get strange?" Elliot asked as he took George's hand in his and intertwined their fingers.

"Well." Jean-Paul dabbed his lips with a napkin, and then started to ladle tomato bisque soup into bright yellow stoneware bowls. "Toss some croutons on top, hon," he directed Raphael as he handed him the first bowl. "Tim told the guy that he owned a florist shop, but didn't tell him the address. I mean, it could've been anywhere in town, right? The guy says, 'Oh, *flowers!* Fraun Sisss simply *adored* flowers. I would buy him a fresh bunch every week. His favorite was calla lilies.' "

"Calla lilies," Raphael sighed. He closed his eyes, and then opened them. "They're in bloom again," he began in a near-perfect imitation of Katharine Hepburn. He clutched his hands to his chest. " 'Such a strange flower, suitable to any occasion. I carried them on my wedding day, and now I place them here in memory of something that has died.' "

Elliot released George's hand and called out, "Bravo!" as he applauded Raphael's recitation.

Raphael shot up out of his chair, took a short, quick bow, and then sat down. "From the film *Stage Door*. Released in 1937. The storyline is as follows: aspiring actresses live in a boarding house and share their ambitions, dreams, and disappointments. The cast included Katharine Hepburn, Ginger Rogers, Lucille Ball, Eve Arden, and Ann Miller, to name a few. But," Raphael said as he raised a finger in the air, "most important of all, writing credits go to Ms. Edna Ferber and Mr. George S. Kaufman. Some day . . ." He let out a sigh and sat back in his chair. "Some day, I *will* write a wonderful screenplay."

"Some day, will our guests be able to eat this soup?" Jean-Paul asked.

Raphael sat up in his chair and raised his nose in the air. "See if I thank you when I accept the Academy Award for Best Screenplay. I'll name everyone else—from my grade school teacher to the teen with a bad attitude who works the counter at the place where I'll make copies of my script. But not *you*." Raphael let out a few feigned sniffs, then grabbed a handful of croutons and dropped them into the soup bowl.

"Not with your hands, lovey," Jean-Paul said. "Use a spoon."

"You did say *toss* the croutons on, babes. Kind of nonchalant. Like I could do it any way I wanted to. You *did not* say spoon them on."

"I thought that was understood."

"That I knew *toss* meant *spoon?*"

"That you'd see the *spoon* next to the bowl of croutons and know to use it," Jean-Paul answered.

"This is interesting," Elliot said as he looked first at Jean-

Paul and then at Raphael. "Is the old married couple having an argument?"

"It's a crouton crisis," George commented.

"More like a standoff," Madrid offered. "To spoon or to scoop? That is the question."

Jean-Paul gave Raphael a playful glare. "Humor the one who's been slaving in the kitchen all day, would you, and just spoon on the croutons?"

"How about I just spoon with you instead, lambcakes?" Raphael grinned.

"This is about as bad as it gets between them," Madrid told Elliot and George.

"You can spoon with me anytime, lover," Jean-Paul told Raphael.

"How about now?"

"We have guests, my sweet young heartthrob. Who are waiting, very patiently, for their croutons to be *spooned* onto their soup."

"But we'll be here all night if I *spoon* them on, and I'm starving," Raphael whined. "Can't we use our fingers *sometime?*" Raphael quickly glanced at George and Elliot. "No comments, please. I'm talking about the food."

Elliot shrugged his shoulders. "Haven't said a word."

"But you *want* to," Raphael prompted him. "Don't you? Don't you, don't you, don't you!"

Madrid turned to Raphael. "Why use fingers when you have a perfectly good working instrument that's attached to your body?"

Raphael batted his eyelashes at her. "Sometimes, my darling, when, um, Raphael Junior is busy elsewhere, orally speaking, you simply *have* to put your fingers *somewhere.*"

Madrid thought for a moment. "I see. Yet another gayboy-factoid I can file away."

"So back to Tim and Fraun Sisss's ex," Jean-Paul began, and then watched Raphael as he made a dramatic showing of slowly scooping one crouton at a time on a spoon, lifting it, dropping the single crouton into a filled soup bowl, and then resting for a few moments afterward. "Oh, for God's sake, just use your fingers, then."

Raphael dropped the spoon and clapped his hands together. "Merci, my sweetness."

Jean-Paul rolled his eyes. "All for you, darling." He filled another bowl and passed it to Raphael. "So then Tim gets together with the guy one night—says 'Hi, how are ya,' and before he could even finish that, the guy says, 'I believe you're *lying* to me. You don't *own* a florist shop. You probably know *nothing* about flowers. Let me tell you who knows *everything* there is to know about flowers. And that's—'"

"Fraun Sisss!" Elliot and George finished.

Jean-Paul smiled at them. "Yes. Fraun Sisss. It turns out that the guy had walked around, as he put it, to 'every damn florist shop in town' and looked for Tim's. He said to Tim, 'And I didn't see *you* in a single one. So why don't you just tell me the truth for once.'"

"For once? He said *for once?*" Madrid asked.

"Yeah," Jean-Paul answered. "Tim says to me, 'This guy's reliving his Fraun Sisss breakup with me, for sure.' But rather than Tim giving the guy the address of his business to prove that he wasn't lying—he does a booming business at his shop, but it's tucked down an alleyway and not visible from the street—he figures that if he does that, this guy will be coming around all the time and talking about all the flowers that Fraun Sisss loved. So Tim tells him that he does, indeed, own a florist shop and knows about flowers. He adds that he has a *degree* in horticulture, which he pursued after he realized that studying forestry—his first love—might bring him closer to nature, but not to any hunky, gay outdoorsmen. You see, Tim had had several very good experiences in the Boy Scouts when he was a lad and—"

"Oh, I love it when you use the word *lad*," Raphael said as he dropped a handful of croutons on another bowl of soup. "It sounds so . . . *mature*." Raphael looked at Madrid. "Sometimes Jean-Paul will ask me, 'Honey, can you bring me that book?' And I will, and then he'll say, '*There's* a good lad.' It makes me feel like a spoiled young prince living in his lordship's castle."

Madrid looked around the room. "Well, it's kind of close."

Raphael sighed and then rested his hand on his chin. "It is, isn't it? My dream has come true. I'm just a lad who has realized his dream."

"Just don't ever call me lassie," Madrid warned.

"I won't," Raphael said, and then nudged Madrid's shoulder. "I promise never to *collie* you lassie."

"And, yes, it's pretty much like *this* whenever the two of *them* are together," Jean-Paul told George and Elliot as they burst into groans.

"Only when we're around you," Madrid answered. "When you're not around, we actually have pretty intelligent conversations."

"About physics and chemistry and stuff," Raphael added, and then popped a crouton into his mouth.

"May I continue?" Jean-Paul asked Raphael.

"Certainly, my love."

"Thank you. So Tim wanted to study forestry—become a forest ranger, dress in an olive-green uniform, and work in a national park—but then he discovered that the majority of students who were studying forestry were dykes. Forest mamas, he called them. Or there were kids who had been raised by parents who had taken them hiking and camping all the time and who wanted to continue that experience in adulthood. And so Tim switched his course of study to horticulture, moved to the city, fell in love with an older man who doted on him, and together they opened the flower shop."

"He died," Raphael said as he patted his chest. "Tim's lover. He had a bad heart. Tim was with him—how many years, hon?"

"Thirteen."

George and Elliot sighed and then joined hands.

"Is he still single?" Madrid asked.

Jean-Paul nodded his head. "Fraun Sisss's ex was the last guy he dated."

"Talk about going out on a low note," George muttered.

"Well, he didn't think so at the time," Jean-Paul answered. "As he explained it to me, 'If this is the caliber of men out there and available, then I'd rather focus on the shop and my home and call it a day.' "

Elliot nodded. "That's the way I felt before I met Georgie. I had tried every which way to meet guys in real life—the clubs, social groups, fix-ups—but had no luck. My friends kept telling me to try the Internet, so I'd spend hours reading hundreds of on-line profiles. I could only find a few people I was interested in striking up a conversation with. Those I did go out with were, simply put, whacked. They didn't have a Fraun Sisss they were hanging onto, but they rarely lived up to the kind of person they said they were. I'll give you a for-instance. One guy said he was 'buff.' Buff, at least to me, means athletic, muscular, fit. So I'm standing at the entrance of this crowded diner one Saturday afternoon where we had arranged to meet, looking for him. I look here, I look there. No Mister Buff. A few minutes later, I felt a tap on my shoulder and turned around and stared at this man who had his stomach sticking out over his belt. All I could think was, 'Ho, ho, ho—it's Santa Claus.' 'It's me. Jim,' Santa says to me. 'Not Slim Jim,' I think to myself. His definition of buff was apparently about a hundred pounds overweight and gym-phobic." Elliot shook his head. "What a waste of time. 'Moderate social drinkers' turned out to be lushes, those who wanted to take it slow were ready to fuck after a five-minute conversation, and—"

"You never told me all this," George cut in. "How many guys *did* you date on the Internet before we started seeing each other?"

"I *met up* with six sickos," Elliot responded. "I wouldn't actually call them dates at all. *You* were the first guy I dated."

"Good answer," Raphael commented.

"True answer," Elliot added.

"So Tim is single?" Madrid asked Jean-Paul.

Jean-Paul nodded his head and then held out his soup bowl to Raphael, who dropped a handful of croutons on it. "Nicest guy you'd ever meet. Really is."

"Didn't you try to fix me up with him at one point?" George asked.

"I did," Jean-Paul answered. "At a New Year's Eve party I had a few years ago. I thought, you're a great person, and he's a great person, so why wouldn't two great people hit it off? But I didn't make a big deal of it. Both of you had made a New Year's resolution to be single, so I just wanted to see if you guys would meet up on your own at the party. You didn't, and that's okay."

"It's *very* okay," Elliot said. "Because now I have him all to myself."

"Is Tim interested in meeting someone?" Madrid asked.

Jean-Paul shrugged his shoulders. "Possibly. I haven't talked to him in a while because I've been traveling so much lately. But I can ask him. Why?"

"I think I might have someone for him," Madrid answered as she got up from the table. "I'll show you. I'll be right back. I just need to get my purse."

"What—does she carry single, gay men around in her purse?" George asked.

"Her purse is the size of a living room," Raphael said. "So chances are she may well have a few single guys tucked in there."

"Here we are," Madrid said as she returned to her chair at the dining room table and dropped an enormous Louis Vuitton bag on the floor. She bent down and began rustling through it.

"That's a purse?" George asked. "I thought purses were smaller."

"You're thinking of clutches," Raphael told him.

George shrugged his shoulders. "Shows you how much I know. I've never had the desire to delve into the world of women's wear."

"Who cares what women wear?" Raphael answered. "It's the accessories women have that are to die for."

"What do you keep in there?" Elliot asked as he leaned forward and peered over the edge of the table.

"Just the essentials," Madrid answered as she pulled out a tall stack of manila folders and laid them on the table.

"The essentials for what? The end of the world?" George asked.

"Girl stuff, gay boy," Madrid answered as she opened up a folder and flipped through several sheets of paper. "Did I tell you that I recently fixed up a straight woman I know? One of my neighbors. Nice woman. A little overweight and standoffish, but still, very nice. I thought, 'She needs someone who's down to earth, who will ground her but bring her out of herself, make her feel happy and noticed.' So I fixed her up with the guy who owns the newspaper and magazine stand down the street from the building. Charlie has his frickin' M.B.A., but he couldn't handle the stress of the corporate world. He wanted to be with people who were real, he told me, and he is. And making a darn good living at it, too. Who would've thought that a newsstand could support someone? I never paid much attention to small businesses before my money got taken away. It's amazing how many little shops make a ton of money."

"You're looking at one of those little shop owners," Jean-Paul said.

"And he supports me quite well, in a style to which I was never accustomed," Raphael added and then blew a kiss at Jean-Paul.

"So did the two straighties you fixed up live happily ever after?" Elliot asked Madrid.

"Actually, yes. One day I asked Regina to go for a walk with me. I took a route that brought us to the newsstand, and then I stood back and just watched it all happen." Madrid stopped riffling through the papers and smiled up at them. "They've been seeing each other for a month now. She couldn't be happier. And she told a couple of her friends what I had done for her, so I'm trying to find them a match now."

"Maddy, the matchmaker," Raphael proclaimed, and then began singing. " 'Matchmaker, matchmaker, make me a match. Find me a find. Catch me a catch.' " Raphael grinned at her. "Are you becoming a yenta?"

"No, there's not a single drop of yenta blood coursing through my veins," Madrid told him. "I'm not meddling or trying to push people together. If someone tells me that they're single and want to meet a nice person—I don't know—it's kind of fun to try to find a potential partner for them." She paused for a moment as she glanced through some papers. "Yes. Here's the one I was thinking about for Tim. This guy is, let's see." She paused as she scanned the profile. "He's into the outdoors. Hiking, sea kayaking—I'm sure *he* shops at L. L. Bean—mountain biking, skiing. He loves camping or just being in a forest surrounded by trees. He says that he misses the fact that there are no forests in the city. He works at an animal shelter, doing fund-raising and public relations. Has had a few long-term relationships. Wants monogamy and commitment. Along with, well . . ." Madrid paused and looked up at them. "The usual honesty, trust, good sense of humor, blah, blah, blah. I thought this might be a good match for Tim because the guy likes the outdoors and has a job that involves a lot of giving. It sounds like Tim is a sensitive, giving man."

"He is," Jean-Paul agreed.

Raphael raised his eyebrows at Madrid. "You've got a *ton* of profiles there, woman. How did you remember this particular guy?"

Madrid shrugged her shoulders. "I don't know. I'll scout around a bunch of Internet matchmaking sites and print profiles of the people who I think show some partnering potential. I remember just about everyone whose profile I print, although sometimes I'll get some of their likes and dislikes mixed up. It's funny, but every once in a while I'll be lying in bed at night, unable to sleep, and I'll think, 'Oh, what about putting this one with that one?' I'll get really excited about the potential match, until I realize that I don't even know the people. So how could I even fix them up? That makes me bummed out sometimes. I just want to write to the people who posted the profiles and say, 'Have you looked at so-and-so? Because if you haven't, I think you might want to give it a shot.' "

"You could do that," Elliot said. "Once the friend of someone who was single and very shy contacted me through my profile and gave me some information about his friend. He wrote and said that maybe I'd hit it off with his friend. I went out on a date—I *met up* with him, I mean—" he quickly corrected himself as he glanced in George's direction. "But we weren't right for each other."

"Of *course* you weren't," George said. "He wasn't *me*."

"That's right, love. He *wasn't* you," Elliot said. "But my point being, Maddy, that you *could* do that if you wanted to."

Madrid shook her head. "I wouldn't be comfortable doing that. That's a little too yenta for me."

"Could I see that profile?" Jean-Paul asked, and then glanced at the profile Madrid handed him. "Hmm. Nice picture. The guy's cute. He's about Tim's height and build. Says here he likes classical music and Windham Hill artists—Tim plays that kind of music in his store all the time. This guy's favorite book was *The Perfect Storm*. That was Tim's favorite, too. He couldn't stop talking about it and tried to get me to read it. The only thing I like about the ocean is fish, preferably scaled, deboned, and cut into serving-size pieces. I was too nervous reading the book because I knew those guys were doomed." Jean-Paul handed the profile back to Madrid. "It sounds like this guy shares a lot of common interests with Tim."

"How many profiles do you have in those folders?" Raphael asked.

Madrid shrugged her shoulders. "I don't know. A lot, I guess. It was a real mess for a while. I couldn't keep track of who was who. Then I made up a folder for men looking for men. And then another one for women looking for men, since I did so well with Regina and Charlie. And then I cross-indexed them, depending on their interests, locations, and personalities."

"My, aren't we organized!" Raphael commented.

"But why *do* all this?" Elliot asked as he waved a hand at the folders.

Madrid replied, "It keeps me busy. What *else* am I going to do with my time? Volunteering worked out so well for me, as everyone in the world knows. When I had money, boys . . ." Madrid paused and sighed. "When I *had* money, I was always out and about. I took trips. I went out to dinner. I went shopping. I was *never* home. But now that I am, as London says, 'income-challenged,' there's nothing I *can* do *but* sit around the house. And that's pretty boring, because I've discovered that I'm not really as interesting as I had once thought I was. So, I do this."

"Oh, pish-tush," Raphael responded. "I find you *very* interesting."

Madrid rolled her eyes. "*You* try spending twenty-four seven with me. I can get really old, really fast."

"Well, you *are* getting older," Raphael smiled. "The big three-oh is right around the—"

Madrid quickly held up her hand. "Don't remind me of that, boy-toy, or I'm going to have to kill you."

Raphael crossed his arms across his chest. "He was *so* young. He was *so* beautiful. Until he was struck down in the prime of his life by a woman who was three *decades* old."

"Oh, thirty's not so bad," George said. "I think the older you get, the more interesting life is. There aren't so many surprises, so many unknowns. You can handle things better, because you've gained experience."

"But it's hard when you're older *and* you're single," Elliot said.

George nodded his head. "It is. But we found each other."

"Actually, Maddy found us."

"You guys were my inspiration for all this," Madrid told them as she waved a hand over her folders. "I figured, if I can fix you two up, maybe I could fix up other people, too."

"So what calls your attention to a particular profile?" Jean-Paul asked.

Madrid thought for a moment. "It's kind of hard to describe. I guess it's just a feeling I have about someone from what they write. I can pick up on whether or not they're genuine. I can read between the lines to figure out if they have a lot of issues or baggage they're carrying around with them or if they've got something unresolved in their lives. I pay attention to what their hopes and dreams are, how they live their lives. And then, well, I focus in on people who have something to offer someone else, who seem to be . . . oh, how would I describe it? *Worthy,* I guess. Worthy in that they would have a lot to give to someone else. And worthy in deserving to be with someone who would see their good qualities."

"You can get all that from a profile?" Elliot asked.

"It seems to me that people could write whatever they wanted to—fact as well as fiction—in order to portray themselves in a certain way, wouldn't you think?" Jean-Paul asked. "I mean, I could say that I'm a moral, upstanding person—"

"When you're really a gay porn film star," Raphael finished.

"That wasn't exactly where I was going with that, but okay," Jean-Paul responded. "I guess what I'm asking, Maddy, is how do you know if someone is telling the truth?"

Madrid showed Jean-Paul a half-smile. "Life experience, hon. You can't be in the position I've been in all of my life—wealthy, well known, and constantly in the limelight—without getting a good feel for people. You learn, pretty quickly, and sometimes at great expense, who's on your side and wants only the best for you, and who wants to take all they can get."

"I guess I'm a taker," Raphael said. "I took your L. L. Bean gift certificate."

Madrid smiled at him. "No, honey, I *gave* that to you."

Raphael beamed at Madrid. "Because I'm so wonderful."

"No. Because *I'm* so wonderful."

"And modest," Raphael added.

"But how can you tell the good, sane people from the bad ones, the insane ones, without really meeting them?" George asked Madrid. "It would seem to me that you'd have to get to know a person, face-to-face, in order to find that out."

"As Tim has. And as I have," Elliot added.

"And as countless people on the Internet have," Jean-Paul added. "It sounds to me like it's anyone's guess who someone really is when you initially meet through a computer."

"That's probably true," Madrid answered. "But I think I've had a lot more surface-level interactions with people in my life. So I've learned how to form opinions about people pretty quickly." She smiled. "When Lon and I were growing up and were out at a social event with my parents, we used to play a game we called Signals. Like traffic signals. We'd watch people at the event and then give them a signal rating. Green for a genuine person. Red for someone who should be avoided. And yellow for those we had suspicions about. Yellow-lights were people who we thought weren't being completely honest. We'd remember everyone at the party and the signal we gave them—maybe that's where I started developing my ability for good recall. Later on, we'd test our ratings by casually bringing up each person we had rated with our parents. We'd say something like, 'Mrs. Phelps wore a really pretty dress last night. What's she like?' And Mother might answer, 'Oh, what a *darling* woman she is. She'd give you the shirt right off her back.' Sure enough, we had given Mrs. Phelps a green light. We were hardly ever wrong, and then only with the yellow-light people, who we weren't really sure about anyway. But we were *never* wrong with the greens or the reds."

"Interesting," Elliot said. "So you've printed out all of these profiles and made folders for them. What do you plan to do with them now?"

"Well, I just found someone who might be a good match for Tim."

"But what about the dozens of other profiles you have there?" George asked.

Madrid shrugged her shoulders. "I don't know. It's just something I'm doing to pass the time each day. I guess I'll keep the profiles on hand. And then if I hear of anyone who is looking for someone I might be able to match them up with—"

"Why not be more proactive?" Jean-Paul broke in.

"What do you mean?"

"Why don't you advertise yourself as a matchmaking service?" Jean-Paul suggested. "Start your own little business."

"With what?" Madrid asked and then pointed to the folders. "A stack of folders with profiles in them that anyone could find on their own?"

"You could put the folders in a *filing cabinet* instead of carrying them around in your Louis Vuitton—unless you want to become some sort of mobile matchmaker," Raphael joked. "A traveling yenta, so to speak."

"So what if all those profiles are readily accessible to everyone?" George asked. "It takes time to go through them all—"

"And money," Elliot added. "You have to join an on-line matchmaking service if you want to respond to anyone on the sites. And all of the high-end matchmaking and dating service businesses require a joining fee plus membership fees. It can be really expensive. And then sometimes you have to make a video and fill out questionnaires and then view videos of potential interests. If you see someone you like, you have to contact them, set up times to meet—blah, blah, blah. It's too much work."

Madrid nodded. "I know. I . . . well . . . I have to confess that I did do a search of some of the matchmaking services in the New York City area. There are quite a few. One of them is an elite dating service for corporate executives. I mean, how dumb is that—to try to match up two corporate executives? That's like matching up two doctors who work in the intensive care unit of a city hospital. If your profession is demanding and chaotic and you barely have time to eat lunch, then what makes you think you're going to be able to have a relationship with someone who's in a similar situation? Sure, you have to look for similarities in a potential partner, but you also have to have enough differences to complement one another."

"You sound like you've been in the matchmaking business for years," George told her.

Madrid took a sip of wine, and then leaned forward. "This executive dating service has all these membership plans, from what they call 'entry level' up to 'presidential club' membership. Presidential, my ass. They essentially do nothing. The cheapest plan is twenty-five hundred dollars for a year, and all they do is list your name in their client database. The priciest membership plan—the presidential—runs ten grand annually."

"Wow!" Jean-Paul exclaimed.

"You'd think that after forking over ten thousand dollars, they'd really *do* something for you," Madrid continued. "What they *do* do is take your money. They call what they do for each client a—" Madrid paused and wagged two fingers from each hand in the air, "heart shopper campaign, but all that means is that they have you fill out a rather lengthy questionnaire. What are your favorite foods? Do you like to travel? Describe your ideal date. Stuff like that. Then they write up your profile for you. Big deal. After that, all they do is what I've been doing in my own time. They screen profiles in their database and on-line, find potential matches, and then fix you up with someone who meets your partnering criteria. If you hit it off, great. If not, it's back to the drawing board. Oh, and they also give you—for *free*—a brochure that offers dating tips that they claim *work*. 'Plan a fun activity' is the most insightful of the ten tips. Another is, 'Dress nicely.' I mean, *duh!*"

"If that's your competition, then you could definitely start your own matchmaking business," Elliot commented.

"And make a lot of money," Jean-Paul added.

Maddy shook her head. "There's too much competition for Web-based matchmaking services. I'd much rather do a one-on-one type of thing. I like talking with people. Plus, I think people communicate better in person than on paper. The Web can be too impersonal."

"So why not do that?" Jean-Paul asked. "Why not open up a matchmaking business?"

"Yeah," Raphael agreed. "You could call it Yentas R Us. Or how about Renta Yenta?"

"I'm being serious, even if my beloved is not," Jean-Paul said. "Start your own matchmaking business, Mad. Open up an office."

"With what?" Madrid asked. "I've got no money. Besides an office, I'd need to advertise. I'd need a faster computer system than the one I have at home. A phone system, office supplies, furniture—"

"We'll get you the furniture," Jean-Paul cut in.

"Oh, yes!" Raphael exclaimed. "We could decorate your office to look really, really elegant. We could make a nice waiting-room area, and then a more intimate room where you'd meet with clients. And you could have the name of your business over the door in some sort of fancy lettering. You'd have to think of a really clever name, a name that captures what you'll be doing. I simply *adore* names that fit a business, especially the ones that are clever. Like I love the name of that dental group—The Whole Tooth. Or that dog psychiatrist. He calls his business Dogma."

"Actually, I kind of have a name," Madrid said, and then began stacking her folders into a pile.

"What's the name?" George asked.

"Oh, you'd all probably think it's silly," Madrid said as she slipped a handful of folders into her bag. "Or sappy. It *is* a little sappy, I think. Kind of maybe too much, now that I think about it."

"What is it?" Jean-Paul asked.

Madrid picked up the rest of the folders, and then looked down at the tablecloth. "I was thinking of naming it Cuor D'Angelo Matchmaking Service. It's Italian for Angel Heart. My Gamma's name is Angelica. She's someone who has always given from the heart." Madrid cleared her throat, then looked up and surveyed the group.

Raphael stared at Madrid with wide eyes. "My God, but that's beautiful."

Jean-Paul stood up from the table and clasped his hands together. "It's wonderful, Madrid. It's a beautiful name. It describes a really *personal* dating service—a service that *does* come from the heart, that *touches* the heart. And I like the Italian name. Italians are all about romance."

"They absolutely are!" Raphael agreed. "Think *Moonstruck*. That movie was all about *amore*. Even when Cher was slapping Nicholas Cage—her *innamorato,* her lover—and yelling at him to snap out of his feelings for her, she was so *passionate* about it. It was coming from her *cuor*—her heart."

"You really *do* like the name?" Madrid asked him.

Raphael smiled at her. "I *love* it!"

George and Elliot nodded.

"It works. It's *perfect,*" Elliot added.

"Now I'm thinking . . ." Jean-Paul paused and started to walk around the dining room. "I have some lovely Italian pieces—a desk that's simply exquisite—and chairs and side tables that we can use to set up a really nice, comfortable space for you and your clients. And art—oh, yes! Do I have some magnificent paintings that you could hang!"

"Jean-Paul, I can't pay you for—"

"You're not paying me for *anything,*" Jean-Paul cut in. "I'm donating it. We'll just put a sign up somewhere that gives the name of my business. 'Furnishings from Duettos on Lexington,' or something like that. With our address and phone number. It's free advertising for me and also opens up some space at the store."

Raphael clapped his hands together. "Oh, this is *so* exciting! It's a whole new venture—a new *adventure!*"

"It sounds terrific, it really does," Madrid said. "But I'd need to put the furniture *somewhere.* I can't afford to pay rent at an office anywhere in the city."

"Didn't the guy who bought out La Mira East from your grandmother tell you that you could have space in there whenever you wanted it?" Raphael asked.

Madrid thought for a moment, then nodded her head. "He did."

"And didn't you say that he had a hair salon in there, a nail place, some sort of day spa?" Raphael continued.

Madrid nodded again.

"What a perfect location!" George said. "Those are high-traffic businesses. A lot of people will see the Cuor D'Angelo Matchmaking Service. Even if they aren't single, *everyone* knows someone who is. Word of mouth could be your best advertising."

"A friend of mine runs a small printing company," Elliot told Madrid. "He could make up some fancy business cards for you. That way, when people stop in they could take your cards and give them to their single friends."

"We could throw a grand opening party for Angel Heart!" Raphael nearly shouted as he sprang up from his chair. "Jean-Paul will cater it—make up lots of heart-shaped something-or-others, honey, to go with the theme of love— and I'll write out your invitations, and—"

"Tim can provide the flowers," Jean-Paul broke in. "Some simple yet elegant arrangements would look lovely on the side tables."

"My brother-in-law works for The Bose Corporation," George volunteered. "He could set up a stereo system in there. Music really sets the mood and creates a nice atmosphere."

"Oh, honey, you're going to be rich again!" Raphael exclaimed. "And all on your very own!"

Madrid sat quietly in her chair. "But I don't *want* to be rich from this, Raphael," she said. "Don't get me wrong—I *want* to do it. And now that we're talking about it, and you guys are getting all excited and are going to help me out with it, I'm getting excited myself. But I just . . . oh, this is so stupid, because I know I don't have a cent to my name right now. If I'm going to do this, though, I just want to make people happy. Is that ridiculous? Making money won't be my goal. Finding partners for people will be. Because it makes me feel good inside when I can do that. Look at you and Elliot, George. Look how happy you two are. That's because of *me*. That makes me feel good. And you wouldn't believe how excited Regina was when I fixed her up with Charlie. She was transformed into a different person. I don't want to charge people a lot of money. I want to attract people who are just good people, you know? People who have a lot to give someone else and don't know how to find that special person."

"Well, you've got to charge *something*," Elliot pointed out.

Madrid nodded her head. "I know. But it's not going to be thousands or even hundreds of dollars. It's going to be reasonable. I don't want to make a living from a person's loneliness or prey on their desire to find someone who will bring them happiness. I just want to give a little, and to get a little. That's all I really want to do."

"You're different," Raphael told Madrid as they sat in the living room after George and Elliot had left and Jean-Paul had shooed the two of them out of the kitchen so he could, as he told them, 'work his domain.' "

"You work it, baby," Raphael encouraged him before he took Madrid's arm and escorted her to the couch in front of a bay window that overlooked the brick courtyard in the back of the house.

"Different how?" Madrid asked.

"Different as in, 'Where the hell is the Madrid I know?' " Raphael answered. "But it's a *nice* different. A *soft* different. A *genuine* different."

"How *different* a different?"

"Well, I don't think you said the word *fuck* once tonight. In fact, I don't think you swore at all. Which is very unlike you. You're always so . . . so *excitable,* I guess would be the word. But now you're very . . ." Raphael smiled, closed his eyes, raised his hands, and touched an index finger to each thumb. He took a deep breath in, and then slowly exhaled and opened his eyes. "You're mellow, baby. Feelin' groovy. Just chillin' with the gay boys."

Madrid laughed. "Me? *Mellow?* I never thought I would hear myself described as mellow."

Raphael nodded. "I know. It's so anti-La Mira, don't you think? The Madrid La Mira I know is usually all over the place. But not you right now. You're very focused. Very concentrated. Serious, but not overly so. It's like—you know what it's like?"

Madrid shook her head.

"It's like you—now don't take this wrong or anything, honey, because you know that I love you to pieces. But it's like you've matured."

"So I'm mellow *and* mature!" Madrid laughed. "How un-La Mira-like is that?"

Raphael laughed along with her. "*Very.* Imagine if the newspapers got hold of that news. 'Extra! Extra! Read all about it! Madrid La Mira Matures!' But, kidding aside. I *like* it. It suits you."

Madrid thought for a moment. "I guess I *feel* different, Raphael. I'm not happy, but I'm not sad, either. I'm just . . . well, I've been doing a lot of thinking lately. About myself. Which, of course, I've always done. It's always been about me, me, me. But this time I've been thinking in a way I haven't before."

"Soul searching?"

"I guess you could call it that. I've been thinking about how I've behaved, how I've been presenting myself to people I know, to the media, to the world. I've really done some pretty stupid things. Some pretty hurtful things. Some pretty pompous things. Things I'm not proud of. I don't think I want to be that way anymore. Because I really don't like what I saw."

"Do you like how you are now?"

Madrid smiled. "It doesn't always feel comfortable. It feels kind of funny. Kind of strange. Like I'm still me, but a different me. It's growing on me. I'm learning things about myself. I'm finding myself interested in things that I hadn't been interested in before. Like, in the past, I'd be rushing here and rushing there and never really paying very much attention to things." She paused for a moment. "I never realized, just as one example, what a pretty view I have from where I live. I moved a chair in front of the windows one afternoon and just sat there for hours. I saw the sky gradually darken and the lights start to blink on in the buildings around me. It was pretty cool."

Raphael smiled and nodded his head. "That *is* cool."

"I'm not cracking up or anything, am I? I mean, is that, like, a normal thing to do? Just sit and stare out the windows?"

"Of course it is. Sometimes Jean-Paul and I will sit in front of the fireplace and just stare into the flames. We won't say a word. Time will pass. We're just in the moment, that's all. I think it feels odd to you because you've lived your life trying to escape from the moment. You always seem to want to add something to the moment. More excitement. More drama. More spice. Sometimes, my friend, the moment is really *all* you need."

Madrid moved closer to Raphael and rested her head on his shoulder. "Thanks, Raphael."

"For what?" he asked as he placed an arm around her.

"For being my friend. For being my friend when I was a shit and—"

"Oh! I stand corrected. There's a swear word!"

"Stop it! I'm trying to be serious."

"Mad, please don't thank me for being your friend. I am and I always will be your friend. No matter what you do or what you say, I will always be there for you. I am Raphael, rock-solid friend."

"But I want to be there for you, too. I don't think I've always been a good friend to you."

"Honey, what you *think* is one thing. But what I *know* is another. I couldn't ask for a better friend. And now that you're changing, I have two friends—a La Mira, and a new and improved La Mira. And I *adore* them both."

11

"This price is *ridiculous*."

Madrid looked up from the paperwork she was filling out in the new-client interview room of the freshly painted, elegantly furnished, lushly carpeted, tastefully decorated, and almost completely finished office space that housed Cuor D'Angelo, Matchmaking Service for All Lifestyles. Her eyes met the eyes of the mid-fortyish woman sitting across from her, while at the same time she also took in the woman's body, hair, and skin—all of which broadcast decades of neglect.

"Excuse me?" Madrid asked.

"*This price is ridiculous*," the woman repeated in a louder, more forceful voice.

"Ruh, roh," Madrid heard Raphael mutter under his breath as he busily spritzed a group of rubber plant trees of varying heights set up in a corner of the room.

Madrid cleared her throat as a warning to him, but the woman kept her puffy-lidded eyes and jowly scowl locked on Madrid. "If you don't want to—" Madrid began.

"Did I *say* I don't want to?" the woman barked out in a deep voice as she shifted her excess weight in the eighteenth-century, high-backed, upholstered armchair on the opposite side of Madrid's desk. She tugged emphatically at the waist of a bright red sweater bordered with clusters of peacefully slumbering adult cats and playful, wide-eyed kittens rolling around in tangled balls of yarn. She succeeded in stretching the bottom of the sweater sufficiently to cover a mound of flesh that extended out over the waistband of her black stretch pants. That task accomplished, she then let out a few deep breaths and hoisted one of her hefty thighs over its mate as she readjusted her weight in the chair. The chair responded with a low creak and a moan.

Raphael gave a quick glance over his shoulder at the sound, inadvertently sending a misty spray in Madrid's direction. "Sorry," he mumbled in apology as Madrid waved a hand in the air, and then turned back to the plants.

The woman rubbed the back of her enormously large hand against her mouth and promptly expelled a short machine-gun burst of deep-chest smoker's coughs. She cleared her throat. "Now I didn't *say* that at all, did I?" she challenged Madrid after she had caught her breath. "I'm *saying,* what you're charging is *ridiculous.*"

"I really haven't heard any complaints from other clients," Madrid countered. "Most clients think the price is quite reasonable."

"I don't give a *crap* what your other clients think. *Should I?* I mean, should I give a rat's ass about what other people think?"

Madrid shook her head.

"Of *course* not," the woman continued. "My mama raised me right. I take *no* crap from *no one,* missy. I do what I want, I say what I want, I march to my own drummer."

"More like your own marching band," Raphael voiced under his breath and then quickly accelerated the speed of his spritzing.

Madrid held her breath as she saw the woman's eyes rove in Raphael's direction.

"What's that you say, young man?"

Raphael shot a quick glance at Madrid, then slowly turned to the woman. "I'm sorry. I was talking to the plants. They grow more—actually, respond quite well, in fact—to music. So I was saying, when I heard you say something about a drummer . . . well, I was saying to myself, 'I wish *they* had their own marching band.' "

"Who gives a crap about the plants?" the woman snapped. "And mind your own beeswax."

"Yes, ma'am," Raphael muttered. He caught Madrid's eye and raised his eyebrows while he mouthed 'beeswax?' to her, and then turned back to the plants.

"I really can't go any lower on Cuor D'Angelo's matchmaking fee," Madrid told the woman. "As it is, I'm barely—"

"Did I *ask* you to reduce the price?"

"Well, no, but you said that the price was ridiculous, and I just want to let you—"

"It *is* ridiculous," the woman emphasized. "You just have to wonder, what the *hell* is that fee all about? What is it paying *for*? I mean, if you think that I'm going to pay you that amount of money—for *what*? Are you going to find me the man of my dreams, or aren't you? I have to question, I have to wonder, at your prices and about the *quality* of the person I would be purchasing."

Madrid raised her eyebrows. "You're not *purchasing* a potential partner—Pam, is that your name?" Madrid asked as she glanced down at the paperwork she had been filling out.

"Does it say *Pam?*" the woman asked. "I wrote down *Pamela*. That's my name. I don't answer to Pam. I don't answer to Pammy. It's Pam-e-la. Or, what I really prefer, is Pamela Jean. But Pamela is fine."

"Okay, Pamela," Madrid answered. "As I was saying, what you're paying for is essentially a very thorough search service. I first review what you desire in a potential partner. That's what we're doing now. Then I conduct an extensive search, both on-line and through Cuor D'Angelo's database—which, by the way, is private and not accessible to any other matchmaking service. The goal is for me to be able to find at least one, sometimes a few, or even several men who match as closely as possible some of the qualities, desires, and characteristics that you're looking for."

"For *that* price?"

"I really don't see what's wrong with the price."

"You *don't?*" Pamela countered. "Well, I'll tell you what's *wrong* with the price. It's cheap. Cheap, cheap, cheap! I've shelled out *a hell* of a lot more dough for other dating services. Even those that are on-line, where you don't have to do anything more than just make up a story to convince all those lying Prince Charmings out there that you're Cinderella. I'm talking *thousands* more, sister."

"Uh-huh," Madrid answered. "And so how did those other, more expensive services work out for you?"

"Good question," Raphael muttered and then spritzed and coughed a few times.

"You're going to drown those plants," Pamela told him.

"I'm simulating a rain forest," Raphael answered as he stepped back from the plants, placed a hand on his hip, and watched as beads of water dripped from the ends of the leaves onto the new carpet.

"Looks more like you're simulating a damned flood," Pamela snapped.

"I know what I'm doing," Raphael answered as he dropped to one knee, placed both hands around the pot holding one of the plants, and then gave it a slight turn. A cascade of water immediately drenched the back of his neck.

"My point entirely," Pamela informed him.

Raphael turned and faced the woman. He shot her a tight smile. "Time to dust," he announced as he pulled a rag from his back pocket and moved across the office, where he started to wipe down an antique side table.

"Too bad you're one of those flamers," Pamela said as she

watched him, and then turned back to Madrid. "Can I add 'tight ass' to the physical description of what I'm looking for in a man?"

"You can add anything you'd like," Madrid answered. "But you have to keep in mind that Raphael is all of six years old. The men in your age category—"

"I know, I know," Pamela broke in. "They're going to look pretty much like me. That means they'll have a bit more heft to them."

Raphael turned to Madrid and made a show of biting his tongue.

"So, Pamela," Madrid began as she swallowed a giggle at Raphael's action. "I was asking you how those other dating services, for which you've said you've paid a lot of money, have worked out for you."

Pamela expelled a quick snort. "I'm here, aren't I?"

"Yes, you are."

"So what does that tell you?"

"It tells me that—"

"I'll tell you what my being here tells you," Pamela broke in. "They fucking *sucked!* I could be a goddamned best-selling author with the lies I've told on some of those sites. Oh, yes, I'm five-feet-two, weigh one-hundred-and-ten pounds, have long, blond hair, and am an aerobics instructor. I look like one, right?" Pamela immediately raised a hand in the air. "Don't answer that. I'm being facetious."

Madrid nodded.

"I could talk for hours about the lies I was told as well. You start out feeling like, 'Maybe this time,' and you write an honest profile. And then, whenever you open up your mailbox and see, 'No new messages,' you start to think, 'Guess not.' I mean, why do you think I did that—that I told those lies? Two can play that game. One guy had the audacity to post a picture of Antonio Banderas with his profile. Like no one's going to look at that and think, 'This guy's full of crap.' So you know what I did? I scanned a picture of

Melanie Griffith and wrote to Mister Antonio, 'I want a divorce.' "

Raphael laughed.

Pamela glanced over at him. "Yeah. I guess it was pretty funny at the time. But when all is said and done, all those sites I visited, all those matchmaking services I signed up for, were a waste of money."

"Most are," Madrid agreed. "I've heard a lot of stories just like yours. So I guess that answers your question about my fees for—"

"It doesn't answer *anything*," Pamela snapped. "Just because the others were expensive and did diddly for me doesn't mean that your being cheap is going to do me any better."

Madrid nodded her head. "You're right. But you have my assurance that I'm going to do the best I can to—"

"The *best?*"

"The best."

"You damn well better," Pamela snapped, and then let out a sigh. "Because I'm really sick of doing this, you know? This is my last shot, honey. Do you understand that? *My last shot.* I'm forty-fucking-six. I've buried both of my parents, I have no siblings, and all of my acquaintances, if I can even call them that, are married. I'm tired of doing things alone and I'm tired of being alone. I won't go out to movies because everyone else is there with someone. A night out for me is going to Home Depot. Mind you, I'm not crying in my beer because I'm single. But it's just gotten really old. I'm giving this one more try. *One more.* And if *this* doesn't work out, I'm going to just say to hell with it and sit on the couch and eat ice cream and Snickers and bags of potato chips every night for the rest of my life, with Mister Biggins curled up next to me. I'll die an old, fat, chain-smoking woman. Probably of a heart attack. Maybe diabetes. Who knows? But right now I think my Persian is worlds better than the perverts I've been dating through all of those other matchmaking places."

"Well, Pam . . . ela," Madrid said. "I understand what you're saying. You're not the first client to come here and say, 'I don't know that I can go through getting my hopes up one more time.' There are a lot of disappointing matchmaking places for singles, and most of them have you doing all the work. It's hard to be objective when you're doing your own searches, especially when, like every other single person in the world, all you really want is to find someone who can share a life with you. I think the biggest mistake people make is trying to force something to work with someone simply because they see a few common points they share. Just because two people like going to baseball games or enjoy foreign films, for instance, doesn't a relationship make. That's not enough."

"I'm not looking for much," Pamela said.

Madrid nodded. "I know. But you've got a lot to offer. You've got a challenging job—"

"Damn straight," Pamela agreed. "I don't take any guff from the truck drivers at the moving company, and believe you me, they get their deliveries out on time. If any customer comes to me with a complaint, I jump down the throat of whatever a-hole was responsible. And after I've given him a piece of my mind, he doesn't fuck up again. If he does, he's out. Because the boss listens to what I tell him. He's gotten rid of a lot of dead wood based on what I've recommended."

"Right," Madrid replied. "So, as I was saying, you have a challenging job."

"I like my job."

"I know you do. And that's good. Because the men in your age category aren't looking for someone to support."

"Yeah, right. Like *I'm* looking for support."

"And you own your own home."

"That I do. Have for the past twenty years. I put on an addition and expanded the garage from a one-car to a two-car with my own hands, I'll have you know. Poured the concrete. Framed it. Schlepped shingles up a ladder and pounded them in myself. Hung the gutters. Most men think those things would be their jobs. But they're screwed if they think they're going to be taking care of me in that regard. I have power tools, and I know how to use them. I've gotten this far in life without needing someone to change my oil or rotate my tires or rip out rotten, termite-infested wood or chain saw trees or split cords of firewood. I'm not looking for Mister Handy Dandy. That's why I wrote down on that questionnaire of yours, 'No men who work in construction or in a trade.' I don't want them to think of me as just another job."

"Yes, I have that noted on your profile," Madrid said. "You're not a high-maintenance woman, Pamela. You're very indepen—"

"High maintenance," Pamela cut in, then ran a tongue over her teeth and sucked air in through a couple of them. "By God, I like that, what you said. I am certainly *far* from being high-maintenance. I think that's a good thing, don't you? I mean, I've been alone for so long that I know how to take care of myself. I'm not going to be a heck of a lot of work." She threw Madrid a lopsided grin. "Honey, I think I'd have a heart attack and die on the spot if I woke up one morning and someone was lying in bed next to me. Actually lying in bed, asleep. Maybe wanting me to put on a pot of coffee or fix us up some ham and eggs and home fries—not throwing on their clothes in the middle of the night after rolling around with me for a couple of hours like they're rushing off to fight a fire and then saying, 'I'll call ya later.' Like that's ever happened. Not the fire, I mean. But calling me later." Pamela paused for a moment, and then shook her head. "Me not being high maintenance—do you think that's attractive to men?"

"I don't see why not."

"Don't they like them all gooey and starry-eyed and helpless and," Pamela stopped, clutched her massive arms to her well-endowed chest, batted her eyes several times, and said in a voice that was a few octaves higher than her own, " 'Oh, poor me, I don't know how to do *a thing* without a man around?'"

"Some men do," Madrid agreed as Pamela lowered her arms. "But not the ones I'll be considering for you." Madrid paused for a moment. "And, truth be told, Pamela, not the ones that I've known. Most men want you to do everything for them. Maybe they'll expend some energy in your direction for a week or so—during that getting-to-know-you honeymoon period in which they try to convince you that they're very sensitive and very giving—but then when they know you're interested, they just sit back and want you to take care of them. That gets really old, really fast. I think you have to strike a balance with a partner—a give and take—do you know what I'm saying?"

"Yeah, yeah, I know what you're saying," Pamela responded. "You do everything for them, and then all you got at your place is another piece of furniture. It's nice to have around, but it doesn't give anything back." Pamela stared at Madrid for a moment, and then sighed. "I mean, I *know* men," she said. "I work with them every fucking day. How do you strike that balance, as you say, when what they're looking for is women like you? Women who are pretty. Skinny. Kinda tall—or at least with long, well-shaped legs. What is it with men and them liking long legs? They want a woman to be all girly, with matching earrings and makeup that's put on just so. I put on makeup, and my face breaks out in hives. Big, red blotches everywhere. Not a pretty sight. And they want you to wear those ladylike shoes. Like *those* will fit on my fat feet. I like my Rockports. They're sensible, and they're comfortable. And men always want you to have a goddamned bright, perky smile, no matter how you're feeling. But, most important of all, they want you to be sexy. Sexy, sexy, sexy. They want *sexy*. Look at *me!*" Pamela exclaimed as she suddenly thrust her hands against her sweater, grabbed at it, and then pulled on it. "I'm fat. I'm short. I'm far, far, far from being pretty. I don't dress ladylike, and I don't act ladylike. I mean—*shit!* You know, maybe this is a *bad* idea. A bad, bad, bad idea. I don't know what I'm thinking, that I'll find someone who could just like me. You hear that? Just *like* me. I've given up on love. I gave up on that years ago. And forget about lust. I'm just not the lusted-after type. Except, apparently, by firefighters."

Raphael let out a quick laugh, and then turned quickly to Pam and said, "Sorry."

"What are you apologizing for, tight buns? It was meant to be a joke."

Raphael flashed her a grin. "It *was* funny."

"Of course it was. I *do* have a sense of humor. Most fat people do. We're jolly, you know?" Pamela sighed. "I crack the guys up at work all the time. But do you think any of them has ever asked me out?" She shook her head. "I've found that after all these years of being an available, single gal—one who's not high-maintenance at all, I now can say— that the only male that likes my company, that truly wants to be close to me, is Mister Biggins. I should just thank you right now for your time and call it a day."

"Pamela, I'll do whatever you want me to do," Madrid answered. "I understand that every time you put yourself out there to try to meet people, you're taking a risk. You're opening up your heart a bit. And it's tough to keep trying time and again, to keep getting your hopes up. You can't help but do that, and so you have to be ready to maybe have some more disappointments with my matchmaking service. I'll do the best I can for you. I will not try to fix you up with someone who won't be a good match for you, who will be a waste of your time and energy. That I can promise you. But please think about this. Now, I'm not a pet person myself—apparently I'm somewhat of an animal murderess, at least when it comes to turtles. But no matter. Here's what I'm wondering. Do you honestly think that Mister Biggins is the *best* companion that you can have for the rest of your life? No offense, but I think you're too sexy for your cat."

"Huh?"

"I said, you're too sexy for your cat."

"What you think about that?" Raphael sang out as he gave a quick spin and turn in Pamela's direction.

Pamela stared first at Raphael, and then at Madrid. "You're making fun of me."

Madrid and Raphael shook their heads at the same time.

"You're a take-charge woman," Raphael said as he walked over to Madrid's desk. "You speak your mind and you let yourself be right out there. Good for you, girl, is what I say. I think some man's going to *love* that. He'll *swoon*. Take it from me. If there's one thing I know, it's men. And men like to be told what to do. Men *like* to be dominated."

"I agree," Madrid said. "All the men I've been with like to be told, 'Honey, do this. Honey, do that.' They can't stop and ask for directions when they're out driving and are clearly lost, but they need someone else to help them navigate through every little twist and turn in life. There are also a lot of men who like women of your . . . stature, Pamela."

"Think Queen Latifah," Raphael grinned. "She's loud and proud."

"I *am* pretty proud of myself," Pamela said.

"You should be," Madrid agreed. "And there are a lot of men who like women who have fix-it skills, who aren't going to be nagging them about doing things around the house. They like women who take care of themselves, who can be independent. That makes you very appealing. And here's another thing to think about. When you give off the air that you don't really *need* someone, you then become *very* attractive to others. People naturally like, naturally gravitate toward the unattainable."

"I don't think I'm *un*attainable," Pamela said. "After all, here I am, right? But I *am* a little particular. I don't want just *any* man. I want a *nice* man. And I wouldn't mind a man who's relatively attractive. He doesn't have to be a model or anything like that—not like those men you've dated," she told Madrid. "All those actors and athletes and famous people. I mean, I know *they're* out of my league."

"Handsome men aren't all they're cracked up to be," Madrid answered. "They're nice to look at, don't get me wrong. But they're . . . well, they're fragile. And self-absorbed. I think they like mirrors best of all."

"And cameras," Raphael added.

Madrid nodded. "Handsome men don't see *you*. They see themselves."

"But still . . ." Pamela began, and then paused. "I wouldn't even *know* what that would feel like, to have some Adonis on my arm. You know what that feels like, missy. But take it from me. *Every* ugly duckling dreams about it."

"Ugly ducklings turn into beautiful swans," Raphael quipped. "Don't forget *that*."

"*That's* a fairy tale," Pamela snapped, and then looked at Raphael and let out a quick bark of a laugh. "A *fairy* tale! Get it?"

Raphael waved his dust rag in the air. "Got it. Very clever." Then he turned his back to Pamela and muttered, "Like I've never heard that one before."

Madrid showed Pamela a half-smile. "It's not always easy to meet a nice person, no matter what you look like. I'm single. I'd like to find a nice man as well. Someone who I could be with for a while. It's hard for me, too, Pamela. Even though," she quickly added as Pamela threw her a frown, "you might not believe that. The men who have been interested in me look at the outside. It's all about appearances with them. And, of course, money. That was definitely a hook—at least, when I *had* it." Madrid sighed. "I guess, to be fair, what I've done as well is focus solely on appearances. And on a person's prestige, on his fame. But I'm starting to learn what you already know so well—that there's much more to a person than what meets the eye. What you have, deep down inside of you, is a lot to offer someone. If you decide to sign on with me, the type of men I'll look for on your behalf will be those who can see what's inside your heart, inside your mind, inside the things in life that you view as important. They will appreciate both the inner and the outer you. And remember, as the contract says, if I can't find, in six months, at least three people who I would consider to be of high interest to you, you'll get a full refund. I'm not going to expect you to wait around forever. Give me six months, and we'll see what happens."

Pamela thought for a moment. Then she sat forward in her chair and patted Madrid's desk with the palm of her hand. "Give me those papers. I'll sign them, and we'll see what happens. I guess I'll trust what you say, that you think you can find someone for me. In the meantime, Mister Biggins will be right by my side."

"Well, you'd better make sure he doesn't get too attached," Madrid said as she handed some paperwork to Pamela. "Because my guess is that he's going to have to be sharing your attention soon."

"Yeah, well, just be sure to put down in that profile you're writing about me that I have to be with a cat lover. No man is going to replace Mister Biggins. He's going to have to share."

" 'I'mmmm always chasing rainnnn-bows,' " Raphael sang out after Pamela had left.

"Stop it," Madrid told him.

"Okay. How's this one? 'To dream, the impossible dream . . .' "

"Don't be mean," Madrid chided as she stood up from her desk and walked to the filing cabinet.

"I'm *not* being mean."

Madrid shot Raphael a glare.

"Okay, well, maybe I am. But, honey, you have got your work cut out for you, trying to find a match for that woman. She *is* a woman, right? Because I detected the faint outline of a moustache on her upper lip. And what comes out of that mouth of hers! She swears like a female Ozzy Osborne. Except, of course, she's not dictionary-challenged the way he is. She should be signing up for an anger-management course, not a matchmaking service. And what was all that talk about power tools and—"

"You *are* being mean. And hypercritical."

"Mad, come *on.* If she wasn't straight, I'd say she was the poster child for Bull-Dykes of America."

"So? She's a person. She wants to find love."

"As do most people. But, honey, let's be realistic. She may be tilting at heart-shaped windmills for the rest of her life. And those windmills are going to be heading for the hills as fast as they can. She could've been one of Teddy Roosevelt's Rough Riders. Admit it. She's *quite* rough around the edges. Good God—all she *is* is edges! Here's Pamela," he said as he held a hand up in the air. "Here's me touching her," he continued as he slid a finger down the side of his hand. "Ow! Ow! Rough! And she seems to have an unnatural attachment to her cat. I thought only lesbians did that. She's going to be a mess—well, she is already—but she's going to be an even *worse* mess when that furball known as Mister Biggins passes through those *purr*-ly gates."

"Now you're being nasty."

"I'm just calling it as I see it. You know, it might be a good idea to set some sort of parameters for who you accept as a client. I don't think you should take in everyone who walks through these doors. Or waddles. Or crawls. Or slithers."

"Like what sort of parameters?"

"Not Pamela, for instance. Honey, I just want you to succeed at this business venture of yours. I really do. But you know as well as I do that some people are going to be very, very difficult to find matches for."

"Succeed? Look at all the clients I signed up at today's open house," Madrid answered as she pointed to a stack of papers on her desk. "And each day this week is booked solid with appointments. I have no doubt that this is already a success."

"I'm not talking about *signing* clients. I'm talking about *finding* them matches. That'll be the measure of your success."

"I'll find them matches."

"Oh, really? Are we looking through the same glasses at Pamela, or are yours rose-colored?"

"Okay, so she's going to be a challenge. I admit that," Madrid said as she walked back to her desk and sat down. "But I believe there's someone for everyone. That's why I added that line to the Cuor D'Angelo Web site. 'Someone for everyone.' "

"Then maybe *you're* tilting at heart-shaped windmills. I just don't want you to get discouraged when you have to refund her money. How does that actually work, by the way? You contact someone after six months and say, 'Give it up. You ain't never gonna be someone's dreamboat?' "

"I'm *not* refunding her money. Or anyone else's, for that matter. You know how much I like a challenge. You tell me I *can't* do something, and the next thing you know, I'm doing just what you told me I couldn't do."

"True. But I thought that applied only to illegal substances and immoral acts."

"Which I've given up, as you know full well. But I'm *not* giving up on the Pamelas of the world. They deserve love as much as anyone else."

"That's very noble of you, Mad. It really is. And might I add that it's at times like this that I wish I could play the violin. Because I think some music should accompany your blind determination. But just be sure not to take this new focus of yours—of doing good for the lonely-hearts of the world—too far."

Madrid smiled. "That's funny that you'd say that to me. Because that's exactly what I told Lon the other night. Her big event at La Mira West for the women and children of Home Safe Home is tomorrow afternoon, and she's running herself ragged over it."

"Is that the Mother's Day dinner?"

Madrid nodded. "Lon was going on and on about how much the women and their kids are going to love the dinner, and how she hasn't been sleeping much at all to prepare for it, and how *next year's* event is going to be even better. Next year's! And then she starts telling me about other dinners she could have for people in need. So I said, 'Hey, slow down. Take a deep breath, and just get through *this* year's first. Remember, you can't feed *everyone*.'"

"And you, my darling, can't find a match for everyone."

"You want to bet on that?"

Raphael thought for a moment. "Normally, I would never bet against you. You're someone who always does what she says she's going to do. But in this case . . . yes, in this case, I'm going to take that bet. I say you *don't* find a match for Miss-slash-Mister Pamela."

"What's the time frame?"

Raphael shrugged his shoulders. "Six months?"

Madrid shook her head. "I want a quick payoff."

"You're *that* confident?"

Madrid nodded her head.

"A month?"

"When's my birthday, lover-boy?"

"I believe that would be in another week, old biddy. The big three-oh, is it not?"

"You know it is. So here's the bet. I'm going to find someone for Pamela *before* my birthday."

"Get out!"

"I will not. This is *my* office. *You* get out."

"In less than a week? You're going to find a match for Pamela in less than a week?"

"Something wrong with your hearing?"

"Something wrong with your grip on reality?"

"*Before* my birthday, bucko. That's the bet. Unless you're scared. Are you scared?"

"Oh, I'm quaking in my Louis Vuitton mocs. How much?"

Madrid shook her head. "It's not for money, brave lad. It's for the honor."

"Oh, puh-leeze," Raphael said as he rolled his eyes at her.

"You must do the honorable thing."

"What's that? Parade up and down the streets of New York yelling, 'Madrid was right! Madrid was right!' "

"No. That would be too easy. I know how much you love a parade. I want you to do something even better. I want you to take out a full page ad. In *The New York Times*. In the Sunday edition. It's going to be one big, fat apology penned by you about how wrong you were about my matchmaking skills. With, of course, in big, bold letters, the name of my business, the phone number, and the Web site address."

"And what do *I* get?"

Madrid showed Raphael a half-smile. "I'll cover your hours at the store one day a week for the next three months so you can write your screenplay."

"Serious?"

Madrid nodded her head. "Serious."

"Deal. This is going to be so great! Because you know I've been wanting to write, but haven't had time."

"Oh, I *know* that. But I'm afraid that will continue to be your dream. I'm *not* going to lose the bet."

"Don't bet on that."

"Oh, but I am. And Raphael?"

"Yes?"

"Remember, I *never* lose."

Raphael placed a finger by his lips and furrowed his eyebrows. "You never lose—is that what you said?"

Madrid nodded her head. "That's what I said."

"Then please refresh my mind again as to what happened with that annual check you receive."

"Low blow."

"Truth."

"You suck."

"Sometimes."

"You're going to lose."

"No, *you* are."

Madrid stood up from her desk. "Time for you to go. I've got work to do. But be sure to keep your cell phone nearby. I'll probably be calling you shortly to say, as graciously as I possibly can, 'I won! I won! I won! I won!'"

Raphael stood up and walked to the door. "And just how many tickets do you want when the play, based on a book written by *moi,* opens on Broadway? One for you, and one for the crow who's going to eat your words?" Raphael gave Madrid a quick wave and tossed an air-kiss in her direction. "Ta-ta."

"Hey, guys!" London yelled over the sound of pots and pans clanging together, dozens of waitstaff scurrying about chaotically as they barked out pleas for more orders of food and filled their trays with clean silverware and water glasses, and a gyrating cooking staff—grillers, line chefs, bakers, and all of the chefs' assistants—scampering up and down the line of ovens and stoves in the massive La Mira West kitchen calling out commands to one another.

"Guys!" London tried again. "Just one minute of your attention, please!"

The noise level downgraded slightly.

"Enough with the baskets of bread, okay?" she asked as she waved an arm in front of her. "There must be a dozen baskets scattered around this serving area countertop, and we need to keep it free."

"Some woman keeps asking for white bread," a female voice called out to London over the din. "So I make up a basket and bring it out to her, and she keeps sending it back. Where am I *supposed* to put it?"

"Must be from the table I'm waiting on, Julie," a male voice replied before London could answer. "*If* it's the same woman. She says to me, 'I want white bread,' and then, when I put a basket of it on the table, she says, 'I don't want *that.*' Lucinda says we're always supposed to put out *fresh* bread whenever anyone asks for more, and so I just keep filling new baskets."

"Yeah, yeah. That's the one, Tom," Julie called back. "I'm just ignoring her now."

"Cinda, FYI. We don't *have* an unlimited supply of bread," Cindy offered up as she clapped two flour-coated hands together, setting a puffy white cloud loose in the air. "I have enough desserts, but we didn't even *think* about needing a lot of bread for this event. I have dough prepared for this week. Do you want me to start baking some sourdough rolls? I don't have time for the pecan sticky buns, though."

"Just keep bringing out the same basket," offered up a woman who was tearing up salad greens.

"I don't have time," Tom answered her. "I'm barely keeping up with the appetites out there."

"No one's eating the damn bread," a new male voice contributed. "No offense, Cindy. But they're concentrating on the meal."

"As well they should," Lucinda called out. "Cindy, just stay focused on the dessert preparation. We'll probably be serving that up in about forty-five minutes or so."

"Gotcha."

Lucinda turned her attention to a man who was bent over an open oven door. "Maurice, how are we holding up on the pork tenderloins?"

"A-okay," Maurice told her. "I need more cranberry-avocado salsa, though. I can serve it without, but that's what's on the menu."

"Coming up with the salsa," someone answered.

"Thank you, Jenny," Lucinda replied. "What about the eggplant, Carlos?"

"Not lookin' good, boss lady. Five more servings—tops," Carlos answered.

"Heat up another roasted carrot-and-parsnip casserole," Lucinda suggested.

"They're eating the carrots and pushing the parsnips onto their bread plates," Tom offered up.

"Well, there's nothing we can do about that," Lucinda answered.

"How are we on the kids' meals?" London asked as she carried an armload of bread baskets to a corner of the kitchen serving area and began stacking them.

"I've got a dozen bacon, turkey, and cheese sandwiches ready to flip on the grill," answered a man who was holding a spatula in each of his hands.

"I'm serving up the last bowl of spaghetti and meatballs," a female voice answered.

"Heat up that pan of mac and cheese that's in the walk-in," Lucinda called out. "Someone grab it, please. It's on the second shelf, left, toward the back." She turned to London. "I thought we had this all figured out. We had enough for everyone, or so we thought."

"The kids're eating like it's their last meal," one of the waitstaff tossed out over her shoulder as she scurried past Lucinda and London and dropped a tray on the counter. "I need four more oinkers, light on the salsa on three, heavy on one!" she called out, and then turned back to London and Lucinda. "I saw one skinny little Vietnamese girl down five bowls of spaghetti in less than fifteen minutes. *Five bowls!* Imagine that! She can't weigh more than forty-eight pounds. Although now she's probably doubled her weight. She wanted more, so I just gave her a grilled sandwich. I swear to God, I don't know where she's putting it all."

"I thought these people were homeless," Julie said as she filled a tray with steaming plates of food. "It's like they haven't eaten in weeks."

"Homeless, hungry—what does it matter?" London asked. "We'll feed them until they can't eat any more."

"Or until we run out of food," Lucinda added. "Whichever comes first."

London picked up another armload of bread baskets. "Sorry about this, Cinda."

"About what?"

"About how we didn't anticipate they'd be so hungry."

"Not to worry, Lon. That's why I made up the mac and cheese. Just in case. We won't run out of food."

"Christ, I hope I have enough desserts," Cindy blurted out as she removed a tray of freshly baked pies from the oven. "Sixteen apples. This is the last of 'em. Eight blueberry pies are chilling in the walk-in, along with a dozen Boston creams. Yesterday we finished with the cookies—we have about two hundred M & M cookies. There are five frosted strawberry angel-food cakes. Ten dozen éclairs. And gallons of ice cream."

"Do you know how many people are on their *third* complete main course?" a waitress asked as she placed both hands against the counter and leaned forward. "Man, my dogs are hurting. We're not having an all-you-can-eat contest, by any chance, are we?"

"Just go with it, people," Lucinda called out above the kitchen sounds, which had cranked back up in volume.

"Oh, we're *going* with it," a male voice yelled back in reply. "All I can say is, thank God we're closed tomorrow. I'm taking the phone off the hook and not getting out of bed unless I gotta pee."

"Where's the white bread?" a waitress shouted as she slammed through the kitchen doors. "There's a woman out there who keeps saying, 'I want white bread. I want white bread—*now!*'"

London picked up a breadbasket from the counter. "I'll bring it out to her. Which table is she at?"

"Eight. But watch out. She's a bit nasty."

"White bread!" Rhonda cried out in a boisterous greeting as she watched London walk up to her table.

"Why didn't you *say* you wanted to see me?" London asked, and then held up the breadbasket. "Instead of asking for this."

"Hey, I didn't ask for no bread," Rhonda chuckled, and then reached out and delivered a quick punch to the arm of the woman who was sitting next to her at the table. "Git up and go visit your kids, Ruth," she commanded.

"I'm still eatin'," Ruth snapped at Rhonda.

"Take yer damn plate wid you, then. Gimme me five here wid white bread."

Ruth grabbed her napkin, scooped up her plate, and shot Rhonda a glare as she got up from the table.

"Oh, yeah, Ruthie. Like that cuts me like a knife. Sit, sit!" Rhonda ordered London as she spanked the seat of the vacated chair with the palm of her hand.

London dropped the breadbasket on the table and slipped into the chair. "If you had asked to see *me*, I would've come out. Do you know how many baskets of white bread were brought out to you? They're now stacked sky-high in the kitchen."

Rhonda released a loud laugh. "I know! Dat's pretty funny, how dey kept bringin' 'em out an' bringin' 'em out. When you wasn't showin' up, I thought to myself, 'How long can dey be doin' dat, bringin' dem baskets out ta me? I think I counted 'bout eight or so."

"Try a dozen."

Rhonda let out another loud laugh. "Excellent!"

"You *do* know that my name is London, right?"

"Honey, you always be white bread to me. I kinda like that name. You don't look like no country to me anyway."

"Actually, London's a city."

"You don't look like no city, neither."

London gave Rhonda a smile and shook her head.

"You be wantin' some bread?" Rhonda said as she waved a palm at the breadbasket.

London sat back in the chair and crossed her arms over her chest. "I'm all set."

"Now don't you think I be lookin' darn pretty?" Rhonda asked her. "This here dress is jus' what I be wantin'."

"It does look nice on you."

"All dese sunflowers are so glorious, don't you think? And dey be matchin' these here flowers on da table. I gotta tell ya, white bread, you done a good job here. A real fine job. The food! My oh my, but it is meltin' in my mouth. Shore is a difference a'tween heatin' it up an' eatin' it fresh from da oven. An' settin' up dem kids at dat whole 'nother table. Dat's another one of dem good ideas. Dey be likin' dat, 'cuz it makes 'em feel pretty darn adult. An' it gives us moms a break from 'em, you know? Like we're at our own special dinner."

"You *are* at your own special dinner," London said and then glanced over at a long line of tables set up in a corner of the main dining room. "Sitting the kids at their own table was my idea. The meal, of course, is all Lucinda's doing. And the desserts are going to be fabulous."

"Dat Lucinda is one special lady," Rhonda said as she picked up her napkin from her lap and wiped it across her face.

London nodded her head. "That she is."

"Yes, she is," Rhonda agreed, and then dropped her napkin next to her plate. "She be a good influence on you, if you let her be, white bread. You oughtta spend more time wid her, is what I be sayin'."

"Oh, I'm spending a lot of time with her. Every day but Monday, here at the restaurant. Although most Mondays we both end up here anyway. She's taught me a lot about cooking. And, truth be told, about how to run a business. She was the one who kept my club going before it switched over to a restaurant."

Rhonda nodded. "I know dat. But I tell ya, Lucinda could keep de *world* runnin'."

"That she could."

"You should be spendin' more time wid her."

"I just told you that I spend every day but—"

"I be meanin' *socially,* white bread. You get my drift?"

London stared at Rhonda for a few seconds. "Not really."

"Um. Didn't think so. What I be sayin' is, I think Lucinda done like you."

"And I like her."

"I mean, she *likes* you."

"And I *like* her."

"You bein' dense now."

"I don't think I'm being dense."

"Well, y'are. I be sayin' you need to ask Lucinda out."

"Out of the restaurant?"

"Good Christy! Dat's what a college degree done buy? I don't think I be needin' one den, thank you very much."

"You're welcome. I guess."

"Okay, dumber den a doornail. Listen up. I say, you need to ask Lucinda out. *On a date,* white bread. 'Cuz she be likin' you in *dat* way. I know she ain't fancy like all dem other ladies you be wid a'fore. But she's a downright good person, a good soul. You be wid someone like her, an' you never be gettin' in trouble again. Like the love of a good man, the love of a good woman be all de same. I ain't no prejudiced person."

"You *do* call me white bread."

"You *are* white. Dat ain't prejudice. Dat accurate.

Anyways, I done know it irks de hell outta you, so dat's why I keep sayin' it."

"Okay. Well, I'm glad you're enjoying this Mother's Day dinner," London said as she sat up in her chair and reached for the breadbasket. "Guess I'll take this back into the kitchen and see if I can help out with the desserts."

Rhonda placed a hand on London's arm. "I ain't done talkin', white bread. Set back down dere. Now, how you feel 'bout Lucinda?"

"I told you. I like her."

"Enough ta be askin' her out?"

"She doesn't want to go out with me, Rhonda."

"You sure 'bout dat?"

"Of course I'm sure. I'm someone she works with. I'm someone who used to be her boss."

"So?"

"So . . ." London began, and then paused. "She, well, I'm sure she's not interested in me in *that* way. She saw what I was like, she knew me . . . well, let's just put it this way. I'm not someone she much admires, for a lot of reasons. We get along great now, so let's just leave it at that."

"People's opinions can change, don'cha think? Dat's 'cuz *people* can change. An' I think you done be goin' through some changes. Don't think she ain't noticed. An' don't think dat even when you was a wildcat, she weren't interested in you. I done see de way she looks at you. I seen de way she is when she's wid you. A'fore you started comin' wid her for the Home Safe Home deliveries, she'd be nice 'n all. *Pleasant,* more is to de point. But not really all *there.* Kinda distracted-like, I guess. Like she got things on her mind she be thinkin' 'bout. But when she's wid you, she be focused. Really *there.* An' she's got herself a little bit of a spring in her step when she's 'round you. Not like a boingy-boingy one. More like a bing-bong, bing-bong. You see?"

"Not really."

Rhonda sighed. "Okay. I be spellin' it out for ya. It's the *way* she looks at you when you ain't lookin' at her, white bread. She *watches* you. She *hangs* on yer words. You got yourself dere someone who would love fer you ta throw her a bone. Dat is, if yer interested. If you're not, den I think yer one dumb woman. 'Cuz you'll never find no one better'n Lucinda. She's a gem of a woman. A real sparklin' diamond. An' I *know* you likes diamonds."

London placed a chin in her hand and thought for a moment. "You're right, Rhonda. Cinda *is* a gem of a person. But not me. I'm no gem."

"But you *be* wid a gem, an' some o' dat sparkle'll rub off on you. She *make* you a better person. Trust me on dat. Whatcha got ta lose? Ask her out. Somethin' simple. A movie. Ain't no harm in dat. Take her out fer an afternoon walk in de park. Or out fer a drive, maybe over de bridge ta Sausilito. Git to know her outside 'a da kitchen, outside 'a work. Yer gonna find a real sweetheart of a woman. You sure will."

"Well, I—"

Rhonda leaned forward and wagged a finger in front of London's face. "But if I hear dat yer not treatin' her right, I'll rip ya from bone ta bone, you hear me?"

London raised her eyebrows at Rhonda. "I think you mean limb to limb."

"Bone, limb—it'll hurt, is all I'm sayin'." Rhonda let out a sigh, sat back in her chair, and then patted her belly. "Now where dem desserts be, white bread? Git hoppin', wouldja?"

"Good night!"

"Good night! And thank you!" Lucinda called back to the last of the kitchen cleanup crew as they made a slow, shuffling exit out of the back doors of La Mira West.

"See you tomorrow!" London added.

"*Tuesday!*" one of the group yelled back. "Geesch! Give us a break, wouldya?"

"Right," London mumbled as she lifted a hand in a wave, then dropped it as she watched the door slam shut behind the group.

"Well!" Lucinda exclaimed as she closed her eyes for a moment, sighed, and then slowly made her way to a kitchen stool and sat down. She surveyed the gleaming kitchen. "No leftovers, Lon. Remember how we thought we'd have a lot of food left? They picked us clean. I was going to heat up that mac and cheese for Tuesday noon, but we finished off that tray. Guess I'll have to make up another batch."

"I can do that," London said as she pulled out another kitchen stool and sat down.

Lucinda turned to London and smiled. "Would you? Could you put that together tomorrow, do you think?"

London nodded her head. "Absolutely. I'll be in tomorrow, and I'll do whatever you want me to."

"Thank you. You're wonderful, Lon. You've been a real help. And this idea of yours—wow! What a hit! The ladies and their children really, really enjoyed it."

"I think we'll get some good press out of it, too."

Lucinda immediately lost her smile. "You're joking, right?"

London shook her head. "No. I think we'll get good press."

Lucinda bit her lip, and then shrugged her shoulders. "Is *that* why you did this, Lon? To get good press?" She shook her head. "Oh, why should I have thought otherwise? Of *course* you did. After all, you want to get your money back—what is it, about a week until your birthday deadline?—so you can return to the luxurious lifestyle to which you were accustomed. Then you won't have to waste your time here, slaving away in a kitchen. How beneath you that must seem!"

"That's not true, Cinda. I only mentioned the press because it will bring more attention to places like Home Safe Home. Maybe other restaurants would want to run similar events. Good press is *always* good. And today's event has nothing to do with me at all."

"Lon, I saw you talking to the reporters. Tell me you weren't talking yourself up."

"I wasn't."

"Right." Lucinda reached her arms behind her back and began to untie her apron.

"I'll prove it to you," London said as she stood up and reached into the back pocket of her white slacks. "Here are my talking points." She glanced down at a piece of paper jammed full with scribbled notes. "Let's see. The Home Away from Homelessness project, which includes a total of twelve shelters in the San Francisco area, also includes The Learning Center, a Life Skills College, and—" London stopped and looked up at Lucinda. "Is this of any interest to you at all?"

Lucinda fumbled with the knot on her apron. "I'm listening."

"Okay." London scanned her notes. "Blah, blah what the program includes. I told the reporter the number of people the program services each year. The breakdown of program participants, which I got when I talked to the director last week. Forty-seven percent are African-American, sixteen percent are Caucasian—or, as Rhonda would put it, white bread—five percent are Asian, twelve are of mixed descent. I told the reporter about—"

"Damn! I can't get this," Lucinda broke in as she tugged on the knot.

"I'll get it," London said as she slipped the paper back into her pocket. "I also told the reporter that you were in charge of the entire event. I gave her Cindy Freeman's name as the person responsible for the desserts. I gave her a list of all the businesses that contributed to the gift baskets. I know you don't believe me—gosh, you've really got yourself bound up here," London commented as she stood behind Lucinda and pulled on the apron ties.

"Oh, just take a pair of scissors and cut it. I've got enough aprons."

"Let me give it a shot."

"I'm too tired. I just want to go home and go to bed."

"Patience, please. I can do this. So, as I was saying, even though you think that this event was something that I pushed for, for my own selfish reasons, that could *not* be further from the truth. I've learned to live for months on the money I earn here. I have plenty. I wear the same clothes every day—white slacks, white shirt, white jacket. The only time I take my flashy car out for a spin is to come here and then to go back home. I haven't been shopping for weeks. I haven't had a pedicure, a manicure, a hair coloring or a styling. I haven't gone to the spa for a day of pampering. I haven't been on a trip."

"Have you forgotten Anguilla already?"

London grinned. "Oh, yeah. Well, I've been *there*. But nowhere else. And even though it may be of little interest to you, I haven't smoked, I haven't used drugs, and as for drinking, now and again I'll have a glass of wine."

"I've noticed those things."

"My point is, I don't need anything right now. I'm getting by, and I'm okay. To be honest, once I started working here, I haven't had time to think about my birthday or the damn deadline Gamma gave Madrid and me. You keep me pretty busy, Cinda. But in a good way. I really like working here. And I like cooking. I was even thinking that maybe I could take some courses, learn more so I can do better here."

"You don't need to go to school to learn what you're learning here. And if there's anything you want to know, just ask me."

"I will. I *do*. There," London said as she held up the apron ties. "You've come undone."

Lucinda turned on the kitchen stool to face London. "Free at last."

London met Lucinda's eyes.

"How come you look so wide awake?" Lucinda asked.

London shrugged her shoulders. "I guess the night hasn't caught up to me yet."

"Well, I'm ready for bed," Lucinda said, and then let out a yawn. She raised her arms above her head and groaned as she stretched them. "I'm not setting the alarm for tomorrow. That means I'll probably be in later than usual."

"Okay."

"Are you ready to get going?"

"Yeah. There's just one thing."

"What's that?"

"Would you like to do something?"

"Now?"

"Well, no. But something?"

Lucinda looked at London and blinked her eyes. "What do you mean?"

"*Sometime.* Would you . . . would you like to do something? Sometime? With me?"

"I guess."

"Like a movie. Or we could go for a walk in the park."

"You don't mean now, right?"

London shook her head. "No. I mean sometime. If you want to. We could do something sometime."

"Okay."

"So you wouldn't mind?"

"Mind what?"

"Doing something? Sometime? With me?"

"London, what the heck are you babbling about?"

London took in a deep breath. "I want to know . . . I want to know if you want to go out. Sometime."

"Go out?"

London nodded her head.

"You don't mean like on a date, do you?"

"Actually, I do."

Lucinda's eyes widened slightly. "You're asking *me* out?"

"Probably quite badly. But yes. That's what I'm fumbling through right now. Having never asked someone out before, I don't quite know how it's done. I know that a wink and a nod can get someone into bed. But I don't know how to get someone to do anything that's not . . . that's not bed, I guess."

"You're asking me out on a *date? Me?* With *you?*"

London swallowed. "Well, that doesn't sound too positive."

"I'm just trying to understand what you're asking."

"Okay. Here it is. I was thinking of us going out on a date. Together. Of you going out with me. Anyway," London turned away from Lucinda and pushed her kitchen stool under the counter, "it was just a thought."

"Do you know how long I've . . . well, no, you probably wouldn't."

"Wouldn't what?"

"Wouldn't—never mind." Lucinda pulled in a breath, and then released it. "Lon, I would like to go out on a date with you."

"You would?"

Lucinda nodded.

London smiled and then knocked the knuckles of a hand against the stainless steel counter. "Ow. Okay. Okay! Yes, okay. Okay! This is good. This is good—it's great! Great! So, you want to go out on a date with me, right?"

Lucinda returned the smile. "Yes, I do. But not tonight."

"No—no! Of course not tonight."

"When?"

"When." London thought for a moment. "When? How can we do this, if we work six nights a week?"

"You mentioned the park. We could do a picnic in the park on a Monday. We could call that a date. If it's raining, we could go to a matinee. That could be a date. A date doesn't have to be at night."

"Right. Okay. Great!"

"One question, Lon."

"What's that?"

"Why?"

"Why what?"

"Why are you asking me out?"

"Because you're . . . you're *you*."

"Yes. I *am* me. But I'm not like any of the other women you've dated before. I'm not sexy or rich or beautiful or—"

"I didn't *date* them, Cinda. I had sex with them."

"So why me?" Lucinda asked, and then let out a soft chuckle. "Because you know you've got a snowball's chance in hell of ever getting me in a sex room."

London wiggled one eyebrow up and down. "Oh, you think?" She immediately held up her hands. "Kidding! I'm just kidding. *Really!*"

"I just like a natural progression to things, Lon. And that means that I need to get to know someone first."

"Yes. Well. Since I don't know what a natural progression really is, I bow to your experience on that."

"So answer my question. Why me?"

"Because you've treated me better than anyone else ever has. Except for Gamma. You're wonderful to me. You don't judge me—well, except about the sex rooms. And my drinking. And the way I used to behave. And how I ignored the club. And my letting in underage drinkers. All right. Well, that's all in the past, isn't it? *Now* you seem to genuinely like me for who I am. And for who I'm *discovering* I am."

"But why me? Do you understand what I'm asking you? I don't want to go out with someone just because they think I'm nice. Most people *do* think I'm nice. But I'd like to know that there's an interest there beyond the nice. Beyond just a friendship. I guess what I'm wondering is, is there an attraction there? An attraction that you might have toward me?"

London met Lucinda's eyes. "An attraction? Well, there was one night here at the restaurant. It was a Saturday. A few weeks ago. It had been busier than usual. The kitchen staff was stressed, the waitstaff was stressed. I swear the food was even stressed. And just when it seemed like things were about to explode in the kitchen, when things had reached a boiling point, you called out to everyone, 'One more hour, folks. Let's just get through another sixty minutes, and I guarantee you, it'll be a whole different world in here.' It was as if the kitchen took in a deep breath and then let it out, and everyone's mood changed."

Lucinda nodded. "I remember that night."

"And then you looked over at me, gave me a slight nod as if to say, 'There. That takes care of it.' You turned back to whatever you were doing, but I kept looking at you and feeling this . . . this *something*. I don't know what it was—but I felt it *inside* me. I had this urge to walk over to you and wrap my arms around you." London looked down at the floor and shook her head. "And the weird thing was, I wanted to feel your arms around me. I imagined what it would be like to hug you, and then I thought about kissing you, and then the grill flared up and you rushed over to make sure everything was okay. *But that feeling!* That feeling has just stuck with me ever since that night. It made me feel good. *You* made me feel good." London looked up at Lucinda. "Was that okay to say?"

Lucinda nodded her head. "It was not only okay, it was the nicest thing anyone's ever said to me. Anyone outside of my family, that is. You can say things like that to me whenever you'd like, Lon."

"Okay."

"And I apologize for accusing you of only thinking of yourself with today's event."

"Why *wouldn't* you think that? I mean, you *know* I'm a selfish, self-centered person."

"I think I *knew* someone who was once like that. But I haven't seen her around much lately."

"Good riddance to her, then."

"Yes, good riddance. Let's lock up and call it a night, shall we?"

London nodded her head. "We shall."

12

"**O**ur birthday is coming at the *worst* possible time," Madrid said as she steered her car down an entrance ramp and then onto the Massachusetts Turnpike.

"Tell me about it," London agreed as she pushed a button to close her window and turned on the air conditioning. "Truck," she pointed out as she glanced up from adjusting the passenger-side fan and then immediately pushed her right foot against the floor carpeting.

"See it."

"Jesus!" London gasped. She leaned back in her seat as she watched the back of a Budweiser semi grow closer. "Would you slow down! Our party isn't until tonight. *What's* the rush?" she demanded as Madrid veered the car into a passing lane and sped past the truck.

"I *feel* rushed."

"Well, we're *not* rushed. We got an early start this morning and it's not even noon. I don't want to be white-knuckling this ride the whole way to Concord. I'm tense enough as it is."

"I *know* how to drive, Lon."

"Everyone who learned how to drive in Massachusetts says that."

"And New York City has only refined my skills. You get no road challenges in San Francisco, do you?"

"None at all. I only have to deal with roller-coaster hills, tons of steep, banked turns, and cable car tracks that become as slippery as black ice whenever it rains."

"As I said, you get no challenges," Madrid answered as she veered to the right to get around a slower-moving vehicle, then pulled in front of it and veered to the left to avoid getting too close to the back of another tractor-trailer truck. She glanced over at London. "Stop hyperventilating. Why don't you push your seat back and take a nap? You looked like shit when you got off the airplane last night."

"Thanks, sis. I can always depend upon you to make me feel better about myself."

"I'm serious, Lon. You still look like you haven't slept in weeks."

"I've been keeping some pretty late nights lately."

"Please tell me you haven't returned to the party days of yore."

"Of yore? What's *of yore?* Oh, never mind. I don't want to know. No, I haven't been partying. *Believe me.* I've mostly been working. And, well, I've kind of been—"

"Then take a nap for the next couple of hours," Madrid broke in as she turned and reached an arm around the back of the driver's seat.

"What are you doing? Don't take your eyes off the road!"

"I'm trying to find my CD case. I want to listen to some music."

"Why don't you just concentrate on the Race to Concord? I think we're in first place."

"You know, maybe if you didn't *watch* my driving, you'd feel better."

"I'd much rather *see* my life flash before my eyes than go

out with my eyes closed. Just as an FYI to me, how the hell fast are you going?"

"It's only a little over the speed limit."

"A little? Well, then, we'll end up only a *little* dead."

"Would you *relax!*"

"I can't. It's not just because of your driving. I feel wound up inside."

"What are you so tense about?" Madrid asked as she veered into the third lane of the highway and passed a line of cars that were already going well over the speed limit.

London shook her head. "I don't know. I guess leaving the restaurant for the weekend. It's the busiest time during the week. I took a look in the reservation book before I left, and we were booked solid, including two parties of ten. That'll keep the place hopping. I hate thinking about people having to work harder because I'm not there. Lucinda doesn't have someone else who can step in and do what I do. I wish I were staying there instead of going home. I feel bad about dumping all the work in her lap."

"She'll do fine without you. She did just fine before you started working there."

"I know."

"And it's just two days."

"Two of the *busiest* days."

"Move or get out of the damn lane!" Madrid shouted at the car ahead of her, which was now being passed by cars on the right. She flashed her high beams on and off at the car. "Idiot!"

"You seem pretty relaxed," London deadpanned as she crossed her legs. "Why are you in such an all-fired rush to get home?"

Madrid shrugged her shoulders, eased up a bit on the accelerator, and settled back into the driver's seat. "I guess I feel the same way you do. *Wound up* is a good way to describe it. And I'm not happy, either, leaving work behind for the weekend. I've just started a new business, and now I'm closing up after only being open for a short time. That's not a good thing. It's not very business-savvy to put out the message, 'I'm open,' and then the message, 'But now I'm closed.' Weekends are pretty busy for me, too. That's when I get a lot of calls or walk-ins. I brought a laptop with me, though, so I'll at least be able to keep up with the searches for the clients I've already signed. Believe me, I'd much rather be in New York than in Concord."

"It does seem pretty ridiculous to have to sacrifice an entire weekend to celebrate our birthday," London said. "We haven't celebrated any of our other birthdays since we left the childhood home behind."

"Gamma wanted it. She wanted us to come home for our thirtieth."

"Wanted it? She absolutely *demanded* it," London corrected her. "She sent me my plane ticket and then called and told me, 'I *expect* you girls to be home for the weekend. We're all going to be together for your thirtieth birthday. This is a *big* one.' "

"Yeah, *all* of us. Like Mother, Dad, and Gamma are *all* of us. Woo-hoo! That's a major celebration, don't you think?"

"Well, that *is* all of us."

"I would think fifty or sixty would be considered *big* ones. I don't think thirty is big, do you?"

London shrugged her shoulders. "I guess it's *supposed* to be big. After all, we're leaving our twenties behind. The twenties are supposed to be filled with angst. Filled with self-discovery and experimentation. Filled with—"

"Crap," Madrid broke in. "All we did is act out. And act up."

"Act immature."

"Act crazy."

"Act spoiled."

"Good riddance is what I say," Madrid said as she sped up when the car in front of her signaled it would be making a move to a slower lane. "To that car, as well as to our twenties. They were fun while they lasted, but . . ."

"But," London echoed, and then sighed. "We got into *a lot* of trouble, didn't we?"

Madrid smiled. "Oh, yeah. That we did. We're the girls formerly known as the big, bad La Mira twins. But we've gotten all that stuff out of our systems now, haven't we? *I'm* not going there again."

"Me neither."

"I don't have the time, and I don't have the energy. All those past times, both the good and the bad, should be things we store in our memory banks. They can be things we can retrieve when we're old ladies sitting in rocking chairs when life is passing us by. Then we can say to each other, 'Hey, remember the time we . . .' "

"I hope we *never* feel that way. That life is passing us by, I mean. I want to be like Gamma when I'm her age. I want to be going places, doing things, enjoying life to the fullest. But I agree with you. Those days are *so* over for me. I remember *being* there, but it seems like those times were so long ago. Like I was a different person then—very different from the way I am now."

Madrid nodded her head and then sighed. "I have to admit, lately I sometimes *feel* like I'm thirty. Ever since Christmas, I feel like I've aged a decade. I feel more like I'm forty than thirty."

"I know what you mean. Life has certainly taken us on a lot of twists and turns since Gamma's money-deprivation experiment began. But we've done okay for ourselves, don't you think?"

"Sure, *now* we have. But look at what it took to get to where we are now. I killed sea turtles."

"*Baby* sea turtles."

"Thanks for the clarification. I had forgotten that they were babies."

"Thanks for telling me that I look like shit."

Madrid stayed quiet for a few moments. "I agree with you, Lon. We *have* done okay for ourselves. I may not be able to name three places in the world where unfortunate people are living in bad conditions—"

"Dire circumstances."

"Right. You remembered Gamma's words exactly. And I may not be able to identify some of the diseases people have, but I *am* able to earn a living and get up each day and feel like I'm *doing* something with my life."

London nodded her head. "I'm certainly not doing anything that will save the world, that's for sure. Not like Gamma ever did. But the Mother's Day dinner for the homeless women and their children turned out to be a great event, and La Mira West is still going strong."

"High-five to thirty, Lon," Madrid said as she held up the palm of a hand.

London patted Madrid's hand with her own. "Why can't we just call *that* our birthday celebration? I didn't want to make a big deal about it. I just wanted to do something simple. I think it's a waste of time for each of us to blow this entire weekend. Gamma knows we're working now. You can't just say, 'I'm going home for the weekend,' and expect the people you work with to be understanding. It's not a very considerate thing to do."

Madrid nodded. "Even when you work for yourself, you don't feel right taking time off. You have to be there for the people who use your service. You can't just pick and choose to be there when it's right for you."

London tossed an arm over the back of Madrid's seat. "Listen to us. *Working* girls. Talking about *work*."

"Who would've thought."

"Who would've thought," London echoed. "The funny thing is, I actually *like* what I'm doing."

"Me, too."

"I never thought I'd be living the way I am now. I get the coffeemaker ready the night before. I set an alarm in the morning. I haven't worn heels or gotten dressed up in I don't know how long. I don't get home until late at night, and when I do my body feels like it got hit by a truck. Which is probably why your driving is making me nervous. I sleep like a rock, without getting high or drunk. I'm asleep before my head even hits the pillow. And then I get up the next day and do it all over again."

"I'm the first business to open in the mini-mall," Madrid said. "And I'm usually the last one to lock its doors. I eat lunch at my desk—*if* I have the time. I love it, though, Lon. I really do."

London nodded her head. "I love what I do, too. I'm learning how to do more things all the time. When I first started out, I was just doing food prep—chopping and grating and things like that. Not very challenging things. Now I'm doing some of the cooking. I'm not actually *making* dishes on my own. But I'm assisting in the preparation of most everything. The other day I learned how to make sugar roses and decorated some cakes with them."

"You *make* those?" Madrid asked. "I thought you just bought them."

"Maybe you can buy them. But we make everything at the restaurant. I don't think Lucinda even buys stock."

"What does buying stocks have to do with a restaurant?"

"Not stocks. *Stock*. As in soup stock."

"I have no clue what that is."

"It's the liquid for the soup. It's made out of boiled vegetables—onions, celery, carrots, seasonings. You add chicken bones to make the stock for chicken soup, beef bones to make onion soup. And then you let it simmer for hours."

"And you *like* doing that? It seems so, I don't know, messy."

"It *is* messy."

"I thought you were like me. I don't *like* messy. I have to have everything just so. I still get my nails done. Yours look like crap, by the way."

"Again, thanks for the compliment. But you can't work in a kitchen and have nice-looking nails."

"And that doesn't bother you?"

"Not really. I have to wear a hairnet, too."

"Get out! *That* must look attractive."

"Who cares what I look like? The important thing is that the food looks good." London waved a hand in the air, clenched her teeth, and raised her chin. "It's *all* in the *pre*-sen-ta-tion, you know."

"Christ, it's a real sad state of affairs when dinner looks better than you do, Lon."

"And the whites that I wear—"

"Oh, God, *stop it,* would you? Don't you just *crave* putting on a nice Steve Fabrikant knitwear suit like the one you're wearing now? Oh, by the way—have you seen the new Germano Zama? It was in this month's *W.* I'd give my *eyetooth for that jacket.*"

"No, but I've read this month's *Bon Appetit.*"

"I'd rather read bon fashion. I can't believe all of your gorgeous clothes are just *hanging* in your closet."

"Where am I supposed to wear them, Mad? I get up every day and go to work in a kitchen, where I see no one but the kitchen staff, and then I go home late at night. I wear starched white slacks and a white button-down shirt. *Every day.* I won't even tell you about my white lace-up shoes—the ones I bought at Target for less than ten dollars."

"Thank you. I don't think I could handle that."

"I start out with nice, clean clothes in the morning, and then end up covered with grease and stains and smell like food and my own sweat by the end of the night."

"Stop it! You're making me nauseous. You *know* how I can't take cooking smells. Even *thinking* about them. I can't believe that you even *like* that!"

London gave a quick laugh. "Go figure. And I can't believe that you *like* fixing people up. You help people *fall in love.* What's up with that? You've always been known as the queen of hard hearts! Fuck 'em and leave 'em—hasn't that always been your motto?"

"Hey, I can't remember you being any less hard-hearted with your past lovers than I've been with mine. And wasn't that *your* motto?"

"Okay, so maybe it was. The key word being *was*. But we're not talking about me right now. We're talking about *you*. The only thing I've fallen in love with lately is cooking. You have no patience whatsoever with anyone other than yourself—and even then you don't have much patience—and you *hate* even the *concept* of feelings. Isn't match-making about relationships and love and all that gooey, starry-eyed stuff that you've always thought was useless and pathetic?"

Madrid sighed. "I know. I used to hate it when someone I was sleeping with wanted to talk about his feelings. Wanted to *process* things. Wanted to get to the *heart* of matters. I just didn't get it."

"Didn't one guy call you the Ice Maiden?"

Madrid nodded. "Yes. That Ice Maiden would be me. I think someone else called me the iceberg that sank the *Titanic*. And another called me Frigidaire. I don't think I was very nice—and certainly not very warm and fuzzy—to *any-one* I was having sex with. Because, to me, that was what it was all about. The Big O was all that mattered to me. But in-variably my bedmates would fall in love with me, and that was my signal to move on."

"You and me both. Although lately I've had—"

"Now it's like I can sit for hours listening to people talk about what they're looking for in a potential partner," Madrid continued. "Or about their past relationships. I find it fascinating. And then it's so cool when you can get an idea of that person, get an idea about another person, and then re-alize, 'You know, those two might hit it off together.' And then, of course, they do. Because my instincts have been dead-on right in every case. Sometimes it's positively scary."

"It means you're good at it."

"I guess I am. Which surprises the hell out of me. Where'd that come from?"

"Where'd my interest in cooking come from?"

"Who knew?" Madrid asked as she shrugged her shoulders. "The other day, one of my clients was telling me about this guy I had fixed her up with. They had gone out on their second date, and he had brought her flowers and candy and had even burned a CD for her with songs that he thought she'd like. I actually *felt* what she was telling me. Like I could understand how touched she had been by what he had done."

"I helped make a soufflé the other day, and it didn't fall."

"Is that a good thing?"

"Absolutely."

"God, we're getting *weird*, aren't we?" Madrid asked.

"Maybe turning thirty means you start turning a little weird. Maybe aging does something to your brain cells."

"Or something to your heart."

"How do you mean?"

"I think my iciness is melting a little. It feels like maybe I'm not so cold inside anymore."

"That's probably good, don't you think, Mad? Considering the business you're in. I don't think you can help people fall in love if your heart isn't into the whole concept to begin with."

"True." Madrid thought for a few moments. "You know, Lon, I don't think we would be having this conversation, let alone doing what we're doing in our lives, if it wasn't for Gamma. I know I wouldn't be."

"Me neither. La Mira West would still be a party-central nightclub. I'd still be using the sex rooms, taking off on trips to exotic destinations, going shopping for hours, and spending thousands and thousands of dollars."

"And we used to do that *all the time*."

London nodded her head. "And not so very long ago, either."

"Do you miss it?"

"What? The money? The sex rooms? The club, the way it used to be? Shopping?"

"All of it."

London thought for a moment. "Do you?"

Madrid immediately shook her head. "Not at all."

"You seem pretty certain."

"I am. Although maybe I do miss the shopping, just a little. For jewelry. For clothes. But you make do. That's what I've discovered. You just make do with what you have, rather than worry about getting more of what you don't have. Does that make sense?"

"Sure it does. I sometimes miss—how can I describe it—I guess the *ease* of how things used to be. The certainty, the predictability of it all. Even though in retrospect I know that the way I lived my life was fairly chaotic and out of control. But it was . . . it was *my* life. It was what I knew, what I had become accustomed to."

"I know what you're saying."

"Sometimes it's hard, living life the way it is now. It feels full of some things, like work. The days and the nights fly by, they're so busy. But I go home at night, and I feel kind of empty. Sometimes I wake up feeling that way, too. I'd like not to feel so alone. Do you know what I mean? Before, there were *always* people to be with. Mostly to party with and have good times with. I'm not saying that I want those times back. But I think I'd like to be with someone in a more—is that your cell or mine?"

Madrid reached behind her seat, fished around in her purse, and then pulled out her phone. She glanced down at it. "Mine," she said, and then pressed a button. "Hello? Who? Oh, hey! I was wondering how it was . . . uh, huh . . . So when did you . . . uh, huh . . . And did you . . . uh, huh . . . So did he . . . uh, huh . . . Will you be . . . uh, huh . . . Okay, so I'll . . . uh, huh . . . Right, right. I take it that . . . uh, huh . . . Okay . . . 'Bye."

Madrid clicked off the phone and slipped it back into her purse. Then she laughed and gave London a quick slap on her shoulder.

"What?"

Madrid made a fist with her right hand, raised it, and stirred it in small circles in the air. "I won, I won, *I won!*"

"What did you win?"

"I won the bet with Raphael!" Madrid exclaimed as she rapped the palms of both hands against the steering wheel. "Oh, he's going to be soooo upset! The *poor* lad. I'm not even going to call him and tell him he lost. I'm going to *love* seeing his reaction. I'm going to wait until I'm home and then invite him out to dinner, and *then* tell him! This is going to be great, Lon. Great, great, great! He's going to have to take out a full-page ad in the Sunday *New York Times* proclaiming what a *wonderful* matchmaker I am. It's going to be the *best* advertising I could ever get for my business. I tell you, no one should *ever* bet against me. When I say I can do something, by-fucking-golly, you damn well better believe I can do it!"

"What the *hell* are you raving about? And could you *please* kick back the speed a notch? You're in the red zone. Christ, you really *can* go over a hundred miles per hour in this car."

Madrid glanced down at the speedometer, and then gasped. "Jesus!"

London turned to Madrid and glared at her. "My sentiments *exactly,* for the past half-hour."

"I'm just so excited!" Madrid exclaimed as she slowed her speed to eighty. "Raphael was there one day when this new client came in to Cuor D'Angelo."

"Did I ever tell you that I think that name sounds like a

sub shop? You should just change it to what it means—Angel Heart."

"I'm not changing the name. Angel Heart sounds like some sort of New Age clinic. No, more like a heart donor organization." She cleared her throat and lowered her voice. " 'When you die, leave your heart to Angel Heart.' "

"But Cuor D'Angelo sounds like—"

"I *know* what it sounds like. And I'm *not* changing the name. *Anyway.* This new client—her name is *Pamela*, not Pam or Pammy, in case you were wondering."

"I wasn't. But go on."

"Pamela is *not* very attractive. How would I describe her? She looks really bulldog-tough butchy, but she's straight. She's a very tough woman. A rough, tough woman. She's overweight. She's a chain-smoker. She's—you know what? She kind of looks like Roseanne Barr, but before all the face-lifts and some of the weight loss."

"Okay."

"So, she comes to me as a new client. Raphael's in the room while I'm interviewing her and working on her profile. After she leaves, Raphael says there's no way I can fix up someone like Pamela with anybody. Well, you know what happens when someone says I can't do something."

"I have a pretty good idea, since I feel the same way."

"The thing is, I've been looking at *thousands* of on-line personals profiles for *months,* so I *know* what's out there. Most of the women are like Pamela. They're older, have let themselves go either a little or a lot, and they've been living on their own for so long that they're pretty independent. Single people run the gamut, but they usually aren't drop-dead gorgeous, either the men or the women."

"Now there's a surprise. And they pay you money to figure that out?"

"Are you going to take me seriously, or not?"

"Mad, I *am* taking you seriously, but it's taking you a god-awful amount of time just to come out and say that you found someone for Pamela. Isn't *that* where you're going with this?"

"Well, yes."

"Okay."

"But I was having such fun telling you the story about how much of a challenge Pamela presented and how I searched and searched and finally found this guy who I *knew* would be just right for her."

"And she liked him."

"Yes, she did. That was her on the phone. She said that she had met up with Bert on Tuesday and they—"

"Bert?"

"Yeah, I know. It's kind of a dud name, isn't it?"

"Tell me he's never heard a Bert and Ernie reference in his life."

Madrid wagged a finger in the air at London. "Never judge a book by its cover, and never judge a person by his or her name. Don't you remember how kids would make fun of our names when we were young? You used to be called London Broil. And because you were called London Broil, I would be called Mad Cow."

"Anyway," London prompted Madrid.

"Anyway. Bert and Pamela arranged to meet for a drink on their first date. Now, I don't recommend going out for drinks on a first meeting. I always think coffee or tea is the way to go because when people are nervous they use alcohol to relax, and sometimes that can get out of hand. But what Pamela wants, Pamela gets. They met at a sports bar for drinks, and they had a nice time. Then Bert called her the next day and asked her out to dinner that night. They went out to dinner, and Pamela just told me now that they've made plans to spend a lot of the weekend together."

"Well, that sounds promising."

"It does. She really likes him. She was positively gushing when she was talking to me. He's a nice guy. Very down-to-earth, very easygoing, a guy who's not looking for Julia Roberts. He's looking for a very sincere, no-holds-barred woman, and—*voila*—I fix him up with Pamela. That would be game, set, and *match!* Isn't that great?"

London smiled at her. "I think it's great that what you do makes you so happy." She patted Madrid's leg, and then settled back in her seat. "My soufflé rises. You fix up a seemingly impossible-to-fix-up client with someone who might turn out to be the man of her dreams. Life is good."

"You know, Lon, I could find someone for you, if you're interested. You said you didn't like that empty feeling, that feeling of being so alone, and I could—"

"I'm actually dating someone, Mad."

"You *are?* And when were you going to tell me this?"

London cleared her throat. "Well, I'm telling you now. But I don't think you're going to be happy when you hear who it is. Who *she* is."

"Oh, Christ—please tell me that you're not dating that anorexic fashion model! I thought you didn't like her at all."

"I don't. And it's not her. It's . . . it's Lucinda."

Madrid turned to London and raised her eyebrows. "Oh?"

London shot a quick glance at Madrid, and then looked down at her lap. "Yeah. I, uh, asked her to go . . . I asked her *out* . . . I asked her to go out with me. I've never done that before and I was so nervous, I could barely get out the words. But I did. Ask her to go out. I asked her to go on a picnic with me. And we *did.* It was nice. And then, this week, well, every night actually, we've been getting together after we finish up at the restaurant. Just getting together, like for a movie at a late-night cinema. We saw *Rocky Horror Picture Show* and it was a hoot because she actually got dressed up like one of the characters and was telling me what all the lines were that you were supposed to say at the movie screen—you kind of interact with the movie, it's hard to describe—and once we just rented a video and then another time we channel surfed and we just hung out and talked for hours—that's why I haven't gotten much sleep—and I really, really like our conversations, she's a really nice person." London stopped, and then looked up and stared out the windshield.

"Are you breathing now?"

London looked at Madrid. "What's that?"

"Are you *breathing* now? Because that was the world's longest sentence."

"Well, I know that you and I always used to make fun of Lucinda, about how uptight she was when she was running the club. And I used to imitate her—remember?—and we always had a good laugh about that. But she's really a very nice person. She's good inside. And she's really attractive. I never saw that before. She's lost a lot of weight, and she has her hair in this nice cut now that really looks great on her, and she's got these intense eyes that just kind of look right into you, like *right* into you, and yet she's so gentle and kind and fun to be with and—"

"Breathe!"

London took in a breath.

"Do you like her?"

London stared at Madrid. "Doesn't it sound like I do?"

"It sounds like you're nuts about her."

"I guess I am. I *know* I am."

"And is she nice to you?"

"*Very* nice. She's great to me."

"Then good. I'm happy for you."

"You *are?*"

Madrid took London's hand in hers and squeezed it. "Of *course* I'm happy for you. You found someone who you enjoy being with, and who enjoys being with you. What's wrong with that? It's something I'd like to find one day. I mean, let's face it, sis. We're fast approaching midlife, and we need to get our heads together. We have our possessions—very nice possessions. We now have our professions, or at least something that keeps us busy and challenged.

Next, I think, is we need to find someone to have in our lives. To have and to hold, as they say. Believe me, I'm right behind you in that. I've been kind of doing searches for myself, too. I haven't found anyone I'm interested in yet, but at least I'm looking."

"Mad, no offense to you or to Gamma or the parental units. But I really wanted to spend my birthday with Cinda. When I got the plane ticket from Gamma, I asked Cinda if she wanted to come home with me. But she said it would be too difficult to keep the restaurant open without her on a weekend. Which I can understand. But all I really wanted to do was just be with her. I feel like I really miss her when I'm not with her. Which is strange, because I see her every day. But I just wanted to hear her say 'Happy birthday' to me. That's really all I want for my birthday."

Madrid nodded her head. "I was pretty sure that Raphael and Jean-Paul would ask me over for a birthday dinner to celebrate. For over a month now, Raphael has been busting me about turning thirty. That's what I wanted to do on my birthday, to spend time with my good friends, but he never said anything to me. Then Gamma called, and I figured, 'What else am I going to be doing on my birthday?' I didn't want to spend it alone, so, here we are. We're thirty years old, Lon. At exactly eight-oh-five tonight, you leave your twenties, and I turn thirty just minutes later."

"And then we only have ten more years to go before we turn forty."

"Okay—now *that's* something I really don't want to think about."

"Then let's put on some music and get this celebration of our next decade started. And step on it, granny. I'm tired of you poking along."

"I just want to go on record as saying that I thought *all* of us jumping out at the same time and yelling 'Surprise!' at the top of our lungs might be too much of a shock to your delicate, thirty-year-old system," Raphael told Madrid as he inched his way out from behind a high-backed chair tucked in a corner of the living room at the La Mira home. "Your face does have that, 'Oh, this is *all* too much' look on it. Are you okay? Honey, I said 'Are you OKAY?' Would you like to sit down?"

Madrid narrowed her eyes at Raphael and crossed her arms over her chest. "Since *when* have you ever been able to keep a secret from me, Gladys? And Gamma, how did you know—how did you find—"

"Lucinda was a piece of cake," Gamma answered as she stepped out from behind a grandfather clock. "After all, I've talked with her about La Mira West. Finding someone in your life who meant a lot to you was harder, Maddy. Then I remembered that you had mentioned a young man named Raphael and his partner Jean-Paul, who you said were your best friends. You told me once that they owned an antique store in Manhattan. So I just Googled the store. That's what you call it, right?"

"That's right, Gamma," Raphael said as he draped his arm around her shoulders. "You are *so* hip. But what I think is even more wonderful—more wonderful beyond belief—is that I kept a secret from Madrid. I *didn't* tell! Look at *me!* I'm Mister Secret Boy!"

"But you tell me *everything*," Madrid responded in a whiney voice, and then stuck out her lower lip.

"Ha, ha! I put one over on you!"

"Oh, you think? Well, just enjoy yourself now, buddy-boy. Because you're going to have to take out an ad in *The New York Times* for Cuor D'Angelo. Ha, ha! Who's laughing *now?*"

"You're joking!"

"Am not! You lost the bet! Pamela and Bert, sitting in a tree, k-i-s-s-i-n-g."

"Oh, that's mature," Raphael sniffed. "And what kind of name is Bert anyway? I think you're making it up."

"Am not!"

"Who's taking care of things at the restaurant?" London asked Lucinda, who had risen from a crouching position behind the living room couch.

"And hello to you, too," Lucinda said with a smile as she walked over to London. She gave her a quick hug and a kiss on the cheek. "Happy birthday."

"But who's—"

"My aunt and uncle," Lucinda broke in. "They used to own their own restaurant in Florida. Now they're snowbirds. They fly back to Redwood City every spring, and the timing couldn't have been better for them to take care of things at the restaurant this weekend."

"So when I asked you to come home with me for the weekend—"

"I already had a ticket. Sent to me by your grandmother. I left on a red-eye after we rented the movie the night before last."

"Now Jean-Paul was absolutely *dying* to be here," Raphael said as he walked over to Madrid and linked his arm with hers. "But one of us had to tend to the store because we have a major, major big-spender client flying in this weekend from Milan. So Jean-Paul sends his love and kisses— kiss, kiss," Raphael said as he tossed two air kisses at Madrid, "and he promises that next weekend we'll celebrate your birthday together at our home."

"I am just *thrilled* to finally meet your friends," Catharine told Madrid and London. "Now this has involved choreography *extraordinaire*, trying to coordinate everything and set up the guest rooms and—"

"Catharine, it's been *nothing*," Gamma broke in. "Just relax and *go* with something a little different, will you? Your life will get back to its normal—and boring—ebb and flow after tomorrow."

"All I was going to say was—"

"How's that cake coming, Lucinda?" Gamma cut in.

"It's probably ready to come out of the oven," Lucinda answered as she looked at Catharine. "The kitchen's . . . ?"

"I'll show you," Gamma told her.

"You're baking the cake?" London asked as she fell in behind Lucinda. "You don't have to—"

Lucinda turned and placed a hand against London's chest. "Stop right there. You're *not* getting a look at this cake until it's done."

"Is it the Boston cream?" London asked as Lucinda exited the room. "The strawberry angel food—"

"Give it up, Lon," Lucinda called back to her. "You'll see it when you see it."

" 'You'll see it when you see it,' " Raphael repeated, and then bobbed his head back and forth at London. "Well, I guess she told *you!* Now we all know who wears the pants in your relationship."

"You didn't tell me that Raphael was an annoying teenager," London replied, and then stuck out her tongue at Raphael.

"Maddy! Your sister's picking on me!"

"Where's Dad?" London asked as she flopped down on the living room couch.

"He'll be in later on tonight," Catharine said as she eased herself gently into a high-backed chair, then spent several seconds straightening out her skirt. "Is anyone ready for a cocktail?"

"I'm all set," Madrid said as she playfully bumped a hip against Raphael's. "You lost the bet! Ha! The first man Pamela goes out with—and zing, went the strings of her heart!"

"Oh, like she's in any sort of position to pick and choose," Raphael sniffed.

"Raphael, do you want a cocktail?" Catharine asked.

"Oh, no, thanks. I'm all set."

"London?"

"No, Kitty. Maybe I'll have wine at dinner. I don't drink much anymore."

"Oh, Lord! You're not in that alcoholics program, are you? Who am I going to drink with tonight? I don't want to have to wait until your father gets home."

"Don't be an idiot, Catharine," Gamma scoffed as she returned from the kitchen. "She's not in Alcoholics Anonymous."

London nodded her head. "I just don't drink as much as I used to, Kitty."

"And that's a good thing, honey," Gamma said as she sat down on the couch next to London. "I think you and Maddy were overdoing it a bit."

"Ya think?" Madrid quipped with a grin. "Gamma, we were overdoing a lot of things, and much more than a bit."

Gamma winked at Madrid. "Ya think?"

Madrid walked over to Gamma and gave her a hug. "Gam, thank you *so much* for doing this. Lon and I were bumming out about our birthdays, thinking that we weren't going to be able to celebrate it with our friends, too. Little did we know that you had already taken care of things."

"I take care of everything for you girls," Gamma said. "You know that I do, don't you?"

Madrid nodded her head. "Yes, we know."

"We know, Gamma," London said. "We know you're *always* looking out for us."

"Can we do presents now, Gamma?" Raphael asked as he looked around the table. "Unless you want a *third* piece of cake, London."

"Wow. You can count pretty high for a youngster, can't you?"

Raphael flashed London a fake smile. "Gee, I think I hate you almost as much as I do your sister."

"I might actually have another piece," Gamma began as she caught Raphael's eye and smiled at him. "Lucinda, this cake is delicious."

"It's Lon's favorite," Lucinda said.

"Mine, too," Raphael said in a monotone. "Can we do presents now?"

"I'm still debating whether or not I should have another piece of cake," Gamma said. "Carlisle? Do you want another piece?"

"I don't know. What do you think?"

"I'm not sure. If you will, then I will."

"Well, if you will, then I will. Unless," Carlisle began, and then paused. "Would you rather do presents now, young man?"

"I don't want to interrupt the great cake debate," Raphael said as he placed an elbow on the table and rested his chin in his hand. "I can wait. I'm a very impatient—I mean—*patient* man."

"I say screw the cake and open the presents!" Catharine said as she took another sip of wine. "Although it's a *very* good cake, dear," she told Lucinda.

"Okay," Gamma replied. "Then screw the cake and open the presents!"

"Goody, goody!" Raphael exclaimed as he shot up from his chair. "So here's my present, Mad," he said as he reached under the table. "It's *really* from Jean-Paul and me. But I'm saying it's from me right now so I get all of the credit." He slowly pulled out a long wooden sign, and then held it up and turned it slowly so everyone at the table could see it. "It's old, honey. And it's from Italy. Isn't it cool? It's got angels and hearts all over it. I thought you'd like it for your office."

"It's *beautiful,* Raphael," Madrid said as she stared at it. "I love the colors. It's going to look great right over my desk, don't you think?"

Raphael nodded his head. "That's what Jean-Paul and I were thinking."

"Very exquisite," Gamma remarked.

"And here's my present to you, Lon," Lucinda said as she drew up an envelope from her lap and slipped it toward London.

London picked up the envelope, opened it, and pulled out a card. She opened it and read it. "Two hours at a day spa!"

"Well, you said that's one thing you really miss—being pampered with things like a facial and a massage," Lucinda explained. "So, I thought you'd like that."

"You should probably get a manicure, too, while you're at it," Madrid added.

"Baby sea turtles," London hissed at Madrid.

"Shut *up!*"

"That's *so* nice of you, Cinda," London said, and then leaned toward Lucinda and kissed her on the cheek.

"And this is from your mother, your father, and me," Gamma announced as she handed London and Madrid wrapped boxes that were the same size.

London and Madrid tore through the gift paper, and then stared down at the object that they each held in their hands.

"Now, it took a little doing," Gamma told them as she rose and then walked over and stood behind them. She put a hand on each of their shoulders. "Your father and your mother and I spent hours looking through stacks and stacks of photo albums."

"*Hours,*" Catharine echoed. "Who *knew* we had *so* many pictures! And we'd look at them and start to remember—wouldn't we, Carlisle?"

Carlisle looked over at Catharine and nodded. "You forget, sometimes, how things happened. *Why* they happened. What things you did together."

"It was nice," Catharine said. "I *liked* doing that." She gave a quick smile to Carlisle, and then turned her attention back to Gamma.

"It turns out, girls—and it's sad for me to say—that we've never had a picture taken together as a family, although I don't know why," Gamma continued. "I guess this family has always gone off in different directions. But I think family pictures are important, and it's even more important to display them. So we first found ones of you girls when you were around ten or eleven, I think. They were the nicest pictures, we thought, and so we decided to build a family picture around those."

"That meant that everything had to fit," Carlisle explained. "Your mother and I had to remember how old we were when you girls were that age, and then find pictures of us."

"And I had to find ones of me, too," Gamma said.

"We spent *hours,*" Catharine reiterated, and then looked at London and Madrid. "But it was fun. We had—I can't tell you *how* many—pictures scattered all over the living room floor. I think I dealt with the clutter very well."

"Actually, you did *quite* well, Kitty," Carlisle told her.

"Thank you, dear."

"Then I took the pictures to a photography studio and had them blended together, to have one picture made up to look like we had gathered together at the same time in front of a camera," Gamma said. "So now, what you girls have is a La Mira family portrait. You can change the frames if you don't like them."

"No, Gam, they're beautiful," London said as she stared down at the picture. "It all *fits*. The frame, the picture. It's hard to believe that these pictures were taken separately. It really looks like we posed together."

"It's amazing, Gamma," Madrid said, and then turned the picture around so Raphael could see it.

"Wow!" he exclaimed. "What hard work that must've been."

"It took hours and hours," Catharine told him. "There were boxes and boxes of pictures. I went so far back that I found pictures of my own parents. I haven't thought about them in years. *In years.*" She took another sip of wine, then ran a finger up and down the stem of her glass. "Your Gamma is right. Family pictures are very important. I had two old pictures of my parents framed because of this little activity. Now I can look at them all the time."

"It's not hard work when you're doing something worthwhile," Gamma said as she patted London and Madrid's shoulders. "Is it?"

"What's this on the back?" Madrid asked as she looked at the back of the picture.

"Oh, that's just a little something that I thought you girls deserved," Gamma said as she returned to her chair and sat down.

London turned over her own picture, and then gently removed an envelope that was taped to the back.

"Lon," Madrid said as she opened her envelope, and then showed her the contents.

"Oh—*oh!*" London exclaimed, and then dropped her envelope on the table and let out a sigh. "But we didn't *do* anything, Gamma. These past five months have just been filled with a lot of mistakes and miscalculations and miserable attempts to try to do some good in our lives."

"On the contrary," Gamma said. "Those things that you call mistakes and miscalculations and miserable attempts—which, by the way, I think are *not* accurate descriptions at all—you're being much too hard on yourselves—were exactly what I *wanted* you to do."

"You wanted me to kill sea turtles?" Madrid gasped.

"*Baby* sea turtles," London clarified.

Madrid quickly turned to London. "Would you *stop* saying that! I *know* they were babies!"

"Of course I didn't want you to *kill* them," Gamma scolded Madrid. "Nor did I think your attempts at volunteering would turn out to be so terribly bad, and then so highly publicized to the world. But so what? You tried something that was completely different for each of you, and while your attempts fell quite short of the intended mark, what you discovered in the process was something wonderful. For each of you. You each now do something in your lives that makes a difference in the lives of others. You bring joy, in different ways. You touch the hearts of others. London, that was extraordinarily generous of you to think up the idea of holding a Mother's Day dinner for Home Safe Homes. And Madrid, you have opened the hearts of people who had given up on love until you showed them that there was someone in the world for them.

"When I lost your grandfather," Gamma continued, "I was devastated. Two very glorious things were taken from me. The love of my life was the first. The giving spirit that he had shown me was the other. Since that horrible day when I received that awful notification that he had been killed overseas, I have resolved to live my life with love for others and with giving in my heart. That is what I was hoping you girls would find, and you have succeeded beyond my wildest dreams."

"It's too much," London said in a soft voice.

Gamma nodded her head. "I know it's been too much, dear. Making radical changes always is."

"No, Gam," London said as she looked at her. "It's too much. The *check* is too much. I don't need this much. *No one* really needs this much."

"She's right," Madrid said. "I mean, I can use *some* of this. But—*good Lord*—what did we ever *do* with this amount of money *every* year?"

"Girls, it's yours," Gamma told them. "It's yours to do with as you please. Invest in a business or in your futures. Donate some to a charity. Help out a friend in need. Start a scholarship program—my goodness, but I can think of a lot of things you can do with that money. It's yours. What you do with it is no longer my concern. Because, quite frankly, I know now that the money is in good hands."

Silence fell over the table.

"I think I'll have that drink now, Kitty," London said as

she retaped the envelope to the back of the picture and then set the picture down on the table and stared at it.

"I think I'm going to cry," Madrid said, then lowered her head.

"The ice maiden melteth," London mumbled as she took Madrid's hand in hers.

"I don't know if I like this feeling," Madrid said as she grimaced. "It feels like my insides are shaking."

"It's okay," London told her.

"Don't cry, Mad," Raphael said. "I'll take that big, bad check from you. I'll buy myself a pony. No, wait—maybe a new Barbie. Maybe *dozens* of them. And *hundreds* of little outfits to dress them up in. Here's Barbie on the beach. Here's Barbie in the disco. Here's Barbie having shrimp on the barbie. I can find *oodles* of ways to spend that money of yours. Really, I *can!* I can help you get rid of that awful, awful check!"

Madrid raised her head and started to laugh. "Raphael, would you stop it!"

"But I just want to *help*. If you start crying, I'm going to cry. I'm *very* impressionable, you know."

"I know," Madrid smiled. "I don't want you to cry."

"Then buy me a pony. *Pleeease!*"

"I'll buy you something better."

"Something better than a pony? Is there anything better in the whole, wide world?"

"How about a college degree? You can concentrate on writing, really learn how to write a screenplay. How does that sound?"

Raphael stared at Madrid. "Are you serious?"

Madrid nodded. "What about Columbia University? Don't they have a good writing program there?"

"My God—yes, *yes,* they do! But I—"

"Then when you get home, fill out an application and let's get your writing career under way. That way you can stop *talking* about writing and start writing."

Raphael placed his hands on his chest. "You are so *sweet!* I think I'm going to cry."

"Don't cry. I'll take you shopping for your pencils and notebooks when we get home. I'll get you Barbie stickers and everything."

"I know one place that deserves a big chunk of this money," London said as she looked at Lucinda. "I'm sure Home Safe Homes will have some use for several thousand dollars, don't you think?"

"I do."

"But before I make a donation, do you think we could get away for a while? Just you and me—to a place where we'd have no restaurant duties?"

"Sure. Did you have any place in mind?"

"Well, there's this island paradise that I really like, and I thought—"

"Anguilla!"

London nodded. "Let's go there for real. Just you and me."

"For real?" Lucinda asked. "You and me?"

"You and me."

"Well," Gamma said as she rose from her chair and raised her wineglass. "To London and to Madrid, on their thirtieth birthdays. Here's to the start of even greater things to come. May you live, my dears, in the way we all should live. May you live *all* the days of your lives."

EPILOGUE

*We are born, so to speak, twice over; born into
existence, and born into life . . .*
—Jean-Jacques Rousseau

*The first thing which I can record concerning myself
is, that I was born . . . These are wonderful words.
This life, to which neither time nor eternity can bring
diminution—this everlasting soul, began. My mind
loses itself in these depths.*
—Margaret Oliphant

*Although it is generally known, I think it's about time
to announce that I was born at a very early age.*
—Groucho Marx

WHEN YOU LOOK IN LA MIRA, WHAT DO YOU SEE?

In which I issue my first—and final—apology

Sorry IS one of the hardest words to say.
Especially when one is wrong.
To avoid saying it, one can move through each day cloaked in a comfortable air of superiority, wearing a feeling that one is far better than another. Or, should feelings of guilt and doubt surface, one can use a well-feigned ignorance about the impact of words spoken or written about another, a sort of shoulder-shrugging attitude that pooh-poohs the very idea that hurt was inflicted. Or one can even issue a verbalized sentiment such as, "I have no idea what you're talking about."

When confronted about a wrong done to another, one can, should one desire to, effectively turn the tables back on the accuser and place blame on the injured party. After all, we are quite adept in our society at making the victims suffer to a far greater degree than *the person who actually inflicts the injury and pain. Statements such as, "You're too sensitive," or "You're blowing this way out of proportion" are always good to use in such cases.*

Deflection, denial—yes, they both work. If you want them to. And, over the years, I have wanted them to. And I have used them quite effectively.

But I don't want to use them anymore.

You see, dear readers, I have been disturbed in the still, dark hours of the night with an uncomfortable gnawing feeling that has deprived me of a good night's sleep for week after week.

All because I have been wrong.

I admit, dear readers, that in this column over the years I have inflicted pain on a number of people. I have aired their shameful weaknesses and revealed their well-guarded secrets. I have criticized mercilessly, and I have sometimes—okay, many times—enjoyed doing such things.

In the past, I have skewered both London and Madrid La Mira. Yes, I said skewered. Now there's a huge difference between merely shoving a knife into the back of another human being and standing right in front of that person and pushing that sharp blade deep into their hearts, deep into their souls. In the first case, you make your hit, wipe off your hands, and walk away. In the latter case, you make your hit and then see the result of your actions. You can see it in their eyes when you next speak with them.

And a person's eyes are, quite truly, the windows to their souls.

What I often forget, despite my years of writing a gossip column that oftentimes results in angry phone calls or even death threats about the back-stabbing and skewering that I have done, is the humanness of the people I write about. Those who have star quality, those whose names and faces we see on movie screens, on television, at lavish parties, at ceremonies and events that most commoners would give their right arm to attend, seem to us to be larger than life. And because they seem to be larger than life, it's in our very nature to try to cut them back down to size.

And so cut we often do. Hence, my analogy of the knife.

Such people also seem to be made up of different nuts and bolts from the rest of us. Because of this, we oftentimes poke at them harder than we would normally do, not realizing they are, indeed, made up of flesh and blood.

And, yet, these people were all assembled at the same birth factories as we were. They each grew up in childhood homes, some good, some bad. They—the lot of them—have experienced life through eyes similar to ours.

Like us, they are capable of experiencing a wide range of emotions. They laugh, and they cry. They love, and they lose. They live, and they learn. As do all of us.

But I keep forgetting that.

And so, with deep regret and heartfelt emotion, I issue a very public apology to **London** *and* **Madrid La Mira.** *Weren't we overjoyed when we learned that their grandmother, the strong and enviously charitable* **Angelica,** *took away their yearly trust fund checks last Christmas? Weren't we highly entertained—sometimes even outraged—when the girls fumbled and stumbled their way through volunteer work? You, dear readers, know that I certainly was, because I wrote column after column expressing my delight.*

And, we must all 'fess up to the fact that as we were enjoying their transition from true billionairesses to billionairesses in name only, we wanted them to fail.

We were rooting against them, loud and clear.

And, for some time, it looked like they would fail, didn't it? They were, in a metaphoric analogy to the start of this year's baseball season, down several runs in the bottom of the ninth, with two outs and no one on base. They were standing in the batter's box with a terrible at-bat statistic and facing a pitcher who had already delivered two strikes, no balls.

And yet, they have certainly proven to us that they have balls, haven't they?

This past weekend, I attended an incredibly joyful event. It was the groundbreaking of two new shelters in San Francisco's highly lauded Home Safe Homes program: the **London La Mira Beach House,** *where children can go to play, to stay overnight near the majestic Pacific Ocean, and to learn about the world of nature, and the* **Lucinda Claremont Women's Home,** *a transition home for those women who are just entering the program after leaving terribly abusive situations that gravely endangered their lives and those of their children. London donated a large portion of this year's check to the construction of these homes and, in a move that was quite uncustomary, took a back seat while the president of the program gave a magnificent speech about what these two new homes will mean to the program's participants.*

And I can't say enough about **Madrid La Mira,** *who has devoted endless hours to her* **Cuor D'Angelo Matchmaking Service for All Lifestyles.** *I have spoken with several clients of hers who are now in long-term relationships—some for the first time in many years. You see, Madrid doesn't shy away from divorced women who have young children who want very much to date, or men who are painfully shy and incredibly insecure, or gay men and women who want more than* *what the clubs and social events that they usually frequent have to offer. She is sincere, she is dedicated, and she now has a higher success rate in bringing people together than her competition.*

And, unlike many of the singles dating services, she offers a money-back guarantee if she hasn't found a potential love interest for someone in six months. Tell me who will do that for you?

And here's another thing that Madrid has done. It's not well-publicized, but my sources tell me that her best friend, a terrific young man named **Raphael Barthelemy,** *whose dream has always been to be a writer but who grew up in a family that couldn't afford to send him to college, has paid full tuition for him to attend Columbia University in the fall. I have also heard, from sources at the university who requested anonymity, that Madrid is in the final stages of working out the details to offer a writing scholarship program for talented inner-city kids.*

May I remind you once again of whom I am speaking? You and I once knew them to be spoiled brats, selfish snobs, relentless party goers who cared only for themselves.

The bottom line, dear readers, is that London and Madrid were each given a surprising and stunning ultimatum last Christmas from their grandmother: shape up, or ship out of the lifestyle to which they had grown accustomed.

And shape up they have. We should all be so blessed, to be able to confront difficulties in life and to rise above them to such great heights. But I know what some of you might be thinking—that their fall came from a position of incredible endowment to begin with, and that most likely there was always a soft cushion in place lest the girls fall too hard.

But how many of us have had to face a difficulty and then work through it with the eyes of the world focusing constantly upon us?

These girls—no, they're now women, as they have recently celebrated their thirtieth birthdays—have proven that there is a grand chasm between who someone once was and who someone now is. And they have also shown that the past, however it was lived, is no indication of how a life is lived now.

Shouldn't we all be given such leeway by those who have known us for many, many years?

Some people are born into privilege, as socialites such as **Paris** and **Nicky Hilton** and **London** and **Madrid La Mira** have been. Some achieve privilege through hard work and incredible sacrifice, such as self-made socialite **Dayssi Olarte De Kanavos,** who has become a fixture on the elite charity circuit.

But, ultimately, how one lives one's life is of utmost importance. One can take privilege and abuse it, as London and Madrid have done in the past, or one can take that privilege and use it to achieve greatness.

When I contacted both **London** and **Madrid** last week to let them know that I was writing a column about them, London's reaction was swift and to the point. "Say what you want about me," she said. "But, please—please—don't forget to give a nice mention to Home Safe Homes." She then launched into a speech that lasted several minutes about the lives that had been touched and changed in positive ways through that program. She also invited me and any number of guests of my choosing to **La Mira West** to dinner. When I reminded her that I had previously written a glowing column about the restaurant, she responded, "Yes, you did. But that was before I became the club's assistant chef. I'd really like your honest opinion now that I'm doing some of the cooking. I'm getting better

*at it, but I know there's room for improvement. I'll let
you be the judge of that."*

Yes, that was a direct quote from a now quite humble, honest, and open **London La Mira.**

This woman, who I have treated so badly in the past through my public airings, expressed to me a sincere interest in hearing my opinion.

That, dear readers, takes class.

And as for **Madrid,** when I contacted her I thought at first that she had hung up on me because there was silence on the other end of the line. I asked if she was still there, then heard her sigh. "Please don't mention anything more about me killing baby sea turtles," she begged. "I really can't read about it or hear about it anymore. I have donated several thousand dollars to the program in the hopes that this year they will be able to pay for the costs of taking on a greater number of volunteers so a higher number of turtles can be guided to the sea."

So, my apologies, **Madrid,** that I have again mentioned something you didn't want me to. But I only did so in order for my readers to learn about your charity to the program.

I conclude this week's column with both a reiteration of my apology to **London** and **Madrid** and a fond farewell to my faithful readers. I am going to make a change in my own life, which I hope will be for the better. Like most writers, I earn a living using my skills on assignments that may not always be to my liking, but which pay the bills. However, I have always yearned to write something that comes from my heart. I have an idea for a book, and so I will be leaving this newspaper to discover if I am, indeed, someone who can write from the heart rather than to the word count, someone who can write on a self-imposed deadline.

So, my dear readers, I leave you with one last sentiment. *I have been incredibly inspired by the amazing changes that have come about in the lives of two young women who have gone from riches in wealth to a richness in their hearts. They have forgiven me, without fanfare, my trespasses against them—my numerous invasions of their privacy and my assaults upon their characters. Change, no matter how it comes about, either through an outside force or by a personal choice, is always difficult. But change, once completed, alters your life forever.* **London** *and* **Madrid** *are proof positive of this.*

I leave you with words that I hope you will find to be inspirational. They were spoken by Richard Hooker, an English theologian, sometime in the late 1550s. He said, "Change is not made without inconvenience, even from worse to better."

London *and* **Madrid***—I wish you the best in your lives.*

My dear readers—I wish you the best as well.

I hope you all can seek change in your lives, and that such change can move you, as it has moved others, from worse to better.